Union Publishing Co. of Ingersoll

Peterborough Directory, Including Ashburnham. 1894.

Union Publishing Co. of Ingersoll

Peterborough Directory, Including Ashburnham. 1894.

ISBN/EAN: 9783741184970

Manufactured in Europe, USA, Canada, Australia, Japa

Cover: Foto ©Andreas Hilbeck / pixelio.de

Manufactured and distributed by brebook publishing software
(www.brebook.com)

Union Publishing Co. of Ingersoll

Peterborough Directory, Including Ashburnham. 1894.

UNION PUBLISHING CO'S

(OF INGERSOLL)

PETERBOROUGH DIRECTORY,

INCLUDING

ASHBURNHAM.

1894.

Containing an alphabetically arranged list of Business Firms and Private Citizens, a classified list of Business and Professional Men, and a Miscellaneous Directory of Town and County Officers, Public and Private Schools, Churches, Banks, Incorporated Institutions, etc., etc.

UNION PUBLISHING CO., OF INGERSOLL,

PUBLISHERS.

PREFACE.

In presenting to our patrons our second Directory of Peterborough and Ashburnham, we hope it will meet with their approval. A thorough canvas of the towns has been made, and every effort used to obtain the name of every person who should be represented in the Directory.

Mistakes will occur, but we are confident that no more thorough canvas of the towns has ever been made.

THE CLASSIFIED BUSINESS DIRECTORY is a complete mirror of the business interests of the towns and represents them to the outside world only as a business Directory can.

THE MISCELLANEOUS DIRECTORY furnishes a large amount of information useful to strangers.

THE STREET GUIDE will be found a valuable addition.

Thanking our patrons for the liberal patronage bestowed on our work, we remain

Yours respectfully,

THE PUBLISHERS.

GENERAL INDEX.

INDEX TO ADVERTISEMENTS.

ABBREVIATIONS:—opp. Opposite.

PETERBOROUGH DIRECTORY.

ABBREVIATIONS.—Bds boards ; cor corner ; acct accountant ; bkkpr book keeper ; co company ; clk clerk ; carp carpenter ; dom domestic ; com trav commercial traveller ; blksmth blacksmith; gent gentleman; h house; jr junior; lab laborer ; mkr maker ; mnfg manufacturing; mngr manager; mnfr manufacturer ; mach machinist ; mldr moulder ; propr proprietor ; rms rooms; st street ; secy secretary , sr senior ; wks works ; wid widow.

Ackerman Benjamin F, harness 204 George h 222 Dalhousie
Ackerman Estelle, l 222 Dalhousie
Adam Frank, bkkpr Lock Works h 13 Queen
Adam Leslie,mach W Hamilton bds 302 Aylmer
Adams Frederick,Canadian General Elec Co h 433 Sherbrook
Adams George, brakeman G T R h 183 Rubidge
Adams Louisa,wks Auburn Mill bds 862 George
Adams R H,policeman h 308 Stewart
Adams T Harry, clerk Robert Fair
Adamson J, lab Bridge Works
Adamson John, lab h 202 King
Adamson Wm P, tinsmith A Hall h 240 McDonnel
Adlam George, butcher l 400 Sherbrooke

AS OTHERS SEE US.

" The Manufacturers' Life is a solid institution".—EMPIRE.

" The Company is evidently in a most satisfactory condition".—THE GLOBE.

" Both the Shareholders and Policy-holders have every reason to be satisfied with the result of last year's business".—THE MAIL.

Adlam John, lab h 400 Sherbrooke
Adlam Seth, wks Lock Works h 394 Sherbrooke
Aetna Fire Insurance Co, Cox & Davis Agents 433 George
Agnew Fred, groom 34 Weller
Ahern George, moulder Lock Works h 249 Stewart
Akey Charles A, wks H B Lindsay l 10 Boliver
Akey Henry, cook h 10 Boliver
Akey Mary J, l 10 Boliver
Akey Wm H,wks Canadian General Elec Co l 10 Boliver
Albeck Annie, dom Oriental Hotel

Albeck Sarah, waitress Oriental Hotel

Aldrich Ada W, l 128 Weller

Aldrich Emma J, l 128 Weller

Aldrich Wm, valuator h 128 Weller

Alexander Charles A, grocer 559 George h same

Alexander Harriet P, (wid James S) l 559 George

Alexander John, carp h 494 Aylmer

Alexander Pennington, carp J H Greer h 277 Reid

Alexander Rodie M, l 559 George

Alford Ada, mlnr Hall, Gilchrist & Co bds 301 Reid

Alford Sarah, (wid John W) h 301 Reid

Allan Nellie, dom, 331 Rubidge

Allen Delia, (wid Edward) h 330 Water

Allen Herbert, Canadian General Elec Co h 119 Lake

Allen H M, trav rms 372½ Water

Allen Maggie, h 75 Hunter

Allen Minnie, h 75 Hunter

Allen Philippa, h 75 Hunter

Allen Wm, (Kingan & Allen) bds 168 Brock

Alliance Fire Insurance Co, Cox & Davis Agents 433 George

Allin Annie, l 19 Cresent

Allin Grace, (wid Samuel F) l 19 Cresent

Allin John F, potter 19 Cresent h same

Allin Maud, l 19 Cresent

Allin Wm G, operator C P R Office l 19 Cresent

Allison Aggie, l 54 Albert

Allison Andrew, grocer 877 Water h 875 same

Allison Caroline, (wid Joseph B) h 180 Simcoe

Allison David, millwright h 887 Water

Allison Eliza A, (wid Wm) h 54 Albert

Allison Fred O, clerk l 180 Simcoe

Allison Sarah, dom 207 Dublin

Allison T H, draughtsman Bridge Works bds 168 Brock

Allison Wm, wks Wm Donel h 272 Dublin

Allsworth Wm, bds 69 Hunter

American House, Patrick E Kennedy prop 184-186 Hunter

American Surety Co The, W H Hill Agent 400 Water

Ames Adline V, school teacher l 181 Edinburgh

Ames George S, cutter Hall, Gilchrist & Co h 595 George

Ames James H, boots & shoes 405 George h 181 Edinburgh

Amey Louisa, (wid Hiram) l 192 Dalhousie

Amos Charles H, clerk G A Schofield bds Water

Anders Edmund, lab h 66 Patterson

Anders Lizzie, Canadian General Elec Co bds 66 Patterson

Anderson Adam R, clerk Wm Madill l 31 Dennistoun ave

THE BANK OF TORONTO,
PETERBORO' BRANCH, P. CAMPBELL, MANAGER.
FARMERS' NOTES DISCOUNTED,

Auderson Agnes, (wid Gilbert) h 46 Bonacord
Anderson Alex, lab Dickson Co
Anderson Alice, dom 68 Murray
Anderson Bella, clk C B Rutley l 46 Bonacord
Anderson Bruce, binder The Examiner
Anderson David, trav h 700 George
Anderson Frankie, dressmkr Robt Fair
Anderson John, appr J H Yelland bds 466 George
Anderson John, carp Dickson Co
Anderson John C, bkkpr P Hamilton Mnfg Co h Ashburnham
Anderson Maggie, dom 190 Brock
Anderson Maud, mlnr Robt Fair
Anderson Rachael, clk J McComb
Anderson Robert, clk W Madill
Anderson Thomas G, wkr Wm Hamilton h 46 Bonacord
Anderson Walter, wks Auburn Mill h 31 Dennistoun ave
Andrew Elizabeth, house keeper 281 Rubidge
Andrews James, student bds 285 Dalhousie
Andrews Mrs, (wid S G) l 309 Park
Angleasye Ellen, l 480 Reid
Angleasye Samuel, baker h 480 Reid
Anthony Albert, bookbinder The Times l 32 Union
Anthony Frank, fruits 387 Aylmer h same
Anthony Wm H, shoemaker 159 Simcoe h 32 Union
Appleby Alexander B, hides etc cor Simcoe & Bethune h Barnado ave

Mnfrs. Life Ins. Co.,
Toronto.
"I received your cheque for $10,000 within three hours after I filed claim papers".
KATHERINE RIDOUT.

Archambauld Eugeon, teamster h 71 Elm
Archambeault Henry, lock fitter Lock Works
Archambault Joseph, l 268 London
Archambult Louie, teamster h 268 London
Archer Mary, l 300 Rubidge
Archer Mrs, (wid Francis C) h 300 Rubidge
Armour Andrew, carp l 201 Harvey
Armour George, river man Dickson Co
Armour Grace, l 201 Harvey
Armour John, h 201 Harvey
Armour John, river man Dickson Co
Armour Miss, finisher Fairweather & Co
Armour John jr, lab Dickson Co l 201 Harvey
Armstrong Alexander A, wks Bridge Works h 73 Albert
Armstrong Allan, teamster Wm Buller h 197 Bethune
Armstrong Annie, milliner Robt Fair l 693 George
Armstrong Annie, (wid George) l 195 Simcoe
Armstrong Archibald, lab h 671 Stewart
Armstrong Bella, clk A G Dickson l 84 Hunter upstairs
Armstrong Benjamin, trav J Allen h 3 Wescott

COX & DAVIS, PETERBORO' - Agents for
Royal Ins. Co., North Brit. & Mer. Ins. Co., Lancashire Ins. Co., Alliance Fire Ins. Co., Guardian, Sun Insurance Office,
Caledonia, London & Lancashire, Western, Phœnix of Hartford, " of Brooklin, Manchester Ins. Co.

SHELF & HEAVY { HARDWARE { ADAM HALL 407 GEORGE STREET.

CENTRAL CANADA LOAN AND SAVINGS CO { MONEY TO LOAN ON EASY TERMS DEPOSITS RECEIVED.

Armstrong Clara, clk Jos Armstrong & Co 1 502 Water

Armstrong David G, clk R H Kells & Co h 171 Antrim

Armstrong Edward, clk Grafton & Co

Armstrong Ettie, mlnr Hall, Gilchchrist & Co bds 98 London

Armstrong George C, clk J Armstrong 1 502 Water

Armstrong George, blksmith C G Elec Co Ld h 84 Hunter upstairs

Armstrong H S, condr St Ry Co

Armstrong John, (J Armstrong & Co) h 782 Water

Armstrong John S, 1 279 Bethune

Armstrong John & Co, (Jno Armstrong) grocers 129 Hunter

Armstrong Joseph, trav h 19 Gilmour

Armstrong Joseph, (Jos Armstrong & Co) h 382 Stewart

Armstrong Jos&Co,(Jos Armstrong) dry goods 396 George

Armstrong Mary, (wid Wm) h 693 George

Armstrong May, mlnr J C Turnbull bds 3 Wescott

Armstrong Minnie, dressmaker M E Frise 1 84 Hunter upstairs

Armstrong Minnie, 1 693 George

Armstrong Moses, dray man b 279 Bethune

Armstrong Robert, clk E F Mason & Co bds 106 Murray

Armstrong Robert M, student Rose & Morrison bds 171 Antrim

Armstrong Rolland, lab Bridge Wks bds 164 Alymer

Armstrong SJ Miss, Millinery, Fancy Goods etc 390 George h same

Armstrong S R, Town Clerk h 207 Dublin

Armstrong Thomas, grain buyer b 502 Water

Armstrong Thomas J, baggage man C P R h 164 Alymer

Armstrong Wm, pattern maker C G Elec CoLd 1 84 Hunter upstairs

Armstrong Wm, wks Canadian General Elec Co h 35 Paterson

Armstrong W W, clk Jno Armstrong & Co bds 502 Walter

Arnberg Wm A, salesman Peterboro Music Co h 635 Water

Arnold Frank K, wks Canadian General Elec Co h 39 Stewart

Arnott John, canoe bldr Peterboro Canoe Co bds Southern Hotel

Arnott Robert, wks Wm Donell h 193 McDonnell

Arsenault James, h 10 Argyle

Arsenault John, wks Auburn Mill 1 10 Argyle

Arsenault Joseph, wks Auburn Mill 1 10 Argyle

Arsenault Thomas, wks Auburn Mill 1 10 Argyle

Aselstine Samuel G, art studio 348 Water h same

Atkinson Frederick, 1 153 Rubidge

THE BANK OF TORONTO,
PETERBORO' BRANCH, P. CAMPBELL, MANAGER.
BUYS AND SELLS CANADIAN AND FOREIGN EXCHANGE.

PETERBOROUGH CITY DIRECTORY. 5

Atkinson James, section man C P R h 153 Rubidge

Atkinson Lou, clk J C Craig bds cor College & McDonnell

Atlas Fire Insurance Co, W H Hill Agent 400 Water

Attrill Thomas P, h 273 Hunter

Auburn Woolen Mill, James Kendrey pres & mang director J I Davidson secy & treas Auburn

Ayling George, bds 262 London

Babb John, carp h 17 rear 35 Homewood ave

Bacon Annie, mlnr J C Turnbull

Bacon H C, wks J F Allin h 75 Ware

Bacon Nellie, l 75 Ware

Bacon Thomas, wks J F Allin l 75 Ware

Bacon Wm, baker 485 Bark h same

Bague James, contractor h 220 Dublin

Bailey Emma, (wid Donald) h 266 Sherbrooke

Bailey Florence, l 351 Charlotte

Bailey Jane G, (wid Thomas J) h e s Monaghan l n Weller

Bailey Lizzie, l 266 Sherbrooke

Bailey Samuel A, mldr Wm Hamilton h 470 Donegal

Bain John, wks Auburn Mill bds 856 George

Baird George, wks Auburn Mill bds 37 Dennistoun ave

Baker Addie, dressmkr Robt Hall bds 4 Sheridan

Baker Charles E, boilermaker Wm Hamilton h 544 Park

Baker Frederick J, bricklayer l 546 Park

Baker George A, mach Bridge Works h 299 Bethune

Baker H Hector S, driver Wm Dickson l 546 Park

Baker John C, blksmith Wm Hamilton h 546 Park

Baker J R, freight clk C P R h s s Lansdowne 6 e Lock

Baker Mollie, stenogr Stratton & Hall bds 378 Rubidge

Baker Robert, butcher l 546 Park

Baker R J, mach Bridge Works

Baker R W, carp Dickson Co

Baker Susan E, dressmaker l s s Lansdowne 6 e Lock

Ball Annie, tlress T Dolan & Co

Ball Annie, wks Wm Lech l 470 Park

Ball Fannie, dom 298 Hunter

Ball George, tailor A Mercer & Co h 391 Smith

Ball John, clk A G Dickson

Ball John cutter h 470 Park

Ball Mary, tlress T Dolan & Co

Ball Mary, l 470 Park

Ball Mattie, tlress T Dolan & Co

Ball Miss, finisher W Lech & Sons

Ballantyne John F, wks Canadian General Elec Co h 93 Paterson

Balmoral Hotel Timothy Cavanagh propr cor Charlotte & Water

Balnett Tusb, nurse Nicholls Hospital l same

Bamford W B, C P R Station agent h 146 Aylmer

Banfield Edward, wks Wm Hamilton l 368 Brock

Bank of Montreal, F J Lewis Mngr 360 Water

Bank of Toronto, P Campbell Mngr s e cor George & Hunter (see adv)

Bannon John, wks Canadian General Elec Co bds 155 Stewart

Bannon Robert, lab h 1 Crescent

Baptie Douglas, confectioner L Potwin h 303 King

Baptie Jane, (wid Alex) l 422 George

Baptist Maggie, dom 459 Reid

Barclay John, carpet weaver 583 George h same

Barclay Mary, clk G M Roger l 583 George

Barker L J Miss, sec Y W C A bds 512 Aylmer

Barlee Jane Miss h 177 Aylmer

Barlow Wm C, mngr retail dept The GeoMatthews Co Ld h 154George

Barnaby Daniel, hostler American House l same

Barnardo's Home, Dr Miss H S Woodgate Superintendent Hazel Brae George

Barnes Edward, baggageman G T R h 270 Sherbrooke

Barrett August, wks Lock Works l rear 385 Bethune

Barrette Christena, (wid) l 197 Perry

Barrette Denisa, (wid Meader) h rr 385 Bethune

Barrette Desierie, lab Dickson Co h 26 Park

Barrette Edward, driver S Barrette l 28 Park

Barrett Fred, lab Dickson Co h 157 Romaine

Barrett George, driller Lock Works

Barrett Mary, (wid) l Southern Hotel

Barrett Mrs, (wid Alex) l 157 Romaine

Barrett Solomon, baker 28 Park h same

Barrett Susan, dom 290 Charlotte

Barrie Alexander, Canadian General Elec Co 282 Dalhousie

Barrie Emline, wks Peterboro Mills l 310 Edinburgh

Barrie Ernest L, mach Canadian General Elec Co bds 297 Sherbrooke

Barrie George, mach h 310 Edinburgh

Barrie G L, wks Peterboro Carbon Co

Barrie Patrick, lab Wm Donell h 384 Aylmer

Barrie Wm C, mach P Hamilton Mnfg Co h 297 Sherbrooke

Barry Esther, (wid Thos) l 100 Weller

Barry Thomas, clk Fairweather & Co h 100 Weller

THE BANK OF TORONTO,
PETERBORO' BRANCH, P. CAMPBELL, MANAGER.
HIGHEST RATE OF INTEREST ALLOWED ON DEPOSITS.

PETERBOROUGH CITY DIRECTORY.　　　　7

Barry Wm, upholsterer bds 101 Simcoe

Bartlett Frederick, architect 140 Murray h same

Bates Frederick, driver W Bates 1 656 Stewart

Bates Jessie, 1656 Stewart

Bates Rebecca Mrs, h 656 Stewart

Bates Stanley, wks W Bates 1 656 Stewart

Bates Walter, baker 654 Stewart 1 656 same

Bateson Mary, dom 232 Dublin

Bathgate Hannah, 1 386 Water

Batten Joseph, blacksmith 189 Simcoe h 173 Bethune

Batten Lottie, tailoress W H Merideth 1 379 Bethune

Batten Minnie, milliner R Hall 1 379 Bethune

Batten R, carriage cleaner G Matthews

Batten Wm, blksmith J Batten h 265 McDonnell

Battersby Wm, tailor Hall, Gilchrist & Co bds 332 Water

Baum Walter C, clk Post Office h 490 George

Baxter F, celler forman G Matthews

Baxter Mrs, (wid Wm) bds 291 Stewart

Baxter Robert, blacksmith Dickson Co h 31 Waterford

Baycott John, operator G T R bds 18 Queen

Beach Ida, dom Commercial Hotel

Beach Robert M, dyer Parkers Dye Works h 29 Louis

Beal Annie, (wid Walter) h 688 George

Beal Harry L, clk Dennistoun & Stevenson bds 688 George

Bean Jennie, dom 305 Park

Beattie Mattie, mlnr Robt Fair

Beatty John, veterinary surgeon 180 Simcoe rms same

Beauregard Alpisone, Canadian General Elec Co bds 229 George

Beauregard Amelia, dressmaker Kells & Co bds 229 George

Beauregard Emma, dressmaker Kells & Co bds 229 George

Beauregard Joseph, lab bds 229 George

Beauregard Louis, lab Canadian General Elec Co h 50 Parnell

Beauregard Philomen, (wid Louis) h 229 George

Beauvias Octavas, riverman Dickson Co

Beavis Albert, teamster Dickson Co

Beavis Charles, carp 1 249 Simcoe

Beavis George, teamster Dickson Co

Beavis John W, wks Wm Hamilton

Beavis Margaret, 1 249 Simcoe

Beavis Thomas, h 249 Simcoe

Beck Annie M Miss, 1 699 Water

Beck Margaret, (wid John W RRev) h 699 Water

Becker Thomas, freight clk C P R

Becket Elizabeth Miss, teacher Barnardo ave School bds 710 George

Bedard James, mach Canadian General Elec Co bds 407 Wolfe

Bee Edith, dom 526 Water

Beeton Wm, clk Robt Fair

Begley Robert, clk T Dolan & Co

Begley Robert, furniture 380 Water bds Ashburnham

Begley Thomas, prtr The Examiner

Belcher B Miss, l 269 Edinburgh

Belcher Florence, l 269 Edinburgh

Belcher John, l 269 Edinburgh

Belcher John E, county & city engineer etc 435 George h 269 Edinburgh

Belcher Samuel, civil engineer bds J E Belcher

Bell Arthur, clk Bank of Commerce bds 5 Dennistoun ave

Bell Arthur R, Bank of Commerce bds 141 London

Bell A S, boat mkr Canadian Canoe Co l 45 Harvey

Bell Francis J. Clerk Division Court h 100 London

Bell Fred, student Canadian General Elec Co bds White House

Bell Frederick E, accountant h 141 London

Bell Harry H, wks Canadian General Elec Co bds 265 Townsend

Bell John C, culler Dickson Co h 45 Harvey

Bell J R, wks Peterboro Carbon Co

Bell Lizzie, l 220 Edinburgh

Bell Mary, dom 352 Stewart

Bell Robert, nightwatch Carbon Wks 265 Townsend

Bell Robert W, physician 494 George h 492 h same

Bell Sarah, (wid John) h 220 Edinburgh

BellTelephone Co ofCanada, J S Knapman Local Mngr 332 George

Bell Thomas H, student l 100 London

Bell Thomas sr, l 100 London

Bell Wm J, lab h 217 Charlotte

Belleghem Annie, milliner R Hall l 583 Bethune

Belleghem Daniel, furniture & undertaker 188 Hunter h 190 same

Belleghem James, l 667 George

Belleghem John, h 667 George

Belleghem John jr, l 667 George

Belleghem Lillie, l 667 George

Belleghem Mary L, l 190 Hunter

Belleghem Wm, cabinetmaker Wm Donell h 583 Bethune

Bellet clk Bank of Commerce rms 167 Brock

Bennet J Williams, barrister h 369 Park

Bennet Wm Rev, h 309 Brock

Bennett John A, agent h 91 Hunter

Bennett Jennie, corset mkr C G Gemmell

Bennett L Miss, box mkr The Examiner

Bentley Wm H, mngr Bentleys Fair bds Grand Central

Bentley's Fair, W H Bentley mngr 340 George

Benton Albert E, printer Examiner b 862 George

Benton Frederick. wks Can Gen E Co l 273 Dalhousie

Benton George, mach P Hamilton bds 14 Boliver

Benton George, lab P Hamilton h 273 Dalhousie

Benton George jr, mach P Hamilton Mnfg Co

Berchard A E. clk Jos Armstrong & Co

Beresford Charles, ptr Can Canoe Co h 19 Parnell

Bernier Joseph, wks Dickson Co h 85 Wescott

Best E, ptr The Examiner

Best Ella, l 426 Donegal

Best Elva L M, l 643 Bethune

Best E J Miss, tailoress Hall Gilchrist & Co bds 210 Antrim

Best Henry, stoves & tinware 324 George h 103 Locke

Best James C, clk Hall Gilchrist & Co h 501 Water

Best John, agent h 426 Donegal

Best L, prtr The Examiner

Best Lousia, l 210 Antrim

Best Marian, l 103 Lock

Best May, l 210 Antrim

Best Mrs (Wid James) h n s Smith 2 w Park

Best Samuel H, h 210 Antrim

Best Thomas H, insurance h 643 Bethune

Best Valentine, h 209 Brock

Best Wm D, [Best & Metherel] h 501 Water

Best & Metherel, [W D Best & J H Metherel] machinists 419 Water

Bettes Hellen, l 468 Park

Bettes James K, tinsmith A Hall h 468 Park

Bickell Fred, conductor St R W bds 66 Waterford

Bickell J K, wks Peterboro Carbon Co

Bickell Samuel, box mnfr bds Morgan House

Bickell Wm H, lab h 464 Donegal

Bickerton John, lab bds rear 10 19 Water

Bickle George, lab h 61 Park

Bickle James R, miller Carbon Wks h 63 Park

Biggs John H, clk W Paterson & Son h 113 Brock

Billett Thomas, Acct Bank of Commerce Brock

Billington John, bookkeeper P Hamilton Mnfg Co h 354 Stewart

Binch Peirce C, mach Wm Hamilton h 263 McDonnel

Bingham James, physician 473 Water h same

Birchard Albert E, clk J Armstrong h 39 Union

Bird Elmira, (Wid John) h 521 Aylmer

Bird James, lab h 9 Cresent

Bird Jane, cook Dickson Co

Bird Maggie Miss, artist l 179 London

Bird Margaret, (Wid Robert) h 582 Bethune

Bird Martha, (Wid John) h 179 London

Bird Michael, painter 1 9 Cresent

Bird Susana,(Wid Mathew) 1 9 Cresent

Birdsall Ada, 1 166 Edinburgh

Birdsall Charlott (Wid Richard E) h 166 Edinburgh

Binnie Wm F, miller W H Meldrun h 767 Water

Bishop Arthur,teamster Dickson Co

Bissouette Frederick, driver A Elliott h 242 Simcor

Blackbourn Annie E, housekeeper 263 Bethune

Blackstock George,egg dealer h 101 Rubidge

Blackstock George A, tool mkr Can Gen Elec Co bds 101 Rubidge

Blackstock MargaretA,wksCanadian General Electric Co bds 101 Rubridge

Blackwell Wm, architect 374 Water h 40 Vincent

Blackey, mach Canadian General Elec Co bds 155 Stewart

Blade Annie, dom 356 Stewart

Blade Ann, 1 645 Downie

Blade Arthur, gardner h 489 Park

Blade Arthur, florist 465 Park h 489 same

Blade Sindey, wks W H Moore h 645 Downie

Blain James, bartndr Palace rms 336 Water

Blair Edward, mldr Lock Works bds Balmoral Hotel

Blair Robert, yardman Little Windsor h same

Blake Annie, dom 237 McDonnell

Blake Marin, dom 550 Aylmer

Blanchard Alexander C A, Prin Peterborough Business College h 21 Gilmour (see adv)

Blanchard J Bell, (wid Sedley) h 304 Brock

Bletcher Henry, fruit agent h 180 Brock

Bletcher Wm B, Canadian General Elec Co bds 180 Brock

Blewett Ada, dressmkr Miss Mann bds R Rae

Blodgett Arthur, shingle mkr Dickson Co

Blodgett James A, lab Dickson Co l 213 Antrim

Blodgett Sarah, dom 217 Brock

Blodgett Thomas, lab Dickson Co l 213 Antrim

Blodgett Zemri, lab Dickson Co h 213 Antrim

Board Fred, lab h 369 Sherbrooke

Boddy Thomas E. Agent C P R Telegraph Co etc 322 George h 213 Brock

Bogan Albert, wks Canadian General Elec Co h 187 Stewart

Bogan Charles, wks Canadian General Elec Co l 187 Stewart

Bogan Clara,wks Auburn Mill l 187 Stewart

Bogan John, painter Canadian General Elec Co l 187 Stewart

Bogan Wm, lab h 187 Stewart

Bolan Bridget, dom 4 Kirk

Boland May, dressmkr Robt Fair

Bolin Bridget, (wid John) h 74 Lake

Bolin Frank, lab l 74 Lake

Bolin Kate, dressmkr bds 74 Lake

Bolin Richard H, lab h 74 Lake

Bolin Susie, Canadian General Elec Co bds 74 Lake

Bolster Flora, nurse Nicholls Hospital h same

Bolster Jessie, asst supt Nicholls Hospital l same

Bolton John, lab h 107 Smith

Bolton Edward, school teacher h 23 Park

Bolton Michael, trustr h 23 Park

Bolton Michael jr. l 23 Park

Bolton Patrick J, wks Canadian General Elec Co l 23 Park

Bone Maurce J, weaver h 193 Auburn

Boomer Frank Mrs, bds 226 London

Booth A, Canadian General Elec Co h 78 Patterson

Booth James, wks Water Works h 287 Perry

Borland Emma M, l 544 Donegal

Borland Gilbert, w s J D T l 544 Donegal

Borland Lizzie, corset m' C G Gemmell

Borland Louis, miller h 544 Donegal

Borland Martha J, l 544 Donegal

Borland Wm, harness mkr B F Ackerman h 99 Weller

Borland Wm C, mach Wm Hamilton h 99 Weller

Boswell E J, student l s w cor Charlotte & Park

Boswell John S, insurance 161½ Simcoe h cor Charlotte & Park

Boucher Beauchamp, student l 543 Water

Boucher Mary Miss, l 543 Water

Boucher Robert P, physician 543 Water h same

Boundy F, plumber Adam Hall

Bourne James, wks G Matthews Co (Ld) h 221 Rink

Bourn Walter, clk Post Office

Bout Mrs, laundress Oriental Hotel

Bowron Jennie, dom 308 Charlotte

Bowron Lizzie, dom 292 Stewart

Boyce Matthew, harness mkr B Shortly h 540 Park

Boyle Mary, (wid Martin) h 96 Lake

Boys Robert, btchr George Matthews Co Ld b 63 Alymer

Bradburn Bevin Mrs, l 231 Dublin

Bradburn Ellen, (wid Wm) h 575 Stewart

Bradburn Hector, trav h 292 London

Bradburn Henry T W E, wks St R R h 231 Dublin

Bradburn Maud Miss, l 293 London

Bradburn Robert, carpT BBradburn h 17 Union

Bradburn Rupert, l 293 London

Bradburn Thomas, Capitalist 336 George h 293 London

Bradburn T Evans, Mngr St Railway h n Monaghan c l

Bradburn Wm H. Mngr Bradburns Opera House bds 293 London

Bradburns Opera House, Wm H Bradburn Mngr George bet Charlotte & Simcoe

Braden Emma, waitress Balmoral

Bradley George, upholsterer D B Belleghem l 104 Dublin

Bradley James, lab h 104 Dublin

Bradley James, tchr Business College bds 104 Dublin

Bradley James jr, caretaker George St Methodist Church l 104 Dublin

Bradshaw Ada, clk W Bradshaw bds 344 Alymer

Bradshaw Annie, (wid James) h 344 Aylmer

Bradshaw Emma, dressmaker Miss Nortcott bds 344 Alymer

Bradshaw Henry, clk F Mercer bds 344 Alymer

Bradshaw Wellington, grocer cor Hunter & Alymer h same

Brady Joseph, lab h 44 Ware

Brady Thomas, grocer 442 George b 704 George

Branch Annie, trav l 166 Sherbrooke

Branch Elizabeth Miss, l 166 Sherbrooke

Brand Nellie, dom 19 Scott

Branch Laura, trav l 166 Sherbrooke

Brault Eugenie, housemaid Montreal House

Brault Harry, lab h 32 Ware

Brault Nellie, waitress Montreal House

Braund Ralph C, grocer 111 Park b same

Bray Annie, mlnr Miss Armstrong

Brealy James, carp h 97 Dickson

Breckenridge Annie, dressmkr l 108 Boundry

Breckenridge David, mach Canadian General Elec Co bds 215 Stewart

Breckenridge Maggie, bds 108 Boundry

Breckenridge Matthew, teamster bds 108 Boundry

Breeze David, (Breeze & Jones) h 665 Bethune

Breeze Maud, l 665 Bethune

Breeze & Jones, (D Breeze & E A Jones) tinsmiths etc 437 Water

Briggs Margaret, l 195 Auburn

Brennan Frederick, wks Lock Works h 356 London

Brennan Frederick H, Physician 217 Brock h same

Brennan Maud Miss, l 217 Brock

Brennan Reginald, polisher Lock Wks

Brennan Richard, miller Dickson Co

Brennan Wm, l 217 Brock

Brenton Fannie, dom 193 Aylmer

THE BANK OF TORONTO,
PETERBORO' BRANCH, P. CAMPBELL, MANAGER.
BUYS AND SELLS CANADIAN AND FOREIGN EXCHANGE.

PETERBOROUGH CITY DIRECTORY.   13

Brenton Frank, wks Wm Hamilton

Brenton Wm, driller Lock Wks

Brewer Charles, lab h 31 Alfred

Brewer Miss, dress mkr Hall Gilchrist & Co

Brickley Sarah, (wid Wm) h 385 Sherbooke

Brickmeyer Sarah, l 551 Gilchrist

Bridgewater A, pattern mkr Bridge Works

Brien Wm, rms Fire Hall

Brion Fred, lab Dickson Co

Brion Hosanna, (Guerin & Brion) h 616 Water

Brisbin G F, lab T Bradburn h 33 Chambers

Brisbin James W, Flour & Feed 161 Hunter h 617 George

Brisbin Millie, dom 457 Water

Brisbin Nettie, l 617 George

Brisbin Walton, harness mkr B Shortly

Brisbois Mary, wks Auburn Mill l 206 Harvey

Brisbois Moses, h 206 Harvey

British AmericanInsurance Co. W H Cluxton Agent 399 George

Britton George, cooper J Britton bds 13 Harvey

Britton John, cooper 13 Harvey h same

Britton Lillie, l 13 Harvey

Britton Marth A, l 13 Harvey

Britton Wm, cooper J Britton bds 13 Harvey

Brodegan Agnes, (wid Robert) bds 196 Brock

Brooks Laura, l 344 McDonnel

Brooks Sarah, (wid Daniel) h 344 McDonnel

Brooks Thomas, Mang Director Peterboro Lock Mnfg Co h 21 Scott

Brough James, bus driver Grand Central h 133 McDonnell

Brousseau Beatrice, l 119 Smith

Brousseau George, barber P M Brousseau bds 119 Smith

Brousseau Louis, barber P M Brousseau bds 119 Smith

Brousseau P M, barber 165 Hunter h 119 Smith

Brown Andrew, wks Canadian General Elec Co h 31 Wescott

Brown Annie, dom 285 Park

Brown Ann J, artist l 612 Stewart

Brown Ann Miss, l 739 Water

Brown Blanch, l 162 Smith

Brown Bros, (Edward & Wm A) grocers 394 George

Brown Burtha, l 737 Water

Brown Charles N, flour & feed 139 Simcoe h 737 Water

Brown Edward, (Brown Bros) h 18 Belmont

Brown Eliza, (wid Templeton) l 737 Water

Brown Elizabeth, (wid Albert) l 381 Sherbrooke

Brown Ellen, (wid James) fancy goods 162 Simcoe h same

FOR BIBLES, HYMN BOOKS, PRAYER BOOKS, ETC., ETC.

Go To SAILSBURY'S.

Brown Francis lab bds 80 Boundry

Brown Fred, pattern mkr W Hamilton bds 33 Louis

Brown Frederick, wks AuburnMills bds 47 Dennistoun ave

Brown Gavin, lunch room 386 Water h same

Brown George tanner W Patterson & Son bds 33 Louis

Brown Harry, brass moulder Lock Works h 56 Harvey

Brown Isabella, (wid James R) h 267 Reid

Brown James, prtr Review bds 33 Lewis

Brown James C, insp PublicSchools County Peterboro h 162 Smith

Brown Jennie, l 33 Louis

Brown John, wks Carbon Works bds 272 Simcoe

Brown John, h 33 Harvey

Brown John, clk Peterboro Hardware Co

Brown John A, potter J F Allin h 56 Wescott

Brown Maggie, l 33 Louis

Brown Margaret, (wid John) h 33 Louis

Brown Martha, milliner l 33 Harvey

Brown Maud, l 56 Wescott

Brown Milley, l 33 Harvey

Brown Redman, lab h 318 Sherbrooke

Brown Robert, porter W H Hamilton h 141 Sherbrooke

Brown Robert A, prtr Review bds 33 Louis

Brown Ronald, t'r Hall, Gilchrist & Co

Brown Samuel, brakeman G T R h 180 Rubidge

Brown Sarah H, school teacher l 612 Stewart

Brown Sophia, (wid John) h 454 Park

Brown Thomas, h 612 Stewart

Brown Wesley, wks St R R Co bds 521 Reid

Brown Wm, groom T Fitzgerald h 345 Stewart

Brown Wm A, (Brown Bros) h 217 London

Brown Wm N, watchman St Ry Co

Brown, physician bds Little Windsor

Brownlie George, l 247 Aylmer

Brownlie James M, driver G Doig l 103 Albert

Brownlie James S, wks Canadian General Elec Co h 103 Albert

Brownlie John, mach P Hamilton h 247 Aylmer

Brownlie Magdalene, dom 80 Boundry

Brownlie Wm, wks Carbon Works l 103 Albert

Brownscombe Felix, secy Can Canoe Co h 165 Murray

Brownscombe Mary A (wid Wm) l 168 Murray

Bruch R, wks Wm Hamilton

Brundrett Wm H, shipper Can Gen Elec Co bds 303 Bethune

Bryson James P, clk Coughlin Bros h 83 Albert

Buchan Wm G, pressman Review h 491 Aylmer

Buchanan Mary, (wid John) h 11 Elm

Buchanan Wm, rep Review bds 330 Water

Buck Francis, driver Henry Bros l 384 Sherbrooke

Buck Thomas, wks Bridge Works l 384 Sherbrooke

Buck Wm, agent h 384 Sherbrooke

Buckland Frank, porter Oriental Hotel

Buckley Nellie, dom 32 Gilmour

Bullen Robert J, driver I X L Laundry l 243 Rubidge

Bullen Thomas, canoe bldr Wm English Canoe Co h 19 Elm

Bullen Wm, tanner W Patterson h 243 Rubidge

Bullen Wm Mrs, grocery 241 Rubidge h 243 same

Buller Ettie, l 260 Murray

Buller Isabella, (wid Joseph) h 211 Park

Buller Lizzie, (wid Joseph) h 260 Murray

Buller Wm H, carter h 274 King

Bullied Charles, lab Dickson Co

Bullied Silas, lab Dickson Co h 19 Waterford

Bunton Wm, insurance h 172 Hunter

Burdett Frank, foreman Lock Works h 181 Dalhousie

Burdick Wm, billiard mrkr Oriental Hotel h 338 Alymer

Burfield Richard, (Jackson & Co) h 247 Hunter

Burgess John, mason Dickson Co

Burk Maggie, tlress W H Meredith bds Auburn

Burk Minnie, dressmkr M McCauley Water

Burke Daniel, wks Lock Works l 841 Water

Burke Ellen, wks Auburn Mill l 841 Water

Burke Julia, wks Auburn Mill l 841 Water

Burke Mary, l 841 Water

Burke Michael, dray man Peterboro Hardware Co h 841 Water

Burke Patrick, wks Dickson Co l 841 Water

Burke Wm, prin Separate School bds Phelan's Hotel

Burley Ann, (Wid Wm S) l 13 Waterford

Burley Robert S, wks Wm English Co bds 13 Waterford

Burnes Edward, driver D Sullivan

Burnes Wm, cook Dickson Co

Burnett Henry D, sup lamp work Canadian General Electric Co h 306 Brock

Burnett James, wks Auburn Mill h 801 Water

Burnett Nellie, l 801 Water

Burney George, clk Grand Central bds same

Burnham Ethel, l 343 Stewart

Burnham George, physician 513 Water h 515 same

Burnham Hamden, rms 583 Water

Burnham Hellen E, (wid Frederick E) l 343 Stewart

Burnham John, Barrister 415 Water h cor Lake & John (Ashburnham)

Burnham Thomas, clk Peterboro Hardware Co

Burns Jennie, waitress City Hotel

Burns John, lab A McDonald

Burns John, wks Wm Hamilton

Burns Michael, carp bds C P R Hotel

Burns Robert, river man Dickson Co bds 179 Harvey

Burritt Daniel H, h 332 Rubidge

Burritt Mrs, laundress I X L Laundry h Bethune

Bush Lowell, carp Canadian General Electric Co bds 96 Lake

Butcher Bella, l 199 Murray

Butcher Charles, cooper l n s Wolsley 3 w Benson

Butcher George, wks W J Green l n s Wolsley 3 w Benson

Butcher James, wks Canadian General Electric Co bds 20 Boliver

Butcher John W, variety store 378 George h 199 Murray

Butcher John W, lab l 553 George

Butcher Maria Mrs, h 199 Murray

Butcher Mark T, clk J W Butcher h 553 George

Butcher Timothy, cooper G Kingdon h n s Wolsley 3 w Benson

Butler Albert, painter l 12 Queen

Butler Bertha, mlnr Robt Fair

Butler Charles, painter h 12 Queen

Butler Charles, clk Hall Gilchrist & Co l 20 Queen

Butler Clara L, (wid Charles R) h 20 Queen

Butler Edward, lab h 77 Lake

Butler Hannah, house keeper 269 Rubidge

Butler James, wks R King bds 290 Charlotte

Butler James, porter J W Moore & Co b Ashburnham

Butler John, bus driver Snowden House h 202 Charlotte

Butler Joseph, wks Canadian General Elec Co l 12 Queen

Butler Margaret E, clk Miss Rudkin l 12 Queen

Butler Patrick, lab F Fairen l 77 Lake

Butler Perry, teamster h 431 Bethune

Buxton A P, pattern mkr Lock Works h 360 Stewart

Buyer John W, freight agent C P R h 59 Alymer

Byers Charles, teamster T Fitzgerald h 336 Alymer

Byers Harry J, photographer h 772 Water

Christie Hugh W, mach Wm Hamilton
Christie Mary J, (wid Hugh) 1 489
    Donegal
Clinkseale Robert, carp h 401 Park
Cooper W, wks Can Gen Elec Co h
    28 Albert
· **Croly T M D,** Refrigerator Mnfr
    Carpenter & Stair Builder 66
    Auburn h same (see adv)

Byers Jemima, (wid John) h 274 Edinburgh

Byers Maria, 325 Aylmer

Byers Miss, laundress Peterboro Steam Laundry

Byers Thomas J, h 325 Alymer

Byrne James, stone cutter h 452 George

Byrne James Mrs, ladies furnishings 452 George h same

Byrnes Eliza, (wid Peter) h 210 Charlotte

Byrnes John, wks Wm Donell bds 210 Charlotte

Byrnes Minnie, wks Auburn Mills bds 210 Charlotte

Cadday Arthur, draughtsman bds 330 Water

Cadigan Annie, dom 178 Dalhousie

Cadigan J, signalman G T R

Cadigan John, carp h 8 William

Cadigan Kate, wks Can Gen E Co l 8 William

Cadigan Lizzie, l 8 William

Cadigan Mary Miss, dressmkr Miss Northcott l Ashburnham

Cadigan Minnie, Miss Auburn Mill h 8 William

Cahill Agnes, clk S Armstrong l 278 Reid

Cahill Amelia, mlnr Miss E Delaney l 278 Reid

Cahill Annie, (Wid James) grocery 262 Simcoe h same

Cahill Honora, (Wid John) h 17 Elm

Cahill Joseph, clk Peterborough Hardware Co l 278 Reid

Cahill Maggie, dom 196 Alymer

Cahill Margaret, l 278 Reid

Cahill Patrick, lab Can Gen E Co h 37 Parnell

Cahill Thomas, deputy Coll Inland Revenue

Cahill Thomas, gas inspector h 278 Reid

Cairnes Clara, school teacher l 41 Paterson

Cairnes George, carp h 41 Paterson

Cairnes George jr, printer Times l 41 Paterson

Cairnes Susan, l 41 Paterson

Cairnes Thomas W H, carp h 17 rear 21½ Paterson

Calder Wm H Jeweler 428 George h 166 McDonnell (see adv)

Caldwell Annie, l 212 Brock

Caldwell Wm, physician 212 Brock h same

Caledonia Fire Insurance, Co Cox & Davis Agents 433 George

Callagham Catharnie, dom 681 Stewart

Callaghan Ella, (Wid John) h 47 Elm

Callaghan Kate, tlress H Le Brun & Co l 99 Elm

Callanane M, section man C P R

Callendar student Can Gen E Co bds White House

Calnan Michael, lab h 139 Aylmer

Calvert Thomas, wks St R R bds 19½ Paterson

Cameron Alexander, harnessmkr B F Ackerman l 143 London

Cameron Alfred J, surveyor l 502 George

Cameron Ann (Wid Duncan) h 381 Sherbrooke

Cameron Annie W, l 502 George

Cameron A R, clk Jno Cameron bds 502 George

Cameron Charles,agent h 502George

Cameron Duncan cutter T Dolan & Co

Cameron George shoemaker h 143 London

Cameron John grocer etc 392 George h cor Brock & Reid

Cameron John A trav h 292 Stewart

Cameron John H, lab h 381 Sherbrooke

Cameron Nellie, dressmaker l 143 London

Cameron Phebe, l 143 London

Cameron Sophia J R, kindergarten teacher l 502 George

Campau Effie, housemaid C P R Hotel

Campbell Charles, mldr P Hamilton Mnfg Co bds 159 Stewart

Campbell Emma, dressmaker 285 Wolfe bds 159 Stewart

Campbell Emma, wksAuburn Mill l n s Barnardo ave l e Stewart

Campbell George, carp Cen Can-Loan & Savings Co h 159 Wolfe

Campbell Hattie, mlnrRobtFair bds 34 Water

Campbell James, blksmith R Hull bds 334 Water

Campbell James, h 334 Water

Campbell James,bookkpr The Rathbun Co bds 106 Murray

Campbell Jemima, dom 457 Water

Campbell Jennie, l n s Barnardo Ave l e Stewart

Campbell John, wks Peterboro Woolen Mill h n s Barnardo Ave l e Stewart

CampbellKate,bkkpr Times bds 334 Water

Campbell P, Mngr Bank of Toronto h 364 Simcoe

Campbell Samuel J, barkpr Croft House bds same

Campbell Thomas, wks Times bds 334 Water

Canada Accident Insurance Co The, W H Hill Agent 400 Water

Canada Life Assurance Co, Cox & Davis Agents 433 George

THE BANK OF TORONTO,
PETERBORO' BRANCH, P. CAMPBELL, MANAGER.
FARMERS' NOTES DISCOUNTED,

SHIELF & HEAVY { ADAM HALL { HARDWARE
407 GEORGE STREET.

CENTRAL CANADA LOAN AND SAVINGS CO { MONEY TO LOAN ON EASY TERMS
DEPOSITS RECEIVED.

Canadian Bank of Commerce, W MansonMngr s w cor George & Brock
Canadian Canoe Co Ltd (The) H O Fisk pres, A R Tibb mngr, F Brownscombe sec-tres, 439 Water
Canadian Express Co, Cox & Davis Agents 433 George
Canadian General Electric Co (Ld), electric supplies Park
Canadian Land & Immigration Co (Ld) of Haliburton, J M Irwin mng dir 435 George
Canadian Pacific Railroad Depot, W B Bamford agent George
Canning Annie, (wid Horatia) h 179 Edinburgh
Canning Margaret, dressmaker Robt Fair l 176 Edinburgh
Canning Richard, hlpr J &W Metherel
Card Walter D, grocer 99 Hunter h 97 same
Carew David, wks Dickson Co bds 583 Water
Carew Fannie, l Carew House
Carew House, Jeremiah Carew prop 219 Hunter
Carew Jeremiah, prop Carew House 219 Hunter
Carew Mary, l Carew House
Carew Nathaniel, bartender Carew House h 92 London
Carey Agnes, l 26 Patterson
Carey James W, boots & shoes 450 George h same
Carey Redmund, h 26 Patterson
Carey Robert, student l 26 Patterson

Mnfrs. Life Ins. Co.,
Toronto.
"I received your cheque for $10,000 within three hours after I filed claim papers".
KATHERINE RIDOUT.

Carlisle Frederick, jeweler W A Sanderson l 32 Union
Carlton M, lab J J McBain
Carlton Middie, lab h 862 Water
Carlton Ralph, painter h 168 McDonnell
Carmichael Duncan N, Physician 132 Brock h 441 Water
Carroll Annie, housemaid Balmoral
Carroll Ellen, (wid John) h378Sherbrooke
Carroll John, appr M O'Brien bds 70 Sherbrooke
Carroll Mark, bell boyOrientalHotel bds same
Carroll Mary, l 378 Sherbrooke
Carroll Michael,butcherJ Grady bds c l
Carroll Patrick, bartender Oriental Hotel bds same
Carroll Stephen, lab h 59 Boliver
Carruthers Annie, tlress Hall Gilchrist & Co l 471 Rubidge
Carruthers Fannie, l 471 Rubidge
Carruthers George, miller W H Meldrum
Carson Letetia, (wid James) h 203 Charlotte
Carson Mrs, laundress I X L Laundry h Charlotte
Carson Robert,wksC G Elec Co bds 407 Wolfe
Car son Robert, wksC GElecCo h 24 Albert

COX & DAVIS, PETERBORO' · Agents for { Royal Ins. Co., North Brit. & Mer. Ins. Co., Lancashire Ins. Co., Alliance Fire Ins. Co., Guardian, Sun Insurance Office, | Caledonia, London & Lancashire, Western, Phœnix of Hartford, " of Brooklin, Manchester Ins. Co.

Carson Wm, porter M Carton

Carter Christopher, wks Auburn Mill 1 189 River Rd

Carter Emily, dom Dr Barnardos Home

Carter Robert, wks Auburn Mill 1 189 River Rd

Carter Wm H, h 189 River Rd

Carton George, pork packer etc 321 George h same

Carton Kitty, clk M Carton

Carton Michael, grocer 206 Simcoe

Carty Mary, dom, 396 Downie

Carveth Ernest, wks Carbon Wks bds 189 Charlotte

Carveth Henry, grocer 212 Hunter h same

Carveth Thomas, carp bds 212 Hunter

Carveth W J N, canoe builder Wm English Canoe Co h 21 Cresent

Cassan Eliza, dom 740 Water

Cassel Joseph, foreman Carbon Wks h 303 Rubidge

Cassidy Edward, 1 409 Aylmer

Cassidy Lillie, mlnr Mrs M Cassidy bds 409 Aylmer

Cassidy Margaret, (wid Edward) 423 George h 409 Alymer

Cassidy Mary, school teacher 1 409 Aylmer

Cassidy Thomas, lab A Donnell h 95 Wescott

Castle H, stoter man E Matthews

Castler Joseph, wks Peterboro Carbon Co

Cavanagh Harry, hack driver bds Balmoral House

Cavanagh James, bartender Balmoral

Cavanagh Richard, bartender Balmoral

Cavanagh Timothy, prop Balmoral Hotel cor Charlotte & Water

Cawthorne Wm B, carriage painter h 136 London

Central Bridge & Engineering Co Ltd, W H Law mngr dir 138 Dalhousie

Central Canada Loan &Savings Co, G A Cox Pres, Richard Hall Vice Pres, F G Cox Mngr, 437 George (see adv)

Chamberlain Margaret, office asst The Times

Chamberlain J Miss, 1 N Monaghan bd Patterson

Chambers George, lab Wm Hamilton h 470 Rubidge

Chambers H, trimmer G Matthews h Ash

Chambers Maggie, stenog The Times bds 526 Water

Chambers Maud, dom 1 514 Aylmer

Chambo Charles, lab h 95 Rubidge

Chapman Ann, (wid Wm) h 339 Downie

Chapman Mary, wks Peterboro Laundry 1 339 Downie

Chapman Samuel, brass moulder 1 339 Downie

Chapman Sarah A, (wid Wm) h 572 Aylmer

Chapman Wm, baker 1 339 Downie

Chartren J, mach Bridge Works

Chatten James H, stone cutter h 544 Downie

Chatten James Mrs, h 245 London

Chatten Jennie, l 245 London

Chatten Lottie, dom 546 Aylmer

Chatten Thomas, mason h 348 Smith

Chatten Wm, lather bds 544 Downie

Chestnut David, ptr T Fitzgerald

China Hall, Macfarlane Wilson Prop 360 George

Chislett Alfred, wood finisher Canada General Elec Co bds 118 Aylmer

Chislett Stephen, wks Canada General Elec Co bds 263 Stewart

Chiverill Charles K, appr H Long bds same

Choate Ellen, (wid Jacob) h 101 Simcoe

Choate Herbert R, wks Lock Works l 101 Simcoe

Choate May, l 101 Simcoe

Choate Samuel, appr Lock Works

Chowen Bruce, wks Peterborough Woolen Mill l 781 Water

Chowen Kenneth, jeweller F S Schneider bds 781 Water

Chowen Richard J, mach Auburn Mill h 781 Water

Christie Ella, mantle mkr Hall, Gilchrist & Co

Christie John R, asst agent C P R Tel Co bds Phelan House

Christie Wm, wks Wm Hamilton

Christoe Joseph, lab b 288 Brock

Chrow Albert, cabinet maker Daniel Bellegham b 689 George

Chrow Annie, clk A H Stratton & Co l 127 Smith

Chrow Ruth, (wid Edward) h 127 Smith

Chynoweth Amelia, dom 303 Brock

City Hotel, Wm Clancy prop 331 & 333 George

Clancie Peter, lab Dickson Co

Clancy James, dray man Peterboro Hardware Co h 714 Water

Clancy John, polisher Lock Works

Clancy John, propr Peterboro House 189 Hunter

Clancy Maggie, tlress H Le Brun & Co bds City Hotel

Clancy Thomas, l City Hotel

Clancy Wm, mach Canada General Elec Co bds City Hotel

Clancy Wm, prop City Hotel 331 George

Claringbold Eliza, l 371 Hunter

Clark A N, acct Water Works Co h 700 Water

Clark Clara, l 700 Water

Clark Edward, l 80 Weller

Clark Elizabeth L, l 700 Water

Clark F R, ledgerkpr Bank of Commerce bds 700 Water

Clark George, wks G T R b 781 George

Clark Johannah, (wid Wm) h 13 Elm

Clarke John, (Clarke & Gibson) h 547 Water

Clarke Minnie E, opr Bell Tel Co l 308 Charlotte

Clark Stanley, wks G T R l 781 George

Clarke & Gibson, (John Clarke & Alex Gibson) jewelers 136 Hunter

Clarke Agnes, (wid Archibald) h 386 Stewart

Clarke Annie L Miss, l 166 Brock

Clarke John, Physician 166 Brock h same

Clarke Rosa Miss, l 386 Stewart

Clatworthy Agnes, l 580 George

Clatworthy James, h 580 George

Cleary Jennie, dressmaker l 201 Stewart

Cleary Wm, farmer h 201 Stewart

Cleeves Edward O B, blksmith Can Gen Elec Co h 249 Wolfe

Clegg Abraham, Furniture etc 427 George h 16 Benson

Clegg Clara, l 16 Benson

Clegg Edward B, Cigars, Tobaccos etc 415 George bds 16 Benson

Clegg Herbert, upholsterer A Clegg bds 4 Sheridan

Clegg Samuel, salesman A Clegg h 295 Stewart

Clemence Christopher S, mach Wm Hamilton h 61 Bonacord

Clement Phoebe, dom 182 McDonnell

Clementi Charles H, collector Customs h cor Park & Charlotte

Clementi Frederick, wks G T R Station bds 671 George

Clementi Mary, l 359 Stewart

Clementi Mary J, (wid Vincent M) l 359 Stewart

Clementi Vincent Rev, h 193 Aylmer

Clerihew George W, trav h 463 Stewart

Clifford Ann, housekeeper 350 Hunter

Clifford Ida, dom 155 Stewart

Close Mary, l s s Lansdowne 4 e Lock

Close Wm, lab h s s Lansdowne 4 e Lock

Cluxton Harold, clk Carbon Works l 376 Brock

Cluxton H C, wks Can Gen Elec Co l 376 Brock

Cluxton L G, bkkpr Lock Works l 376 Brock

Cluxton Mrs, (wid George) h 376 Brock

Cluxton Wm, Cheese Exporter 399 George h 343 Stewart

Cluxton Wm H, Insurance etc 399 George h 238 Antrim (see adv)

Clysdale Annie, dom 335 Rubidge

Clysdale Emma, housekeeper 270 Charlotte

Coates Mary A Miss, dressmkr Miss E Delaney

Cobb Albert H, druggist h 412 London

Cobb Joseph H, h 551 Aylmer

Cochrane Ella, l 697 Aylmer

Cochrane George. licence inspector 415½ Water b 697 Aylmer

Cochrane Sarah, l 277 Rubidge

Cochrane Thomas, agril implt agent etc 388 Water h same

Cockraft E E, wks Can Gen Elec Co bds 583 Bethune

Code B Miss, Secy Dr Barnardo's Home

Coe Jennie, l 160 Aylmer

Coffill Maggie, dom 415 Rubidge

Coleman Elizabeth, h 639 Reid

Collens Lizzie, dom 543 Water

Collier A, wks Can Gen Elec Co bds 80 Gilmour

Collinge Sarah, tlress W H Meredith h 211 Murray

Collins Charles D, student l 194 McDonnell

Collins James, lab Dickson Co

Collins J D, h 194 McDonnell

Collins Mabel, l 194 McDonnell

Collins Mary, dressmkr Robt Fair l e s Boundry c l

Collins Mary, (wid Patrick) h 31 Paterson

Collins Michael C, (Collins & Co) h 225 Hunter

Collins Patrick, bartender American House bds same

Collins Sarah, bds 24 Albert

Collins Wm, farmer h e s Boundry (c l)

Collins & Co, (M C Collins) grocers 225 Hunter

Coltart Annie, dressmkr Mrs Byrnes bds 99 Aylmer

Coltart Wm Swks George Matthews Co (Ld) h 99 Alymer

Cotton Robert, clk J W Moore & Co h Aylmer

Commerical Hotel, Arthur Rountree prop 440 George

Commercial Union Fire Insurance Co, W H Cluxton Agent 399 George

Comstock Aaron, Furniture Mnfr & Undertaker 300 George h 305 Water (see adv)

Comstock George, wks Canadian General Elec Co h 357 King

Comstock Lottie, l 305 Water

Comstock Sarah, l 305 Water

Comstock Wm, clk A Comstock bds 305 Water

Condon Bridget, l 174 Alymer

Condon Eliza, l 174 Alymer

Condon Francis, dressmkr l 174 Alymer

Condon Hannah wks Canadian General Elec Co bds 16 Albert

Condon James, lab h 16 Albert

Condon John, pump mkr 196 King h 281 Perry

Condon Margaret, (wid Michael) b 174 Alymer

Condon Margaret, l 16 Albert

Condon Matilda wks Canadian General Elec Co bds 16 Albert

Connall Beatrice, dressmkr Wall & Connall bks Ashburnham

Connal Bessie, l 270 Brock

Connal James H, clk P Connal & Co bds 270 Brock

Connall Kate, (Misses Wall & Connall) bds Ashburnham

Connal Peter, (Peter Connal & Co) h 270 Brock

Connal Peter & Co, (Peter Connal & W G Ferguson) grocers 380 George

Connal Thomas, clk Peterboro Hardware Co l 270 Brock

Conners Thomas, engr Water Works Co h 909 Water

Connecticut Fire Insurance Co, W H Cluxton Agent 399 George

Connin Anna Miss, boarding house h 479 Water

Connor Bros, (M & J) livery rr 303 George

Connor Hugh, condr Str Ry h 239 George

Connors James, (Connor Bros) bds Hub Hotel

Connors Martin, (Connor Bros) h Hub Hotel

Connors Walter, mach Wm Hamilton bds 29 Homewood ave

Conoran Mary, dom 377 Park

Conroy John, butcher 213 Hunter h Ashburnham

Conroy Timothy, lab h 264 Murray

Conway Mary, (Wid Patrick) l 80 Boundry

Conway Wm E, Mngr Grafton & Co bds White House

Cook Albert J, sawyer h 109 McDonnel

Cook Cassie, dressmaker l 560 Water

Cook James R, mach Wm Hamilton l 560 Water

Cook Jennie A, l 560 Water

Cook K E Mrs, l 267 Ried

Cook Lizzie, dom 308 Park

Cook Melissa, (Wid John) h 560 Water

Cook R, wks Wm Hamilton

Cook Wid Richard P h 200 George

Cookson Edward, mach Wm Hamilton l 508 Aylmer

Cookson Matilda, (Wid Edward) h 508 Aylmer

Cookson Minnie, h 508 Aylmer

Cooney B, blksmith Bridge Works

Cooney Lillie, dressmaker Miss Geary bds 527 George

Cooper Wm H, wks Auburn Mill h 200 Auburn

Cope Lizzie, dom 297 Hunter

Cope Mary, dom 16 Miller

Corbett Alexander, Miss St R R Co h 295 King

Corbet Lizzie Mrs, cook Grand Central

Corbin W S, wks Times h 30 Louis

Corbitt Peter, pedler h 16 Parnell

Corly Charles, wks Can Gen E Co h 22 Wescott

Corcoran Augustus C, polisher Lock Works h 269 Charlotte

Corcoran Bryan, lab h 479 Stewart

Corcoran Maggie sorter A Murty bds 479 Stewart

Corcoran Margaret, dressmkr l 479 Stewart

Corkery Catherine, l 169 Perry

Corkery John, dep post master b 57 George

Corkery Margaret, (wid Jeremiah) l 169 Perry

Corkery Mary, dressmaker Miss O'Brien l 169 Perry

Corkery Peter, clk H Le Brun & Co bds Balmoral Hotel

Corkery Thomas, carp h 270 King

Corneil Susan, dressmaker l 177 Dublin

Corrigal Catharine Miss, h 36 Union

Corrigal Charlotte, l 36 Union

Corrigal Elizabeth, l 36 Union

Costello D, prtr The Examiner

Costello Lida, l 176 Simcoe

Costello Michael, h 176 Simcoe

Costello Patrick, lab bds 184 Brock

Cottingham John, miller W H Meldrum bds 184 Brock

Cottingham Sam, wks Wm Hamilton

Cottingham Samuel, mldr Wm Hamilton b 12 Cambridge

Cotton R G, insurance h 507 Aylmer

Couch John, painter h 98 Albert

Couch Thomas, wks Wm Hamilton h 488 Reid

Coughlin Bros, (Michael & John) marble works 209 Hunter

Coughlin Daniel, carp h 11 Gilmour

Coughlin Michael, (Coughlin Bros) bds Phelan House

Coulter Bessie, dressmaker Miss O'Brien l 356 Downie

Coulter Maggie, l 356 Downie

Coulter Mary, music teacher bds 313 Bethune

Coulter Robert, lab h 356 Downie

Coulter Sarah, dom 455 Water

Coulter Victora, dom 273 Hunter

County Court Office, John Moloney Clerk Court House Sqr

Cours Wm, butcher J Mervin bds w s Boundry l s C P R

Coursey Bridget, (wid Anthony) h 15 Louis

Coursey Patrick, btchr Geo Matthew Co (Ld) bds 15 Louis

Coursoy Thomas, lab bds 15 Louis

Court House & Goal College, bet Murray & Brock

Courtemanche Dolly, clk G J Horkins

Courtney Grace, dom 755 Water

Cousins John, lab h 226 Murray

Coutchers Philiman (wid) h 89 Paterson

Cowan Isabella, (wid James) h 49 Inverlea

Cowan Samuel G, student h Inverlea

Coward Mary A, (wid Cornelius) l 193 Smith

Cowie Harry, prtr The Examiner bds 219 Simcoe

Cowie Wm, bookbinder The Examiner h 219 Simcoe

Cox Aaron, valuator Central Canada Loan Co h 19 Scott

Cox Alice, l 616 Aylmer

Cox Edward W, hardware l 19 Scott

Cox Estela, l 223 Murray

Cox Frederick J, painter W Cox l 616 Aylmer

Cox George A, (Cox & Davis) h Toronto

Cox Hanna E, (wid James) h 223 Murray

Cox Wm G, wks Lock Works l 616 Aylmer

Cox Wm S, painter h 616 Aylmer

Cox & Davis, (Geo A Cox & A L Davis) General Insurance, Railway & Steamship 433 George (see adv)

C P R Hotel, Wm J Overend prop 170 & 172 Simcoe

C P R Telegraph Co, TE Boddy Agent 322 George

C P R Ticket Office, T E Boddy Agent 322 George

Cragg Edward Rev, h 576 Aylmer

Cragg Frank, l 576 Aylmer

Craig A, pattern mkr Bridge Works

Craig B, lab Bridge Works

Craig George, carp P Hamilton Mnfg Co

Craig James, baker J C Craig bds 663 George

Craig John C, confectioner 426 George h 663 George

Craig John D, furniture 441 George h 493 Alymer

Craig Wm J, baker 663 George h same

Crain Wm, lab Dickson Co

Crandall Howard, wks Can Gen Elec Co bds 471 Rubidge

Crandell H S, wks Can Gen Elec Co bds Snowden House

Crane John clk Ontario Bank h 178 Dalhousie

Cranfield Joseph wks Geo Matthews Co Ld h 76 Lake

Crawford A mach Bridge Works

Crawford Walter L, wks Bridge Works h 31 Walnut

Creamer Wm, h 214 London

Crebbin Wm, bkkpr J R Donell h rear 292 Park

Creddick Sarah, dom 593 George

Cristo Joseph, brick maker h 12 Elm

Croft House, Wm Croft prop 402 Water

Croft Jane, (wid Patrick) h 201 Rubidge

Croft Wm, propr Croft House 402 Water

Croley Louis, stenog Dickson Co h Auburn

Cromie Aggie, mach A Mercer &Co l 121 Brock

Cromie Annie, school teacher l 121 Brock

Cromie Jane, (wid Charles) h 121 Brock

Cromie Maggie,dressmkr M E Frise l 121 Brock

Cromie Susan, mantlemkr J C Turnbull l 121 Brock

Cronan Thomas, tinner J Murty h Park

Cronan John, gardener h 51 Elm

Cronan Nellie, dom 360 Simcoe

Cronin Norah, dressmkr R H Kells l 51 Elm

Cronin Timothy, plasterer l 51 Elm

Crosby J W, Pianos, Organs etc 342 Water h same (see adv)

Crosby Percy D tuner J W Crosby bds 342 Water

Crosby Wm H, trav bds 188 Dalhousie

Crosley Abigail Mc, (wid Henry H) h 188 Dalhousie

Crossley Amey, l 19 Gilmour

Crossley Annie, bkkpr Peterboro Laundry l 381 Aylmer

Crossley Ellen, (wid Thomas) dressmkr h 384 Water

Crossley Holden, bookkpr R Hall h 19 Gilmour

Crossley James, melter P Hamilton Mnfg Co h 381 Aylmer

Crossley Jennie, l 19 Gilmour

Crossley Maggie, dressmkr l 384 Water

Crossley Wm, driver Peterboro Laundry l 381 Aylmer

Crosson Adelaide, dom 483 Water

Crough Maggie, laundress bds 137 London

Crouter George, lab Dickson Co

Crouthers George, miller W H Meldrum bds 69 Hunter

Crowe Agie, l 66 Waterford

Crowe Albert, cabinet mkr D Bellegham

Crowe Charles, wks Dickson Co

Crowe Chas, wks Wm Hamilton

Crowe Emma, (wid Edward) laundress T B McGrath h 209 Hunter

Crowe Francis, l 66 Waterford

Crowe John, lab Dickson Co l 66 Waterford

Crowe Joseph, mldr Wm Hamilton h 11 Cross

Crowe Maud, wks Lock Works bds 109 McDonnel

Crowe Nettie, dom 29 Queen

Crowe Sarah, dressmkr l 66 Waterford

Crowe Sylvester H, boarding house h 66 Waterford

Crowe W H, cabinet mkr Peterboro Canoe Co h Ashburnham

Crowley Eliza, h 178 Aylmer

Crowley Ellen, dressmaker l 71 Elm

Crowley Mary, (wid David L) h 6 Aylmer

Crowley Mary, (wid David) grocery 108 Lake h same

Crowley Mary Miss, dressmkr h 70 Elm

Crowley Patrick, h 126 Romain

Crowley Wm, wks H Calcutt h 6 Aylmer

Crowley Wm, wks H Calcutt bds 108 Lake

Crown Timber Office, J B McWilliams agent 378 Water

Culling Cornelius, shoemaker Foot & McWhinnie h 107 Albert

Cumming Bessie, city collector 127 Simcoe bds Charlotte

Cumming Elizabeth tax collector 1 334 Charlotte

Cumming Elizabeth, (wid Wm) h 334 Charlotte

Cumming Ina G 1 334 Charlotte

Cumming John, clk A Elliott 1 334 Charlotte

Cummings A, lab Bridge Works

Cummings Alice, (wid Thomas) 1 189 Reid

Cummings Thomas, lab C P R h 189 Reid

Cunace C S, wks Peterboro Carbon Co

Cuncannon Annie, dom 80 Westcott

Cuncannon John B, wks Can Gen Elec Co h 82 Wescott

Cunning Lillian Mrs, 1 635 Water

Cunningham Bolton, clk Brown Bros bds 284 Brock

Cunningham Frank S, clk Fairweather & Co h 173 Edinburgh

Cunningham George, painter h 49 Hunter

Cunningham G Mrs, confectionery h 49 Hunter

Cunningham Jane, (wid Samuel) 1 173 Edinburgh

Cunningham John J, wks Joseph Cunningham 1 284 Brock

Cunningham John Mc, lab h 284 Brock

Cunningham Joseph F, baker rear 210 Charlotte h 27 Rutherford ave

Cunningham J P, (Turner & Cunningham) h 544 Bethune

Cunningham Lottie, dom 376 Stewart

Cunningham Pheobe, dom 392 Charlotte

Cunningham Thomas, barber 326 Arcade bds 185 Edinburgh

Cunningham Wm H, miller W H Meldrum 1 284 Brock

Curran Alicia, 1 360 Downie

Curran Charles D, wks Carbon Works h 155 Stewart

Curran James, mason bds C P R Hotel

Curran John S, lab h 360 Downie

Curry Cora, 1 273 McDonnel

Curry Wm S, carpet weaver 273 McDonnel h same

Curtin Jane, (wid Timothy) 1 785 George

Curtis George, lab h 571 Reid

THE BANK OF TORONTO,
PETERBORO' BRANCH, P. CAMPBELL, MANAGER.
BUYS AND SELLS CANADIAN AND FOREIGN EXCHANGE.

PETERBOROUGH CITY DIRECTORY.　　　29

Curtis George, bricklayer h 690 Aylmer

Cushing Daniel, lab A McDonnell h 330 Sherbrooke

Cushing Mary E, l 330 Sherbrooke

Cushing Michael, wks Oriental Hotel l 330 Sherbrooke

Cushing Wm, l 330 Sherbrooke

Customs House, C H, Clementi collector s e cor George & Simcoe

Daigneault Angelina, wks Auburn Mill l 53 Smith

Daigneault Joseph, wks Auburn Mill l 53 Smith

Daigneault Mary, wks Auburn Mill l 55 Smith

Daigneault Peter, lab h 53 Smith

Dainty George, teamster J D Craig

Dalaire Duffield, lumberman bds 221 Perry

Dalaire Joseph, lumber man h 221 Perry

Dalaire Joseph, l 221 Perry

Dale Thomas, carp h 56 George

Daley Jeremiah, wks Lock Works h 99 Elm

Daley Michael, wks Lock Works l 99 Elm

Daly Eugene, lab h 92 Weller

Daly Fannie, l 92 Weller

Daly Kate, l 92 Weller

Dancy Samuel R, lab h 273 Simcoe

Daniels Ettie, dom 293 Townsend

Daniels Frederick, farmer h 336 Aylmer

Dannard George, wks Lock Works h 479 Donegal

Dannard John, wks Lock Work l 479 Donegal

Dannard Lizzie, school teacher l 479 Donegal

Dannard Mary, dressmaker l 479 Donegal

Dark Hugh, wks Wm Hamilton h 124 Rubidge

Daten James S, carp J Montgomery h 223 Rink

Daubez Edith, l 39 Sheridan

Daubez Henry, J h 39 Sheridan

Daubez Mina, l 39 Sheridan

Danett wks Williams, bds 106 Murray

David Wm S, bkkpr Can Gen E Co bds 235 George

Davidson Adam, bartender Southern Hotel h 344 Simcoe

Davidson Andrew, h 25 Louis

Davidson Andrew, painter l Cotton l 587 Aylmer

Davidson Bella, clk R Fair l 198 Edinburgh

Davidson Charles, tailor W J Green bds 267 McDonnel

Davidson Dickson druggist Ormond & Walsh l 124 Dickson

Davidson Elsie, clk J W Butcher l 198 Edinburgh

Davidson Flora H, l 815 George

Davidson Florence, bkkpr Hall Gilchrist & Co l 509 Water

Davidson George, wks Can Gen E Co h 587 Aylmer

Davidson George, wks Auburn Mill h 860 George

Davidson Harry, clk H S McDonnell l 509 Water

Davidson James, wks Auburn Mill h 2 Anson

Davidson John I, sec Auburn Mill h 815 George

Davidson J C Rev M A, Rector Of Peterborough (St Johns) h 64 Hunter

Davidson Laura J, l 124 Dickson

Davidson Maggie, clk C B Routley l 198 Edinburgh

Davidson Maggie, l 587 Aylmer

Davidson Margaret, (Wid Samuel) h 198 Edinburgh

Davidson Margaret M, teacher Central School l 815 George

Davidson Mary, l 198 Edinburgh

Davidson Minnie, clk J W Moore & Co bds 25 Lewis

Davidson Robert S, Treas Peterboro Hardware Co h 202 Dalhousie

Davidson Susan G, kindergarter directoress Rubidge St School l 815 George

Davidson Walter, clk Stratton & Hall l 509 Water

Davidson Wm, miller h 124 Dickson

Davies Benjamin, gardner h 499 Aylmer

Davies B Mrs, dressmaker 499 Aylmer h same

Davis A L, (Cox & Davis) h 35 Belmont

Davis Alice, l 35 Belmont ave

Davis Charles, sawyer Dickson Co

Davis Eva, l 191 Brock

Davis Jane, (Wid Rev George H) h 191 Brock

Davis Jane Mrs, h 588 Aylmer

Daw student Can Gen E Co bds White House

Dawe D D C, printer Review h 31 Gilmour

Dawner Asa B, carp h 20 Kirk

Dawner Geo, lab l 20 Kirk

Dawson Adam, contractor h 483 Donegal

Dawson Alfred, grocer 355 George h 45 McDonnel

Dawson Alice, retoucher P H Green bds Ashburnham

Dawson Annie, dressmkr Misses Kingdon & Menzies

Dawson Annie, l 72 Bonacord

Dawson B, appr Bridge Wks

Dawson Charles, supt Bridge Works h 44 George

Dawson Charles N mach Bridge Works l 44 George

Dawson Edwin, clk Cox & Davis

Dawson George H, pattern maker Wm Hamilton l 44 George

Dawson Hillier, wks Peterboro Carbon Works bds 74 Chamberlain

Dawson Jeremiah, lab h 179 Harvey

Dawson Jennie, dom 603 Stewart

Dawson John, wks Wm Hamilton l 72 Bonacord

Dawson J A, mach Bridge Works

Dawson Lizzie, dressmkr J C Turnbull l 72 Bonacord

Dawson Sarah, dom 155 Stewart

Dawson Thomas, wks WmHamilton h 72 Bonacord

Dawson Wm A, wks Peterboro Carbon Works h 74 Chamberlain

Day Ettie, l 200 Edinburgh

Day Henry, h 200 Edinburgh

Dayman Wm H, clk Alex Elliott h 219 Stewart

Daynard John A, wks Bridge Works h 113 Albert

De Laire J, mldr Lock Works

Decher George, driver J C Craig bds 79 Smith

Deenen Ellen, (wid John) h rear 96 Aylmer

Deitcher Annie, dom 29 Homewood avenue

Delaire John, moulder Lock Works h 15 Cross

Delaire Minnie, l 470 Donegal

Delaire Patrick, shoemaker 336 McDonnel h 382 same

Delaney Ellen, dom w s Boundry 1 s C P R track

Delaney E Miss, dry goods etc 403 George bds cor Brock & Downie

Delaney John, h 437 Downie

Delaney Kate Mrs, grocery 853 Water h same

Delill Charles, plasterer h 24 Union

Delong Samuel, plasterer h 87 Albert

Demontette Joseph, blksmith PHamilton Mnfg Co

Deneen Elizabeth, (wid Timothy) l 943 Water

Deneen Maurice, river man h 885 Water

Deneen Timothy, l 885 Water

Denne Emily, l 723 George

Denne Eva, l 723 George

Denne Gertie, clk A H Stratton & Co l 723 George

Denne Hattie, l 723 George

Denne Henry, h 723 George

Denne T H G, flour & feed 135&137 Charlotte h 293 Park

Dennistoun Annie Miss, l 755 Water

Dennistoun Catherine, (wid James F) h 755 Water

Dennistoun Georgie, l 755 Water

Dennistoun Hellen, l 755 Water

Dennistoun Jessie, l 755 Water

Dennistoun Lewis, l 755 Water

Dennistoun Mamie, l 755 Water

Dennistoun R M, (Dennistoun & Stevenson) h 748 Water

Dennistoun & Stevenson, (R M Dennistoun & Arthur Stevenson) Barristers etc 417 Water (see adv)

Deno Joseph, lab 1 143 Romaine

Deno Louis, cook h 143 Romaine

Denoon E Miss, stenog G Matthews

Denoon John, Butcher 561 George h 29 Division

Deremo Wilber A, wks Can Gen Elec Co h 86 Park

Deremo Wm L, carp h 29 Wescott

Derocher Isaiah, lab The Rathbun Co

Derrick Frank E, wks Can Gen Elec Co h Customs House upstairs

Derry Thomas, harnessmkr h 343 McDonnel

Derry Thos, mldr Wm Hamilton 1 433 McDonnel

Derry Walter, wks Wm Hamilton

Dery Wm, wks W J Hall h 437 McDonnel

Desautel Damas, blksmith W E McCall b 40 George

Desautels David, telegraph operator 1 40 George

Desautel Edward, clk John Burnham bds 40 George

Desautelle Lexie, dress mkr Miss Delaney

Desault Louis, lab h 41 Smith

Desaultels Nellie, dressmaker 1 40 George

Desautels Rigna, tailoress H LaBrun & Co 1 5 Lake

Desaultels Zotique, lab b 5 Lake

Detcher Burt, clk W Detcher 1 865 Water

Detcher George, driver W J Craig 1 79 Smith

Detcher Isabela, wks Lech & Sons 1 540 Gilchrist

Detcher Maud, 1 865 Water

Detcher Wm, grocer 1 Victoria ave h 865 Water

Detcher Wm, lab h 540 Gilchrist

Devett Matthew, lab G McWilliams

Devine Edward, lab Can Gen Elec Co h 82 Patterson

Devine John, forman on drive Dickson Co

Devitt Arthur, supt Peterboro Woolen Mill h 762 Water

Devlin Wm J, harness 160 Hunter h 324 King

Deyell David, cabinetmkr D Bellegham h 181½ London

Dianeen Lillie, 1 Queens Hotel

Dianeen Mary, 1 Queens Hotel

Dianeen Richard, wks Wm Dianeen bds same

Dianeen Wm, propr Queens Hotel cor Charlotte & Alymer

Dick Jessie, waitress C P R Hotel

Dicks George, mason h 189 Patterson

Dicks George jr, bricklayer h 135 Patterson

Dicks James, mach Canadian General Elec Co bds 139 Patterson

Dicks Lillie,wks Carbon Works bds 139 Paterson

Dicks Noah, wks Carbon Works bds 139 Paterson

Dickson A G, Dry Goods 395 George bds Oriental(see adv)

Dickson Charlotte, h 84 Murray

Dickson Co (Ld), T G Hazlitt pres & mang director lumber mnfrs 47 London

Dickson Martha, h 84 Murray

Dickson Wm,farmer b n s Smith c l

Diegle Georgia, wks Auburn Mill l n s Wolsley 2 w Benson

Diegle Joseph, wks Auburn Mill l n s Wolsley 2 w Benson

Diegle Lena,l n s Wolsley 2 w Benson

Diegle Louis, wks Auburn Mill h n s Wolsley 2 w Benson

Digman Kate M L, l 208 Charlotte

Dineen Tim, clk Miss Rudkins

Dinsdale Mary, dom 124 Dickson

Distin George W,painter h 33 Aberdeen Ave

Diston Thomas, mach P Hamilton Mnfg Co

Ditcher Grace, (wid Joseph) h 79 Smith

Division Court, F J Bell Clerk 415½ Water

Dix Ada, dom 270 Charlotte

Dix Lillie, wks Peterboro Carbon Co

Dix Nora,wks Peterboro Carbon Co

Dixon Albert E, (Edmiston & Dixon) h 681 Stewart

Dixon Charles, groom Dr Yelland l 147 Murray

Dixon Emily, l 686 Stewart

Dixon F H, secy W H Hill

Dixon George, wks E McGrath bds 539 George

Dixon George, clk A E Micks

Dixon John, range mkr Adam Hall

Dixon Margaret,(wid Joseph) h 686 Stewart

Dixon Reginald, clk Edmiston & Dixon bds 686 Stewart

Dobbin Eliza, (wid Wm) h 178 Edinburgh

Dobbin Eliza, (wid Wm) h 461 George (upstairs)

Dobbins F H, Mngr Dir Peterboro Review P & P Co Ld h 44 Weller

Dobbin L, plumber Adam Hall

Dobbin Lemuel, millwright W H Meldrum h Ashburnham

Dober Frederick, clk Wm Cluxton h Ashburnham

Dobson Eva, school teacher l 146 Murray

Dobson George, clk R Neill h 146 Murray

Dobson Mark, mason Dickson Co h 330 Smith

Dodds Ella,student bds 559 Aylmer

Dodds E E, United States Consul bds Morgan House

Dodds E K, clk T Dolan & Co

Doherty Maggie, l 300 Simcoe

Doherty Mary, (wid John) h 300 Simcoe

Doig David, junk 214 Hunter h Park

Doig David jr, pedler D Doig bds same

Doig George, milkman bds 103 Albert

Dolan James, h 341 George

Dolan Robert, lab bds 101 Rubidge

Dolan Thomas, (T Dolan & Co) h 358 Brock

Dolan T & Co, (Thos Dolan) Clothiers 399 George

Dominion Express Co, T E Boddy Agent 322 George

Donaldson Ellen, (wid Samuel) l 762 Water

Donaldson Miss, dressmkr Hall Gilchrist & Co

Donovan D, wks Lock Works bds 479 Donegal

Donell J R, planing mill Dickson Race h 640 Bethune

Donell Wm J, planing mill 165 Dublin h 618 Bethune

Donlay John, section foreman G T R

Donnelly Harry, pressman Examiner bds 313 Bethune

Donnelly John, section foreman G T R h 313 Bethune

Donnelly Maud, dressmkr Miss Kingdon & Menzies

Donoghue Daniel, mach Lock Works h 298 Simcoe

Donohue Mrs, (wid Robert) l 735 Water

Donovan Dennis, mldr Lock Works bds C P R Hotel

Donovan Dennis jr, polisher Lock Works

Donovan John M, grocer 356 Charlotte h 323 Downie

Doris Albert, jointer Dickson Co l 83 London

Doris James, packer Dickson Co l 83 London

Doris John A mach Dickson Co l 83 London

Doris John R, carp Dickson Co h 83 London

Doris Nellie, dressmaker l 83 London

Doris Patrick, mach Dickson Co l 83 London

Dormer Edward G, wks Dickson Co bds 209 Rubidge

Dormer G, appr Bridge Works

Dormer Isaac, lab Dickson Co

Dormer John, storekeeper Bridge Works

Dormer L, appr B F Ackerman

Doris B, yardman Live Oak Hotel

Doris Bernard, h 48 Elm

Doris James, carp Dickson Co h 109 Elm

Doris Johanna, wks Can Gen Elec Co l 195 Reid

Doris John, lab Dickson Co

Doris J R, carp Dickson Co

Doris Margaret, wks Can Gen Elec Co l 195 Reid

Doris Mary, dom 222 Dalhousie

Doris Patrick, shinglemkr Dickson Co

Doris Patrick J bartender Pullman Hotel bds same

Doris Thos J, wks Wm Hamilton h 36 Cedar

Doris Wm, lab h 195 Reid

Doris Wm F, harnessmkr B F Ackerman l 195 Reid

Douglas Andrew, contractor h 52 Gilmour

Douglas Ellen, dressmkr 84 Hunter h same

Douglas Hattie, bds 574 Aylmer

Douglas John, h 119 Willer

Douglas John C, l 52 Gilmour

Douglas John J, bkkpr Winch Bros l 119 Weller

Douglas, l 52 Gilmour

Down Mary, (wid Henry) l cor McDonnel & Bethune

Downer Addie, clk R Neill l 144 Murray

Downer Agnes, clk R Neill l 144 Murray

Downie Eugene, bartender Phelens Hotel h 379 Stewart

Downing Joseph E, wks Auburn Mill h 16 Lisburn

Doyle Louisa, dom 387 Reid

Doyle Bert, ptr Can Gen Elec Co bds 50 Parnell

Drake Sarah, (wid John) h 188 Rubidge

Drake Rosa, (wid Harry) grocer 87 Hunter h same

Drake Wm, stonemason h 198 Perry

Dredge Charles, lab h 13 Victoria ave

Mnfrs. Life Ins. Co., Toronto.

"I received your cheque for $10,000 within three hours after I filed claim papers".

KATHERINE RIDOUT.

Dredge Eliza, wks Auburn Mill l 13 Victoria ave

Dredge George, lab h 23 Sheridan

Dredge Walter, wks The Examiner l 13 Victoria ave

Drew Richard, wks Can Gen Elec Co bds 302 Aylmer

Drew Thomes, foreman Can Gen Elec Co bds 302 Alymer

Drocher Israel, lab Rathbun Co h 495 Bethune

Drope Wm J, teacher Collegia te Inst h 591 George

Dugan Abbie, l 232 Brock

Druley Louis, wks Can Gen Elec Co h 297 Townsend

Drummond J, lab Bridge Wks

Drury Amelia, l 88 Simcoe

Drury Lydia, l 88 Simcoe

Drury Robert, lab P Hamilton Mnfg Co h 38 Patterson

Drury Wm, mngr Gas Works h 88 Simcoe

Drury Wm jr, l 88 Simcoe

Duckworth George, mach Can Gen Elec Co bds 391 Sherbrooke

Dudman Charles S, watchman Dickson Co h 676 Water

Dugan Abbie, l 232 Brock

Dugan Alexander T, carp h 22 Gilmour

Dugan Benjamin E, wks Can Gen Elec Co l 22 Gilmour

Dugan Francis Miss, h 232 Brock

Dugan John, lab l 22 Gilmour

Duignan John, insp Dickson Co Ld h 184 Dalhousie

Dumble D W, (Dumble & Johnston) h 365 McDonnel

Dumble Frederick, l 310 McDonnel

Dumble & Johnston, (D W Dumble & W F Johnston) Barristers 435 George

Dumonetet Alfred, wks Lock Works l 222 Park

Dumontet Joseph, blksmith P Hamilton h 138 Perry

Dumonetet Wm, carp Wm Donnel h 222 Park

Duncau A, bottler D Knox bds Southern Hotel

Duncan Daisy, dressmkr l 109 Smith

Duncan Elizabeth, (wid James) h 68 Wescott

Duncan Essie, wks Lock Works l 68 Wescott

Duncan George H, printer bds 350 Water

Duncan James, driver l X L Laundry bds 86 Lock

Duncan John, miller W H Meldrum h 109 Smith

Duncan Nellie, l 68 Wescott

Duncan Robert, dray man h 115 McDonnel

Duncan Thomas, mach Canadian General ElecCo h 354 Sherbrooke

Duncan Wm, wks J Watt bds 20 Queen

Dundas Alfred, engr h 155 Stewart

Dundas Harry, harness mkr 166 Simcoe h 694 George

Dundas Wm, harness mkr H Dundas bds 694 George

Dunford Albert, carp h 414 Sherbrooke

Dunford Elizabeth, (wid Charles) h 323 McDonnel

Dunford John, mngr A E Mosley h 32 Louis

Dunlop Andrew C, h 483 Water

Dunlop Emma, l 19½ Patterson

Dunlop Ida, dressmkr l 19½ Patterson

Dunlop Mary Miss, l 483 Water

Dunlop Minnie, wks Canadian General Elec Co l 19½ Patterson

Dunlop Thomas, lab h 19½ Patterson

Dunn Annie, l 367 Bethune

Dunn Bridget, (wid Francis) h 861 Water

Dunn Catherine, (wid James B) h 367 Bethune

Dunn Charles, wks Auburn Mill h 857 George

Dunn Eveline, clk R Fair l 9 John

Dunn John, lab Dickson Co

Dunn John, wks Auburn Mill l 861 Water

Dunn John M, carp Dickson Co h 9 John

Dunn Justus, grocer 163 Charlotte h same

Dunn Katie, dressmkr l 367 Bethune

Dunn Mary, l 367 Bethune

Dunn Michael, barkeeper Grand Central bds same

THE BANK OF TORONTO,
PETERBORO' BRANCH, P. CAMPBELL, MANAGER.
BUYS AND SELLS CANADIAN AND FOREIGN EXCHANGE.

PETERBOROUGH CITY DIRECTORY. 37

Dunn Thomas, propr Bodega 139 Hunter h same

Dunnett Charles, butcher h 180 Auburn

Dunnigan Francis, agent h 69 Harvey

Dunsford Enos, carp h 303 Sherbrooke

Dunsford George, h 113 Simcoe

Dunsford Ley, wks Can Gen E Co Rooms 338 Stewart

Dunsford M J Mrs, grocer 240 Rubidge l same

Duquette Ellen, (Wid J B) h 165 Sherbrooke

Durand Marth (Wid James) l 273 Hunter

Duvall Samuel, mason h 317 Smith

Dwyer Ellen Mrs, laundress h 41 Albert

Dwyer John, forman Dickson Co h 708 Water

Dwyer John A, h 375 Sherbrooke

Dwyer Rose M, mantle mkr bds 375 Sherbrooke

Dwyer Thomas J, school teacher bds 375 Sherbrooke

Dygnan John, inspr Dickson Co bds 184 Dalhousie

Dyson Mary Mrs, cook Snowden House

Eagleson Alexander, lab P Hamilton Mnfg Co h 258 Reid

Eagleson George, clk E B Stone bds 58 Harvey

Eakins James, wks Dickon Co h 664 George

Eano Michael, lab Dickson Co h 115 Elm

Earle George, clk R Neill

Earle O Barton, insurance h 694 Water

Early George J, photographer 374½ George h same

Early Thomas, lab Dickson Co bds 66 Waterford

Earskin Frank, lab Dickson Co

Earskin Wesley, filer Dickson Co

Earskin Wesley, h 100 Dublin

Eastland Bertha, wks C G Gemmell bds 401 Wolfe

Eastland Catherine A, (Wid Poole) h 199 Simcoe

Eastland Frederick, boiler mkr Wm Hamilton h 401 Wolfe

Eastland Hannah Miss, l 401 Wolfe

Eastland Maria P, (Wid Henry) h 199 Simcoe

Eastland T, wks Wm Hamilton

Eastwood Margaret, (wid Vincent) l l 232 Dublin

Eastwood Vincent, clk Peterboro Hardware Co h 232 Dublin

Edgar Lillie, dressmkr M E Frise

Edgar Thomas, fire insurance agent W H Hill

Edgcumbe Eleda, bkkpr J Edgcumbe l 687 Water

Edgcumbe James, grocer 682 George h 687 Water

Edmison Annie, l 458 Rubidge

Edmison George, (Edmison & Dixon) h 458 Rubidge

FOR BIBLES, HYMN BOOKS, PRAYER BOOKS, ETC., ETC.

Go To SAILSBURY'S.

Edmison George jr, clk J D Tulley l 458 Rubidge

Edmison Herbert, clk J McKee l 458 Rubidge

Edmison James, lab h 138 Rubidge

Edmison Jane, (wid Richard) h 138 Rubidge

Edmison Maud, l 458 Rubidge

Edmison & Dixon, (Geo Edmison & A E Dixon) Barristers 397 George (see adv)

EDMISON & DIXON,

(Geo. Edmison &, A. E. Dixon)

Barristers, Solicitors, Notaries, Etc.

397 George,   -   -   cor. Hunter.

Edmonds Alexander, h 338 Stewart

Edmonds Mary, l 338 Stewart

Edmondson Henry, overseer J Stephenson Coal Co h 116 Weller

Edmondson Lucy, corset mkr Mrs Gemmel l 116 Weller

Edmondson Wm, boilermkr Wm Hamilton l 116 Weller

Edmunds Archibald, fireman G T R h 35 Stewart

Edwards E B, (Edwards & Murray) h n Monaghan c l

Edwards Jas W, painter h 20 Gilmore

Edwards M, driver D Knox

Edwards & Murray, (E B Edwards & W H Murray) barristers 435 George

Elliott Euphemia, clk T C Elliot l 147 London

Elliot Thomas C, knitting works 382½ George h 147 London

Elcombe Edward W, clk W J Hall h 600 George

Elcombe R Edwin taxidermist 176 Harvey h same

Elliott Alex, Grocer etc 353 George h cor Park & Gilmour

Elliott Arthur, mldr W Hamilton bds 184 Brock

Elliott Benjamin, mldr Can GenElec Co bds 184 Brock

Elliott Charlotte, l 184 Brock

Elliott Christina, l 147 Romaine

Elliott David, mach Can Gen Elec Co bds White House

Elliott George, contractor h 250 Charlotte

Elliott Grace, (wid Benjamin) h 184 Brock

Elliott Jason, lab h n s Weller l w Monaghan

Elliott John, lab h 563 George

Elliott John C, harnessmkr B F Ackerman h 147 Romaine

Elliott Laura, dom 147 Murray

Elliott Thomas H, wks Can Gen Elec Co h 351 Bethune

Elliott Wm, harnessmkr T H Denuel bds 101 Simcoe

THE BANK OF TORONTO,
PETERBORO' BRANCH, P. CAMPBELL, MANAGER.
HIGHEST RATE OF INTEREST ALLOWED ON DEPOSITS.

PETERBOROUGH CITY DIRECTORY. 39

Ellis Annie J, wks Auburn Mill 814 Water

Ellis Eliza, dom 187 London

Ellis Frank, yardman OrientalHotel bds same

Ellis James, insurance agent h 814 Water

Elves James, machinist 232 Hunter bds 213 Charlotte

Elvin M Miss, matron Dr Barnardos Home

Emerson Charles M, trav Wm Hamilton h 340 Rubidge

Emerson E M, wks Wm Elliott

Emery Wm, wks F Mason bds Ashburnham

Emmerson Ann, (wid Wm) h 28 Division

Emmerson Annie J, clk W H Wrighton l 138 London

Emmerson Hannah, clk Foot & McWhinnie

Emmerson Jon, h 138 London

Emmerson John E, tool mkr Lock Works h 338 Downie

Emmerson Maud, dom 222 McDonnel

Emmerson Thomas, wks Wm Hamilton h 341 Downie

Emmett George, hostlerCroft House bds same

Emond Bertha,wksParisianLaundry l 375 Stewart

Emond Eugene, lab F McDonnel h 375 Stewart

Edmond Mary, wks Parisian Laundry l 375 Stewart

English Caroline, (wid Wm) h 264 Water

English Francis, tailor Hall Gilchrist & Co l 220 London

EnglishGoldsmith, agent h 220 London

English James, fireman City Dept h 176 Charlotte

English Kate, l 176 Charlotte

English Maggie, dressmkr l 220 London

English Samuel W, mngr Wm English Canoe Co h 178 Charlotte

English Walter J, bds 264 Water

English Wm Canoe Co, S W English mngr 182 & 184 Charlotte

Ensign Corset Co, (Mrs L Ensign) Corset Mnfrs 176 Simcoe

Ensign Lettie Mrs, (Ensign Corset Co) h 176 Simcoe

Errett Annie, l 80 Gilmour

Errett Richard W, insurance 392 Water h 80 Gilmour

Errett Olive, l 80 Gilmour

Erskine Alexander,carp h 196 Brock

Erskine Anna B, l 196 Brock

Erskine Minnie, dressmkr l 196 Brock

Erskine Robert, clk Mulholland & Roper bds Ashburnham

Ervin Elizabeth, (wid) l 16 Elm

Evans Edith, wksCanadian Gen Elec Co bds 44 Paterson

Evans Enos D, carp Dickson Co h 44 Paterson

Evans George, tlr Hall Gilchrist & Co bds 44 Paterson
Evans Harry, carp h 36 Wescott
Evans Russell, mach Canadian General Elec Co bds 44 Paterson
Evans Wallace, carp rms Fire Hall
Evans Walter, carp h n Monaghan
Evans Wm, carp bds 213 Charlotte
Evens David, deliver J Denoon l 170½ Dublin
Evens David, butcher J Denoon h 165 Edinburgh
Evens E, carp Dickson Co
Evens Hugh T, butcher 554 Bethune h same
Everett Henry T, watchmaker 16(Simcoe bds 195 Murray
Everett Herbert, motorman St Ry h 70 Weller
Everett Russel, l 195 Murray
Everett Wm, clk St R R Co h 195 Murray
Examiner Printing & Publishing Co Ltd (The), J R Stratton M P P Pres, F J Jamieson Mngr 419 George (see adv)
Examiner The, The Examiner P & P Co Ltd Props 419 George (see adv)
Eyres Mary, school tchr l 168 Antrim
Eyres Wm, h 168 Antrim
Fady Bridget, (wid George) h 37 Albert

Fady Hattie, wks Canadian General Elec Co l 37 Albert
Fady Jennie, dressmkr R Fair l 37 Albert
Fady Mary, wks Canadian General Elec Co l 37 Albert
Fady Randolph, wks Canadian General Electric Co l 37 Albert
Fagan Christopher, wks Dickson Co h 80 Bour.dry
Fair Josie, dressmkr Robt Fair bds 81 London
Fair Robert, operator G T R
Fair Robert, Dry Goods Etc 383 George h 105 Dickson
Fair Sarah, l 105 Dickson
Fair Thomas, teamster A Hall h 218 London
Fairbairn Jane R, (wid T M) l 465 Park
Fairen Frank, prop Pullman Hotel 339 George
Fairen James W, billiard marker F Fairen h Stewart
Fairman Harriett, (wid George) h 212 Auburn
Fairman J, wks Auburn Mill l 212 Auburn
Fairman Susan, wks Auburn Mill l 212 Auburn
Fairley James, mach Canadian General Elec Co h 24 Boliver
Fairweather Agnes, (wid Wm) h 48 Gilmour
Fairweather Isabella, l 48 Gilmour
Fairweather James W T, (Fairweather & Co) bds 48 Gilmour
Fairweather Jessie, l 48 Gilmour

Fairweather Robert H, Bkkpr
Fairweather & Co bds 48 Gilmour
Fairweather & Co, (J W T
Fairweather) Hatters and Mnfg
Furriers 361 George (see adv)

FAIRWEATHER & CO.,
Manufacturing Furriers and Hatters,
of Peterboro' and Lindsay.

Ordered Fur Garments and Remodeling or
Repairing of Old Furs receives our special
attention. FAIRWEATHER & CO.,Y,
COR. GEORGE & SIMCOE STS.

Fallice Charles E, tailor P Simons
bds 58 Elm
Fallis Frank, wks Carbon Works
bds 101 Rubidge
Fallon Michael, lab Dickson Co
Fallon Nellie, waitress Balmoral
Fanning Hattie, h 407 Wolfe
Fanning James M, bookkeeper bds
833 Water
Fanning John, clk Thos Kelly bds
Morgan House
Fanning Robert, teamster Wm Ham-
ilton h 465 Downie
Fanning Samuel J, harnessmaker B
F Ackerman l 465 Downie
Fanning Sarah, h 407 Wolfe
Fanning Stewart, mach Wm Hamil-
ton l 465 Downie
Fantine Francis, lab h 486 Park
Farnell Joseph, lab h 54 Albert
Farnum David, h 20 College

Fassett Charlotte, clk Stratton &
Hall bds 583 Water
Faulcher Frank, porter Geo Carter
Faulkner Sylvester G, insurance 379
Water h 188 Murray
Fausett John, teamster h 857 Water
Fawcett Annie, l 168 Brock
Fawcett Michael, lumberman h 168
Brock
Fax Maggie, dom 176 Brock
Federal Life Assurance Co,
H B Mebarry District Agent 161
Simcoe
Fee Harry, tlr W H Meredith bds
380 Water
Fee Thomas, expressman h 368
Sherbrooke
Fegg J A, baggageman C P R h 34
Albert
Felli Philimine, (wid Eli) h n s Ro-
maine l w R R track
Ferguson Adam, clk Kingan &
Allen l 254 Stewart
Ferguson Alithea M Miss, h 359
Stewart
Ferguson Edith E, school teacher l
19 Aylmer
Ferguson Evelin G, clk Bell Tele
phone Office l 19 Aylmer
Ferguson Edward, cab driver A E
Mosley bds 195 Simcoe
Ferguson Flo M, l 19 Aylmer
Ferguson Frederick, clk Kingan &
Allen l 356 Stewart

Ferguson Georgena, (wid Bruce) h 356 Stewart
Ferguson John J, barber h 183 Antrim
Ferguson Maggie waitress Southern Hotel
Ferguson Minnie, dom 352 Simcoe
Ferguson W, section foremanG T R
Ferguson Wm, insurance h 19 Aylmer
Ferguson Wm G, (Peter Connall & Co) h 254 Stewart
Fessenden Cortez, prin coll institute h 602 Rubidge
Fice Minnie, dom 210 McDonnel
Fife Herbert, wks Electric Light Co h 77 Harvey
Fife Herbert Mrs, bkkpr W H Meldrum
Fife James A, teacher coll inst h 87 Benson
Fife Joseph A, physician 631 George h same
Finn Dennis lab h 211 Rink
Finn John, lab h 113 Lake
Finn Maggie, l 211 Rink
Finn Miss, dressmker h 101 Chamberlain
Finn Nora, dom 813 Water
Finn Patrick, lab l 211 Rink
Finney Ada Mrs, (wid Dr) nurse Nicholls Hospital l same
Finney Edward, porter Thomas Brady

Finnie Ettie, mlnr J C Turnbull
Fire Hall, 133 Simcoe
Fisher James, lab h 1 Sheridan
Fisher Wm, blksmith T Fitzgerald bds 213 Charlotte
Fisk Albert, bds 560 Water
Fisk Homer O, electrician bds 560 Water
Fitch H, lab Bridge Works
Fitzgerald Ellen, tlress A Mercer & Co bds 40 George
Fitzgerald Emma, dressmkr Miss Morgan l Ashburnham
Fitzgerald Ernest, clk P Hamilton Mnfg Co l 687 George
Fitzgerald G, wks Peterboro Carbon Co
Fitzgerald George, (Fitzgerald & Stanger) h 32 Sheridan
Fitzgerald Gerald D, physician l 206 Smith
Fitzgerald James W, civil engr h 206 Smith
Fitzgerald James W jr, surveyor l 206 Smith
Fitzgerald John, cigar mkr A Murty bds Ashburnham
Fitzgerald Richard, tlr H Le Brun & Co bds Balmoral Hotel
Fitzgerald Robert, wks The Peterboro Canoe Co h 687 George
Fitzgerald Samuel S, carriage mnfr T Fitzgerald h 257 Stewart
Fitzgerald Thomas, trimmer Fitzgerald & Stanger bds 106 Murray
Fitzgerald Thomas E, agent P Hamilton Mnfg Co h 159 Stewart
Fitzgerald Tobias, livery 224 Charlotte h 225 same

Fitzgerald & Stanger, (George Fitzgerald & John Stanger) carriage mkrs 131 Brock

Fitzpatrick Edward, lab h 769 Water

Fitzpatrick John, lab h 85 Lake

Fitzpatrick Mary, tlress H Le Brun & Co l 85 Lake

Flaherty Edward, clk Dickson Lumber Co h 180 Antrim

Flaherty Edward, dray man h 115 Smith

Flaherty Eugene, wks Review l 180 Antrim

Flaherty James, carp l 115 Smith

Flaherty Jerrie, wks Lock Works l 115 Smith

Flaherty Katie, wks Peterboro Woolen Mill l 180 Antrim

Flaherty Maggie, l 180 Antrim

Flaherty Martin, lab bds 47 Elm

Flaherty Mary, l 180 Antrim

Flaherty Michael, wks Auburn Mill l 115 Smith

Flaherty Winnie, wks Auburn Mill l 115 Smith

Flannery John, wks Auburn Mill h 210 Auburn

Fleetwood Wm, btchr J J Howden h Ashburnham

Fleming Andrew Mrs, grocery 113 Rubidge h same

Fleming A H, wks Peterboro Carbon Co

Fleming Delila, (wid David) bds 141 Sherbrooke

Fleming Maud, dressmaker Hall, Gilchrist & Co l 113 Rubidge

Fleming Wellington, wks Carbon Wks bds 113 Rubidge

Fletcher Archie, driver E F Mason & Co l 30 College

Fletcher Wm A, insurance agent h 30 College

Flynn Agnes, dressmkr bds 96 Lake

Flynn James, blksmith h 96 Lake

Fobert Timothy, l 32 Parnell

Foden John H, lab h 145 Park

Foley Bridget, cook Peterboro House

Foley Catherine, (wid Timothy) h 371 Stewart

Foley Ellen, (wid John) l 37 Parnell

Foley Ellen, l 37 Parnell

Foley George, agent Singer Sewing Machines h 389 Aylmer

Foley Nellie, dom Oriental Hotel

Foley Peter J, canvasser G B Sprule

Foot Amelia B, l 246 McDonnel

Foot Frederick, (Foot & McWhinnie) h 246 McDonnel

Foot Harry F, trav l 246 McDonnel

Foot Mary, milliner Miss Delaney l 246 McDonel

Foot & McWhinnie, (Fred Foot & Robt McWhinnie) Boots & Shoes 420 George (see adv)

Forbes Alexander, cooper Royal Oil Co h 22 Aylmer

Forcier Nanson, h 83 Wescott

Ford Lydia, (wid Joseph) h 226 London

Forresters Hall, 180 Simcoe

Forster Carrie, (wid Harry) b 144 Murray

Forester Charles, blksmith Bridge Wks h 225 George

Forster Wm, engr Bridge Wks h 228 George

Forsyth George, driver Parkers Dye Wks bds 34 Louis

Forsyth George Forsyth & Son h 641 George

Forsyth Hellen, l 641 George

Forsyth Mary Miss, bds 285 Dalhousie

Forsyth Wm, wks Forsyth & Son l 641 George

Forsyth Wm A, baker rear 641 George h 643 same

Forsyth & Son, George & Wm bakers 631 George

Fortune Robert J, lab l 91 Lock

Fortye R H, secy Peterboro Hardware Co h cor Park & Gilmour

Fortye Thomas, wks Lock Wks bds Phalen's Hotel

Fosey Mary A, dom 378 McDonnel

Foster John, lumler culler b 864 George

Foster John, wks freight shed G T R l 297 Bethune

Foster Kate, dom 300 London

Foster Richard, yardman G T R b 297 Bethune

Foster Wm, farmer bds 67 Park

Foster Wm J, blksmith Bridge Wks h 355 Sherbrooke

Fountain Arch, lab Point St Charles Ice Co

Fountain Frank, lab Dickson Co

Fountain Louis, lab Point St Charles Ice Co

Fowler Annie, l 483 Aylmer

Fowler Annie, l 302 Alymer

Fowler Bruce, clk Bank of Toronto bds 483 Aylmer

Fowler Catharine, (Wid Wm) h 287 King

Fowler Catharine, (Wid Wm) l 277 Stewart

Fowler David, lab bds 78 Chamberlain

Fowler F B, collection clk Bank of Toronto Rms Upstairs cor Hunter & George

Fowler George, grocer 481 Aylmer h 483 same

Fowler George, clk W G Fowler & Co h 481 Aylmer

Fowler James B, h 302 Alymer

Fowler Maggie, l 273 Rubidge

Fowler Sarah, finsher Fairweather & Co bds 78 Chamberlain

Fowler Wm, h 273 Rubidge

Fowler Wm, lab h 78 Chamberlain

Fowler Wm C, bkkpr bds 78 Chamberlain

Fowler Wm G, (W G Fowler & Co) bds 481 Alymer

Fowler W G & Co, grocers 159 Hunter

Fox Ella, dom 166 Brock

Fox F Leslie h 177 London

Fox James, foreman Dickson Estate h 58 Harvey

Fox Lizzie, l 58 Harvey

Fox Rosa, l 58 Harvey

Foy Fred H, harnessmkr B F Ackerman bds 346 Alymer

Foy George A, harnessmkr B F Ackerman bds 346 Alymer

Foy Henry Mrs, h 346 Alymer

Foy Kate, mach B F Ackerman bds 346 Alymer

Frame John, carp G T R h 89 Gilmour

Francis Alethea Miss, l 265 Hunter

Francis Francis H Mrs, (wid Michael) h 265 Hunter

Frank Mary, clk R H Kells & Co bds 512 Alymer

Frankland Elizabeth, (wid Robert) l 31 Dennistoun ave

Franks Thomas, yardman C P R Hotel l same

Fraser Ada, l 89 Alymer

Fraser Aggie, dom 631 George

Fraser John, blksmith Wm Hamilton h 89 Alymer

Fraser Wm, lab h 408 McDonnel

Fraser Wm, jeweler Clark & Gibson

Fredenburg H, pressman The Review

Fredenburgh Hiram, lab l 501 Bethune

Fredenburg James, lab Wm Donell h 610 Bethune

Fredenburgh Tobias wks The Rathbun Co h 501 Bethune

Fredenburgh Wm, wks J J Turner & Son h 76 Chamberlain

Free Lena, l 13 Waterford

Free Lizzie, (wid James) l 13 Waterford

Freeborn Francis J, lab h 65 McDonnel

Freeborn George, h 832 George

Freeborn Ida, dom 16 College

Freeborn Vernon E, wks Peterboro Woolen Mill Co l 832 George

Freeborn Wm G, wks Peterboro Woolen Mill Co l 832 George

Frise Eliza, tailoress W J Green l 176 McDonnel

Frise John, lab h 176 McDonnel

Frise Lillie, milliner Hall Gilchrist & Co l 176 McDonnel

Frise Minnie E, dressmaker l 176 McDonnel

Froats Louisa, l 63 Lock

Froats Maggie, clk Can Gen Elec Co l 63 Lock

Froats Miles, cutter H Le Brun & Co h 63 Lock

Froates Minnie, l 63 Lock

Frost Albert, driver Morris & Howden bds n Monaghan c l

Frost George E, clk G A Schofield

Frost John, (Frost & Heath) h 207 King

Frost & Heath, (Jno Frost & A G Heath) General Machinists etc 287 George (see adv)

Frowde James, contractor h 63 Homewood ave

Fry George W, painter l 304 Park

Fry Isabella R, h 304 Park

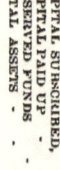

Fry John painter l 304 Park
Fry Mary, l 304 Park
Fulcher Frank, wks R P Boucher bds same
Fuller Grace, milliner J C Turnbull l 123 Chamberlain
Fuller Hugh. cabinetmaker l 123 Chamberlain
Fuller James, cabinetmaker A Comstock h 123 Chamberlain
Fuller Mortimer, baker Wm Stock l 123 Chamberlain
Fuller Percy, wks Carbon Works l 123 Chamberlain
Fulton John, clk bds 350 Water
Fyfe Robert J, clk Ormond & Walsh
Gadouas Joseph, lab Can Gen Elec Co h 33½ Parnell
Gadouas Joseph jr, wks Can Gen Elec Co bds 33½ Parnell
Gagnon Annie, dressmkr Mrs Phalen l 49 Smith
Gagnon Joseph, carp h 49 Smith

Gainer John, lab Bridge Works h 28 Patterson
Gainey Cornelius, barber W J Morgan bds Ashburnham
Gainey Maurice, cigar mkr A Murty bds Ashburnham
Galley Hellen H, l 458 Aylmer
Galley Howard A, mach Wm Hamilton bds 458 Aylmer
Galley Wm, mach Wm Hamilton h 458 Aylmer
Galley Wm C, upholsterer bds 458 Aylmer
Galna Margaret, (wid Wm) l 368 Brock
Galvin Ellen, dressmaker bds 862 Water
Galvin Garrett, h 185 Auburn
Galvin James, Coal & Wood C P R Yards b 183 Stewart
Galvin Mary, (wid John) h 650 Stewart
Galvin Miss, finisher Fairweather & Co
Gamble John, h 200 Antrim
Gamble Margaret l 200 Antrim
Gannon Ann, h 15 Sheridan
Gannon Ann, (wid Dennis) h 341 George
Gannon Kate, l 341 George
Garbutt George, trav bds Snowden House
Garginson Thomas, h 488 Aylmer
Garland Joseph J, pntr b 778 Water
Garlick A D, bartndr Snowden House h 332 Water
Garrow James, mach Wm Hamilton h 466 Park
Garrow Sarah J, drsmkr l 466 Park

Garsides James,plasterer h 36 Albert

Garvais Adlor, wks G N W Telegraph Co l 11 Romaine

Garvais Alphonse l 11 Romaine

Garvais Uzail,lab A McDonald h 11 Romaine

Gaskin A, wks G Matthews

Gaskin S, press man G Matthews

Gaskin Stephen,btchr h 178 Auburn

Gaskins Alfred,brklyr h 25 Lisburn

Gaskins Emma, (wid Wm) l 25 Lisburn

Gaskins Emma,wks Peterboro Mills l 25 Lisburn

Gauthier George,lab l 199 Charlotte

Gauthier Virginia, (wid Joseph) h 199 Charlotte

Gay Lettie Miss, drsmkr 376 Water l same

Geary EA Miss, drsmkr 371½ George h same

Geary Mary,tailoress bds 373 George

Geary Wm jr,cabtmkr M McFadden h 34 Union

Gemmell C G, corset mnfr 325 George h same

Gemmell John, corset cutter C G Gemmell bds 329 George

Gemmell Peter, clk Robt Hall

Gemmell Thomas, carpet mnfr h 325 George

Gentile Salvidore, h 17 Parnell

Gere W E, mach Canada General Elec Co bds 118 Aylmer

German Stanton,clk H S Macdonald

Geroux Moses, clk Thos Kelly h 444 George

Geroux Timothy S grocer 208 Charlotte h same

Gerians B, prtr The Review

Gibbs Elsie, l 31 Chambers

Gibbs G Miss, visitor Dr Barnardo's Home

Gibbs Harry,driver R Gibbs bds 31 Chambers

Gibbs Hugh,lumberman h 203 Rink

Gibbs John, ptr Stanger & Fitzgerald h 31 Chambers

Gibbs John, painter R Mein

Gibbs John jr, prtr Fitzgerald & Stanger

Gibbs John A jr, carriage painter h 250 McDonnel

Gibbs Laura. l 32 Chambers

Gibbs Robert, livery 25 Chambers h 31 same

Gibbs R H Mrs, l 203 Charlotte

Gibbs Wm, blksmith R Mein h Ashburnham

Gibson Alexander, (Clarke & Gibson) h 585 George

Gibson Grace, dom 360 Charlotte

Gibson John, lab Carbon Works h 23 Parnell

Gibson John J, wks Carbon Works bds 23 Parnell

Gifford James, shoemkr h n Monaghan c l

Gifford Peter,shoemkr W H Anthony h n Monoghan c l

Gilbeau Minnie, dressmkr bds 199 Charlotte

Gilbeau Wm, driver Wm Buller bds 199 Charlotte

Gilbert Alfred, toolmkr Canadian General Elec Co h 100 Alymer

Gilbert George, clk C P R h 144 London

Gilbert Madeline, l 248 Hunter

Gilchrist Annie Miss, l 451 Water

Gilchrist John J, (Hall Gilchrist & Co) h n s Murray e end

Gilchrist Maturia, dom 804 George

Giles Ella, dom 147 London

Giles John, general store 315 George h same

Giles Martha, clk J Giles bds 315 George

Gilgore Wm, wks James Kendry h w s Water c l n

Gill Lillie, 467 Water

Gillespie Ada, tchr Public School bds 231 George

Gillespie Adam H, tinsmith A Hall l 32 Division

Gillespie Alex, foreman P Hamilton Mnfg Co bds 179 Sherbrooke

Gillespie Annie, dom 298 Brock

Gillespie Annie, mlnr R Fair bds 231 George

Gillespie Charles, jeweler Clark & Gibson l 14 Wescott

Gillespie Elizabeth, (wid John L) h 32 Division

Gillespie Hellen Mrs, h 14 Wescott

Gillespie James B, carp P Hamilton Mnfg Co

Gillespie John, engr P Hamilton Mnfg Co h 231 George

Gillespie Jennie, clk T H Hooper bds 327 George

Gillespie Jennie, clk R Fair bds 231 George

Gillespie Lizzie, dom 87 Benson

Gillespie Lottie, tlress W H Meredith l Brock

Gillespie Louis, E wks Can Gen E Co bds 59 Wescott

Gillespie Thomas, carp P Hamilton Mnfg Co h 68 Lock

Gillman R, lab Bridge Wks

Gillman Robert, lab Dickson Co

Giroux Albert, lineman Bell Tele Co bds 208 Charlotte

Girard Alphonse, baker 84 Lake bds same

Giroux George H, acct Trent Valley Canoe h 306 Stewart

Gladman Charles, canoe bldr Peterboro Canal Co

Gladman Frederick W, barrister 134½ Hunter bds 24 Harvey

Gladman Thomas, bookkeeper A Hall b Harvey

Glass John, wks G T R h 585 Aylmer

Glass Joseph, mldr P Hamilton Mnfg Co h 269 Townsend

Glass Joseph jr, wks Can Gen E Co bds 269 Townsend

Glass Robert, bds 155 Stewart

Glasson H, wks Times bds 213 Charlotte

Gleason Dennies, wks F Fairen rms Balmoral

Glenney Hattie, waitress Grand Central bds same

Glover R, clk The Examiner

Goacher James, teamster J Galvin h Sherbrooke

Goacher Thomas, mason h 424 Sherbrooke

Goard Electa, l 341 Charlotte

Goard Thomas H, mach P Hamilton Mnfg Co h 341 Charlotte

Godard Georgenia, school teacher bds 490 George

Godfrey Jessie, h 184 Auburn

Godfrey W, wks Geo Matthews Co Ld h 305 George

Goheen George, coller maker B F Ackerman l 155 Stewart

Goheen Milton, harnessmaker B F Ackerman l 155 Stewart

Goldie H B, prtr The Review

Goldie T, ptr Peterboro Canoe Co h Ashburnham

Goldsmith Perry D, Physician 190 Brock h same

Goldsmith Perry G, student bds 190 Brock

Goldsmith Thomas, l 190 Brock

Good Charlotte, dom 343 Stewart

Good Ezra, mach Can Gen Elec Co h 173 Stewart

Goodenough R, watchman B Matthews

Goodfellow Archibald, wks Dr Greer bds 195 Simcoe

Goodfellow James, boarding house h 195 Simcoe

Goodfellow Miss, fur sewer Fairweather & Co

Goodfellow Sarah A, (wid Robert) h 78 McDonnel

Goodliffe Sarah, (wid John) l 195 Charlotte

Goodwin Alfred, lab J Hartley h n Monaghan c l

Goodwin Emma, dressmaker Robt Fair

Goodwin James, lab h Lundy Lane (c l)

Gordon Albine, wks Can Gen Elec Co l 72 Lock

Gordon Clement, carp h 72 Lock

Gordon C H, prtr Times bds 332 Water

Gordon Henry, wks Can Gen Elec Co h 42 Park

Gordon James, night watchman h 253 Stewart

Gordon James W, billiard marker F Fairen l 253 Stewart

Gordon Mary L, wks J J Turner & Son l 72 Lock

Gordon Margaret Mrs, l 184 Auburn

Gordon Percy Miss, wks Fairweather & Co l 72 Lock

Gordon Rock, carp h 119 Crescent

Gorham Patrick, sectionman C P R

Gorman James, lab Dickson Co h 31 Union

Gorman Maggie, wks Morgan House bds same

Gorman Mary, (wid Hugh) l 31 Union

Goselin Alexina, 1 29 Crescent

Goselin E, store man G Matthews

Goselin Esidore, lab h 45 Romaine

Goselin Francis, lab h 139 George

Goselin Frank J, Butcher 245 George h 29 Crescent (see adv)

Goselin Joseph, butcher h 41 Crescent

Goselin T, wks G Matthews Co Ld

Gough A J, (Gough Bros) h 379 Hunter

Gough Bros, (R P & A J) Clothiers etc 375 & 377 George

Gough Mary, 1 359 Hunter

Gough Richard P, (Gough Bros) h 379 Hunter

Gould Ralph, printer The Examiner bds 69 Hunter

Gould Wm H, butcher h 86 Boundry

Goyett Telesphore, lab h 199 Charlotte

Grady James, butcher 244 Charlotte h c l

Grady James, moulder Lock Works l e s Lock c l

Grady John, teamster McDonuel's Mill h 101 Lake

Grady Michael, lab C P R h e s Lock c l

Grady PatrickJ, hackman l 167 Charlotte

Grady Wm, tailor E LeBrun & Co l e s Lock c l

Grafton & Co, W E Conway Mngr Clothiers 387 George

Graham Allen, clk T Dolan & Co bds 11 Walton

Graham Ann, (wid Robert) h 547 Water

Graham Bertie, 1 326 Water

Graham Bros, (George & James) Proprs Oriental Hotel 167, 169 & 171 Hunter

Graham Christopher, bell boy Oriental Hotel bds 15 Queen

Graham Clara, dom 755 Water

Graham Edward, baggage man G T R h 251 Rubidge

Graham Elizabeth, tlress A Mercer & Co

Graham Frank, clk Oriental Hotel h 15 Queen

Graham George, (Graham Bros) l Oriental Hotel

Graham James, (Graham Bros h 62 Murray

Graham James G, contractor h 122 Dublin

Graham John W, bds 631 Water

Graham Joseph, lab Dickson Co

Graham Margaret, dressmaker 592 George h same

Graham Mary, bds 625 Water

Graham Mattie, housekeeper Oriental Hotel

Graham Noble, carp bds 69 Hunter

Graham Robert Mrs l 302 Hunter

Graham Sewana, clk Mulholland & Roper bds 20 Queen

Grand Central Hotel, David Lackie Propr 345 & 347 George (see adv)

Grand Trunk Railway, WmHayden agent Charlotte

Grange George, wks Wm Hamilton h 197 Brock

Granger Arthur, fireman G T R h227 Perry

Grant Charles, moulder Lock Works h 376 Dublin

Grant John C, trav l 228 Dublin

Grant Keneth M, news agent G TR l 228 Dublin

Grant Wm W, Government Cheese Exporter l 228 Dublin

Grant Wm Rev, h 228 Dublin

Grassett H J, teller Ontario Bank h 280 Hunter

Gravelle Annie, dom 36 Albert

Graves Mary, cook Balmoral Hotel

Gray Christenia, (wid Wm) h 168 Rubidge

Gray Jessie, cooper h 61 Harvey

Gray Joseph H, wks Geo McWilliams h 198 Charlotte

Gray Richard M, wks Can GenElec Co h 168 Rubidge

Great Northwestern Telegraph Co, Cox & Davis Agents 433 George

Green Albert, fur cutterFairweather & Co

Green Albert E, painter l 174 McDonnel

Green Alice, (wid Joseph) h 18 Stewart

Green Annie M, bkkpr P H Green bds same

Green Arthur, butcher G Matthews & Co bds 142 Romain

Green Edward, blind mnfr326 Water h same

Green Eliza, wksCan GenElecCobds 173 Park

Green Frank, tinsmith A Hall l 238 Dublin

Green Frederick, appr The Times bds 173 Park

Green Frederick W, wks R A Sloan l 238 Dublin

Green Garnet G, photographer P H Green l 338 Dublin

Green George, mach Can Gen Elec Co bds 173 Park

Green Hattie, l 173 Park

Green John, barrister 37½ George bds Grand Central

Green John, l 18 Stewart

Green Joseph, h 18 Stewart

Green Lottie, clk Hall, Gilchrist & Co l 387 Reid

Green Lula, tlress W H Meredith l 211 Murray

Green Mary A, (wid Charles E) h 211 Murray

Green Mary A, bookbinder The Examiner l 174 McDonnel

Green Milton, clk Fairweather &Co

Green P H, Photographer 140½ Hunter h CommunicationRd Junction, Reid & Stewart

Green Robert H, market clerk Mkt Sqr h 387 Reid

Green Wm, moulder l 211 Murray

Green Wm, btchr G Matthews Co (Ld) h 173 Park

Green Wm F, wks E Green bds 326 Water

Green Wm J, painter h 238 Dublin

Green Wm J, merchant tailor etc 145 Hunter h 380 Stewart

Green Wm jr, btchr G Matthews Co (Ld) bds 173 Park

Green Wm M, painter h 174 Mc Donnel

Greene Henry, trav J J Turner & Son h 109 Park

Greene May, l 109 Park

Greene William, wks Wm Hamilton

Greene Wendell, clk Carbon Works l 109 Park

Greenwood G S, supt Trent Valley Canal bds Oriental Hotel

Greenwood H S, asst supt Trent Valley Canal bds Oriental Hotel

Greer Jennie Miss, h 512 Alymer

Greer John, h 701 George

Greer Johnson H, Electrician & Dealer in Electrical Supplies 134 Brock h 57 Harvey (see adv)

Greer Margaret J, l 701 George

Greer Maria, l 701 George

Greer Mary, wks Canadian General Elec Co bds 160 Romaine

Greer Thomas N, physician 357 Aylmer h 359 same

Greystock Katie, clk Mrs McEachren bds 422 George

Grieve Alexander, h 47 Dennistoun Avenue

Grieves Mary, (wid Peter) h 321 Sherbrooke

Grieves Nellie, dom 380 Stewart

Griffin Fred, harness mkr B F Ackerman

Griffin James, harness mkr B F Ackerman

Griffin May, corset mkr C G Gemmell

Griffin Minnie, dressmkr 202 Charlotte bds 213 same

Griffin Mrs, (wid Joseph) h 108 Weller

Griffin Samuel J, bds 270 Dublin

Griffin Wm, tlr Peter Simons & Co bds American Hotel

Griffith Bella, bkkpr A H Stratton & Co l 179 Antrim

Griffith Mary Miss, h 179 Antrim

Grose Ann, (wid John) h 206 Charlotte

Grose John, lab Bridge Works bds 206 Charlotte

Grose Mary, wks Canadian General Elec Co bds 206 Charlotte

THE BANK OF TORONTO,
PETERBORO' BRANCH, P. CAMPBELL, MANAGER.
BUYS AND SELLS CANADIAN AND FOREIGN EXCHANGE.

PETERBOROUGH CITY DIRECTORY.   53

Grose Susie,wks Peterboro Laundry ods 206 Charlotte

Grover Alfred L, clk J C Turnbull h 25 Boliver

Grubbe Robert W, teller Bank of Toronto h 47 McDonnel

Grue Annie, dressmkr l 363 McDonnel

Grue John W, blksmith W Logan bds cor Alymer & Simcoe

Grundy Ann, (wid Henry) h 498 Alymer

Grundy Ethelwyn, l 264 Hunter

Grundy Fannie, l 498 Alymer

Grundy Hellen, l 264 Hunter

Grundy Henry, h 264 Hunter

Guarantee Co of North America, W H Cluxton Agent 399 George

Guardian Insurance Co, Cox & Davis Agents 433 George

Guay Joseph, lab 46 Park

Guerin Isaie,(Guerin & Briou)h 125 George

Guerin Adolph, baker A Girard

Guerin Adolphus, lab Dickson Co h 118 Boundry

Guerin Alexena,dom Montreal House

Guerin Alfred, wks Lock Works 28 Park

Guerin Archie, lab h 197 Perry

Guerin Clemeet, wks P Hamilton Mnfg Co h 71 Ware

Guerin E, lab Dickson Co

Guerin Edward, lab h 152 Romaine

Guerin Edward, wks Lock Works l 125 George

Guerin Fred, driller Lock Wks

Guerin Georgena,wks Lock Wks l 118 Boundry

Guerin Georgina, mach J J Turner & Son

Guerin Joseph, lab bds 32 Ware h 207 Rink

Guerin Lousia, wks Can Gen E Co l 118 Boundry

Guerin Mary, wks Can Gen E Co l 197 Perry

Guerin Mary, (Wid Clement) l 197 Perry

Guerin Napoleon, lab h 7 Louis

Guerin Newell, lab l 197 Perry

Guerin Tenece, butcher Winch Bros h 138 George

Guerin & Briou, (Isaie Guerin & Hosanna Briou) barbers 349 George

Gummo George, blk smith J Isbister bds 204 Brock

Gumpricht George J, piano tuner h 535 Aylmer

Gunn Charles, wks P Hamilton Mnfg Co l 403 London

Gunn Thomas, brushmaker 557 Gilchrist h 403 London

Gunsolus Charles, harnessmaker 346 Water h same

Guthrie Mary, dom 21 Scott

Guy Bert, clk Sailsbury & Co bds 223 George

Guy Bert, barber W J Morgan bds George

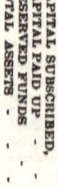

Guy Charles F, fruit dealer bds 223 George

Guy Elizabeth, (wid Richard) h 223 George

Guy Jennie, l 223 George

Guy Wm, groom A E Mosley bds 344 Aylmer

Hagerman Hannah, l 253 Bethune

Hagerman John, eng G T R h 253 Bethune

Haggart James E, carp Wm Donell h 575 George

Haggart John, auctioneer h 167 Brock

Haggart Minnie, dressmaker bds 113 Brock

Haggert Jacob, wks Can Gen Elec Co bds 263 Stewart

Haggerty Bridget, l 91 Elm

Haggerty Ellen, tlress T Dolan &Co l 91 Elm

Haggerty Margaret, (wid Patrick) h 91 Elm

Hall Adam, Hardware, Stoves Tinware, Plumbing etc 407 George h 300 London (see adv)

Hall Albert, clk Jos Armstrong &Co

Hall Alice M, l 342 Rubidge

Hall Amelia, l 286 Simcoe

Hall Annie, l 248 Hunter

Hall Annie, wks Carbon Co l 195 Rubidge

Hall Annie J, l 813 Water

Hall A S Miss, l 286 Simcoe

Hall David, barber 163 Simcoe h 261 McDonnel

Hall Dorothy, teacher Central School l 286 Simcoe

Hall Edith, music teacher l 20 Waterford

Hall Edward H D, (Hall & Hayes) h 354 King

Hall Ellen, (wid Albert) h 17 Queen

Hall Emma, l 33 Benson

Hall Frank, clk J A Hall bds 248 Hunter

Hall Frederick, deputy sheriff bds 248 Hunter

Hall Frederick, lab l 43 Smith

Hall George, lab l 43 Smith

Hall George W wks Can Gen Elec Co h 240 Simcoe

Hall Gilbert, wks Can Gen Elec Co bds 583 Bethune

Hall, Gilchrist & Co, (Richard Hall, John J Gilchrist & S D Hall) Dry Goods etc 130-132-134 Simcoe (see adv)

Hall Harriett, l 17 Queen

Hall J, agent bds Phalens Hotel

Hall J, lab Bridge Works

Hall James, shipper C B & E Co (Ld) h 12 Harvey

Hall James A, sherriff h 248 Hunter

Hall Jane G, [wid James] h 342 Rubidge

Hall John H, student l 813 Water

Hall John J, coll Inland Revenue h 286 Simcoe

Hall John W L, tinsmith Geo Hutchinson l 20 Waterford

Hall Kate M, l 300 London

Hall Lawrence, harnessmkr B F Ackerman bds Balmoral Hotel

Hall Lilian, clk R Hall 1 305 Stewart

Hall Lillie, 1 248 Hunter

Hall Madeline, 1 33 Benson ave

Hall Mary A, [wid Henry C] h 20 Waterford

Hall Richard, [Hall Gilchrist & Co] b 813 Water

Hall Robert, Dry Goods, Millinery etc 385 George h 305 Stewart

Hall Robert R, (Stratton & Hall) h Ashburnham

Hall Rosanna, 1 220 Brock

Hall Samuel, lab h 195 Rubidge

Hall Samuel D, (Hall, Gilchrist & Co) bds 813 Water

Hall Sarah, 1 195 Rubidge

Hall Wm H, lumber h 33 Benson avenue

Hall W Kelsey, clk W H Moore 1 286 Simcoe

Hall Wm J, grocer 355 George h 220 Brock

Hall W T, clk A Hall bds 300 London

Hall, wks Can Gen Elec Co bds 251 George

Hall & Hayes, (Edward H D Hall & Louis M Hayes) barristers 116 Hunter

Hallahan Johanna, wks Can Gen Elec Co bds 195 Reid

Hallahan Maud, wks Can Gen Elec Co bds 195 Reid

Halliday Amy, 1 457 Water

Halliday Charles J, clk Customs House bds 457 Water

Halliday Elizabeth, dom 48 Gilmour

Halliday James T I, physician 457 Water h same

Halliday Margaret, 1 457 Water

Halliban Minnie, wks Can Gen E Co 1 181 Reid

Hallihan Patrick, h 181 Reid

Hallihan Patrick Mrs, grocery 181 Reid h same

Halpin Cornelius, carp bds 34 Lake

Halpin Cornelius, lab b 34 Lake

Halpin George, clk J Lynch bds 215 Hunter

Halpin John, blacksmith 211 Hunter h 215 same

Halpin M, wks Wm Hamilton

Halpin M H, woodworker J H Yelland h 39 George

Halpin Michael H, grocer 39 George h same

Halpin Thomas, moulder Wm Hamilton h 169 Edinburgh

Hamilton Albert, wks Wm Hamilton bds 368 Brock

Hamilton Annie Mrs, 1 459 Reid

Hamilton Edith J, bkkpr W H Hamilton bds 205 Sherbrooke

Hamilton F, mach Bridge Wks

Hamilton Fred, flour packer W H Meldrum h Ashburnham

Hamilton James, wks Wm Hamilton

Hamilton Jessie Mrs, 1 459 Reid

Hamilton John C, lab Bridge Wks h 98 Lake

Hamilton Percey, clk W H Hamilton bds 255 Sherbrooke

Hamilton Peter, (Peter Hamilton Mnfg Co) h 263 Water

Hamilton Peter Mnfg Co, (Peter & R D Hamilton) implt mnfrs s w cor George & King

Hamilton Robert, wks P Hamilton Mnfg Co bds Grand Central

Hamilton Robert L, pattern mkr Bridge Works rooms cor Bonacord & Monaghan Road

Hamilton Robert R, h 111 Stewart

Hamilton Robert sr, (Peter Hamilton Mnfg Co) bds Grand Central Hotel

Hamilton R A, gen agt W H Hill h 37 Harvey

Hamilton R D, Peter Hamilton Mnfg Co h 273 George

Hamilton W, lab Bridge Works

Hamilton Wm, P Hamilton Mnfg Co h 255 Sherbrooke

Hamilton Wm, P Hamilton Mnfg Co h 459 Reid

Hamilton Wm, engr G T R bds Balmoral Hotel

Hamilton Wm H, Metropolitan Grocery 138 Simcoe bds 255 Sherbrooke

Hamilton Wm jr, P Hamilton Mnfg Co h 459 Reid

Hamilton Wm Mnfg Co Ld, Wm Hamilton jr pres, George Munro vice pres A E Lech secy 479 Reid

Hamilton Wm jr, wks Wm Hamilton

Hamilton S, student Dr Johnston bds 480 Aylmer

Hamilton W J, mach Wm Hamilton Mnfg Co h 14 Cambridge

Hammond Harriet, (wid John E) h h 252 Smith

Hand-in-Hand Fire & Plate Glass Insurance Co, W H Hill Agent 400 Water

Handrin Mrs, mach Peter Simons

Hanes T, mngr Singer Mnfg Co h 430 George

Hankinson Eva, tlress W H Meredith bds 40 Union

Hankinson George, agent Singer Mnfg Co bds 426½ George

Hankinson Mary, (wid Wm) h 40 Union

Hankinson Mr, canvasser G B Sproule

Hankinson Winnie, dressmkr bds 40 Union

Hanley Maggie, waitress American House

Hanlon Julia, wks Can Gen Elec Co 1 22 Elm

Hanlon Patrick, h 22 Elm

Hanna James, cabinet mkr Can Gen Elec Co bds 25 Louis

Hannam Samuel, carp h 72 Lake

Hanrahan Bridget, l 183 Bethune

Hanrahan John J, wks P Hamilton Mnfg Co h 183 Bethune

Hanrahan Margaret, (wid Edward) tailoress P Simons bds 241 Stewart

Hanrahan Mary, wks Lock Works l 183 Bethune

Hanrahan Mary, tailoress Hall Gilchrist& Co bds rear 56 Waterford

Hanrahan Michael, driver G RStratton h 354 Downie

Hanrahan Timothy, lab l 183 Bethune

Hanratty J J, district agent Standard Life Assurance Co 336George bds Oriental Hotel

Hanthorn Annie, (wid David G) l 247 Aylmer

Hardill Wm, moulder Wm Hamilton h 45 Elm

Hardwick Geo, moulder WmHamilton h 490 Gilchrist

Hardwick I, wks Wm Hamilton

Hardwick John, lab h 7 Cross

Hardy C O, canvasser G B Sproule

Hardy Harry, clk Wm Madill bds 267 Hunter

Harkness J, prtr The Examiner

Harmer Frank, carp l 62 Chamberlain

Harmer Lottie, l 62 Chamberlain

Harmer Thomas, h 62 Chamberlain

Harper David, wks P Hamilton Mnfg Co l 495 Aylmer

Harper Florence,milliner J C Turnbull l 495 Aylmer

Harper Hattie, wks Review l 495 Aylmer

Harper Hugh, insp Canadian General Elec Co h 334 Downie

Harper John, city editor The Times bds 500 Aylmer

Harper J R, clk Adam Hall bds Croft House

Harper Thomas G, blksmith Canadian General Elec Co h 202 Charlotte

Harran Arthur, l 243 Hunter

Harran Edward, lab h 243 Hunter

Harran Edward jr, l 243 Hunter

Harran Rosa, l 243 Hunter

Harran Walter, wks J Walsenhome l 243 Hunter

Harriman Lizzie, dom 347 Charlotte

Harris Edward, wks Canadian General Elec Co h 20 Albert

Harris Joseph, condr St Ry bds 208 Charlotte

Harris Sarah, house keeper 100 London

Harrison Thomas J, lab h 554 Downie

Harrison Wm, lab Dickson Co

Hart John, clk J Giles b 226 Edinburgh

Hart John, ptr P Hamilton Mnfg Co h Lundy Lane

Hart, driver Wm Stock

Hartford Fire Insurance Co, W H Cluxton Agent 399 George

Hartley Charles, grocer 547 George h Ashburnham

Hartley Edith, l 52 Murray

Hartley Egerton J, pianos etc l 52 Murray

Hartley Jennie, l 234 Antrim

Hartley John J, bricklayer h 234 Antrim

Hartley, agent G B Sproul l h e 163 Romaine

Hartley Rebecca, (wid John A) h 52 Murray

Hartley Rowland T, l 52 Murray

Hartley Wm, painter h 316 Sherbrooke

Hartley Wm, lab Dickson Co

Hartley Wm G, wks Auburn Mill h 786 Water

Hartman Herbert T, draughtsman Canadian General Elec Co h 289 Park

Harvey Daniel, wks Wm Hamilton Mnfg Co h 201 Murray

Haskill Allen, Shaving Parlors 164 Simcoe h 336 Downie

Haskill Frederick, condr G T R h 277 Rubidge

Hatcher James, moulder P Hamilton Mnfg Co h 183 Dublin

Hatfield Miss, l 735 Water

Hatrick Edward, cattle dealer h 90 Lansdowne

Hatten Mrs, (wid) h 394 Charlotte

Hatton George W, (Hatton & Wood) h n Monaghan c l

Hatton & Wood (Geo Hatton & R E Wood) barristers s w cor George & Hunter

Hauschilds Samuel, glassblower Can Gen Elec Co bds Oriental Hotel

Hawkins Ella, l 24 College

Hawkins Ira Prof, cutting school 426 Water bds 4 Sheridan

Hawkins John A, mach Wm Hamilton h 282 Hunter

Hawkins Mary, (wid James) h 24 College

Hawley Henry H, l 326 Charlotte

Hawley L M Miss, music teacher l 326 Charlotte

Hawley Milo A, h 326 Charlotte

Hawley Minnie, dom 263 Water

Hay G N, clk Stratton & Hall l 544 Water

Hay Martha Mrs, l 544 Water

Hay Minnie, clk Hall, Gilchrist&Co l 544 Water

Hay Robert, clk A P Pousette h 502 Water

Hay Thomas A S, civil engineer etc Bank Commerce Bldg h 192 Mc-Donnel

Hayden Wm, agent G T R h 307 Bethune

Hayes Edward, lab Dickson Co h 826 Water

Hayes Edward jr, wks Peterboro Woolen Mill l 826 Water

Hayes Emma, dressmkr Miss Delaney

Hayes James, canoe bldr Can Canoe Co bds 36 Louis

Hayes John, mason rms Fire Hall

Hayes John E, stonemason h 179 Park

Hayes John F, mason h 36 Louis

Hayes Louis, (Hall & Hayes) h 210 McDonnel

Hayes Maggie, l 36 Louis

Hayes Michael, mason h 436 Sherbrooke

Hayes Wm, rep string instruments 114 Simcoe h same

Hayslip Mary, wks Auburn Mill bds 193 Auburn

Hazlitt Agnes Miss, 1 570 Water

Hazlitt T G, pres Dickson Lumber Co (Ld) h 570 Water

Head Arthur, lab P Hamilton Mnfg Co

Head James, gardener Nicholls Hospital 1 same

Head Walter, groom Dr Johnson bds 480 Aylmer

Head Walter, groom R H Nesbitt rms 13 Chambers

Heal John, lab Dickson Co

Heanan Alice Mrs, cook Grand Central 1 9 Cresent

Heap Alice M, wks Peterboro Woolen Mill 1 686 George

Heap George, printer Review 1 686 George

Heap Sarah, (wid George) h 686 George

Heap Wm, carp G McWilliams 1 686 George

Heath A G, wks Carbon wks rms 161½ Simcoe

Heath A S, (Frost & Heath) b 285¼ George

Heath Byron, wks Carbon Works bds 64 Aylmer

Heath H B, wks Peterboro Carbon Co

Heath Luman, mach Carbon Works bds 64 Aylmer

Heath Milo D, mach Can Gen Elec Co h 27 Lake

Heathcote S G, wks Wm Hamilton Mnfg Co bds 479 Water

Heather Francis W, pedler h 322 Water

Hedenberg H B, wks Can Gen Elec Co bds Oriental Hotel

Heels J, signalman G T R

Heenan Patrick, wks Can Gen Elec Co h 107 Rubidge

Heffernan Annie, dressmaker Hall & Gilchrist 1 82 Hunter

Heffernan Ellen, dressmaker Miss O'Brien 1 189 Stewart

Heffernan John, butcher Winch Bros 1 189 Stewart

Heffernan Lizzie, waitress Phelans Hotel

Heffernan Maggie, stenogr Denniston & Stevenson bds 85 Hunter

Heffernan Matthew J, wks Can Gen Elec Co 1 189 Stewart

Heffernan Michael, lab h 374 Charlotte

Heffernan Michael jr, lab 1 374 Charlotte

Heffernan Nellie, dressmkr Miss O'Brien

Heffernan Patrick, b 189 Stewart

Heffernan Patrick, wks Robert Morrow h King c 1

Heffernan Patrick, blksmith h 85 Hunter

Heffernan Patrick jr 1 189 Stewart

Heffernan Philip, wks Lock Works l 374 Charlotte

Heffernan Wm, wks Lock Works l 374 Charlotte

Helm Wm, h 658 Bethune

Helson Albert, wks Ashburnham h 34 Harvey

Helson H Miss, prtr The Review

Henderson Elsie, (wid Robert) h212 Brock

Henderson Hannah, dom 206 Aylmer

Henderson Robert, lab W H Meldrum Ashburnham

Henderson Sarah, dom 305 Stewart

Henderson Thomas, h392McDonnel

Henderson Wilson, supt Water Works h 440 Park

Hendricks Charles, I l 202 Edinburgh

Hendricks Ellen, (wid Isaac D) h 202 Edinburgh

Hendricks Ida, photographer l 202 Edinburgh

Hendron George, carp h 299 Townsend

Hennessey Daniel, lab h 56 Victoria ave

Henry Annie, bds 204 Sherbrooke

Henry Anson, bartender Oriental Hotel bds same

Henry Bros, (M L & P) Grocers etc 339 & 341 George

Henry Ernist,clk J Stevenson Coal Co bds 204 Sherbrooke

Henry George, teamster h 191 Charlotte

Henry John, plastererl 6 Cambridge

Henry John sr, plasterer l 6 Cambridge

Henry Mary, l 204 Sherbrooke

Henry Myles L, (Henry Bros) bds 204 Sherbrooke

HenryPeter,clkKenny h318Charlotte

Henry Peter, (Henry Bros) h Charlotte

Henry Thomas, h 204 Sherbrooke

Henry Thomas J,wks St R R h 383 Aylmer

Henry Thomas J, clk Henry Bros bds 204 Sherbrooke

Henry Wm,plasterer h 6 Cambridge

Henthorn John, wks Peterboro Carbon Co

Henan Alice Mrs, asst Cook Grand Central

Herridge Albert C, printer Reveiw h 625 Water

Herring Wm, artist h 699 George

Herring Wm, porter Bank Montreal

Herron Walter, groom R J Wolsten holme bds Aylmer

Hetherington Isaac, blksmith Wm Hetherington bds 456 Aylmer

Hetherington John, shoe maker 523 George h 863 Water

Hetherington John S, wksThePeterboro Woolen Mill l 863 Water

Hetherington Mary H,wks Auburn Mill l 863 Water

Hetherington Nellie J, wks Peterboro Woolen Mill l 863 Water

Hetherington Percy, clk Peterboro Steam Laundry

Hetherington Stephen G, turner Wm Donell h 225 Dublin

Hetherington Thomas, wks Wm M Hetherington l 456 Aylmer

Hetherington Wm, stableman Morgan House bds same

Hetherington Wm M, blksmith 467 Aylmer h 456 same

Hetherington Wm P, wks Peterboro Laundry l 225 Dublin

Heuback Frederick, cabinet mkr D Bellegham h 538 Bethune

Heuback May, dressmkr l 538 Bethune

Hewie Andrew, wks Auburn Mill h 190 Auburn

Hewitt George C, mach Canadian General Elec Co (Ld) h 140 London

Hibberd Henry, cashier Canadian General Elec Co h 358 Hunter

Hickey Annie, l 296 Park

Hickey Bridget, (wid Thomas) h 129 Elm

Hickey Dennes, lab h 139 Elm

Hickey Edward, tailor H Le Brun & Co h 129 Elm

Hickey Elizabeth, (wid Daniel) h 296 Park

Hickey James, wks Lock Work l 129 Elm

Hickey John, l 71 Elm

Hickey Joseph, shoemkr, h 769 George

Hickey Katie, tlress P Simons & Co bds 179 Park

Hickey Michael, tailor H Le Brun & Co h 149 London

Hickey Minnie, l 129 Elm

Hickey P J, shoemkr 178 Hunter h 769 George

Hickey Thomas, mach P Hamilton Mnfg Co h 296 Park

Hicks James, student Canadian General Elec Co bds White House

Hicks Wm H, cheese mkr h 592 George

Higgins Jennie, milliner R Fair l w s Water last h n end

Higgins John C, millwright h n s Water last h n end

Higgins Lizzie, dressmkr l w s Water last h n end

Higgins Wm, clk A E Micks l w s Water last h n end

Hill Hattie, l 380 Brock

Hill Mary, (Wid Edwin C) grocery 292 Park h 380 Brock

Hill Rolland, driver Brown Bros h 580 Bethune

Hill Wm, carp J R Donell h 21 Union

Hill Wm H, Mngr Central Ont Sun Life Assurance Co 400 Water h 657 Bethune (see adv)

Hiller Robert J, wks Canadian General Elec Co h 336 Reid

Hilliard Charles, l 1013 Water

Hilliard George, farmer h 1013 Water

Hilliard T W, wks Canadian General Elec Co bds 80 Gilmour
Hillier Daniel, lab h 159 Park
Hillier Harrold, clk E A Peck l 159 Park
Hillier John, h 220 Edinburgh
Hillier Lillie, wks Canadian General Elec Co l 159 Park
Hillier Lillie, wks Canadian General Elec Co l 159 Park
Hillier Phemie Miss, dressmkr l 159 Park
Hillier S J, plasterer h 20 Patterson
Hilson Albert, lab Dickson Co
Hinds Wm, carp J R Donell
Hinscliffe Wm, clk Gough Bros h 31 Sheridan
Hoag Julia, (wid John) l 266 Sherbrooke
Hobbins Dennis, drayman Peterboro Hardware Co h 17 Walton
Hobbins Eliza, dom 714 Water
Hodge Miss, laundress Peterboro Steam Laundry
Hodgson Clara L, clk W H Hill l 7 Elm
Hodgson Ernest, blksmith l 7 Elm
Hodgson Herbert, wks Wm Hamilton l 7 Elm
Hodgson Lois Mrs, h 7 Elm
Hogan Emma, dom 435 King
Hogan Thomas, teamster Dickson Co bds 58 Harvey

Hogan Winnie, dressmkr M E Frise
Hollahan Dennis, driver M T Ostrom
Holland Agnes, dom 139 Hunter
Holland Bridget, (wid John) l 378 London
Holland C, way master J J McBain
Holland Daniel, h 378 London
Holland Ella, cook 226 Brock
Holland Fred W, bartender Morgan House bds same
Holland Richard, blksmith Can Gen Elec Co h 437 Sherbrooke
Holland Stephen, propr Southern Hotel 295 George
Hoolihan Ella, mlnr Miss E Delaney
Holmes Homer T, shoemkr W H Anthony h 241 Stewart
Honsey Edward wks Wm Hamilton
Hooey Annie, (wid George) h 346 Dublin
Hook Wm, driver F Mitchell l 575 George
Hook Wm Mrs, h 495 Aylmer
Hoolihan Lizzie, clk Beutleys Fair bds 11 Gilmour
Hooper Thomas H, baker etc 327 George h same
Hooper Walter, milkman h 504 Rubidge
Hoover A F, music teacher h 212 McDonnel
Hope George, hostler Peterboro House l same
Hope Mary, (wid James) h 184 London
Hope Tilley, l 184 London
Hopkins A, prtr The Examiner
Hopkins D E, agent London Life h Ashburnham

THE BANK OF TORONTO,
PETERBORO' BRANCH, P. CAMPBELL, MANAGER.
HIGHEST RATE OF INTEREST ALLOWED ON DEPOSITS.

Hopkins Margaret, (wid Wm J) l 1035 Water

Hopkins Thomas, lab h 592 Aylmer

Hord Wm H, supt Little LakeCemetery h same

Horkins George J, District Mngr Mnfrs Life & Accident Insurance Co 134½ Hunter h 334 Rubidge (see adv)

Hornbeck Wm, bus driver Oriental Hotel bds same

Horner Thomas, wks G T R bds Balmoral Hotel

Horsefield Alice, dressmkr JCTurnbull l 124 Cedar

Horsfield Geo, mach Wm Hamilton h 124 Cedar

Horsfield Mary. (wid Hiram) l 124 Cedar

Hoskel Allen, barber h 336 Downie

Hoskins Charlotte, (wid) bds 479 Water

Hough Alice A, stenogr Rochester Star Nursery

Houlehan Bridget, (wid Daniel) h 460 Donegal

Houlehan Dennes,wks MT Ostrom l rear 684 Reid

Houlehan James, lab h rear684Reid

HoulehanMargaretE,mlnr Miss Delaney l 460 Donegal

Houlehan Mary, wks BFAckerman l 460 Donegal

Hounsell Charles, tinsmith Geo Hutchinson l 180 Edinburgh

Hounsell George,wks A Clegg l 180 Edinburgh

Hounsell Jane, (wid John) l 180 Edinburgh

Hounsell Percy, bookbinder The Times h 180 Edinburgh

Hounsell Regnald T, printerReview h 976 Smith

Hourigan J, lab Bridge Wks

Hourihan Annie, dom, 369 Brock

Housey Edwin, mach WmHamilton h 541 Gilchrist

Hough Alice M,stenogr CLTrotter l 289 Rubidge

Hough Jane,(wid Alfred) h 289 Rubidge

Hough Martha J, dressmaker M E Frise l 289 Rubidge

Hoven John, lab h 403 Smith

Howden Edward, painter bds 351 McDonnel

Howden Emma, l 678 Bethune

Howden John J, butcher 461George h Ashburnham

Howden Robert, h 678 Bethune

Howden Thomas, l s s Lansdowne 7 e Lock

Howden Wesley,wks Bridge Works h 194 Sherbrooke

Howden Wm, butcher l s s Lansdowne 7 e Lock

Howden Wm G,(Morris & Howden) h n Monaghan c l

Howell Louisa Mrs,clk J Craig h 69 McDonnel

Howland John, butcher J Denoon

Howland R, lab Dickson Co

Howley Annie, dom 290 Charlotte

Howley Kate, dom 81 Crescent

Howson Alice, (wid James) h 668 Stewart

Howson George H, insurance h 188 Edinburgh

Howson Isabella A, dressmkr l 668 Stewart

Hoyt Carrie, nurse Nicholls Hospital l same

Hubbard Wm, carp h 195 Harvey

Hubbs Caleb E, Agent The Rathbun Co h 189 Brock

Hubbs F, prtr The Examiner

Hubel Wm, l h 363 McDonnel

Hudson Buttle, artist etc 134 Brock h 629 Stewart

Hudson Edmund, repair shop 138 Brock h Wescott

Hudson Emma, bds 390 George

Hudson Fred, pressman Times bds 79 Locke

Hudson Minnie, wks Can Gen Elec Co bds 79 Locke

Hudson Richard, repr E Hudson h 79 Locke

Hudson Wm, carp h 634 Rubidge

Hudson Wm E, second hand furniture h 94 Westcott

Huff Martha, dressmkr M E Frise

Huffman Albert, wks Can Gen Elec Co bds 116 Albert

Huffman Charles, cabinet mkr Can Gen Elec Co h 196 Dalhousie

Huffman Christopher, grainbuyer J J McBain h 410 Sherbrooke

Huffman Jane, (wid T L) h 116 Albert

Huffman Joseph, foreman Peterboro Canoe Co bds 116 Albert

Huffman Lizzie, tlress Wm J Green l 116 Albert

Huffman Lou, l 116 Albert

Hughes James H, builder h 306 Park

Hughes Joseph, carp h 306 Park

Hughes Laura, dom Croft House

Hughes Mary, waitress Croft House

Hull Robert, blksmith 300 Water h 302 same

Hull Thomas, wks Carbon Works h 223 Bethune

Hull Wm, lab h 383 Donegal

Humber Charles, wks Auburn Mill l 835 Water

Humber Evelena, l 835 Water

Humber Orenzo, millwright h 835 Water

Humerson Thomas, wks Wm Hamilton

Hunt Bertha, l 213 Stewart

Hunt F E, engr George Matthews Co (Ld) h 213 Stewart

Hunter David, tmstr Dickson Co

Hunter David M, trav h 113 Gilmour

Hunter E J, (wid Dr J) l 118 Gilmour

Hunter Jennie, l 200 Auburn

Hunter Maggie, wks Auburn Mill bds 193 Auburn

Hunter Robert H, (Lane & Hunter) h 693 Water

Hupie Stephen, dray man h 743 Water

Hurd Stephen, lab Dickson Co

Hurley John, h 370 Charlotte

Hurley J P, City Agent Grand Trunk Railway 433 George bds 201 King (see adv)

Hutchinson Jennie, l 20 Boliver

Hutchinson Lillie, wks Canadian General Elec Co l 20 Boliver

Hutchinson Wm, h 20 Boliver

Hutchinson Wm jr, wks P Hamilton Mnfg Co l 20 Boliver

Hutchison Wm S, lab P Hamilton Mnfg Co

Hurley Kittie Miss, music tchr l 269 Reid

Hurley Maggie, mlnr Miss Delaney bds 201 King

Hurley Mary, (wid Edward) h 201 King

Hurley Minnie Miss, music tchr l 269 Reid

Hurley T Mrs, h 269 Reid

Hutchinson Annie, l 578 Stewart

Hutchinson Deborah, (wid Thomas) h 578 Stewart

Hutchinson Ernest, tinsmith G Hutchinson l 578 Stewart

Hutchinson George, stoves 140 Hunter h 28 Sheridan

Hutchinson Harry, wks G Hutchinson l 28 Sheridan

Hutchinson Jennie, dom 205 Brock

Hyde Mary, cook 334 George

Hyde Theresa, waitress 334 George

Hynlstrainz Carl, wks Wm Hamilton

Hyslop A, lab Dickson Co

Imperial Insurance Co, W H Hill Agent 400 Water

Ingles Wm repr St Ry h 214 King

Ingram Robert, lab h rear 1019 Water

Innes Wm L, (Ranney & Innes) bds 168 Brock

Innis Robert, h 356 Rubidge

Insurance Co of North America, W H Cluxton Agent 399 George

Irland Seal, carp h 104 Lock

Irvine James, basket maker h 11 Parnell

Irvine John O, carp h 33 Cresent

Irvine Wm, l 11 Parnell

Irwin Andrew, lab Gas Co

Irwin James M, lumber 435 George h U assau Mills

Irwin John, lab P Hamilton Mnfg Co h 44 Parnell

Irwin John G, caretaker Post Office h same

Irwin John G jr l Post Office Bldg

Irwin Retta, l 504 Stewart

Irwin Robert S, cabinet mkr Can Gen Elec Co l Post Office Bldg

Irwin Roland, l 504 Stewart

Irwin Rubert, insurance bds 198 Charlotte

Irwin Thomas, contractor h 504 Stewart

Irwin Walter H, wksCanGenElecCo bds 198 Charlotte

Irwin Wm, lumber merchant h 40 Sheridan

Isaac Wm, wks Can Gen Elec Co h 176 Dublin

Isbister Alice, dressmkr Miss McIntosh bds 204 Brock

Isbister George, blksmith Stange & Fitzgerald bds 204 Brock

Isbister Jacob, blksmith, 395 Aymer h 204 Brock

Isbister Wm, wks L Potvin bds 204 Brock

Ivory Wm, opr C P R bds Balmoral Hotel

I X L Laundry, Thos B McGrath prop 390 Aylmer

Jackson Andrew butcher J H Howden l l Lansdowne

Jackson Anne Mrs, music teacher l 498 Aylmer

Jackson Archibald S, l l Lansdowne

Jackson Benjamin A, h 415 Rubidge

Jackson Emily, dom 227 Sherbrooke

Jackson Hester A, (wid John S) h 193 Reid

Jackson James, butcher G Matthews h 91 Smith

Jackson James S, wks Can Gen E Co l 193 Reid

Jackson Joshua, mldr P Hamilton Mnfg Co

Jackson Percy, bds City Hotel

Jackson Robert H, (Jackson & Co) h 247 Hunter

Jackson Walter E, wks Can Gen E Co l l Lansdowne

Jackson Wm, lab Carbon Wks h 111 Rubidge

Jackson Wm, mach Can Gen E Co h l Lansdowne

Jackson Wm, baker h 25 Ware

Jackson Wm H, lab h 17 Cresent

Jackson & Co, (R H Jackson & R Burfield) Pianos etc 378 Alymer

James Charles, gingerbeer mnfr h 391 Sherbrooke h same

James John, wks Wm Hamilton h 15 Sheridan

James moulder Can Gen E Co bds 155 Stewart

James Thomas, wks Can Gen E Co bds 57 Alymer

James Wm, signalman G T R h 225 Stewart

Jamieson Francis J, mang Examiner h 19 Harvey

Jamieson Samuel, printer Examiner h 14 Harvey

Jamieson Susie, l 14 Harvey

Jamieson Bros, (John & Matthew) props Little Windsor Hotel 144 Brock

Jamieson F J, mngr Examiner P & P Co Ltd

Jamieson John, butcher J Mervin h 85 Alymer

Jamieson John, (Jamieson Bros) 1 Little Windsor

Jamieson Matthew, (Jamieson Bros) l Little Windsor

Jamieson Minnie, l 224 Rubidge

Jamieson Robert, prtr Examinerbds 224 Rubidge

Jamieson Samuel, shoemkr Foot & McWhinnie

Jamieson Samuel, newsforman Examiner

Jamieson Thomas, shoemkr h 224 Rubidge

Jarrow Jas, wks Wm Hamilton

Jarves Miss, fur sewer Fairweather & Co

Jarvis Steven, clk Carbon Works bds 101 Simcoe

Jayes John, bartender Morgan House h 376 Water

Jeffers John, h 384 McDonnel

Jeffers Julia (wid Patrick) h 227 King

Jefferson Mary, (wid John) h 133 Aylmer

Jeffery Wm, lab h rear 344 Aylmer

Jeffries John, teacher coll inst h 553 Downie

Jenkins Annie, l 384 Stewart

Jenkins G, wks Peterboro Carbon Co

Jenkins Mary Miss, h 384 Stewart

Jenkins Nellie, tchr Central School l 384 Stewart

Jervis E, lab A McDonald

Jewett Edith, wks Can Gen Elec Co bds 206 Perry

Jewett Edna, l 206 Perry

Jewett Wm wksCanGenElec Co bds 206 Perry

Jewett Wm C, caretaker Y M C A h 206 Perry

Jewett W D, mngr Snowden House bds same

Jinkinson John, lab h 43 Elm

Jinks Benjamin, wks Can Gen Elec Co h 348 Charlotte

JinksJohn clk TKelley l 197Antrim

Jinks Margaret, (wid John) h 197 Antrim

Jinkins John W, bkkpr H Calcutt h 472 Reid

Job Andrew, tinsmith Geo Hutchinson bds 20 Waterford

Job James, dray man h 598 Donegal

Job Jennie, dressmkr Robt Fair

Job John, farmer bds 460 Park

Job Thomas, lab h 43 Ware

Job Wm, confectioner 169 London h same

Johnson Benjamin, shoemkr R Neill

Johnson James, lumberman bds C P R Hotel

Johnson Mary, dom 167 Brock

Johnson Thomas, veterinary surgeon h 480 Aylmer

Johnson W R, clk W W Johnson h 26 Waterford

Johnston Alfred J, druggist JnoNugent h 211 London

Johnston Andrew, pattern. mkr P Hamilton Mnfg Co h 262 Dalhousie

Johnston Annie, (wid Robert) l 403 Sherbrooke

Johnston Benjamin, shoemaker R Neill h 260 Reid

Johnston Benjamin jr, wks H W Watson l 260 Reid

Johnston Charles, wks Dickson Co l 80 Weller

Johnston Ernest, wks Peterboro Woolen Mill Co l 110 Dublin

Johnston Fred S, wks Auburn Mill h 11 Victoria ave

Johnston George, l 110 Dublin

Johnston Hannah, (wid James) h 19 Lisburn

Johnston James, moulder Lock Works l 80 Weller

Johnston James, plasterer h 110 Dublin

Johnston Jen Miss, l 94 Gilmour

Johnston Jessie, mlnr Robt Hall bds 4 Sheridan

Johnson John, wks Wm Hamilton h 373 Park

Johnson Kate, l 260 Reid

Johnson Lousia, l 80 Weller

Johnston Lousia, (wid Wm L) l 97 Hunter

Johnston McGregor, wks Can Gen E Co bds 155 Stewart

Johnston Mable, l 110 Dublin

Johnston Phillip, carp l 260 Reid

Johnston Robert, lab G T R bds 139 Elm

Johnston Thomas, vet surg 13 Chambers h 480 Alymer

Johnston Wm, lumberman h 80 Weller

Johnston Wm J, carp l 19 Lisburn

Johnston W S, wks Can Gen Elec Co bds 327 Simcoe

Johnston W F, (Dumble & Johnston) h 533 Downie

Johnston W W, dry goods 410 George h 94 Gilmour

Jones Ambrose, lab h 153 Romaine

Jones A H, wks Peterboro Carbon Co

Jones David, wks G Matthews Co h 9 Parnell

Jones Edward A, (Breeze & Jones) h 373 Bethune

Jones Epsy, dom bds 324 Water

Jones Fred E, livery 193 Hunter bds 90 Hunter

Jones Hillard, millwright Wm Hamilton h 267 McDonnel

Jones John, agt Metropolitan Ins Co

Jones Joseph, millwright Wm Hamilton h 90 Hunter

Jones Lillie, drsmkr Miss M King l 373 Bethune

Jones Martha, dom Grand Central bds same

Jones Maud, l 90 Hunter

Jones Minnie, clk E Melville & Co bds 90 Hunter

Jones R, helper, G Matthews Co Ld
Jones Ralph, wks Peterboro Mills h 196 Lisburn
Jones Robert, tinsmth A Hall h 559 Aylmer
Jones Thomas H, student Can Gen Elec Co bds 291 Stewart
Jordan Andrew, (Jordan Bros) bds 47 Congress
Jordan Bros, (Samuel, Andrew, David) Florists 43 Argyle (see adv)
Jordan David, (Jordan Bros) bds 47 Congress
JordanSamuel (Jordan Bros) bds 47 Congress
Jory Mary (wid Joseph) h 539 Downie
Judge James, lab h 478 Rubidge
Judge John, wks G Edmison l 478 Rubidge
Judge John S, wks Lock Works h 337 Aylmer
Judge Winnie, waitress Phelan's Hotel
Kane George H, carp h 394 London
Kane Patrick, wks Canada General Elec Co h 160 Rubidge
Karch Herline Miss, bds Phelans Hotel
Karsh Miss, tlress H Le Brun & Co
Keane Ellen, (wid Wm) dressmkr 156 McDonnel h same
Keane Mary A, (wid Christopher) milliner 376 Water h same
Keane Wm H, tlr A Mercer & Co bds 156 McDonnel
Kearn Wm J, trav Gough Bros h 46 Elm
Kearns Bridget, (wid Wm) h 467 Rubidge

Kearns Maggie, l 467 Rubidge
Kearns Patrick, thrasher h 344 Smith
Kearns Patrick, tmstr l 467 Rubidge
Keating Wm, shoemkr J W Carey
Keenan John, painter h 51 Harvey
Keirnan Thomas, lab bds 40 Louis
Kelley Burt, conductor G T R bds 18 Queen
Kelley James, wks Canada General Elec Co l 257 Rubidge
Kelley James, agent bds 69 Hunter
Kelley John, h 257 Rubidge
Kelley Maggie, l 257 Rubidge
Kelley Maud Miss, clk County Court Office bds 172 Brock
Kelley Wm, lab Dickson Co
Kells Richard H, (R H Kells & Co) h 187 London
Kells R H & Co, (Richard H Kells) Dry Goods 369 George
Kelly Alice, dress mkr Miss Delaney
Kelly Lizzie, tlress W H Meredith
Kelly Maud, clk County Court Office l 172 Brock
Kelly Thomas, Dry Goods Etc 365 George h 352 Simcoe (see adv
Kemp Edwin A, tinsmith A Hall h 478 Park
Kemp George, wks Auburn Mill l 181 Auburn
Kemp John, wks Auburn Mill l 181 Auburn
Kemp Samuel, shoemkr J H Ames

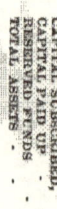

Kemp Thomas, miller h 181 Auburn

Kemp Thomas jr, wks Auburn Mill l 181 Auburn

Kemy Wm, lab h 548 Bethune

Kemp Wm, wks G Carton h 83 Romaine

Kendred Lottie, drsmkr Miss Mann

Kendrey Edward, wks Auburn Mill bds 875 Water

Kendrey Emmet, wks Auburn Mill h 847 Water

Kendrey Herbert, l 891 Water

Kendrey James, mngr Auburn Mill h 891 Water

Kennealy Alice, dressmaker l 207 Perry

Kennealy John, teamster A McDonald

Kennealy John, lab h s s Lansdowne l e Lock

Kennealy Josephine, milliner Miss Delaney bds City Hotel

Kennealy Margaret Mrs, l s s Lansdowne l e Lock

Kennealy Patrick, teamster A McDonald

Kennealy Patrick, lab h cor George & Wescott

Kennealy Teresa, l 6 Aylmer

Kennealy Wm, agent H Calcutt h 384½ Water

Kennealy Wm J, wks A McDonald h 10 Cresent

Kennedy Addie, tailoress H LeBrun & Co l 138 Antrim

Kennedy Alexander, h 445 McDonnel

Kennedy Arnott, section man G TR

Kennedy D, teamster Point St Charles Ice Co

Kennedy Daniel, lab h 207 Perry

Kennedy Honora, l American Hotel

Kennedy James, wks Can Gen Elec Co l 445 McDonnel

Kennedy John, finisher Can Gen Elec Co bds C P R Hotel

Kennedy John E, wks Can Gen Elec Co l 445 McDonnel

Kennedy Joseph, harnessmaker B F Ackerman bds 332 Water

Kennedy Joseph D, wks Can Gen Elec Co h 281 McDonnel

Kennedy Katie, school teacher l 200 London

Kennedy Lizzie Miss, tailoress P Simons &Co h 138 Antrim

Kennedy Maggie, school teacher l 200 London

Kennedy Maggie, mlnr Hall, Gilchrist & Co l 445 McDonnel

Kennedy Mary, bookkeeper Rathbun Co l 445 McDonnel

Kennedy Patrick, stage driver h 200 London

Kennedy Patrick E, prop American House 184 Hunter

Kennedy Samuel, lab h 423 Smith

Kennedy Wm J, blacksmith 161 Charlotte h 219 same

Kenner H H, teacher Collegiate Institute rms 156 McDonnel

Kenrick Charles BRev M A, Curate St Johns Church h 27 Sheridan Terrace

Kent Lubin, h 362 Hunter

Kent Thomas J, boilermaker Bridge Works h 226 Romaine

Kent Wm, wks Can Gen Elec Co bds 295 King

Kerneghan Adam W, contractor h 72 Boliver

Kerneghan David, painter h 497 Aylmer

Kerneghan Dolly, clk R Neill bds 195 Charlotte

Kerns Timothy, lab h 74 Patterson

Ker Jennie, laundress Nicholls Hospital l same

Kerr A L Mrs, housekeeper 441 Water

Kerr George, carp Dickson Co bds C P R Hotel

Kerr Hannah Mrs, h 301 George

Kerr James, wks Lock Works l 505 Rubidge

Kerr Maggie, (wid Stroud) h 421 Water

Kerr Petie, mach Wm Hamilton bds 29 Homewood ave

Kerr Rebecca, (wid Wm) h 16 Elm

Kerr Robert H, clk Hall, Gilchrist & Co h 79 Harvey

Kerr Ross, wks Can Gen Elec Co bds 273 Charlotte

Kerr Sarah Miss, h 505 Rubidge

Kerr Walter, huckster bds 421 Water

Keteon Wm, shoemkr J W Carey bds Balmoral Hotel

Kidd, John, wks B F Ackerman h 160 Aylmer

Kidd Joseph, hrnsmkr BF Ackerman bds 332 Water

Kidd R J, mngr B F Ackerman

Killingback Arthur, coach clnr GTR h 373 Aylmer

Kimbel Hattie Mrs, cook Morgan House

Kincaide Clara, l 38 Harvey

Kincaide Ellen, l 38 Harvey

Kincaid George, foreman J R Donell h 38 Harvey

Kincaide John, contr h 38 Harvey

Kincaide Wm, lab F Fitzgerald, h 247 Simcoe

Kinch Albert, (Moffatt & Kinch) bds Croft House

Kindred Charles A, mldr Lock Works h 295 Bethune

Kindred Ettie, clk G Emerson l 69 Hunter

Kindred Eva, l 69 Hunter

Kindred Lottie V, drsmkr Miss Mann l 69 Hunter

Kindred Minnie, drsmkr l 69 Hunter

Kindred Trucie, music tchr l 69 Hunter

Kindred Wm A, hotel 69 Hunter

King Aggie, tlrs P Simons & Co bds 384 Water

King Bridget, (wid Thomas) h 336 Water

King DeCourey, student R King l 290 Charlotte

King Fannie, nurse Nicholls Hospital l same

King Herbert, clk Hall & Stratton l 545 Downie

King James, mach Moffatt & Kinch l 351 McDonnel

King John, miller W H Meldrum h 845 Water

King John, moulder Moffat & Kinch h 351 McDonnel

King John, stone cutter h 479 Park

King John jr, pattern mkr Can Gen Elec Co l 351 McDonnel

King J H, stenogr Stratton & Hall

King Maggie, dressmkr J Armstrong & Co bds 334 Water

King Minnie, l 548 Downie

King Peter, mach h 548 Downie

King Richard, moulder Moffat & Kinch l 351 McDonnel

King Richard, physician 290 Charlotte h same

King Wm, mach P Hamilton Mnfg Co bds 302 Aylmer

Kingan Jane J Miss, h 271 Brock

Kingan Mary J, l 271 Brock

Kingan R G, (Kingan & Allen) h 417 Stewart

Kingan & Allen (R G Kingan & W L Allen) hardware s w cor George & Simcoe

Kingdon Alice, (Kingdon & Menzies) bds 453 Sherbrooke

Kingdon Emma, dressmaker M E Frise

Kingdon Wm, h 453 Sherbrooke

Kingdon & Menzies Misses, (Alice Kingdon & Katie Menzies) dressmakers 374½ George

Kingscote Alfred, Mnfr Awnings, Tents etc 344 Water h same (see adv)

Kinner Caleb, insurance bds 346 Aylmer

Knapman John S, Local Mngr Bell Tel Co h 195 London

Knapp H W, civil engr Bridge Wks bds Snowden House

Knapp Marshall W, collector G B Sproule Ashburnham

Knapp Mrs, (wid James) l 203 Charlotte

Knapp Wm, appr The Examiner

Knowles Frederick B, insurance h 27 Homewood ave

Knowles Henry L, wks Can Gen Elec Co l 27 Homewood ave

Knowles Lillian, l 27 Homewood ave

Knox Bertha, dom 335 Stewart

Knox David, soda water mnfr 26 Queen b same

Koster Clara, l 580 Aylmer

Koster Francis, wks Can Gen Elec Co l 58 Aylmer

Koster John, painter l 580 Aylmer

Krug Edwin, mach Can Gen ElecCo bds 215 Stewart

Kyle James, wks Bridge Works h 227 George

Kylie Martin lab Dickson Co h rear 50 Waterford

Labbe Henry, carp h 73 Wescott

La Belle Harry, prtr The Times

La Belle Maurice, prtr The Times

Grand - Centr

HOTEL

PETERBOROUGH, ONT.

DAVID LACKIE, Pr

Opposite Bradburn's Opera House, George St.

Rates---$1.50 Per Day.

Lacheur Geo, plater Lock Works l 281 Reid

Lacheur Henry, printer The Examiner l 281 Reid

Lacheur John, janitor South Ward School h 281 Reid

Lacheur Mary J, l 281 Reid

Lacheur Wm J, express driver l 281 Reid

Lackie David, Prop Grand Central Hotel 345-347 George (see adv)

Lackie Edward, clk R Hall bds Grand Central

Lacomb Josie, wks Can Gen Elec Co bds 24 Parnell

Lafavre O, lab Bridge Works

Laford Baptiste, bartender City Hotel h 341 George

Lagenesse Jerome, steamboat engr h 214 King

Lagior Joseph, cook h rear 547 George

Laidlaw Andrew, tailor A Mercer & Co bds 327 Simcoe

Laine Annie, dom 132 Lansdowne

Laing George, grocer 182 Simcoe h 331 Rubidge

Laing Robert, caretaker St Pauls Church h 112 Murray

Laing Scott, clk Kingan & Allen bds 4 Sheridan

Laing Torrance, clk A Hall l 112 Murray

Laing Wm, wks P Hamilton Mnfg Co h 472 Sherbrooke

Lamb Annie, clk W J McCallum bds 330 George

Lamb Mr, clk W J McCallum rms 336 Water

Lamb Mary, (wid Alexander) l 400 Sherbrooke

Lambe Alfred B, engineer Can Gen Elec Co bds 291 Stewart

Lambert Katie, wks Can Gen Elec Co bds 93 Wescott

Lambert Rose, l 93 Wescott

Lambert Samuel, steamboat capt h 92 Wescott

Lamoy E Miss, l 358 Brock

Lamoy Narcise, lab Dickson Co

Lancashire Alfred, clk J C Turnbull

Lancashire Insurance Co, Cox & Davis Agents 433 George

Lane Charles T, insurance agent h 542 Water

Lane Emma, l 470 Sherbrooke

Lane Harry, clk Rochester Star Nursery l 470 Sherbrooke

Lane John, lab h 943 Water

Lane Laura, dressmaker Miss Rae bds 470 Sherbrooke

Lane Lillie, l 542 Water

Lane Lizzie, tailoress P Simons & Co l 943 Water

Lane Philip, agent b 470 Sherbrooke

Lane R J, (Lane & Hunter) b 795 George

Lane Thomas, wks Auburn Mill l 943 Water

Lane & Hunter, (R J Lane & R H Hunter) grocers 144 Hunter

Lang Frederick A, wks Auburn Mill l n s Wolsley 4 w Benson

Lang James, h n s Wolsley 4 w Benson

Lang James S, clk J Nugent bds 23 Gilmour

Lang Margaret, (wid Wm) h 23 Gilmour

Lang Thomas, blksmith Fitzgerald & Stanger 1 Wolsley

Lang Wm, gardener Richard Hall 1 same

Langford Percil, 1 740 Water

Langford Wm, contractor h 740 Water

Langford Wm, butcher J Mervin bds w s Boundry 1 s C P R track

Langford Wm jr, clk Hall & Hayes 1 740 Water

Lankinsheor Alfred, clk J C Turnbull bds 267 Hunter

Lannin Annie, 1 340 Stewart

Lannin Joseph, h 340 Stewart

Lannin Joseph, barber C P R Hotel h 177 Antrim

Lannin Mary, dressmaker 1 340 Stewart

Lannin Thomas, bkkpr 1 340 Stewart

Lannin Wm, wks Can Gen Elec Co 1 340 Stewart

Lanorgan Ann, [wid Nicholas] h 238 Rubidge

Lansing John C, pattern mkr Wm Hamilton h 227 Antrim

Laplante Baptiste, 1 20 Parnell

Laplante Cordelia, 1 49 Cresent

Laplante Ernest, lab Dickson Co

Laplante Frank japanner Lock Works bds 230 Rubidge

Laplante Frank, lab Geo Carton

Laplante Fred, wks P Hamilton Mnfg Co bds 230 Rubidge

Laplante John, [Laplante & Letellier] bds 84 Lake

Laplante Noah T, h 49 Cresent

Laplante Odino, carp h 20 Parnell

Laplante Thomas, Bailiff 415½ Water h 230 Rubidge

Laplante & Letellier, [Jno Laplante & Leger Letellier] butchers 326½ Arcade

Larmer Thomas opr Telephone Co h 558 Water

Larmour Frederick, wks Lech & Sons bds 219 Brock

Larmour Mrs, [wid Robert] h 219 Brock

Larocque Andrew, carp h 15 Wescott

Larocque J B, prop Montreal House cor Aylmer & King

Larome Frank, ptr bds 392 Aylmer

Larome Josephine, tlress T Dolan & Co bds 392 Aylmer

Larome Michael, lab h 392 Aylmer

Larone Joseph, teamster Dickson Co h 58 Waterford

Larue Joseph, yardman Phelan's Hotel

Lasher H, lab J J McBain

Lashley Wm, mngr Singer Sewing Machine Co h 768 Water

Lasure Arthur, lab h 34 Parnell

Lathangue David, driver Lane & Hunter

Latimer John W, trav h 308 Park

Lavasseur Daniel, lab P Hamilton Mnfg Co h 54 Parnell

Lavery Patrick, lab h 258 Antrim

Lavigne Joseph, line repairer G N W T Co h 499 Bethune

Law Harry, wks Canadian General Elec Co h 175 Park

Law John, wks Canadian General Elec Co h 175 Park

Law John J, core mkr P Hamilton Mnfg Co h 37 Stewart

Law Wm, H mng Dir Central Bridge Works h 205 Aylmer

Lawler, wks Canadian General Elec Co bds 64 Aylmer

Lawless Wm, wks C G E Co Ld bds 66 Waterford

Lawrence Ernest, driver Fire Dept rms Fire Hall

Lawrence Louise, dom 212 Brock

Lawson George W, lab h rear 179 Murray

Layfield Edmond, carp Edison Works h 38 Gilmour

Layfield Robert E, pay clk Canadian General Elec Co h 303 Bethune

Leahy James, l 431 Bethune

Leahy Mary, (wid Wm) h 431 Bethune

Leahy Michael, lab C Winn bds 929 Water

Leahy Patrick, lab P Hamilton Mnfg Co

Learmonth George, h 367 Sherbrooke

Learmonth Wm, l 367 Sherbrooke

Leary Robert H, Livery, Sale & Boarding Stable w s Water l s Hunter h 588 Stewart (see adv)

Mnfrs. Life Ins. Co., Toronto.

Le Bar Asa, lab h 340 Aylmer

Le Bar Hattie, dressmkr bds 340 Aylmer

Le Bar James, mason bds 340 Aylmer

Le Bar John, harnessmkr bds 340 Aylmer

Le Bar Louis, tlr A Mercer & Co bds 340 Aylmer

Le Bar Louis, wks T Fitzgerald

Le Bar Vessie, bds 340 Aylmer

Le Belle Harry, prtr Times bds Balmoral Hotel

Le Belle Maurice, prtr Times bds Balmoral Hotel

Le Brun Charles, (Le Brun & Brown) h 344 George

Le Brun Henry, (H Le Brun & Co) h 360 Simcoe

Le Brun H & Co, (H Le Brun & Joseph Picard) Clothiers etc 381 George

Le Brun & Brown, (C Le Brun & Ed Brown) Palace Restaurant 344 George

Lech Albert E, sec Wm Hamilton h 4 Kirk

Lech K G, (W Lech & Sons) h 415 Stewart

Lech Wm, (W Lech & Sons) h 302 Hunter

Lech Wm E, (W Lech & Sons) bds 302 Hunter

Lech W & Sons, (Wm, Wm E & K G) Hatters, Furriers etc 413 George

Lee Adaline clk A H Stratton & Co l 709 George

Lee Emma J, l 709 George

Lee Mary, (wid Thomas) h 236 Rubidge

Lee Mrs, (wid Richard) l 289 Park

Lee Jane, (wid John) l 705 George

Lee John, carp Auburn Mill h 705 George

Lee Mary J Mrs, h 710 George

Lee Robert T, l 709 George

Lee Sam, laundry, 169 Simcoe h same

Lee Susie, tailoress W J Green 1857 Water

Lee Thomas, carp h 709 George

Lee Wm T, clk J W Moore & Co bds 710 George

Leefe B W, tellerBank ofCommerce bds 167 Brock

Lefeve Alphonse, wks G Matthews Co l 17 Wescott

Lefeve Ernest, lab h 878 Water

Lefeve wks Bridge Works l 17 Wescott

Lefeve Frank, lab h 17 Wescott

Legrande R, dressmkr Wall &Connall

Le Grandeur Albertine, dom 57 George

LeGros Charles, Cigars, Tobacco etc 329 George h 9 Gilmour [see adv]

LeGros Virgiene, [wid Frank] l 57 Wescott

LeHane Ada, l 413 Downie

LeHane Alfred H, lock fitter l 418 Downie

LeHane Johannah, [wid Thomas] dressmaker b 413 Downie

LeHane Nettie, dressmaker l 413 Downie

Leitch Christenia, (wid John) l 509 Water

Lemay Ernestine, dressmkr Robt Hall bds 358 Brock

Lemay Francis, lab G T R bds 379 Bethune

Lemay Maggie, wks Lock Works l 379 Bethune

Lendrum Elizabeth M, l 689 Water

Lendrum Georgenia, dressmaker Miss Mann l 689 Water

Lendrum John, h 689 Water

Lendrum Ramenie, dressmaker Miss Mann l 689 Water

Lendrum Wm, l 689 Water

Leonard Alfred, printer Times l 36 Wolfe

THE BANK OF TORONTO,
PETERBORO' BRANCH, P. CAMPBELL, MANAGER.
BUYS AND SELLS CANADIAN AND FOREIGN EXCHANGE.

PETERBOROUGH CITY DIRECTORY.   77

Leonard Catharine, (wid Thomas) h 136 Wolfe

Leonard Jennie, l 136 Wolfe

Leonard Kate, l 136 Wolfe

Leplante Ernest, wks Dickson Co h 97 Wescott

Leplante Fred, mach P Hamilton Mnfg Co

Lesley Wm, lab h 540 Donegal

Letellier Achille, baker h 84 Lake

Letellier Adolphe, student bds 84 Lake

Letellier Leger, (Laplante & Letellier) h 84 Lake

Lethangue David, lab h 418 Sherbrooke

Letts Harry, bds 322 Charlott

Levaque Michel, wks Dickson Co h 11 Louis

Levasseur Emille Mrs, bds 221 Peny

Levasseur Joseph, diver P Connell & Co h 257 Bethune

Levasseur Joseph, wks Bridge Works l 257 Bethune

Levelette Baptiste, lab h 880 Water

Levick Annie H, dressmaker l 244 Antrim

Levis W A, pedler D Doig bds same

Lewarne George, appr G B Sproule

Lewis Ann, (wid Wm) l 223 London

Lewis David, lab Can Gen E Co h 272 Water

Lewis F J, Mngr Bank of Montreal h 123 Simcoe

Lewis Lydia, l 352½ Water

Lewis Thomas, grocer 352½ Water h same

Lewis Wm, driver dom E & Co h 235 George

Libby Walter, lab Wm Hamilton h 21 Parnell

Lilley Emeline, l 246 Antrim

Lilley J C, painter h 246 Antrim

Lilley Wm H, wks Auburn Mill h 186 Lisburn

Lillico D, prtr The Examiner

Lillico James, wks CanGenECo h 215 Stewart

Lillico Richard, printer Examiner bds 273 Rubidge

Lillico R W, teamster h 122 Boundry

Lillico Wm, clk Wm Hamilton bds 273 Rubidge

Lindsay Annie, dom 344 Rubidge

Lindsay Annie, dom 376 Brock

Lindsay H P, (Lindsay & Might) h 659 George

Lindsay & Might, (H P Lindsay & Wm Might) Real Estate etc 326 George

Link Francis, l 238 Charlotte

Linton John A, brakeman G T R h 265 Stewart

Lipsett Arthur, lab Dickson Co

Little Windsor, Jamieson Bros props 144 Brock

Little Wm, barber C Le Gros bds cor Park & Weller

Littyl Margaret, (wid Wm) h 294 Reid

Live Oak Hotel, James H O'Shea propr 201 & 203 Hunter

FOR BIBLES, HYMN BOOKS, PRAYER BOOKS, ETC., ETC.

Go To SAILSBURY'S.

Liverpool, London, Globe Fire Insurance Co, W H Cluxton Agent 399 George

Livick Mary Miss, h 244 Antrim

Llood Mary, housekeeper 21 Queen

Lloyd Wm, watchman Can Gen Elec Co h 423 Sherbrooke

Lloyd Wm, wks Can Gen Elec Co h 24 Parnell

Lloyds Plate Glass Insurance Co, W H Cluxton Agent 399 George

Lobb Susan, (wid Sandy) l 19 Lisburn

Locco Philip, fruits 172 Hunter h same

Locke Joseph, wks Can Gen Elec Co h 88 Park

Lockhart Andrew, clk Jno Armstrong

Lockhart Andrew, miller h 259 McDonnel

Lookhart John, carriage maker h 73 Harvey

Lockington Emman, wks Can Gen Elec Co bds 480 Aylmer

Lookington Essie, (wid James) l 480 Aylmer

Lockington James, lab h 225 Park

Lockington Maggie, wks Can Gen Elec Co bds 480 Aylmer

Lockington Mary A, tailoress H Le Brun & Co l 225 Park

Logau Etta, bds 500 Aylmer

Logon Frank, mldr Lock Works bds 221 Brock

Logan Fred, clk H Le Brun & Co bds 221 Brock

Logan James, steamfitter h 322 Water

Logan John, mach P Hamilton Mnfg Co h 175 Sherbrooke

Logan John S, blksmith P Hamilton Mnfg Co h 393 Park

Logan Kate, dom 293 London

Logan Minnie, wks Ensign Corset Co

Logan Minnie, clk China Hall bds 221 Brock

Logan Robert, blksmith P Hamilton Mnfg Co h 214 Dalhousie

Logan Wm, wks Peterboro Carbon Co

Logan Wm, carriage maker cor Brock & Aylmer h 221 Brock

Logan Wm A, clk bds 16 Stewart

Londerville Annie, asst matron Protestant Home l 470 Stewart

Londerville Eliza, matron Protestant Home h 470 Stewart

London Assurance Fire Insurance Co, W H Hill Agent 400 Water

London & Lancashire, Cox & Davis Agents 433 George

London & Lancashire Fire & Life Insurance Co, W H Cluxton Agent 399 George

Lonergan James, brass mldr Lock Works bds 37 Parnell

Long Annie, clk Harry Long bds same

Long Birdie, corset maker C G Gemmell

Dyspepsia and Indigestion is a very prevalent complaint in this fast living age. If you are troubled with it, take Nugent's Dyspepsia Remedy.

GEORGE STREET, - - - - 389 IS THE NUMBER.

THE BANK OF TORONTO,
PETERBORO' BRANCH, P. CAMPBELL, MANAGER.
HIGHEST RATE OF INTEREST ALLOWED ON DEPOSITS.

PETERBOROUGH CITY DIRECTORY. 79

Long Emily, mach Corset Factory l 558 Bethune

Long Francis, (wid Albert) h 558 Bethune

Long Harry, Confectionery Etc 414 George h same

Long James, confectioner 386 George h 22 Sheridan

Long Miss, mach Fairweather & Co

Long Mary, clk Harry Long bds same

Long Wm J, cabinet maker J Donnell h 710 Water

Long Wm L, driver l 710 Water

Longo Antoin, fruit pedlar l 172 Hunter

Lord, wks Can Gen Elec Co bds 301 Reid

Losey Edward, lab bds 580 Aylmer

Losey Milton, lab bds 580 Aylmer

Louden James, mldr P Hamilton Mnfg Co h 161 Park

Louden John, mldr P Hamilton Mnfg Co h 166 Perry

Lough Annie, l 232 Edinburgh

Lough Hattie H, teacher Barnardo Ave School l 232 Edinburgh

Lough Mary E, teacher Rubidge St School l 232 Edinburgh

Lough Wm, h 232 Edinburgh

Lount Frederick A, clk Bank of Toronto h 368 Simcoe

Lousey Eliza, waitress Morgan House

Loveday J Miss, visitor Dr Barnardos Home

Low Amelia, dom 542 Downie

Lowden James, moulder P Hamilton Mnfg Co

Lowden John, moulder P Hamilton Mnfg Co

Lowe Charles B, grain buyer h 827 Water

Lowes Clarinda, [wid Wm H] h 322 Charlotte

Lowes Milton, groom R A Sloan l 322 Charlotte

Lowes M, lab J J McBain

Lowry Miss, finisher W Lech & Sons

Lowry Maggie, dom Phelans Hotel

Lowry Samuel W, weaver 172 Hunter h 12 Boliver

Ludgate Theodore, clk Crown Timber Office h Ashburnham

Lumsden Charlotte Mrs, h 426½ George

Lumsden Hettie, music teacher l 426½ George

Lumsden Jennie, bkkpr l 426½ George

Lumsden Libbie Miss, dressmaker 426½ George l same

Lundy Douglas J, clk J J Lundy h cor Aylmer & Dalhousie

Lundy Francis, lather l cor Boundry & Lundy

Lundy John J, capitalist h Ashburnham

Lundy Joseph, h cor Boundry & Lundy c l

Lundy Joseph jr, lather l cor Boundry & Lundy c l

Luny Catherine K, (wid John) h 209 Rubidge
Luny Lucretia A, l 209 Rubidge
Lush Edwin T, wks N Lush l 599 Aylmer
Lush Frank, printer Examiner l 193 Smith
Lush Henry, shoemkr J W Miller h 193 Smith
Lush Herbert H, wks N Lush l 599 Aylmer
Lush Nemiah, baker 599 Aylmer h same
Lush Sarah J, l 599 Aylmer
Lush Thomas, baker 186 Dublin h 182 same
Lush Tom, wks Can Gen Elec Co l 193 Smith
Lyle Mary B, (wid Charles) h 259 Reid
Lyle Morley W, wks Canadian Canoe Co h 256 McDonnel
Lynch Dolly, mlnr Miss E Delaney
Lynch Edward, carp P Hamilton Mnfg Co bds 195 Simcoe
Lynch Edward, wks Lock Works l 672 Stewart
Lynch Edward, baker l 4 Elm
Lynch Frances J, school tchr h 269 Rubidge
Lynch Frank, tlr T Dolan & Co
Lynch Fred, cigar mkr A Murty bds 672 Stewart

Lynch James, druggist 168 Hunter bds cor Park & Elm
Lynch John, tlr A Mercer & Co h 4 Elm
Lynch John J, grocer 387 Park h 377 same
Lynch Katie, l 4 Elm
Lynch Maggie, bkkpr Gough Bros l 4 Elm
Lynch Mary A, (wid James) h 672 Stewart
Lynch Michael, tmstr Dickson Co
Lynch Peter, hostler Balmoral Hotel
Lynch Wm, wks Lock Works l 672 Stewart
Lyons Wm H, wks Wm Hamilton h 50 Bonacord
Lytle Ann J, l 669 Water
Lytle Mary, tlress Hall Gilchrist & Co
Lytle Margaret, (wid Wm) h 669 Water
Lytle Thomas, tmstr h 324 Charlotte
Lytle Wm, clk Telephone Office l 324 Charlotte
McAlpine Mary, dom 443 George
McAndrews Mary, (wid James) l 28 Louis
McAnern Mary, dom 286 Simcoe
McAuliffe Bessie, milliner Miss E Delaney l 906 Water
McAuliffe Cornelius, wks Auburn Mill h 906 Water
McAuliffe Florence, h 40 Louis
McAuliffe John, tailor H Le Brun & Co l 906 Water
McAuliffe Mary A, (wid Patrick) weaver Auburn Mill l 286 Edinburgh

McAuliffe Robert, wiper G T R bds 40 Louis

McAuliffe Wm. moulder Lock Works l 906 Water

McAvelia Patrick, lab h 334 Dublin

McBain Jennie, l 280 King

McBain John J, grain 237 Charlotte h 304 King

McBain Margaret, (wid Wm) h 280 King

McBurney Annie, dressmkr Miss Mc Intosh l 659 George

McBurney George S, mach J R Donell h 4 Sheridan

McCabe Daniel, rep Times

McCabe Martha, wks Canadian General Elec Co l 199 Perry

McCabe Samuel, filer h s e cor Lock & Lansdowne

McCabe Thomas, baker l 199 Perry

McCall Wm, shoemaker b 544 Dowine

McCall Wm E, blacksmith 291 George h 221 Charlotte

McCallum Alexander, h 368 Brock

McCallum Alexander, draughtsman Wm Hamilton h 163 Murray

McCallum Alice, l 27 Gilmour

McCallum Margaret, (wid Malcolm) l 368 Brock

McCallum Mary, (wid Edward L) h 27 Gilmour

McCallum Mary, l 27 Gilmour

McCallum Wm J, restaurant etc 330 George h same

McCann Margaret, (wid James) l 225 Hunter

AS OTHERS SEE US.

" The Manufacturers' Life is a solid institution".—EMPIRE.

" The Company is evidently in a most satisfactory condition ",—THE GLOBE.

" Both the Shareholders and Policy-holders have every reason to be satisfied with the result of last year's business".—THE MAIL.

McCarney Wm, J moulder P Hamilton Mnfg Co h 21 Bethune

McCarty Daniel Mrs, bds 500 Aylmer

McCarthy Annie, wks Can Gen E Co bds 137 Lake

McCarthy Annie Miss, wks Grand Central Hotel l 167 Simcoe

McCarthy Bridget, (wid John) h 292 Simcoe

McCarthy Jeremiah, lab h 137 Lake

McCarthy Johanna, tailoress A Merser & Co l 292 Simcoe

McCarthy Mary, tailoress A Merser & Co l 292 Simcoe

McCauley Emma, dom 205 Aylmer

McCauliff F J, clk Miss Rudkins

McCauliff Wm, mldr Lock Works bds American House

McCaulley Matidia Mrs, dressmaker 125 Brock h same

McClean Caroline, l 372½ Water

McClelland Charles S, jeweler J McClelland bds 397 Reid

McClelland John, jeweler etc 388 George h 397 Reid

McClellan Joseph, jeweler 323 George h same

McClellan Joseph H, jeweler Joseph McClellan bds 323 George

McClellan Leonard, dairyman bds 323 George

McClellan Louisa, l 323 George

McClellan Lucy, 1 397 Reid

McClellan W, prtr The Review

McClellan Wm, mach Wm Hamilton 1 397 Reid

McColl Alfred, harness mkr B Shortly

McCollum Mary, clk Hall Gilchrist & Co

McComb James, glove mnfr etc 137 Hunter h 782 George

McConkey Austin, barber J Lannon bds 203 Dalhousie

McCony Arthur, 1 87 Smith

McCony Frederick, lab h 87 Smith

McCormick Annie, wks Auburn Mill 1 816 Water

McCormick Frederick, wks M Quinlan 1 816 Water

McCormick Jerry, wks Auburn Mill 1 816 Water

McCormick John, lab h 816 Water

McCoy Annie, dressmaker h 161 London

McCoy Ryerson, lab h 173 Murray

McCrea George R, carriage trimmer h 793 Water

McCreary James, principal 3rd Ward School h 11 Walton

McCrorie Wm J, wks Can Gen Elec Co h 59 Wescott

McCullough James, lab h 317 McDonnel

McCullough John, bricklayer 1 317 McDonnel

McCullough Katie, dressmaker R Fair 1317 McDonnel

McDermot Susan, rms 379 Stewart

McDonald Alfred, Sawmill & Ice Dealer Point St Charles h 2 Cresent

McDonald Alice Mrs, waitress Grand Central bds same

McDonald Bernard, cooper 21 Queen h same

McDonald Delphina, (wid John) 1 2 Cresent

McDonald Duncan, h 61 Argyle

McDonald Edward, cooper B McDonald 1 21 Queen

McDonald Grace, 1 61 Argyle

McDonald Henry, engineer J J McBain h 247 Wolfe

McDonald Jennie, 1 61 Lake

McDonald John, mngr A B Appleby h 371 Bethune

McDonald John, wks C P R Freight House h 27 Queen

McDonald John S, moulder Can Gen Elec Co bds 409 Wolfe

McDonald Louis, carp h 40 Bonacord

McDonald Margaret, (wid Patrick) h 61 Lake

McDonald Margaret,, (wid Malcolm) h 385 Bethune

McDonald Mary, dressmkr Hall, Gilchrist & Co 1 61 Lake

McDonald Mrs, finisher A Parker

McDonald Peter, wks Lock Works 1 21 Queen

McDonald Thomas, cooper B McDonald 1 21 Queen

McDonald Tilley, dom 35 Bonacord

Point St. Charles Ice Comp

PETERBOROUGH, ONT.

McDonald & Merci

PROPRIETORS.

ICE DELIVERED TO ALL PARTS OF THE T
by the Week, Month or Season.

Bell Telephone No. 176.   Rates Very Reaso

McDonald & Mercier, (A McDonald & A Mercier) Point St Charles Ice Co, Point St Charles (see adv)

McDonell Annie, (widGeorge) h203 Simcoe

McDonell Dolly Miss, l 300 Simcoe

McDonell Elenor, (wid Wm) l 359 Stewart

McDonnel Manan F, dom 535 Aylmer

McDonough Annie, dom Croft House

McDonough James, bds 360 Aylmer

McDonough James, lab l 20 Parnell

McDonough John, clk Gough Bros

McDonough John, lab WaterWorks h 43 Boliver

McDonough John J, brass moulder Lock Works l 43 Boliver

McDonough Joseph, polisher Lock Works l 43 Boliver

McDonough Mary, laundress Peterboro Steam Laundry l 43 Boliver

McDonough Michael, moulder l 43 Boliver

McDonough Mrs, laundress I X L Laundry h Aylmer

McDonough Myles, lock fitter Lock Works

McDonough Nellie, waitress Peterboro House

McDonough Patrick, shoemkr Gough Bros

McDonough Thomas, waiter Oriental Hotel

McEachern CharlotteMrs, (widJohn) fancy goods 422 George h same

McElwain Ann, (wid Matthew) l 51 Harvey

Mnfrs. Life Ins. Co., Toronto.

"I received your cheque for $10,000 within three hours after I filed claim papers".

KATHERINE RIDOUT.

McElwain Grace, (wid Andrew)l 809 George

McElwain Wm H, contractor h 809 George

McEntee Annie, dom 417 Stewart

McEntee Mrs, (wid John) h 93 Weller

McEntee Norah, dom 118 Gilmour

McEvoy, draughtsman Can Gen Elec Co bds 168 Brock

McFadden Agnes, clk Gough Bros l 414 Dublin

McFadden Annie, dressmaker 365 George bds 391 Smith

McFadden Clement, mach Wm Hamilton l 514 Water

McFadden Edward, tailor A Mercer & Co l 414 Dublin

McFadden Frederick, clk A G Dickson l 414 Dublin

McFadden John, clk Gough Bros l 414 Dublin

McFadden Martin, furniture etc 186 Hunter h 34 Elm

McFadden Martin, h 414 Dublin

McFadden May, clk Robt Hall l 514 Water

McFadden R W, harnessmkr B Shortley h 514 Water

McFadden Sarah, dressmkr Miss Nevin bds Smith

McFadden Thomas M contractor h 199 London

McFadden T C, wks Wm Hamilton
McFarlane Andrew, wks Wm Hamilton
McFarlane Chas D, wks Wm Hamilton
McFarlane John, hostler Southern Hotel
McFarlinJohn, carp h 274 Dalhousie
McGarrity Arthur, moulder Wm Hamilton h 286 Edinburgh
McGarrity Maggie, dressmkr l 286 Edinburgh
McGarty Lawrence, lab h 26 Gilmour
McGee Aggie, housemaid Oriental Hotel
McGee Albert, wks Wm Donell bds 527 George
McGee John, lab h 19 Cresent
McGee John jr, l 19 Cresent
McGee Lizzie, house maid Grand Central bds same
McGee Maggie, dom 386 Stewart
McGee Wm, driver Morris & Howden bds n Monaghan c l
McGill Charles, mngr Ont Bank b 226 Brock
McGill Fred, mldr Wm Hamilton bds 184 Brock
McGill James, miller bds Balmoral Hotel
McGill Vernon, student l 226 Brock
McGill Walter, trav b 15 Rutherford ave

McGinty Charles, policeman h 96 Aylmer
McGinty Thomas, lab l 96 Aylmer
McGlynn John, baker 381 Bethune h same
McGrath David, lab Dickson Co h 114 London
McGrath Edward, physician 539 George h same
McGrath John, spinner Auburn Mill l 114 London
McGrath Miss, mantle mkr Hall Gilchrist & Co l 114 London
McGrath Nellie, dressmkr Miss O'Brien l 114 London
McGrath Thomas B, propr I X L Laundry 390 Aylmer h 382 same
McGregor Bessie, tlress W H Green l 509 Water
McGregor Cecila, (wid Gregor) restaurant 350 Water h same
McGregor Gregor, cook Pullman Restaurant bds 350 Water
McGregor Kate, dressmkr l 350 Water
McGregor Nellie, tlress bds 350 Water
McGregor, appr W H Meldrum h Ashburnham
McGregor Robert F, contractor h 509 Water
McGregor Wm C, clk h 261 Hunter
McGuina Mary, tlress l 17 Elm
McIlroy S, signalman G T R
McIndoe Hugh, grocer 718 & 720 Water h Ashburnham
McIntosh Alexander, diver A Dawson h 486 Gilchrist
McIntosh Alex, porter W J Hall

McIntosh Angus, carp Dickson Co h 21 Division

McIntosh Bessie, waitress Morgan House

McIntosh Harry, wks Canadian Gen Elec Co bds 19 Gilmour

McIntosh Mary, (wid John) h 142 Murray l same

McIntosh Tena, dressmkr 142 Murray

McIntyre Archibald A, contractor h 16 College

McIntyre Charles F, wks Can Gen Elec Co h 328 Charlotte

McIntyre Elizabeth, (wid James) h 171 River Rd

McIntyre Fred, blksmith J H Yelland bds 466 George

McIntyre Joseph A, miller W H Meldrum h 704 Water

McIntyre Malcolm, carp A A McIntyre bds 16 College

McIntyre Samuel, wks Auburn Mill 1 171 River Rd

McJarrity A, wks Wm Hamilton

McKay, mach Can Gen Elec Co bds 155 Stewart

McKee Edith, l 315 Rubidge

McKee Ida, l 510 Water

McKee John, Druggist 384 George h 174 London (see adv)

McKee John, h 510 Water

McKee Robert B, Pres Peterboro Hardware Co h 315 Rubidge

McKee Thomas, carp Dickson Co h 771 Water

McKee W George, wks St Ry Co h 663 Water

McKelvey James, h 338 Water

McKelvey Maggie, dressmaker bds 338 Water

McKendry Aggie, t1ress P Simons & Co

McKenzie Andrew, mach Can Gen Elec Co h 38 Albert

McKenzie Andrew, mach Can Gen Elec Co h 191 Rubidge

McKenzie John, wks Can Gen Elec Co bds 433 Sherbrooke

McKenzie Wm I, student Can Gen Elec Co bds 291 Stewart

McKeown Charles O, millwright h 88 Hunter

McKeown Harry, millwright bds 90 Hunter

McKewean, millwright bds 875 Water

McKim Archibald, l 254 McDonnel

McKim James, fitter Wm Hamilton h 254 McDonnel

McKim James, mach Wm Hamilton h 343 McDonnel

McKim Rebecca, stenog l 254 McDonnel

McKim Robert, boilermaker l 254 McDonnel

McLarin Maggie, wks Peterboro Woolen Mill bds 875 Water

McLaughlin Ellen, milliner bds 332 Water

McLean P, bookkeeper G Matthews

McLennan Roderick, gardner Wm Hamilton h 215 Townsend

McMahon Bridget, h 19 Lake

McMahon Bridget, dressmkr bds 93 Lake

McMahon John, lab C P R h 93 Lake

McMahon Mary, wks Can Gen E Co bds 93 Lake

McMahon Michael, l 19 Lake

McMahon Norah, wks Can Gen E Co bds 93 Lake

McMahon Thomas J, bds 93 Lake

McManus Nellie, dressmaker bds 338 Aylmer

McManus Terrance F, lab h 386 Murray

McMartin Annie, dressmaker Hall Gilchrist Co l 708 Water

McMartin Charles, millwright l 584 Water

McMarter Dennis, millwright h 584 Water

McMaster Floyd, carp h 185 Harvey

McMaster Kate, dom 356 Rubidge

McMaster Wm, carp h 98 Wescott

McMillan Albert, l 48 Park

McMillan Bruce, wks G T R bds Carew House

McMillan Elizabeth, (wid Joseph) h 48 Park

McMillan Isabel, (wid James) l 98 London

McMullen David H, wks Telephone Office l 465 King

McMullen Jane, (wid Samuel) l 236 Rubidge

McMullen Lillie M, dressmaker Miss O'Brien l 465 King

McMullen Thomas, lab h 465 King

McMullen Wm, Asst Supt Metropolitan Insurance Co h 174 Park

McNab Annie, l 170 Aylmer

McNab James, roadmaster G T R h 170 Aylmer

McNab Jessie, l 170 Aylmer

McNamara Bridget, dressmkr Miss Delaney l 82 Aylmer

McNamara John, bricklayer l 82 Aylmer

McNamara Joseph, bricklayer l 82 Aylmer

McNamara Lizzie, dress H Le Brun & Co l 82 Aylmer

McNamara Patrick, bricklayer h 11 Bethune

McNamara Patrick J, bricklayer h 82 Aylmer

McNamara Thomas, bricklayer l 82 Aylmer

McNarn Wm, butcher 236 McDonnel h Wolfe

McNaughton Bella, l 544 Bethune

McNaughton Christena, (wid James) h 544 Bethune

McNaughton John, boots & shoes 263 Sherbrooke h 261 same

McNaughton Mary E, clk J McNaughton bds same

McNeil Andrew, trav h 1 Homewood avenue

McNeil Isabella, 1 35 Sheridan

McNeilley John, wks Bell Telephone Co h 393 Aylmer

McNichol Ellen, 1 358 Hunter

McPherson Augus, carp h 73 Patterson

McPherson Angus J, clk 1 73 Paterson

McPherson John, h 287 Stewart

McQuaw H, lab Dickson Co

McRae Robert, trimmer T Fitzgerald

McSella Mrs, house keeper 206 Smith

McVeigh Dorothy, dom 371 Reid

McVeigh Emma, dom 371 Reid

McWha Bella, cook Southern Hotel

McWha Wm, groom Dr Halliday 1 same

McWhinnie Robert, (Foot & McWhinnie) h 198 London

McWilliams Burt, baker W Bates bds 656 Stewart

McWilliams George, printer The Examiner

McWilliams George, pumps Dickson Roadway h 91 London

McWilliams George jr, wks G McWilliams 1 91 London

McWilliams James, lab h 91 Lock

McWilliams James, 1 24 Ware

McWilliams J B, crown timber agent 378 Water h 565 Water

McWilliams Leslie W, pressman Review 1 91 London

McWilliams Robert J, wks Can Gen Elec Co h 299 King

McWilliams Theodore, clk Peterboro Hardware Co bds 565 Water

McWilliams Thomas, teamster h 24 Ware

MacDonald Ada, clk A H Stratton & Co 1 465 Reid

MacDonald Hugh S, druggist etc 402 George h 338 Rubidge

MacDonald Neil, h 468 Reid

MacFarlane Andrew, foreman Wm Hamilton h 29 Homewood ave

MacFarlane Charles, mach Wm Hamilton 1 29 Homewood ave

MacFarlane M, 1 29 Homewood ave

MacFarlane Mary, 1 29 Homewood avenue

Mack Mary, (wid James) 1 94 Gilmour

Mackay F D, editor The Review bds Grand Central

Mackin Joseph, wks Can Gen Elec Co Ld bds Grand Central

MacWilliams Andrew Rev, pastor St Andrews Church h 439 Rubidge

Mabee, miller W H Meldrum

Madden Florence, dressmkr Misses Kingdon & Menzies 1 263 Stewart

Madden Maria, (wid John) h 263 Stewart

Madill Agnes, dom 52 McDonnel

Madill Etta, dom 64 Hunter

Madill Lottie, dom 106 McDonnel

Madill Mary J, dressmkr J C Turnbull bds 271 McDonnel

Madill Wm, druggist 142 Hunter h
221 London

Madill Wm, lab h 271 McDonnel

Maguire Aaron S, h 20 Benson

Maguire Laura, mach B F Ackerman

Maguire Mable, clk A H Stratton &
Co l 20 Benson

Maguire Olive, dressmkr Miss Lumsden bds 20 Benson

Maher Ada, dressmkr Robt Hall
h Lansdowne

Maher Edward, lab h 29 Parnell

Mahoney Bridget, l 115 Lake

Mahoney Catherine, (wid John) h
115 Lake

Mahoney Daniel, lab A McDonald h
s s Lansdowne 2 e Lock

Mahoney John, wks Can Gen Elec
Co l 379 Downie

Mahoney Lizzie, milliner J C Turnbull l 379 Downey

Mahoney Michael, lab h 21 Lake

Mahoney M E, milliner J C Turnbull

Mahoney Nellie, clk J Long bds 22
Sheridan

Mahoney Thomas, agent London Life
h 379 Downie

Mahoney Thomas jr, l 379 Downie

Mahood Bella, dom 273 George

Mahood Hanna Miss, dressmkr h
579 George

Mahood Jane, dom 465 Park

Main Thomas J, boilermaker Wm
Hamilton h 516 Aylmer

Maitland Robert, fireman G T R h
147 Park

Major Annie, dressmkr Miss O'Brien

Major Louis, painter h 580 Aylmer

Makin Annie, dom 330 Water

Mallett C S, asst supt Can Gen Elec
Co bds 308 Charlotte

Mallock Annie, dom 274 Hunter

Manchester Insurance Co,
Cox & Davis Agents 433 George

Maniece Robert, insp Dickson Co

Maniece Thomas, lab Dickson Co

Maniece Wm, foreman mill Dickson
Co

Manley Henry J, cabinetmkr J D
Craig h 175 Edinburgh

Manley Mary, l 175 Edinburgh

Mann Clotilda E, dressmkr bds 169
Murray

Mann George Mrs, h 518 Water

Mann Hanna, (wid Johnathan) h
673 Water

Mann Jane, (wid Aaron) h 209 Dalhousie

Mann John, lab The Rathbun Co h
169 Murray

Mann Maggie, l 434½ George

Mann Mattie, bkkpr J C Turnbull
bds 209 Dalhousie

Mann Minnie, dressmkr J C Turnbull bds 209 Dalhousie

Mann Robert, wks Auburn Mill h 19 Division

Mann Sarah Miss, dressmkr 434½ George h same

Mann Stephen, b 434½ George

Manning Abb, wks Canadian General Elec Co h 17⁹ Dublin

Manning Edward, clk A H Stratton & Co l 631 Water

Manning Elizabeth, (wid Charles) h 631 Water

Manning George, painter l 631 Water

Manning Samuel, h 222 McDonnel

Manning Sidney, wks C G E Co(Ld) l 631 Water

Manning Thomas, prtr The Examiner

Manning W H, Dentist 146 Hunter h 222 McDonnel

Manore Nellie, clk Miss Armstrong

Manson Wm, Mngr Bank of Commerce h 385 Reid

Marino Frank, fruits 228 Hunter h same

Mark Kenward, bkkpr h 106 Murray

Mark Maggie, school tchr l 106 Murray

Marks Eliza, milliner Miss E Delaney

Marks Irvin, blksmith h 504 Aylmer

Marks Kate, (wid Thomas) h 500 Aylmer

Marks Lyle, milliner Miss Delany l 504 Aylmer

Marks Wm, wks Wm Hamilton h 539 Gilchrist

Marlow Alfred, appr J Lannon bds 850 Water

Marshall Charles, carriage trimmer l 460 Park

Marshall Francis, weaver l 460 Park

Marshall Harry, lumber man l 460 Park

Marshall John H, carriage Trimmer h 460 Park

Marshall Martha, (wid John) house keeper 196 Aylmer

Marshall Robert, lumber man l 460 Park

Marshall Thomas J, lumber man l 460 Park

Martin Albert, printer The Examiner l 249 Dalhousie

Martin Belfer, wks Ensign Corset Co

Martin Bertha, dressmaker Prof I Hawkins bds 4 Sheridan

Martin Donald, wks Auburn Mill l 1035 Water

Martin Ettie, bookbinder Review l 282 Park

Martin Frederick, wks H Pigeon bds 270 Charlotte

Martin H, foreman binder The Review

Martin Ipsa Miss, bookkeeper Singer Mnfg Co l 7 Romaine

Martin James, h 1035 Water

Martin James S, carp h 229 Edinburgh

Martin John, carp Dickson Co

Martin Kate, (wid Richard B) h 7 Romaine

Martin Lena, wks Can Gen Elec Co l 7 Romaine

Martin Littia B, l 282 Park

Martin Littia, (wid Thomas B) h 282 Park

Martin Lizzie, dom 168 Brock

Martin Mary J, tailoress T Dolan & Co l 1035 Water

Martin Maxwell, clk G N W Telegraph Co l 7 Romaine

Martin May, bookbinder Review l 282 Park

Martin Miss, dressmaker Hall, Gilchrist & Co

Martin Mortimer, wks A McDonald l 9 Romaine

Martin Mortimer, teamster Point St Charles Ice Co

Martin Mrs, (wid John) h 111 Weller

Martin Rebecca, dom 891 Water

Martin Richard B, wks Water Wks Co h 217 Stewart

Martin Robert, carp Dicksou Co

Martin Robert J, carp l 249 Dalhousie

Martin Ruth, dom 473 Water

Martin R B, pipeman Water Works Co h Stewart

Martin Thomas H, bookbinder Review l 282 Park

Martin Wm, clk McF Wilson l 282 Park

Martin Wm J, carp Dickson Co h 249 Dalhousie

MartynIpsa, (wid Martin) 285 George h same

Martyn Sidney, painter bds 380½ Water

Mason Bertha, l 60 Murray

Mason David, clk Hall, Gilchrist & Co h 218 Sherbrooke

Mason Edith, bkkpr E F Mason & Co l 60 Murray

Mason E F, (E F Mason & Co) bds 60 Murray

Mason E F & Co, (E F Mason) Grocers 429 George

Mason Francis, florist 440 Water h 49 Argyle

Mason Louisa, V, (wid Wm J) h 60 Murray

Masters Carmon, weaver J Barclay l Murray

Mastin Salatiel, wks T Lush h 177 Dublin

Matchett James, lab G T R h 82 McDonnel

Mateland George O, carp l 262 London

Mateland Marian, (wid Malcolm) h 262 London

Mateland R, fireman G T R

Mather A J, lab P Hamilton Mnfg Co

Matheson Dougald, lab Wm Hamilton h 280 Edinburgh

Mathias Charles, mach Bridge Works bds 330 Water

Mathias C D, appr Bridge Works

Mathison John, blksmith Wm Hamilton bds 583 Water

Matschke Bernard, wks Fairweather & Co h 114 Dublin

Matthews Frank, wks Geo Matthews Co Ld h 218 Wolfe

Matthews George S, supt Packing House Geo Matthews Co Ld bds White House

Matthews George Co Ld The, Pork Packers 356 George h Lindsay

Matthews R, conductor G T R

Matthews R Charles, bkkpr Geo Matthews Co Ld bds cor Charlotte & Rubidge

Matthews T Frank, Mngr The Geo Matthews Co Ld h 218 Wolfe

Maude James L, mach P Hamilton Mnfg Co b 6 Weller

Maude Mable C, l 6 Weller

Maurice W H, conductor G T R

Maxwell Jennie, dom 607 Stewart

Maxwell Robert, lab P Hamilton Mnfg Co h 565 Bethune

Maxwell Sarah, l 565 Bethune

Maxwell Wm J, h 377 Bethune

May Miss, fur sewer Fairweather & Co

Maybee Ephraim W B, millwright l 833 Water

Maybee John W, millwright h 833 Water

Mayhew James, tlr T Dolan & Co bds 209 Simcoe

Meagher Bridget, dom 332 Rubidge

Meagher Dennis, lab h s Lansdowne 3 e Lock

Meagher Edward, lab Dickson Co

Meagher Harry, l 118 Lansdowne

Meagher John J, wks Can Gen Elec Co l 118 Lansdowne

Mnfrs. Life Ins. Co., Toronto.

"I received your cheque for $10,000 within three hours after I filed claim papers".
KATHERINE RIDOUT.

Meagher Mary E, dressmkr R Hall l 118 Lansdowne

Meagher Patrick, lab h 118 Lansdowne

Meagher Patrick jr, lab l 118 Lansdowne

Meagher Rosana, wks J J Turner & Son l 118 Lansdowne

Meagher Thomas, lab A McDonald

Mechanics Institute, George Peters Librarian 379 Water

Meehen Louis, porter Grand Central

Meek Charles, trav rms 156 McDonnel

Meeks Hulda, dom 322 Charlotte

Meggait Lizzie, mlnr Robt Hall

Meharry Hugh B, District Agent Federal Life Assurance Co 161 Simcoe h 190 London

Meharry Letitia, (wid Robert) h 658 Aylmer

Meharry Lettie E, l 190 London

Meharry Lottie, l 658 Aylmer

Meharry Minnie, wks Auburn Mill l 181 River Rd

Meharry Robert, gardener A Stevenson h n s Charlotte c l

Meharry Wm H, teamster h 181 River Rd

Meharry Wm J, wks Peterboro Mill l 181 River Rd

Mein George, driver A Parker

Mein Henry A, lab bds 34 Louis

Mein J, boat mkr Can Canoe Co

Mein John, baker H Long bds 34 Louis

Mein Louis, porter Grand Central h 206 Charlotte

Mein Robert, carriage maker 57 Hunter h 27 Sheridan

Mein Robert, carriage maker h 395 Park

Mein Wm, dyer Parkers Dye Wks bds 34 Louis

Mein Wm M, stone mason h 34 Louis

Meldrum Wm H, Prop Auburn Mills Water h 52 McDonnell

Melrose Adam P, trav h 777 Water

Melrose Ida B, milliner R H Kells & Co l 777 Water

Melrose Wm J, wks Peterboro Woolen Mill l 777 Water

Melville Ada, clk R Mills bds over 166 Simcoe

Melville Alexander H, furrier h over 166 Simcoe

Melville E Miss, (E Melville & Co) bds 273 Charlotte

Melville E & Co, (Misses E Melville & Hattie White) fancy goods 424 George

Melville Harry, clk R Neill

Menzies Hellen Mrs, h 131 McDonnel

Menzies Jane, (wid James) h 279 Sherbrooke

Menzies Jennie, l 279 Sherbrooke

Menzies John, h 228 Stewart

Menzies Katie, (Kingdon & Menzies) bds 379 Sherbrooke

Menzies Mary, clk Hall & Hayes l 291 Rubidge

Menzies Miss, wks Camden Elec Co bds 301 Reid

Menzies Wm, advertising staff The Examiner h 291 Rubidge

Menzies Wm jr, l 297 Rubidge

Mercantile Fire Insurance Co, W H Hill Agent 400 Water

Mercer Andrew, (A Mercer & Co) h 369 Hunter

Mercer A & Co, (Andrew Mercer) Merchant Tailors 401 George

Mercer Bell, l 324 Rubidge

Mercer Frank, fruits, fish etc 276 George h 358 Stewart

Mercer Walter, brakeman G T R h 386 Downie

Mercier Albert, lab Point St Charles Ice Co

Mercier Athanas, (McDonald & Mercier) h 13 Lake

Meredith W H, Merchant Tailor 393 George bds Grand Central (see adv)

Merser A, signalman G T R

Merrill W L, clk Gough Bros

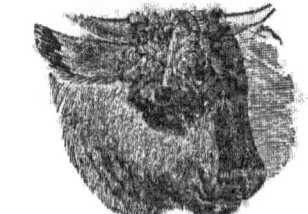

Mervin John, Meat Market 234 Hunter h n Monaghan c l (see adv)

Mervin Sidney, (wid Alexander) l w s Boundry l s C P R track

Metcalf Emma, dom 94 Gilmour

Metcalfe Fred, harnessmkr Wm Metcalfe bds 251 Simcoe

Metcalfe John, lab bds 322 Charlotte

Metcalfe Maud, l 251 Simcoe

Metcalfe Wm, saddler 140 Brock h 251 Simcoe

Metge Georgina, (wid Wm) h 372½ Water

Metheral A, wks Canadian General Elec Co h 32 Albert

Metherel Frederick J, carp C G E Co (Ld) l 148 Murray

Metherel James H, (Best & Metherel) bds 148 Murray

Metheral John P, h 148 Murray

Metheral Joseph (J & W Metherel) h 474 Aylmer

Metheral J & W, (Joseph & Wilton) carriage mkrs 464 Aylmer

Metherel Mable, l 148 Murray

Metherel Minnie, l 148 Murray

Metheral Wilton, (J & W Metheral) h 478 Aylmer

Metherel Wm blksmith P Hamilton Mnfg Co l 148 Murray

Metropolitan Life Insurance Co, Wm McMullen Asst Supt 374 George

Michiel Lavina, clk Thos Michiel bds 11 Louis

Michiel Thomas, grocer 167 Simcoe h 11 Lewis

Micks Alonzo E, hardware etc 137 Hunter h 73 Harvey

Middleton Mary, dom n s Murray e end

Might Bertha, school teacher l 13 Division

Might Emma, clk Cox & Davis l 13 Division

Might Frederick J, clk J C Turnbull l 209 London

Might George, clk Hall, Gilchrist & Co l 13 Division

Might James, h 209 London

Might Wm, (Lindsay & Might) h 13 Division

Miller Ada, l 35 Louis

Miller Alexander, brass finisher Can Gen Elec Co h 108 Stewart

Miller Charles, h 611 Stewart

Miller Finch W, band master h 92 Aylmer

Miller Frederick, lab h 25 Cedar

Miller Fred C, ptr English Canoe Co bds 35 Louis

Miller George, l 92 Aylmer

Miller George, wks Peterboro Carbon Co

Miller Harvey, lab A McDonald

Miller James, grocer etc 241 George h same

Miller James, piano agent bds Phelans Hotel

Miller John, lab h 162 Antrim

Miller John, sawyer A McDonald

Miller John C, clk R Neill h 28 Harvey

Miller John P, lab Dickson Co

Miller Joshua, mldr P Hamilton Mnfg Co bds 108 Stewart

Miller J W, shoemaker 438 George h 35 Louis

Miller Lillie, mantle mkr Hall, Gilchrist & Co bds 35 Louis

Miller Lizzie, dom 1013 Water

Miller Margaret, (wid Duncan) 1 182 McDonnel

Miller Mary A Mrs, h 23 Gilmour

Miller Minnie, mlnr Hall, Gilchrist & Co bds 35 Louis

Miller P, wks Dickson Co bds 19 Waterford

Miller Sarah J, 1 611 Stewart

Miller Wm, drayman h 25 Elm

Miller Wm, h 124 Dublin

Miller Wm, blksmith P Hamilton Mnfg Co b 308 Water

Milligan Charles, mach G McWilliams

Milligan Frederick, wks Dickson Co

Milligan Miss, mantle mkr Hall Gilchrist & Co

Millikin Bella, tlress A Mercer & Co

Millikin Albert, lab Dickson Co

Millikin Daniel, lab Dickson Co

Millikin Fred, lab Dickson Co

Millikin John, painter h 210 Dublin

Millikin Samuel, wks Dickson Co h 102 Dublin

Milloy Peter, lab Can Gen E Co h 230 George

Mills Bros, (Jos Mills) Hatters, Furriers etc 374 George (see adv)

Mills Joseph, (Mills Bros) h 371 Hunter

Milne George, mach P Hamilton Mnfg Co h 176 Sherbrooke

Milne George A, wks Can Gen E Co bds 176 Sherbrooke

Milne Wm, prtr Examiner bds 176 Sherbrooke

Mimms Thomas, enginer G T R h 315 Bethune

Minicolo Edward, pedler P Minicolo bds 67 Elm

Minicolo Philip, grocer etc 206 Charlotte h 67 Elm

Minore Lillie, dressmkr J C Turnbull bds 297 King

Minore Mary, h 297 King

Minore Nellie, milliner Miss Armstrong h 297 King

Minorgan George, moulder P Hamilton Mnfg Co h 121 Stewart

Minorgan Jessie, h 121 Stewart

Minorgan John G, mach Can Gen E Co l 121 Stewart

Mitchell Albert, lather l 3 Romain

Mitchell Alvin E, wks Carbon Works h 18 Albert

Mitchell Arthur, barber J Mitchell bds 3 Romaine

Mitchell Charles H J, printer The Times h 186 Edinburgh

Mitchell Fred J R, grocer 141 Hunter h 226 McDonnel

THE BANK OF TORONTO,
PETERBORO' BRANCH, P. CAMPBELL, MANAGER.
HIGHEST RATE OF INTEREST ALLOWED ON DEPOSITS.

PETERBOROUGH CITY DIRECTORY. 95

Mitchell German A, sewing machine agent 420 Water h 342 Stewart

Mitchell Joseph, barber 131 Hunter h 3 Romaine

Mitchell Joseph jr, painter l 3 Romaine

Mitchell Robert, lab Dickson Co

Mitchell Sidney, clk Post Office bds 420 Water

Mitchell Wm, painter l 3 Romaine

Mitchell Wm, tinsmith A Hall h Antrim

Moffatt Andrew, horse dealer h 204 Sherbooke

Moffatt Annie, cashier Grafton & Co

Moffatt Christena, l 334 Charlotte

Moffatt Christina, (wid John) l 585 George

Moffatt Christopher, ɒwks Canadian General Elec Co bds 215 Stewart

Moffatt Grace, (wid Andrew) l 294 Sherbrooke

Moffatt Lizzie, dressmkr l 294 Sherbrooke

Moffatt Robert L, (Moffatt & Kinch) h 443 Downie

Moffatt Wm, horseman bds American House

Moffatt & Kinch, (Robert L Moffatt Albert E Kinch) founders 395 McDonnel

Moher Daniel J, lab P Hamilton Mnfg Co h 24 Patterson

Moher Mary, dressmkr Miss Frise bds 24 Patterson

Moker Ellen, dom 602 Rubidge

Moker Wm, lab h Water opp Victoria ave

Moloney Johanna, (wid Michael) l 172 Brock

Moloney John, Clerk County Court h 172 Brock

Moncrief Addie, finisher A Parker

Moncrief W, appr Peterboro Canoe Co

Moncrief Wm, blksmith P Hamilton Mnfg Co

Mougraw James, barber A Haskill bds C P R Hotel

Monrow Robert, h Sherbrooke 1 w Monaghan

Montgomery Andrew, h 210 London

Montgomery Dolly, dom 366 George

Montgomery Edith, dressmkr Miss McCauley l 60 Waterford

Montgomery Etta, l 210 London

Montgomery Eva, l 210 London

Montgomery James, contractor h 309 Bethune

Montgomery John, driver Fire Dept h 306 Water

Montgomery John, wks Carbon Co h 383 Bethune

Montgomery John, lab h 60 Waterford

Montgomery John B, l 210 London

Montgomery Mary, l 210 London

Montgomery Maria, wks Auburn Mill bds 563 George

Montgomery Minnie, bkkpr Carbon Works bds 219 Stewart

Montgomery Thomas, wagon mkr J Halpin bds 252 Charlotte

Montgomery Wm, carp bds 69 Hunter

Montgomery W J, teller Ontario Bank bds 338 Stewart

Montreal House, J B Larocque prop cor Aylmer & King

Moore Archibald R, lather h 248 Charlotte

Moore Benjamin, wks Peterboro Carbon Co

Moore Benjamin, lab P C & P Co (Ld), l 550 Water

Moore Benjamin, lab Dickson Co h 550 Water

Moore C E, (J W Moore & Co) h Ashburnham

Moore David, carp h 61 Smith

Moore David H, forest ranger Crown Timber Office h 207 Brock

Moore George fireman G T R h 217 Rubidge

Moore George, lab Dickson Co

Moore Harry, driver J J McBain h 365 King

Moore James, wks Wm Hamilton h 169 Park

Moore James H, wks Can Gen Elec Co bds 169 Park

Moore James Mrs, housemaid Balmoral Hotel

Moore Jane H, wks Auburn Mill bds 169 Park

Moore Jemima, (wid Andrew) h 91 Smith

Moore John W, (J W Moore & Co) h 29 Queen

Moore J W & Co, (Jno W & C E Moore) Grocers etc 351 George (see adv)

Moore Mary, dressmkr l 61 Smith

Moore Mary Miss, l 310 London

Moore, h 391 Aylmer

Moore Nellie, housemaid 334 George

Moore Sarah, l 209 Brock

Moore Thomas J, carp h 327 Simcoe

Moore T W, marble works 317 George h 231 Stewart

Moore Wm, blksmith h 470 Aylmer

Moore Wm, wks Can Gen Elec Co bds 19 Gilmour

Moore Wm, bricklayer l 91 Smith

Moore Wm H, Barrister etc 149 Hunter h 310 London (see adv)

Moorish Wesley, night porter Oriental Hotel bds same

Moran Johannah Miss, h 735 Water

Morency Edward, engr Lock Works

Morency Isadore, engr Lock Works h 219 King

ESTABLISHED 1855. **THE BANK OF TORONTO.** Capital $2,000,000
P. CAMPBELL, MANAGER, PETERBORO' BRANCH.
A GENERAL BANKING BUSINESS TRANSACTED

PETERBOROUGH CITY DIRECTORY. 97

Morency John, engr Carbon Co 1 316 Bethune

Morency Joseph, lab h 213 Dublin

Morgan Annie Miss, dressmkr h 148 Antrim

Morgan A P, Prop MorganHouse 123 Hunter

Morgan Harry, mach PeterboroCanoe Co

Morgan House, A P Morgan Propr 123 Hunter

Morgan Lottie, 1 Morgan House

Morgan Robert, miller h 297 Murray

Morgan Silvia, dressmkr 147 Hunter l Ashburnham

Morgan Miss, mach Fairweather & Co

Morgan Wm J, barber 436 George h 142 London

Morphet Annie, cashier Grafton & Co l 417 Downie

Morphet Edmond, telegraph operator h 417 Downie

Morphet Herbert W, acct Central Can L & S Co h 419 Downie

Morris Ellen E, (wid John) 1 215 Park

Morris Wm H, conductor G T R h 215 Park

Morris Wm C, wks Can Gen E Co h 13 Union

Morris Wm D, (Morris & Howden) h n Monaghan (c l)

Morris & Howden, (W D Morris & W G Howden) meat market 133 Hunter

Morrissey Alice, (wid Edward) h 378 Rubidge

Morrissey Andrew J, l 378 Rubidge

Morrissey Mary C, 1 378 Rubidge

Morrison Elgin, dom 191 Brock

Morrison John, carp G T R h 257 Wolfe

Morrison M A, (Rose & Morrison) h 542 Downie

Morrison Robert, wks Can Gen E Co h 76 Wescott

Morrow Bella, l 34 Weller

Morrow Bernard, registrar h 59 McDonnel

Morrow Eliza, finisher Fairweather & Co l Aylmer

Morrow Emma, l 34 Weller

Morrow Emma, l 176 Dalhousie

Morrow Fannie, l 176 Dalhousie

Morrow Harold A, civil engr Trent Valley Canal bds n MonaghanC L

Morrow Ida, wks Fairweather & Co bds 155 Stewart

Morrow John, clk Robt Hall

Morrow May, teacher central school 1 170 Edinburgh

Morrow Mrs, (wid Wm A)h 34 Weller

Morrow Robert F, Dentist 358 George h 176 Dalhousie (see adv)

Morrow Thomas, realestate 134½ Hunter h 170 Edinburgh

Morrow Wm F, clk Registar l 59 McDonnel

Morrow W G, Secy Central Canada Loan & Savings Co h 34 Weller

Morton Archie, painter h Lundy Lane c 1

Moscrip Margaret, (wid Andrew) h 192 Dublin

Moscrip Nettie, clk R Hall 1 192 Dublin

Moscrip Rachel, mlnr R H Kells & Co l 192 Dublin

Mosley Ashton E, Livery 193 Simcoe rms 165 McDonnel (see adv)

A. E. MOSLEY,
Livery and Hack Stables,

193 SIMCOE. - - 'PHONE 198.

Mosser Kitty, laundress Snowden House

Mowry Aldus, patern mkr h 291 Dalhousie

Mowry Ina, milliner Miss Armstrong l 171 Perry

Mowry John, mach P Hamilton Mnfg Co h 86 Lake

Mowry John, wks Carbon Works h 57 Chamberlain

Mowry Maud, clk Sailsbury & Co bds Ashburnham

Mowry Mercello, mach Canadian Gen Elec Co h 171 Perry

Mowry Mortimer, clk Robert Hall bds 171 Perry

Mowry Mortimer, mach P Hamilton Mnfg Co h 16 Stewart

Mowry Orlando, wks Canadian General Elec Co h 420 McDonuel

Moyse Josephean, (wid Wm) l 183 Dublin

Mudge Richard, mldr Lock Works h 299 Sherbrooke

Mudge Wm, brass finisher Lock Works h 267 Simcoe

Mulholland Ida, 1 362 Simcoe

Mulholland James, mach P Hamilton Mnfg Co h 221 George

Mulholland Robert, (Mulholland & Roper) h 362 Simcoe

Mulholland & Roper, (Robert Mulholland & J H Roper) Bankers, Notes&Checks Cashed, Drafts Drawn on Merchants Bank of Canada 143 Hunter

Mullen Sarah, dom 146 Aylmer

Mulligan George W, music tchr h 274 Hunter

Mulligan Robert, mldr P Hamilton Mnfg Co h 227 Bethune

Mulligan Samuel, lab h 46 Parnell

Muncaster Robert W, jeweler h 375 Brock

Mundy Charles, lab h 77 Smith

Munro Charles C, school tchr l 22 Division

Munroe George, vice pres Wm Hamilton Mnfg Co (Ld)

Munro George, foreman Wm Hamilton h 352 Brock

Munro George, h 22 Division

Munroe George K, pressman Examiner l 22 Division

Munro Nihill, pattern mkr Wm Hamilton h 547 Downie

Munro Robert S, printer Examiner l 22 Division

Murphy Connor, shoe mkr J T Stinson h 12 Kirk

Murphy Debro, (wid Patrick) h 50 Lake

Murphy John, lab J H Meldrum bds C P R Hotel

Murphy John, stableman R Gibbs bds same

Murphy Kate, wks Ensign Corset Co l 12 Kirk

Murphy Margaret, mach J Carey l 12 Kirk

Murphy Michael, cook h 413 London

Murphy Michael, lather l 12 Kirk

Murphy Michael D, barber h 493 Bethune

Murphy Norah, dom 411 Reid

Murphy Samuel, lab h 81 Lake

Murphy Sarah, drsmkr Miss E Delaney

Murphy Stephen J, blksmth 85 Hunter rooms 15 Sheridan

Murphy Wm, yardman Carew House l same

Murray Charles, stableman R Gibbs bds same

Murray Frank, wks Lock Works bds 378 Rubidge

Murray James, lab P Hamilton Mfg Co h 134 Rubidge

Murray John, wks Can Gen E Co h 39 Parnell

Murray Michael, blksmth Bridge Works h 217 Townsend

Murray W H, (Edwards & Murray) h 61 Weller

Marty A, cigar mnfr 174 Hunter h 42 Elm

Murty James, stoves and tinware 174 Hunter h 40 Elm

Myles Aggie, mlnr Robt Fair

Nash Harry, wks Matthews & Sons h 229 Park

Nash Mary Miss, h 380 Downie

National of Ireland Fire Insurance Co., W H Hill Agent 400 Water

Neads James, bkkpr Can Gen Elec Co Ld h 188 Antrim

Nearey Martin, lab h 225 Rubidge

Neild John, mach G McWilliams

Neild Mary, dressmkr R Fair

Neild Wm, foreman G McWilliams

Neill Robert, Boots & Shoes 350, 352 & 354 George, h cor Rubidge & Charlotte

Neil Wm, wks Can Gen Elec Co bds 583 Water

Nelson Joseph, bartndr C P R Hotel bds same

Nelson Wm, lab h 346 Smith

Nelson Wm F, ledgerkpr Ontario Bank rms over Ontario Bank

Nellis Joseph, lab h 176 Edinburgh

Nesbitt Hendeson, jailer h Jail

Nesbitt R H, livery & boarding stable 13 Chambers h cor Smith & Park

Nesbitt R H, (Westlake & Nesbitt) h Smith

Nethercutt Mary J, (wid John) h 2 Queen

Nethercutt Rebecca, clk Post Office 1 2 Queen

Nevin Mary A, drsmkr 213 Simcoe 1 same

Newell Maggie, lndrs Oriental Hotel

Newall Mamie, crst mkr C G Gemmell

Newbecker James, ptr M Carton bds Southern Hotel

Newell Maggie, wks Auburn Mill bds 814 Water

Newell Martha, dom Snowden House

Newell Martha, dom 270 Brock

Newton Henry, furniture 432 George h same

Newton Julia, (wid John) h 583 Downie

Nichols Ann M Miss, h 216 McDonnel

Nicholls Hospital, Mrs O'Donovan supt Argyle

Nicholls Mary A, teacher Central School 1 216 McDonnel

Nicholls Nathan, contractor h 227 McDonnel

Nichols Aaron, trav P Hamilton Mufg Co h 203 Dalhousie

Nichols Annie, dressmaker Miss Griffin bds 352 Water

Nichols Louisa, dom 105 Dickson

Nichols Paul, appr T Fitzgerald bds 352 Water

Nichols Rebecca, (wid Alexander) h 267 Hunter

Nichols Robert, lab h w s Park 1 s G T R Track

Nichols Thomas, carp h 332 Edinburgh

Nicol S J, (wid Andrew) h 84 Aylmer

Nimmo Florence, 1 378 Stewart

Nimmo Richard, Dentist 420½ George h 378 Stewart

Noble Alexander, plumber Noble & Co bds 28 Lewis

Noble Alex, wks Peterboro Carbon Co

Noble Armina, (wid James) dressmaker 384½ Water h same

Noble Arthur, wks Peterboro Carbon Co

Noble E A, wks Can Gen Elec Co bds 80 Gilmour

Noble George, (Noble & Co) h 28 Louis

Noble Irene, 1 384½ Water

Noble Isaac G, driver Macfarlane Wilson h 149 London

Noble James, wks Can Gen Elec Co bds 155 Stewart

Noble James E, plumber Noble & Co h 111 Albert

Noble & Co, (G H Noble) plumbers etc 214 Hunter

Nolan Bridget, dom 359 Hunter

Norrie W, checker G T R

North British & Mercantile Insurance Co, Cox & Davis Agents 433 George

THE BANK OF TORONTO,
PETERBORO' BRANCH, P. CAMPBELL, MANAGER.
BUYS AND SELLS CANADIAN AND FOREIGN EXCHANGE.

PETERBOROUGH CITY DIRECTORY.   101

Northcott Betsey, (wid Wm) h 189 Charlotte

Northcott Sarah, dressmaker 189 Charlotte bds same

Northern Fire Insurance Co, W H Hill Agent 400 Water

Northey A, lab Bridge Wks

Norton Robert, blksmith h 258 Brock

Norwich Union Fire Insurance Co, W H Hill Agent 400 Water

Nott Edwin A, printer The Examiner h 346 Stewart

Nugent John, Druggist 389 George h 205 Brock (see adv)

O'Brien Alexander, lab Dickson Co

O'Brien Annie, l 288 Park

O'Brien Annie, wks Parkers Dye Wks bds 384 Aylmer

O'Brien Annie, milliner Miss Delaney l 777 George

O'Brien Catharine Mrs, cook C P R Hotel

O'Brien Catherine Mrs, h 262 Murray

O'Brien Edward, btchr J Conroy h Ashburnham

O'Brien Edward, moulder h 268 Park

O'Brien Emma finisher A Parker

O'Brien G, condr St Ry Co

O'Brien J, wks St R R bds 138 George

O'Brien James, carp h 411 Downie

O'Brien James, lab h 55 Lake

O'Brien James, section foreman C P R h 20 Aylmer

O'Brien Jennie, dom 587 George

O'Brien Johannah, (wid Dennis) l 411 Downie

O'Brien Johannah, (wid Michael) b 342 Downie

O'Brien Johannah, dressmkr l 342 Downie

O'Brien John, lab Water Wks Co h 45 Lake

O'Brien John, wks Can Gen Elec Co h 79 Lake

O'Brien John, wks Rev J D Casey

O'Brien John, lab b 223 Romaine

O'Brien John L, moulder Lock Wks h 505 Aylmer

O'Brien Kate, waitress Oriental Hotel

O'Brien Lillie, dressmaker l 777 George

O'Brien Lizzie, school teacher l 411 Downie

O'Brien Lizzie Miss, dressmaker 386 George bds 777 same

O, Brien M, wks Wm Hamilton

O'Brien Maggie, dressmkr l 342 Downie

O'Brien Maggie, dressmaker l 355 George

O'Brien Maggie, waitress Live Oak Hotel

O'Brien Maggie, dom 479 Water

O'Brien Maggie, tlress Hall, Gilchrist & Co

O'Brien Margaret, (wid Patrick) h 188 Perry

O'Brien Mary, dom 110 Dickson

O'Brien Mary, (wid James) h 55 Lake

FOR BIBLES, HYMN BOOKS, PRAYER BOOKS, ETC., ETC.

Go To SAILSBURY'S.

O'Brien Michael, butcher 233 Charlotte h Consession

O'Brien Michael, teacher Collegiate Institute h 786 George

O'Brien Michael, drayman h 777 George

O'Brien Nellie, dom Oriental Hotel

O'Brien Nellie, dom 690 George

O'Brien bds 384 Aylmer

O'Brien, wks Can Gen Elec Co bds White House

O'Brien Philip, h 454 Sherbrooke

O'Brien Wm, teamster Dickson Co

O'Connell Aggie, dom 18 Queen

O'Connell Annie, clk Miss Rudkins

O'Connell David, tailor H Le Brun & Co

O'Connell Katie, clk Miss Rudkins

O'Connell Maggie, clk J T Stenson bds Ashburnham

O'Connor Bridget, l 334 George

O'Connor Catherine, (wid John) b 160 Romaine

O'Connor His Lordship Right Rev R Alphonse, Bishop of Peterboro h 350 Hunter

O'Connor Martin, h 334 George

O'Connor Minnie, wks Can Gen Elec Co bds 160 Romaine

O'Connor, bds 334 George

O'Donnell Edward, bookkeeper l 680 Water

O'Donnell Michael, lab h 22 Patterson

O'Donnell Michael, h 213 King

O'Donnell Michael, teamster h 680 Water

O'Donnell Patrick, teamster Dickson Co

O'Donnell Wm, weaver l 680 Water

O'Donohue Miss, tailoress Hall, Gilchrist & Co

O'Donovou Marie Mrs, lady supt Nicholls Hospital l same

O'Heron Maurice, wks Auburn Mill l River Rd c l

O'Houlighan Mich, mach B F Ackerman

O'Keiffe Annie, l 299 Rubidge

O'Keefe Catherine, (wid Patrick) l 267 Perry

O'Keefe James, lab h s s Lansdowne 5 e Lock

O'Keefe John, h 784 Water

O'Keefe Kate, l 784 Water

O'Keefe Patrick, wks Carbon Wks bds 267 Perry

O'Keefe Wm, wks Bridge Wks bds 267 Perry

O'Leary Daniel, teamster l 621 George

O'Leary Fanny, dressmaker Robt Hall bds 621 George

O'Leary Minnie, dressmaker l 621 George

O'Leary Wm, carp h 621 George

O'Mara Emily, l 17 Harvey

O'Mara Patrick Mrs, h 17 Harvey

O'Neil Annie, mlnr R H Kells & Co bds 184 Dalhousie

O'Neil Mary, dom 202 Dalhousie

O'Neil Patrick, lumberman Dickson Co l 184 Dalhousie

O'Neill Bridget, mlnr bds 29 Chambers

O'Neill John, h 29 Chambers

O'Neill Minnie, forewoman Parkers Dye Works bds 29 Chambers

O'Shea James H, prop Live Oak Hotel 201 & 203 Hunter

O'Sullivan Margaret L, (wid John) h 539 George

O'Sullivan Marion P, l 539 George.

O'Reilly Agnes, dressmaker l 420½ George

O'Rielly Maggie Miss, dressmkr 420½ George h same

Odette J B, canoe bldr Wm English Canoe Co h 25 Cresent

Odette Marsell, lab h 141 George

Odette Mary, clk Bentleys Fair

Oke J B, (J B Oke & Co) bds 18 Queen

Oke J B & Co, F H Philp Mngr Commission Merchants 356 Water (see adv)

Oldham Thomas S, wks Wm Hamilton h 421 London

Oliver E, lab J J McBain

Oliver Eliza, h 799 George

Oliver M, clk J C Turnbull

Oliver Samuel, lab h 163 Antrim

Oliver Selina, laundress l 165 Edinburgh

Oliver Selina, (wid Zinri) l 165 Edinburgh

Ontario Bank, C McGill mngr cor Water & Simcoe

Ontario School of Shorthand, A Blanchard C A Prin- 368 & 370 Water (see adv)

Oriental Hotel, Graham Bros Proprs 167-169 & 171 Hunter

Ormond Charles, (Ormond & Walsh) h cor Murray & College

Ormond Sarah, (wid Charles) h 68 Murray

Ormond & Walsh, (Chas Ormond & Wm Walsh) druggists 362 George

Osborne Clara, wks Auburn Mill l 572 Aylmer

Osborne Hattie, wks Auburn Mill l 572 Aylmer

Osborne Lafayette, baggage master G T R h 243 Stewart

Ostrom Albert, clk Ostrom & Co bds Balmoral Hotel

Ostrom Alfred, clk Marshall & Ostrom l 351 Charlotte

Ostrom M T, fruit etc 418 George h 16 Weller

Ostrom Mrs, (wid G K) h 351 Charlotte

Ousterhout George, miller W H Meldrum h Ashburnham

Outram Wm, clk G Matthews Co (Ld) h 440 Sherbrooke

Overend Wm J, prop C P R Hotel 170 & 172 Simcoe

Owens Charles L, clk W W Johnston bds 4 Sheridan

Owens Ella M, l 366 Water

Owens Henry, pump mnfr 124 Simcoe h 366 Water

Owens P W, clk B F Ackerman bds 4 Sheridan

Owens Wm W, inventor bds 192 Dalhousie

Page Edgar, carp Can Gen E Co h 71 baliver

Pakenham Edward, millwright Dickson Co h 36 Manning ave

Pakenham Gilbert, wks Electric Light Co l 36 Manning ave

Pakenham James, carp Dickson Co

Pakenham Maud, teacher Ashburnham schoo' l 36 Manning ave

Palace Restaurant, Le Brun & Brown Proprs 344 George

Palmer James T, painter l 46 Lake

Palette Bridget, cream mkr J Watt

Pamenter Malin, inspector Can Gen E Co h 58 Wescott

Panter Frederick, wks Carbon Works l 128 Rubidge

Panter Herbert, l 128 Rubidge

Panter Joseph, carp h 128 Rubidge

Panter Robert, lab l 128 Rubidge

Paquette Eugene, cook h 11 Wescott

Parker Alfred, Prop Parkers Dye Works 177 Charlotte h same (see adv)

Parker Wm D, acct Ontario Bank rms 372½ Water

Parker's Steam Dye Works, A Parker Prop 177 Charlotte (see adv)

Parks Frederick W, moulder Wm Hamilton h 430 Donegal

Parks Nelson T, lab h rear 547 George

Parnall Martin, lab h n s Wolsley 5 w Benson

Parnell Richard, lab l n s Wolsley 5 W Benson

Parnall Sarah, (wid Richard) h 671 George

Parrington John B, teamster R Stephenson h 266 Simcoe

Parrington Joseph, tmstr Rehill Bros h 258 Wolfe

Parrish Wm H, btchr George Matthews Co (Ld) bds Southern Hotel

Parsons Ernest, wks Canadian General Elec Co bds 263 Stewart

Parson John, clk Bank of Montreal bds Oriental Hotel

Pascall Lillie, tlress P Simons & Co l 188 Perry

Pascall Maud, l 188 Perry

Pascoe Alice, l 583 Water

Pascoe Lillian, l 583 Water

Pascoe Thomas, watchman Lock Works h 583 Water

Paterson Aggie, l 224 Hunter

Paterson Euphemia, (wid Walter) h 224 Hunter

Paterson Euphemia, bkkpr J Mervin bds 224 Hunter

Paterson Eva, l 224 Hunter

Paterson James, (W Paterson & Son) h 224 Hunter

Paterson Mary, l 224 Hunter

Paterson Walter & Son, (James Paterson) tanners 412 Aylmer

Patterson Alexander B, lab h 501 Aylmer

Patterson Allie, l 162 Smith

Patterson Andrew W, inspector Canadian General Elec Co h 217 Park

Patterson Annie, l 71 Romaine

Patterson David, wks St R Ry h 785 George

Patterson Flora, cashier Hall Gilchrist & Co l 370 Hunter

Patterson George, agent T W Moore h 71 Romaine

Patterson George, bkkpr Grand Central bds same

Patterson George H, coller mkr B F Ackerman l 501 Aylmer

Patterson Ida, l 71 Romaine

Patterson James, mach, h 370 Hunter

Patterson Jenett, (wid Thomas) l 370 Hunter

Patterson Maud, l 501 Aylmer

Patterson Nettie, clk Hall Gilchrist & Co l 370 Hunter

Patterson Rubina, milliner l 370 Hunter

Patterson Thomas, l 217 Park

Patterson, auditor Can Gen Elec Co h 299 King

Paton Florence, dom 284 Brock

Paton George, fuel agent G T R h 292 Brock

Patton Annie, wks Can Gen Elec Co bds 111 Rubidge

Patton Bella, wks Can Gen Elec Co l 20 Stewart

Patton Ella wks Can Gen Elec Co bds 111 Rubidge

Patton Lavina, wks Can Gen Elec Co h 20 Stewart

Patton Lillie, wks T C Elliott l 20 Stewart

Patton Lizzie, clk J Long, bds 22 Sheridan

Patton Maggie, wks T C E'liott l 20 Stewart

Pauley Maria, waitress Southern Hotel

Pauley Maria, dom 437 Downie

Paumer Emel, baker G Schneider bds 569 George

Pawson George E, boilermaker Wm Hamilton h 270 Smith

Paxman George, prtr The Review bds C P R Hotel

Payne Ellen, dom 411 Reid

Payne George, nurse l 459 Reid

Payne Jediah, l 74 McDonnel

Payne Lazarus, h 74 McDonnel

Payne Mary A, (wid Urah) h 819 George

Payne Ross, butcher Wm McNarn bds Wolfe

Payton Alfred J, pump mkr E H Payton h 166 Antrim

Payton Edward, pump mkr h 62 Patterson

Payton Edward H, pumps 174 Charlotte h same

Payton James, lab h 166 Antrim

Payton Wm contr St Ry h 50 Patterson

Peace John, wks Wm Hamilton

Peace P H, h 9 Walton

Peacey Wm, gardener h 18 Cedar

Peacock Joseph, lab Wm Hamilton h 359 Sherbrooke

Pearse A Miss, teacher Dr Barnardos Home

Pearse Edgecourt, county treasurer h 586 Rubidge

Pearson Edith, clk Hall, Gilchrist & Co

Pearson Mrs, l 676 Water

Peate Alfred, (Peate Bros) bds 187 Simcoe

Peate Bros, (Frank & Alfred) upholsterers etc 187 Simcoe

Peate Frank, (Peate Bros) bds 187 Simcoe

Peck Annie, wks Auburn Mill l 797 Water

Peck Edward A, Barrister 358 George h cor Market & Maria Ashburnham (see adv)

Peck George, wks Auburn Mill l 797 Water

Peck Gilbert, butcher bds 797 Water

Peck John F, wks Auburn Mill h 797 Water

Pellatt John, lab bds 465 Donegal

Pelling Wm, engineer G T R

Pellit Margaret, (wid Frank) h 213 Charlotte

Pendleton Harry S, bds 330 George

Pennington Clarence, wks Can Gen Elec Co h 154 Rubidge

Pentland Joseph B, Dentist 386 George h 16 Benson

Peoples Samuel, lab G T R h 73 Elm

Perkins Walter H, mach Wm Hamilton b 54 Bonacord

Porks George S Mrs, l 94 Gilmour

Perrin Fannie, bkkpr R H Kells & Co bds 313 Bethune

Perrin Lottie, tchr Public School bds 313 Bethune

Perry Ellen, tchr Public School bds 451 Water

Perry J, dom 815 George

Perry Margaret, (wid Charles) l 451 Water

Perry Maud, opr Bell Tel Co bds 451 Water

Perry Robert F, clk Lock Works h 451 Water

Pese John, mach Wm Hamilton h 15 Cedar

Peterborough Business College, Alex Blanchard C A Principal 368 & 370 Water (see adv)

Peterborough Canoe Co Ld, W H Hill Pres, Geo A Schofield Secy-Treas, J Z Rogers Mang Dir 290 Water (see adv)

Peterborough Carbon & Porcelean Co Ld, J W Taylor mngr 270 Townsend

Mnfrs. Life Ins. Co., Toronto.

"I received your cheque for $10,000 within three hours after I filed claim papers".

KATHERINE RIDOUT.

Peterborough Hardware Co (Ld), R B McKee Pres, H Phelan V Pres, R H Fortye Secy, R S Davidson Treas 368 George & 140 Simcoe

Peterborough House, John Clancy Prop 189 Hunter

Peterborough Light&Power Co, T G Hazlett pres, T E Bradburn V Pres A Stephenson Secy, office 417 Water

Peterboro'Lock Mnfg Co, Jas Stevenson Pres, Juo Carnegie V Pres, Thos Brooks Mng Dir, F Adams Secy-Treas 198 Simcoe

Peterborough Music Co, Turner & Cunningham Props, Pianos, Sewing Machines, Music etc 404 George (see adv)

Peterborough Review(The), The Peterborough Review Printing & Publishing Co Ld pubs 164-166 Hunter (see adv)

Peterborough Review Printing & Publishing Co Ld The, F H Dobbin Mng Dir, J Carnegie Pres 164 & 166 Hunter (see adv)

Peterborough Steam Laundry, A Parker Mngr 179 Charlotte (see adv)

Peterborough Water Works Co, Jno Burnham pres, G W Hatton secy 253 Hunter

Peterborough Woolen Mill, James Kendry propr Water n

Peterborough & Ashburnham St Ry Co Ld, T E Bradburn Pres & Genl Mngr F Nicholls V Pres, A P Pousette Secy-Treas 336 George

Peters Absalom, marble cutter T W Moore h Ashburnham

Peters Charles, sargent mayor 5 7 Battlion h 186 Murray

Peters George, librarian Mechanics Institute h Ashburham

Peters Maggie, dom 469 Water

Peters Walter, prtr Examiner h 266 Murray

Pethick Elizabeth, (wid Henry) bds 548 Bethune

Phair Thomas, driver Adam Hall

Phelan Edward, Propr Phelans Hotel 181 Simcoe

Phelan Henry, Vic Pres Peterboro Hardware Co h 335 Rubidge

Phelan Kate, cook Oriental Hotel

Phelan Water, clk Peterboro Hardware Co

Phelans Hotel, Edward Phelan Prop 181 Simcoe

Phillips Charles, butcher 232 Rubidge bds C P R Hotel

Philp F H, (J B Oke & Co) bds Hunter

Phoenix Insurance Co of Hartford Cox & Davis Agents 433 George

Phoenix of Brooklin, Cox & Davis Agents 433 George

Picard Adolphis, tlr H Le Brun & Co

Picard Alfred, plasterer bds Montreal House

Picard Joseph, (H Le Brun & Co) h 423 Downie

Pickford Edgar W, curate St Johns Church h 345 Rubidge

Pickles Elizabeth, laundress h 695 George

Pigeon Henry, Physician 270 Charlotte h same

Pillar John, lab h 29 Argyle

Pillar Rebecca, l 29 Argyle

Pilling Sarah, l 14 Boliver

Pilling Wm, engr G T R h 14 Boliver

Plummer Alfred R, mach P Hamilton Mnfg Co h 274 Sherbrooke

Plummer Alfred R jr, mach P Hamilton Mnfg Co l 274 Sherbrooke

Plummer Elizabeth C, mlnr J C Turnbull l 274 Sherbrooke

Plunkett Agnes, (wid Thomas) h 210 Edinburgh

Pogue Charles, wks Can Gen Elec Co h 18 Bonacord

Pogue George G, fireman Can Gen Elec Co h 154 Romaine

Pogue John, lab Dickson Co

Pogue Mary A, (wid Joseph) h 188 Dublin

Pogue Nelson, mldr Wm Hamilton bds 188 Dublin

THE BANK OF TORONTO,
PETERBORO' BRANCH, P. CAMPBELL, MANAGER.
BUYS AND SELLS CANADIAN AND FOREIGN EXCHANGE.

PETERBOROUGH CITY DIRECTORY. 109

Point St Charles Ice Co., Mc-Donald & Mercier,ProprsPoint St Charles (see adv]

Pointer F, bookkeeper Auburn Mill h 787 Water

Pointer WmD,wks Wm Hamilton b 21 Walnut

Police Station, 355 Water

Pollard Joseph, baker 238 Simcoe h same

Pollard Minnie, l 238 Simcoe

Pollock Lizzie, l 20 Queen

Pomeroy H, wks Canadian General Elec Co bds 80 Gilmour

Pomfret Albert,wks Canadian Gen eral Elec Co h 356 Sherbrooke

Poole Bernard R,veterinary surgeon 352 Water h same

Poole Edwin Col, h 255 George

Poole Minnie, l 255 George

Poole Mrs, mach B F Ackerman

Pope Annie, (wid Robert) l 292 Simcoe

Pope George G, insurance h 709 Water

Pope Miss, dressmkr Hall Gilchrist & Co

Pope Robert, street inspector h 267 Stewart

Pope Wm, lab h 367 McDonnel

Porter David, h 285 Dalhousie

Porter John, grocer 292 Dalhousie h same

Porter Lottie, wks Ensign Corset Co

Porter Minnie, wks Ensign Corset Co l 292 Dalhousie

Post Office, H C Rogers postmaster n w cor Hunter & Water

Potter Sylvester, engr Canadian General Elec Co h 309 Rubidge

Potts Alexander,wks Canadian Gen eral Elec Co bds 173 Murray

Potvin Edward, wks Canadian Gen eral Elec Co bds 253 Wolfe

Potvin Frederick, barber Guerin & Briou h 209 Simcoe

Potvin Louis, lab h 75 Lake

Potvin L Mrs, grocery 73 Lake h same

Potvin Mary, dressmkr l 75 Lake

Potvin Peter, wks Canadian Gen eral Elec Co h 253 Wolfe

Pouliotte Bridget, wks J Watt l 319 McDonnel

Pouliotte Frederick, lab h 319 Mc Donnel

Poussette Alfred P, Barrister etc 379 Water h 305 Park (see adv)

Poussett Edward M, bkkpr Wm Hamilton h 398 Charlotte

Poussett Francis Miss, l 398 Charlotte

Poussett Sarah, (wid Edward W) h
398 Charlotte

Powell Bella, dressmkr bds 325
Aylmer

Powell Charles, mach Canadian
General Elec Co h 267 Townsend

Powell George W, butcher 684 George h Wasseau Rd c 1

Powell James, blksmith R Hull h
Ashburnham

Powell Otho, prop Palace Restaurant 344 George h same

Powers John, yardman White
House

Poyne Chas, wks Wm Hamilton

Poyne Nelson, wks Wm Hamilton

Pratt Lillie, school teacher l 271
Simcoe

Pratt Maggie, dressmaker l 271
Simcoe

Pratt Thomas E, wks Wm English
Canoe Co h 627 Water

Pratt Thomas G, carp h 271 Simcoe

Prattey George, watchman Auburn
Mills h 155 River Rd

Prest Arnold, brass finisher Can Gen
Elec Co bds 118 Aylmer

Prest John, brass finisher Can Gen
Elec Co bds 118 Aylmer

Preston Albert, teamster W H Meldrum

Preston Alexander A, driver W H
Meldrum h 81 London

Preston Ruby, wks Can Gen Elec Co
bds 76 Lake

Primeau John, barber J H Primeau
h Ashburnham

Primeau Joseph H, barber 162 Hunter
h Ashburnham

Pringle Josephine, music teacher l
372 Rubidge

Protestant Home, Miss E Londerville matron 470 Stewart

Pulfer Susana, dom 166 Edinburgh

Pullman Hotel, Frank Fairen
Prop 339 George

Purser Richard, steamboat purser
bds Little Windsor

Queen Fire Insurance Co, W
H Hill Agent 400 Water

Queens Hotel, Wm Dianeen prop cor
Charlotte & Aylmer

Quinlan David, h 297 McDonnel

Quinlan Elizabeth J, dressmaker l
297 McDonnel

Quinlan Michael H, harness 180
Hunter h 316 Dublin

Quinlan Thomas, teamster Dickson
Co

Quinn Annie, dom 304 Brock

Quinn James, carp h 15 Cresent

Quinn Minnie, dressmaker Miss Mercier bds 213 Charlotte

Quinn Mirah, l 15 Cresent

Quinn M Miss, asst secy Dr Barnardos Home

Quinn Wm, repr Bell Tele Co bds 267 Hunter

Quirk Rebecca S, (wid Hugh) grocer 236 Charlotte h 238 same

Rabey Edward, lab bds 26 Louis

Rabey Martha, wks Turner & Son bds 26 Louis

Rabey Maud, l 26 Louis

Rabey John, wks Carbon Works bds 26 Louis

Rabey Wm, lab Carbon Works h 26 Louis

Rae Ada, mantle mkr Hall Gilchrist & Co

Rae Ada, dressmkr Miss Rae bds 308 Stewart

Rae Elizabeth, dressmkr 146 Simcoe bds 309 Stewart

Rae Joseph J Rev, pastor Charlotte St Methodist h 302 Reid

Rae Millie, tlress W J Green bds 308 Stewart

Rae Robert, turnkey h Jail

Rains Frank, wks B F Ackerman bds 251 George

Ralph Alexander, wks Carbon Works h 62 Lake

Ralph Alex, groom R H Leary

Ralph Wm T, wks Canadian General Elec Co bds 62 Lake

Raney Edward, wks G T R bds 258 Brock

Ranger Joseph, btchr Laplante & Letellier bds w end Parnell

Ranger Moses, lab h w end Parnell

Ranney Aggie, (wid Charles) l 32 Gilmour

Ranney George W, (Ranney & Innes) b 32 Gilmour

Ranney & Innes, (G W Ranney & W L Innes) Surveyors etc 372½ Water

Raper John, carp h 43 Paterson

Rathbun Co The, C E Hubbs Agent, Lumber Mnfrs 248 Murray

Rawlings George, potter J F Allin h 9 Wescott

Ray Fred, clk S Ray bds 330 Water

Ray Samuel, Tobacconist 135 Hunter h 544 George (see adv)

Record George, tlr T Dolan & Co

Record Richard, finisher D Bellegham

Redding Alexander, ptr bds 377 Stewart

Redding Elizabeth, dressmkr J Armstrong bds 377 Stewart

Redding George, lab h 377 Stewart

Redman May, dom 285 Park

Redman Robert, tea agent h 469 Donegal

Redman Wm, hack driver bds 9 Hunter

Redmond Joseph A, butcher 245 Rubidge bds Southern Hotel

Redmund Richard, lab h 45 Payne

Redmond Wm J, Cabman

Redner Thomas, locksmith 443 George h same

Regan Emily, (wid James) h 289 Murray

Regan Emma, dressmkr l 288 Murray

Regan Hugh, lumberman h 2 Anson

Rehill David, l 149 George

Rehill Letitia, l 149 George

Rehill Samuel, h 149 George

Rehill Thomas A, (Rehill Bros) l 149 George

Rehill Wm G, (Rehill Bros) l 149 George

Reid Alex, lab Dickson Co

Reid David F, clk G Carton l 55 Wescott

Reid Edward, h 55 Wescott

Reid Frank, clk Geo Carton

Reid George G, agent h 189 Dublin

Reid Harriett, l 76 Lansdowne

Reid James, teamster Dickson Co

Reid James h 76 Lansdowne

Reid John, mach Can Gen Elec Co b 184 Perry

Reid Lucy, l 76 Lansdowne

Reid Mary A Mrs, grocery 189 Dublin h same

Reid Mat, lab Dickson Co

Reilly Hugh, tlr P Simons & Co b 394 Aylmer

Reilly Michael, contr Lock Works

Renwick Bella, dom 35 Belmont ave

Renwick James h 414 McDonnel

Renwick Susie, dom 100 Weller

Revi Ida, waitress Snowden House

Reynolds Alfred, painter l 415 Downie

Reynolds Francis, wks Carbon Wks h 425 Bethune

Reynolds John, livery 272 Simcoe h same

Reynolds John, lab G T R h 499 Stewart

Reynolds John, section foreman G T R h 699 Stewart

Reynolds Joseph, wks Carbon Wks l 272 Simcoe

Reynolds Louisa, wks Carbon Works l 272 Simcoe

Reynolds May, bkkpr A Elliott l 415 Downie

Reynolds Matilda, (wid Wm) h 415 Downie

Reynolds Sarah, (wid John) l 180 Brock

Reynolds Wm F, mason h 13 Cambridge

Reynolds Wm H, l 415 Downie

Rhea Thomas, wks Auburn Mill h 194 Auburn

Rheel Susana, (wid John) l 155 Stewart

Rhynas Elizabeth, clk H McIndoe bds Ashburnham

Rice John, lab h rear 24 Union

Richardson Dawson, clk G T R Freight Office l 500 George

Richardson Edith, l 475 Rubidge

Richardson Issac, care taker G A Cox h 475 Rubidge

Richardson John, wks Canadian Canoe Co l 475 Rubidge

Richardson Joseph, teamster J W Brisbin h 192 Dalhousie

Richardson Lizzie, l 475 Rubidge

Richardson May, tchr Business College bds 500 George

Richardson Ralph, cattle buyer h 500 George

Richardson Thomas, mach Wm Hamilton h 28 Cedar

Rickerby Alice, dom 398 Charlotte

Rickerby John, mason h 573 Downie

Rickerby Mary, l 573 Downie

Ricketts Jacob, wks Lock Works h 224 Sherbrooke

Rickey A W, clk Mills Bros bds 120 Alymer

Rickey Bruce, clk Mills Bros

Rickey George, grocer 120 Alymer h same

Rickey George, blksmith A McDonald

Rickner Aaron, brass finisher Can Gen E Co h 33 Ware

Riddley Frederick, driver F Merser bds 478 Rubidge

Riley Mamey, l 296 Stewart

Riley Michael, lock fitter Lock Works h 296 Stewart

Ringer Alfred R, carp h 589 Reid

Ringer Arthur, clk E B Clegg

Ringer Robert, canoe bldr Peterboro Canoe Co

Rishea Harry, lab Can Gen E Co h 150 Romaine

Rishea Louis, beam hd W Patterson & Son

Rishor Charles, bkkpr M Carton bds 196 Dalhousie

Ritchie Albenia, dressmkr Wall & Connall

Ritchie Dorathea, (wid John) h 279 Dublin

Ritchie James D, clk Ontario Bank rms Harvey

Ritchie, carp W H Meldrum h Ashburnham

Ritchie Lillian S Miss, music tchr l 279 Dublin

Ritchie Lizzie, waitress Snowden House

Ritchie Louis, tanner Patterson & Son h 95 Patterson

Ritchie Mary, (wid Wm) l 26 Gilmour

Ritchie Michael, mason h 142 Romaine

Ritchie R J, carp Peterboro Canoe Co h Ashburnham

Ritchie Thomas, lab l 26 Gilmour

Ritchie Thomas, wks Peterboro Canoe Co bds 101 Simcoe

Roach Aggie, ironer I X L Laundry

Roach Daniel, wks Peterboro Woolen Mill 1 849 Water

Roach Ella, wks Auburn Mill 1 849 Water

Roach Ellen, (wid Patrick) h 849 Water

Roach Eva, 1 849 Water

Roach Lizzie, dressmkr M McCaulley 1 George

Roach Maggie, dom Phelans Hotel

Roadhouse Stephen, prtr P Hamilton Mnfg Co h 24 Louis

Roadhouse Wm, clk Gough Bros bds 24 Louis

Robert B lla Mrs h 18 Union

Roberts Fred, lab Lock Works

Roberts H, wks Canadian General Elec Co h 293 Townsend

Roberts May, dressmkr 1 18 Union

Roberts Wm H, contractor h 496 Stewart

Robertson Annie, 1 202 Perry

Robertson Annie, 1 209 Murray

Robertson A G, boat mkr Canadian Canoe Co

Robertson Charles, wks Canadian General Elec Co h 100 Stewart

Robertson Fred L, veterinary surgeon 227 Charlotte bds 225 same

Robertson John, moulder Wm Hamilton h cor Bonacord & Monaghan Rd

Robertson John jr, moulder Wm Hamilton 1 cor Bonacord & Monaghan Rd

Robertson John M, carp h 202 Perry

Robertson John M, carp h 209 Murray

Robertson John sr, wks Wm Hamilton

Robertson Josiah, agent h 17 Chamberlain

Robertson J J, wks Wm Hamilton

Robertson Marian, 1 202 Perry

Robertson Mariah, 1 209 Murray

Robertson Robt, wks Wm Hamilton

Robertson Ruth, 1 526 Water

Robertson Sadie, dressmaker bds Simcoe 178

Robertson student Can Gen E Co bds 301 Reid

Robertson Wm, tailor 1 cor Bonacord & Monaghan Rd

Robertson W, condr St Ry Co

Robertson Wm, mldr Lock Works

Robertson Wm H, Pres Times Printing Co h 526 Water

Robinson Abbie, 1 778 George

Robinson Andrew, wks P Hamilton Mnfg Co bds 58 Albert

Robinson Birdie, wks Parkers Dye Wks 1 197 Brock

Robinson Edith, nurse Nicholls Hospital 1 same

Robinson Ellen, (wid Thomas) 1 197 Brock

Robinson Fanny, bds 304 King

Robinson Frederick J, pattern maker Can Gen E Co 1 263 Bethune

Robinson George, carp J R Donell

Robinson Harry, carp P Hamilton Mnfg Co

Robinson Harry, barber 390 Water h 567 Ried

Robinson John, woodfinisher Can Gen E Co bds 118 Alymer

Robinson Maggie, clk A Parker

Robinson Margaret, maid Nicholls Hospital l same

Robinson Margaret A, l 57 Smith

Robinson Mary A, (wid Joseph) h 57 Smith

Robinson Minnie, dom 113 Simcoe

Robinson Miss, wks Times Office bds 494 Aylmer

Robinson Robert, pattern maker Wm Hamilton h 263 Bethune

Robinson Thomas, driver Peterboro Steam Laundry

Robinson Thomas W, h 778 George

Robinson T Mrs, h Patterson n Monaghan

Robinson Wm, mldr Lock Wks bds Balmoral Hotel

Robinson Wm, carp h 58 Albert

Robinson Wm P, coudr St Ry Co h 165 Sherbrooke

Robinson Wm S, tinsmith Can Gen Elec Co h 582 Aylmer

Robson Andrew R, mason h 31 Cross

Robson Bella, l 176 Dublin

Robson Emma, dressmaker J C Turnbull bds 176 Dublin

Robson Jane, (wid John) h 176 Dublin

Robson Jennie, dom 657 Bethune

Robson John, carp Wm Donell l 170 Dublin

Robson John T, mason h 27 Cross

Mnfrs. Life Ins. Co., Toronto.

" I received your cheque for $10,000 within three hours after I filed claim papers".

KATHERINE RIDOUT.

Robson Kate, tlress W H Meredith bds 470 Aylmer

Robson Lillie, milliner R H Kells & Co l 176 Dublin

Robson Mabel, l 176 Dublin

Robson Robert, wks Bridge Works h 19 Cedar

Rochester Star Nursery, T W Bowman Prop, C L Trotter Mngr 415½ Water

Roddy Nelson, brass finisher Lock Works

Rodgers Ann, cook Croft House

Rodgers Ellen, (wid James) l 262 Murray

Rodgers John, h 262 Murray

Rodgers Wm, wks Wm English Canoe Co bds Croft House

Rodman Joseph, engineer h 68 Boliver

Roger George M. Barrister etc 375 Water h 465 Park (see adv)

Roger Isabella Miss, l 465 Park

Roger Rachel H, l 465 Park

Rogers D M, clk Post Office
Rogers Ellen, (wid James) h 262 Murray
Rogers H C Postmaster h Ashburnham
Rogers John, l 262 Murray
Rogers Joseph, nightwatch Snowden House
Rogers J Z, Mng Director Peterboro Canoe Co h Ashburnham
Rogers R B, supt Trent Valley Canal h Ashburnham
Rogers Robert G, pedlar h 106 Albert
Romano Antonio, fruit 445 George h same
Rome Caroline, wks Can Gen Elec Co bds 371 Sherbrooke
Rome Charlotte, (wid George) h 371 Sherbrooke
Rome John, wks Can Gen Elec Co bds 371 Sherbrooke
Rook Myra, dom 112 McDonnel
Roper J H, (Mulholland & Roper) h 396 Downie
Roper Maggie Miss, l 396 Downie
Rose Andrew, (Rose & Morrison) h 25 Dennistoun ave
Rose Donald W, mach l 497 Donegal
Rose George, bricklayer h 275 Reid
Rose Jennie, l 497 Donegal
Rose John, mach Wm Hamilton h 497 Donegal

Rose John, lab Carbon Works h 65 Park
Rose Lillie, wks Can Gen Elec Co bds 65 Park
Rose Stephen, wks Peterboro Carbon Co
Rose Stewart W, lab P Hamilton Mnfg Co h 166 Sherbrooke
Rose Susan, (wid Albert) l 95 Rubidge
Rose Wm B, ptr J H Yelland h 375 Aylmer
Rose & Morrison, (Andrew Rose & M A Morrison) dentists 140½ Hunter
Roseborough Robert, h n s Wolsley 7 w Benson
Ross Catharine, (wid John) h 29 Bonacord
Ross James, binder Examiner
Ross Robert H, clk Hall, Gilchrist & Co bds 168 Brock
Roszel George I, chief police h 596 George
Round Enoch wks Electric Light Co h 175 Dublin
Rountree Arthur propr Commercial Hotel 440 George
Rountree Thomas, shoemaker 416 Water h same
Routh Sarah, (wid Frederick) h 471 Rubidge
Routley C B, fancy goods 379 George h 416 Stewart
Rowe Mrs, (wid Robert) h 607 Stewart
Roy Mable, l 335 Stewart
Roy Robert M, wks G T R h 294 Stewart

Roy Robert M, stores insp G T R h 335 Stewart

Roy R M jr, clk Bridge Works

Royal Insurance Co, Cox & Davis Agents 433 George

Rubidge Daisey Miss, stenog Can Gen E Co bds 409 Wolfe

Rubidge Elizabeth, l 291 Stewart

Rubidge Florence, l 291 Stewart

Rubidge Florence, painter G B Sproule

Rubidge George W, tobacconist 382 George h 294 Rubidge

Rubidge John, h 291 Stewart

Rubidge Margaret, l 291 Stewart

Rubidge Margaret, retoucher G B Sproule

Rubidge Minnie, l 193 Aylmer

Rudkins K Miss, Dye Goods 412 George bds 185 King

Rudkins Wm, wks Lock Works h 185 King

Rumming David, canoe bldr Peterboro Canoe Co

Rumming David H, bricklayer h 623 George

Rumming Ettie, mach Mrs Byrne Ashburnhan

Rundle Arthur L, bookkeeper Can Gen E Co (Ld) h 582 Water

Rundle Edwin, teacher colley Inst h 489 Aylmer

Rundell Wm G, barber J Mitchell bds 3 Romaine

Runnels A E, clk A G Dickson

Rush Harry, insurance agent h 51 Brock

Rush Heny M, wks Can Gen E Co h 202 Dublin

Rush Thomas O, insurance 374 Water h 249 Aylmer

Russell Ernest, mach Can Gen E Co bds 190 Reid

Russell James, wks Bridge Works h 178 Aylmer

Russell John, dray man h 43 Chamberlaine

Russell John, harnessmaker B F Ackeman h 110 Murray

Russell Robert M, carp l 43 Chamberlain

Russia Louisa, waitress Oriental Hotel

Rutherford Alexander, carp bds 69 Hunter

Rutherford Christopher, carp Thos Rutherford h 213 Simcoe

Rutherford Ernest, wks St R R l 25 Union

Rutherford Florence, clk Bell Telephone Office l 32 Benson ave

Rutherford Jessie, l 32 Benson Ave

Rutherford Mary A, (wid Arthur) h 32 Benson ave

Rutherford Sarah, l 891 Water

Rutherford Thomas, contractor h 25 Union

Ruttan David J, contractor h 95 Aylmer

Ryan Bridget, l 199 Dalhousie

Ryan Ester, (wid Wm) l 12 Union

Ryan John, wks Canadian General Elec Co bds 199 Dalhousie

Ryan John, grain buyer W H Meldrum h 409 Wolfe

Ryan Kate, tchr Seperate School bds 199 Dalhousie

Ryan Kate, dressmkr l 378 London London

Ryan Maggie, stenogr Hall & Hayes bds 199 Dalhousie

Ryan Michael, h 199 Dalhousie

Ryan Wm, lab h 12 Union

Rye H B, boat mkr Can Canoe Co

St Andrews Church Presbyterian, Rev A MacWilliams pastor Rubidge opp Brock

St George Georgie Miss, l 208 Perry

St George Harriet, (wid) h 208 Perry

St Peters Cathedral (R C), RevD J Casey Rector cor Hunter & Reid

Sabin Henry E, plasterer bds 46 Chamberlain

Sabin James E, h 677 Water

Sabin Rose E, dressmkr l 46 Chamberlain

Sabin Thomas, plasterer bds 46 Chamberlain

Sabin Thomas J, tuck pointer h 46 Chamberlain

Sager Eli, patent medicines h 29 Harvey

Sager John, l 29 Harvey

Sailsbury Wm,(Sailsbury & Co) h 352 Stewart

Sailsbury &Co,Books Stationery etc 372 George (see adv)

Sanderson George, grocer 235 McDonnel h 237 same

Sanderson Harry, wks Carbon Works bds 144 Rubidge

Sanderson J, prtr The Review

Sanderson Lizzie, dom 274 King

Sanderson Margaret, (wid Thomas) l 19 Parnell

Sanderson Rachel A, l 237 McDonnel

Sanderson Richard J, wks Auburn Mills h 144 Rubidge

Sanderson Wm A, Jeweler & Optician 367 George h 369 Brock (see adv)

Sargeson Evelyn, box mkr Examiner bds 195 Simcoe

Sargent Mrs, bds 223 Murray

Saunders Eliza Miss, forewoman Peterboro Laundry bds 231 Bethune

Saunders Joseph, lab Wm Hamilton h 103 Romaine

THE BANK OF TORONTO,
PETERBORO' BRANCH, P. CAMPBELL, MANAGER.
HIGHEST RATE OF INTEREST ALLOWED ON DEPOSITS.

PETERBOROUGH CITY DIRECTORY.   119

Saunders Wm, wks Carbon Wks h 40 Lake

Sauve Delima, (wid Joseph) h 36 Ware

Sauve Joachim, l 53 Smith

Savigny Ethel J, l 113 Gilmore

Savigny George, carp h 70 Wescott

Savigny John, clk Thos Brady bds 101 Simcoe

Savigny Lorne, clk Hall, Gilchrist & Co h 113 Gilmour

Savigny Thomas A, clk l 113 Gilmour

Savigny Wm, prtr P Hamilton Mnfg Co bds 332 Water

Savin Rose, wks Knob Dept Lock Works

Sawdye Robert C, lab Dickson Co h 550 Water

Sawers Augustus, h 333 Charlotte

Sawers Augustus jr, surveyor l 333 Charlotte

Sawers Campbell W, Barrister 139 Simcoe h 298 Brock (see adv)

Saw yer John, fireman h 181 Park

Sawyer John, h 230 London

Sawyers Wm, Can Gen Elec Co bds 181 Park

Saxby Wm, plasterer h 507 Bethune

Schapp Bridget Mrs, dom 463 Stewart

Schneider Frank S, jeweler 391 George bds 567 same

Schneider George, baker 521 George h 567 same

Schneider George F, clk G Schneider bds 567 George

Schofield George A, Druggist 408 George h 546 Aylmer

Schreiber George, wks Lock Wks h 546 Downie

Scollie W J, canoe bldr Peterboro Canoe Co

Scott Addie, l 112 Stewart

Scott Charlotte, (wid Robert) h 645 Downie

Scott Christine Miss, h 297 Hunter

Scott George, carp P Hamilton Mnfg Co h 112 Stewart

Scott George S, mldr P Hamilton Mnfg Co h 231 Bethune

Scott Harriett, (wid Thomas) l 81 Gilmour

Scott J, cellar man G Matthews

Scott John, teamster l 43 Chamberlain

Scott Leslie, wks Can Gen Elec Co bds 112 Stewart

Scott Mary, dom 385 Reid

Scott Mary, bkkpr J J McBain bds 112 Stewart

Scott Robert M, mldr P Hamilton Mnfg Co bds 112 Stewart

Scott Susan, (wid Andrew) 1 227 Bethune

Scott Walter, wks H Owens h 452 Charlotte

Scott Wm, Physician 176 Brock h same

Scott Wm H, brakeman G T R h 81 Gilmour

Scott Wm J, h 199 Reid

Scriver Annie E, housekeeper 258 Dublin

Scriver James B, lab h rear167Murray

Scriver Maggie, dom 306 Brock

Scriver Robert J, lab h 689 Stewart

Scully John, wks Bault Wks h 252 Charlotte

Sedgwick Mary, (wid Thomas)h 122 Dublin

Sedgwick Mrs, tlress A Mercer & Co bds London

Serro Michael, surveyor A McDonald h 199 Perry

Seward Mrs, (wid Lewis) h 340 Water

Seymour Charles J, stenog h 617 Bethune

Shanahan Ellen, dressmaker Miss L Geary 1 617 Downie

Shanahan John, dray man h 617 Downie

Shanahan Kate, dom 174 London

Shangraw Henry, lab bds 69 Hunter

Shannan Daniel, h s e corDalhousie & Rubidge

Shannan Ellen, (wid Patrick) nurse rms 379 Stewart

Shannon Fred, opr Can Gen ElecCo bds Phelans Hotel

Sharpe John, messenger Bank of Commerce h 350 Dublin

Sharpe Margaret, l 350 Dublin

Sharpe Samuel, painter h 224 Dublin

Sharp Wm, engr Peterboro Laundry h 368 Downie

Shaw Arthur, wks Dickson Co l 200 Harvey

Shaw Donald A, artist 170Charlotte h 188 Dalhousie

Shaw Elizabeth, (wid Mark) h 200 Harvey

Shaw Fred, brakeman G T R bds Queens Hotel

Shaw John, wks The Peterboro Woolen Mill Co l 200 Harvey

Shaw Mark, wks Auburn Mill l 200 Harvey

Shaw R A, wks Can Gen Elec Co bds 409 Wolfe

Shea Lizzie, dom 315 Rubidge

Sheehan Annie, l 11 Alfred

Sheehan Dennis, lab h 11 Alfred

Sheehan Ellen, wks Lock Works l 306 Simcoe

Sheehan Katie, finisher Fairweather & Co bds 11 Alfred

Sheehan Margaret, (wid Cornelius) h 306 Simcoe

Sheehy Margaret,(wid Richard)h 43 Lake

Sheehy Mary A, l 43 Lake

Sheeby Richard, bricklayer h 223 Perry

Shelbourn Maud, housekeeper 39 Stewart

Shelton Richard, foreman brass mldr Lock Works

Sheppard Frederick, tinsmith A Mick h 18 Alfred

Sheppard Robert H, wksCanGenElec Co h 390 Sherbrooke

Shera Robert, carp J R Donell h 621 Water

Sheridan Robert, mill forman Dickson Co

Sherlock Francis, l 42 Boliver

Sherlock Lucuis, bookkeeper R Neill h 42 Boliver

Sherlock Margaret, l 42 Boliver

Sherran Joseph, hostler Connor Bros bds Hub Hotel

Sherrer Essie, dom 414 George

Sherriff H J, act acct Bank Montreal bds Oriental Hotel

Sherrin Bertha, opr Bell Tele Co

Sherrin Wm, horse trainer bds 334 George

Sherwood Alfred, lab h 3 Ware

Sherwood Annie L, l 392 Charlotte

Sherwood Arthur, lab h 410 Aylmer

Sherwood Charlotte E, (wid Wm E) 392 Charlotte

Sherwood Joseph H, mason h 675 Stewart

Sherwood George H, mason h 676 Stewart

Sherwood Wm J, trav h 587 George

Shevlin John P, painter 229 King h same

Shiells George, contractor h 556 Aylmer

Shiells Lizzie, wks The Examiner l 556 Aylmer

Short Jane Miss, housekeeper 263 Water

Short Maggie, dom 35 Belmont ave

Shortly Benjamin, Harness Maker Etc 373 George h 550 Aylmer

Shortly Edith, l 550 Aylmer

Shortly Orville B, Bkkpr B Shortly bds 550 Aylmer

Shuerer Annie, dom 225 Charlotte

Shuter Emily H, dressmaker l 183 Harvey

Shuter Mary Mrs, h 183 Harvey

Siddel James, mach Can Gen Elec Co bds Montreal House

Sim Ellen, l 243 McDonnel

Sim John, carp h 243 McDonnel

Sim John jr, express agent G T R l 243 McDonnel

Simmons Charles, lab J Patterson h 513 Reid

Simons Annie, artist l 163 Charlotte

Simons Catherine, saleslady Hall, Gilchrist & Co l 311 Rubidge

Simons Daniel tlr P Simons & Col 311 Rubidge

Simons James, upholsterer l 311 Rubidge

Simons John, painter bds 163 Charlotte

Simons Nettie, milliner R H Kells & Co

Simons Peter, (P Simons & Co) h 311 Rubidge

Simons Pete & Co, (Pete Simons) merchant tailors 416 George h 311 Rubidge

Simons Peter jr, tlr Pete Simons

Simpson Andrew, wks The Peterboro Woolen Mill Co l 696 Water

Simpson James, wks Peterboro Woolen Mill Co l 696 Water

Simpson James, lab h 1 Chamberlain

Simpson John, wks The Peterboro Woolen Mill Co h 696 Water

Simpson Lizzie, l 696 Water

Simpson Miss, mlnr Hall, Gilchrist & Co bds Oriental Hotel

Sims Arthur, baker Forsythe & Son l 739 Water

Sims Edith, dom 657 Bethune

Sims Joseph C, shoemaker Foot & McWhinnie h 739 Water

Sinclair Neil S, bartender T Dunn h 179 Sherbrooke

Singer Mnfg Co, T Hanes mngr 430 George

Skinner James, opr C P R bds Morgan House

Skitch W F, opr G N W Tel Co bds 98 London

Sloan Edith, dressmaker l 451 Stewart

Sloan George, carp Dickson Co h 211 King

Sloan Hattie, l 451 Stewart

Sloan James A, h 451 Stewart

Sloan Jessie, milliner R H Kells & Co l 451 Stewart

Sloan John, shoemkr J W Carey

Sloan Maggie, l 451 Stewart

Sloan R A, livery Simcoe h 485 Aylmer

Smale Mary, dom l Homewood

Smart Aggie, dom 362 Simcoe

Smart Joseph T, wks Can Gen Elec Co h 88 Aylmer

Smart Mary A, dressmkr l 88 Aylmer

Smart Wm, wks Can Gen Elec Co l 88 Aylmer

Smeaton Alfred A, mach Can Gen Elec Co h 57 Aylmer

Smith Abram H, lab Geo Matthews Co Ld h 35 Parnell

Smith Ann, (wid George) l 11 Parnell

Smith Annie, dressmkr Miss Nevin bds 33 Harvey

Smith Annie, dom 565 Water

Smith Arthur, harnessmkr B F Ackerman h 215 Dublin

Smith Arthur J, agent J W Crosby bds 209 Rubidge

Smith A St A, clk Bank of Toronto h 733 George

Smith Charles, groom F E Jones bds McDonnel

Smith Charles B, Fruiter 166 Charlotte h cor George & Antrim

Smith Cinderilla, (wid Wm) h 156 London

Smith Clara, (wid James) h 291 Townsend

Smith Daisy, l 161 Antrim

Smith De Codin, (wid James) l 559 Stewart

Smith Edith, bkkpr M T Ostrom bds Ashburham

Smith Ernest, driver P J Grady bds 167 Charlotte

Smith Frank, blksmith 179 Murray h rear same

Smith George, yardman Morgan House l same

Smith George, mason h 558 Bark

Smith George, ptr h rear 179 Murray

Smith George A, secy-treas Central Bridge Co h 344 Rubidge

Smith Hannah, l rear 179 Murray

Smith Henry J, supt London Life 172 Hunter bds Oriental Hotel

Smith James, driver J J Howden

Smith James C, plumber h 311 George

Smith Jason, condr St Ry Co

Smith Jason, Grocer 332 Mc-Donnel h 521 Reid

Smith Jennie, housemaid Grand Central bds same

Smith John, lab bds 383 Donegal

Smith John, wks Wm Hamilton

Smith John, h 251 George

Smith John, wks Wm English Canoe Co bds 291 Townsend

Smith John J, clk G Rubidge bds Balmoral Hotel

Smith J N, wks Can Gen Elec Co bds Oriental Hotel

Smith J W, wks Crown Timber Office bds Oriental Hotel

Smith Laura, maid Nicholls Hospital l same

Smith Mabel, maid Nicholls Hospital l same

Mnfrs. Life Ins. Co., Toronto.

"I received your cheque for $10,000 within three hours after I filed claim papers".

KATHERINE RIDOUT.

Smith Maggie, dressmakr l rear 179 Murray

Smith Mary, l 251 George

Smith Mary, dom 392 Stewart

Smith Minnie, waitress Grand Central bds same

Smith Minnie, maid Nicholls Hospital l same

Smith Nellie, dressmkr bds rear 179 Murray

Smith Nellie, l 251 George

Smith Rosa, l 251 George

Smith R H, mason bds 22 Gilmour

Smith Walter, wks G Matthews Co Ld bds 146 George

Smith Wm C, principal public schools h 784 George

Smith, mach Can Gen Elec Co bds 155 Stewart

Smyth James C, teacher School h 22 Aberdeen ave

Smyth Wm, principal Pub Schools h 28 Aberdeen ave

Snowden Herbert, clk Snowden House

Snowden House, Wm Snowden Prop 190 Charlotte

Snowden Wm, Prop Snowden House 190 Charlotte

Snyder Charles J, deputy coll Customs bds 51 McDonnel

Snyder Henry, lab bds 462 Donegal

Snyder Sarah Miss, l 51 McDonnel

Snyder Wm, h 51 McDonnel

Sollitt Eliza A‘ teacher Business College l 58 Elm

Sollitt Francis, mach Wm Hamilton l 58 Elm

Sollitt James, painter Bridge Works h 58 Elm

Somerville F L, draughtsman Trent Valley Canal bds Stewart

Southard Silvia, l 22 Dennistoun ave

Southard Smith, school teacher l 22 Dennistoun ave

Southard Vincent, h 22 Dennistoun ave

Southby, wks Can Gen Elec Co bds 223 George

Southbley H, wks Can Gen Elec Co bds Grand Central

Southern Hotel, Stephen Holland prop 275 George

Southworth Harritt, (wid Alfred) l 595 George

Souvais Fred, barber C Le Gros bds Balmoral Hotal

Sovey Israel, barber C Le Gros bds Balmoral Hotel

Speer Wm W, carp h 601 Rubidge

Speers John, brakesman G T R bds Queens Hotel

Spence Daniel M, carp A A McIntyre bds 16 College

Spence David, moulder Wm Hamilton bds 538 Bethune

Spence John, lab h 27 Walnut

Spence John, lab Dickson Co

Spence John, h 35 Bonacord

Spence Stanley, lab W H Meldrum

Spencer Minnie, dressmaker l 629 Downie

Spencer Wm, harnessmkr W J Devlin bds Little Windsor

Spencer Wm, lab h 629 Downie

Spencley George, mason h 344 Smith

Spencley Martin, mason h 684 Reid

Sperry Anson, lumber man b 997 Water

Sperry Bertha, l 997 Water

Springer Wm C, pattern mkr Lock Works h 215 Simcoe

Sproule Annie, l n e cor Lock & Lansdowne

Sproule Daisey, l n e cor Lock & Lansdowne

Sproule George B, Photographer 170 Charlotte h Lock

Sproule Joseph, b 132 Lansdowne

Spratt Frederick, lab h 881 Water

Spry Lewis, timsmith 214 Stewart h 210 same

Squres Edward W ,clk R Neill l 75 Albert

Squres Walter J ,plumber h 75 Albert

Squres Walter J jr ,clk R H Kells & Co l 75 Albert

Squres W J Mrs ,grocery 79 Albert h 75 same

Stabler Henry C, contractor h 804 George

Stalker Mary, dom 310 London

Stanbury Ella, dom 232 Brock

Stanger John,(Fitzgerald &Stanger) h 98 London

THE BANK OF TORONTO,
PETERBORO' BRANCH, P. CAMPBELL, MANAGER.
BUYS AND SELLS CANADIAN AND FOREIGN EXCHANGE.

PETERBOROUGH CITY DIRECTORY.   125

Stanley E A, supt Can Gen Elec Co h 336 Rubidge

Stanton Charles, mach Moffatt & Kinch l 485 Donegal

Stanton George, mach Wm Hamilton h 435 Donegal

Stanton Hector, wks Can Express Co l 88 Wescott

Stanton Maggie Mrs, cook Phelans Hotel

Stanton Robert, driver G Matthews Co h 86 Wescott

Stanton W, signalman G T R

Staples Alfred, trav h 156 Edinburgh

Staples Daniel, painter h 9 Elm

Staples J E, clk R H Kells & Co

Staples Wm D, painter h 88 McDonnel

Stapleton Charles, auctioneer h 467 Water

Stapleton Henry C, auctioneer l 467 Water

Stapleton H C Mrs, bookkeeper McF Wilson bds 294 Rubidge

Stapleton Mamie, l 467 Water

Staunton Madge, c'k l 34 College

Staunton Sadie, music teacher l 34 College

Staunton Wilford J, clk R Fair l 34 College

Staunton Wm A, signalman G T R h 34 College

Staunton W A Mrs, nurse l 34 College

Steele Agnes, l 476 Park

Steele Elizabeth, l 476 Park

Steele James, l 476 Park

Steele James, carp h 110 Simcoe

Steele John, barber 217 Hunter h 476 Park

Steele Katie, l 110 Simcoe

Steers James E, mldr Carbon Works h 67 Park

Steer Wm G, building sand h 96 Chamberlain

Stenson Charles, clk J T Stenson bds 349 Reid

Stenson Emma, l 349 Reid

Stenson Frederick, clk J T Stenson l 349 Reid

Stenson James T, Boots & Shoes 364 George h 349 Reid

Stent M E Miss, Dr Barnardos Home

Stenton George, wks Wm Hamilton

Stenton Geo jr, wks Wm Hamilton

Stenton J, wks Wm Hamilton

Stenton Robert, driver The George Matthews Co (Ld)

Stephens Christopher, wks Bridge Works h n Monaghan c l

Stephens Eva, clk McF Wilson l 26 Division

Stephenson Jerrie, carp bds 875 Water

Stephens John H, contractor 21½ Paterson h 19 same

Stephens Margaret, (wid John H) h 26 Division

Stephens Martha, l 26 Division

FOR BIBLES, HYMN BOOKS, PRAYER BOOKS, ETC., ETC.

Go To SAILSBURY'S.

Stepheuson, wks Canadian General Elec Co bds 376 Brock

Stethem Archibald, wks George Stethem bds 227 Sherbrooke

Stethem George, (George Stethem & Son) h 227 Sherbrooke

Stethem George A,(George Stethem & Son) bds 227 Sherbrooke

Stethem George & Son, (George & George A) hardware 134 Hunter

Steuart Wm F, photographer h 699 Reid

Stevens C, pattern mkr Bridge Works

Stevens Kate, (wid Jacob) music tchr h 372 Rubidge

Stevens Louise, clk R Neill

Stevenson Annie, dom 458 Rubidge

Stevenson Arthur,(Dennistoun & Stevenson) h n Monaghan c 1

Stevenson George, insurance agent h 473 Water

Stevenson George L, agent h 183 Edinburgh

Stevenson James,(J Stevenson Coal Co) h 216 Simcoe

Stevenson Jessie, l 183 Edinburgh

Stevenson J Coal Co, R Stevenson Mngr 368 Water

Stevenson Susie, school tchr l 183 Edinburgh

Stevenson M C Miss, l 216 Simcoe

Stevenson M E Miss, l 216 Simcoe

Stevenson Rufus, Mngr J Stevenson Coal Co h 376 Stewart

Stewart Alexander,carp l 270 Brock

Stewart Jennie, wks 187 Simcoe

Stewart Joseph, policeman h 80 Wescott

Stewart Lizzie, (wid John) l 40 Sheridan

Stewart Lizzie, dom 40 Sheridan

Stibbings Robert, brick mkr h 191 Reid

Stillman Keneth, lab bds 322 Charlotte

Stinson George T, clk Ormond & Walsh l 349 Reid

Stinson Hattie, dom 293 Park

Stinson John C, wks Wm Donell h 219 Dublin

Stinson Lizzie, wks Auburn Mill h 206 Edinburgh

Stinson Maggie, l 206 Edinburgh

Stinson Sarah J, wks Auburn Mill l 206 Edinburgh

Stinson Thomas,moulder Wm Hamilton h n s Bonacord 2 e Monaghan Rd

Stenson Wm, tlr A Mercer & Co h 338 Aylmer

Stirling Eliza F, (wid John) l 617 Rubidge

Stirling Wm, l 93 Paterson

Stock Minnie, l 283 Sherbrooke

Stock Wm, baker 283 Sherbrooke h same

Stockdale Frederick W, wks T H Hooper l 474 Donegal

Stockdale Wm, lab Gardner & Ullyot h 474 Donegal

Stocker Walter, bill poster h 23 Louis

Stone Erastus B, Barrister etc 374½ Water h 116 Dublin (see adv)

Storm Loresndia, (wid Peter) h 7 Chamberlain

Stortz Clara, wks Auburn Mill l rr 19 Elm

Stortz Joseph, lab Lock Works h rr 19 Elm

Stothart Wm, carp h 197 Harvey

Strachn Robert, jeweler W Sanderson h 584 Bethune

Strain G, lab Dickson Co

Stratton Albert H, (A H Stratton & Co) bds 118 Gilmour

Stratton A H & Co, (A H Stratton) proprs Peterborough Book Store 417 George

Stratton J R, publisher h 206 Aylmer

Stratton Mary L, l 118 Gilmour

Stratton Roey, l 118 Gilmour

Stratton Rosanna (wid James)h 118 Gilmour

Stratton W A, (Stratton &Hall) bds 118 Gilmour

Stratton & Hall, (Wm A Stratton & R R Hall) Barristers 134½ Hunter (see adv)

Strickland A W, teller Bank of Montreal bds Oriental Hotel

Strickland Henry, butcher G W Powell bds Wasaw Rd c l

Strickland R H, wks Trent Valley Canal bds Ashburnham

Strong Wm, lineman Bell Tel Co bds C P R Hotel

Stroud Bros, Frederick Yule Mngr tea 370 George

Stubbs James, carp W Donell h 655 George

Stubbs Wm J, student bds 655 George

Sullivan Aggie, milliner l 153 Edinburgh

Sullivan Bessie, l 949 Water

Sullivan Bridget T, l 420 Charlotte

Sullivan Daniel, grocer 297 Rubidge h 299 same

Sullivan Daniel, grocer 639 George h 153 Edinburgh

Sullivan James, carp h 184 Edinburgh

Sullivan Johanna, (wid John) h 35 Sheridan

Sullivan John, driver C N Brown h 420 Charlotte

Sullivan John, school tchr h 273 Dublin

Sullivan John, wks Peterboro Woolen Mill 1 949 Water

Sullivan Kate 1 35 Sheridan

Sullivan Margaret, (wid) 1 81 Lake

Sullivan Michael, woodyard 639 George h 153 Edinburgh

Sullivan Minnie, dressmkr Miss O'Brien

Sullivan Patrick, grocer 949 Water h same

Sun Life Assurance Co of Canada, W H Hill District Mngr 400 Water (see adv)

Sun Fire Office, Cox & Davis Agents 433 George

Sutherland James, bkkpr The Examiner h 88 Albert

Sutherland Robert, steam fitter Carbon Works bds 88 Albert

Sutherland Silvia, dressmkr M McCaulley Dennistoun ave

Sutherland Susanna, 1 252 Charlotte

Sutton Burtha, 1 234 Murray

Sutton Edith, dressmkr J C Turnbull 1 234 Murray

Sutton Edward, carp J Donell h 234 Murray

Sutton Joseph, carp 1 234 Murray

Swain George, wks Canadian General Elec Co h 22 Boliver

Swanson James, lab Dickson Co

Swanton J, lab Bridge Works

Swanton Hattie, dom 459 Reid

Sweeney Aggie, waitress Phelan's Hotel

Sweeney Bridget, cook White House

Sweeney John, clk Brown Bros 1 249 McDonnel

Sweeney Kate, dom Live Oak Hotel

Sweeney Michael, lab h 249 McDonnel

Sweeney Sophia, 1 246 McDonnel

Sweet Blanch, wks Canadian Gen Elec Co bds 27 Rutherford ave

Swinton Maggie, wks Auburn Mill bds 864 George

Taber Charles J, shipper Lock Works h 690 George

Taffis Ann, 1 556 London

Taggart Albert A, lab l 1019 Water

Taggart Harriett C, l 1019 Water

Taggart Harriett E, (wid Francis C) h 1019 Water

Taggart Robert P, lab l 1019 Water

Tamblin, helper G MatthewsCo(Ld)

Tamblin Robert, stone mason h 177 Sherbrooke

Tangney John, lab h 305 McDonnel

Tangney Margaret, (wid Jeremiah) l 816 Water

Tanner Wm, ptr Carbou wks bds 201 Rubidge

Tassie Sarah, (wid Wm) h 677Water

Taylor Annie, l 313 George

Taylor Ernest, brass finisher Lock Wks bds 313 George

Taylor F Williams, Acting MngrBank ofMontreal h 347Charlotte

Taylor George, h 313 George

Taylor Herbert, l 313 George

Taylor Ida, l 77 Gilmour

Taylor James, contractor h 77 Gilmour

Taylor John R, condr St Ry h 217 Charlotte

Tayor J W, mngr CarbonWks h469 Water

Taylor Philip, lab Can Gen Elec Co h 49 Paterson

Taylor Rose, clk Stroud Bros bds 57 Albert

Taylor Wm, lab h 46 Lake

Taylor Wm, fireman Can Gen Elec Co h 357 Sherbrooke

Taylor Wm, engr C P R h 57 Albert

Tebb Arthur R, mngr Canadian Canoe Co h 614 Reid

Tebb Lucy, dom 34 Weller

Tebb Richard, farmer h 397 Sherbrooke

Tebb Sarah, (wid Edward T) h 167 Antrim

Tebb Sarah, (wid Edward) l 614 Reid

Tebb Thomas W Mrs, l 32 Benson ave

Tebb Wm, cutter A Mercer l 614 Reid

Tebb Wm A, cutter A Mercer & Co l 167 Antrim

Teirney Thomas, wks WmHamilton bds 478 Rubidge

Telford Robert, lab 66 Albert

Telford Thomas, h 66 Albert

Temperance & General Life Insurance Co, H P Lindsay Gen Agent 326 George

Temple Emma, dom 289 Park

Terman Herbert, baker l 614 Downie

Terrill Lyman H, Gunsmith 82 Hunter h same

Thackery John,marble cutterCoughlin Bros bds Carew House

Theobald Amy, l 12 Albert

Theobald Charles, mldr P Hamilton Mnfg Co bds 12 Albert

Theobald John, builder h 67 Albert

Theobald Thomas, lab P Hamilton Mnfg Co b 12 Albert

Thibault Edward, lab 1 372 Stewart

Thibault Emidos, btchr F J Goselin bds 29 Cresent

Thibault Joseph, driver F J Goselin 1 372 Stewart

Thibault Joseph, lab h 372 Stewart

Thomas Etta, 1 348 Stewart

Thomas Heneretta, 1 187 Rubidge

Thomas Lousia, school teacher 1 187 Rubidge

Thomas Wm C, harnessmaker B F Ackerman h 187 Rubidge

Thompson Agnes J, (wid James) h 177 Edinburgh

Thompson Annie, dom 294 Rubidge

Thompson A E, h 165 Smith

Thompson Bella, bkkpr R Fair 1 165 Smith

Thompson Doretha, dressmaker J C Turnbull 1 177 Edinburgh

Thompson Eliza, (wid Edward) 1 165 Smith

Thompson Ellen, (wid Wm) 1 805 George

Thompson Elva, dressmkr Misses Kingdon & Menzies

Thompson Etta, 1 705 George

Thompson George H, clk Cox & Davis 1 165 George

Thompson Gill. wks Geo Matthews Co Ld h 117 Aylmer

Thompson Henry, books etc h 593 George

Thompson J, condr St Ry Co

Thompson James, asst clk Grand Central bds same

Thompson Jennie, dom 367 Hunter

Thompson Jennie, wks Can Gen E Co 1 76 Gilmour

Thompson John, lab G T R h 12 Parnell

Thompson Joseph, wks St R R bds 19½ Paterson

Thompson Kate, dom 352 Brock

Thompson Maggie M, dressmkr 1 177 Edinburrgh

Thompson Mary, (wid Robert) 1 359 Aylmer

Thompson Nina, dom 618 Bethune

Thompson Peter, plumber A Hall h 76 Gilmour

Thompson Prudencia, (wid Wm) h 203 London

Thompson Robert C, mach Wm Hamilton h 93 Aylmer

Thompson Wm, clk Ontario Bank bds 267 Hunter

Thompson Wm, insurance h 805 George

Thompson Wm J, clk Cox & Davis 1 165 Smith

Thomson Andrew, mach 1 123 Stewart

Thomson Gertrude, 1 27 Waterford

Thomson John, millwright h 27 Waterford

Thomson Lottie, l 27 Waterford

Thomson Robt C, wks Wm Hamilton

Thomson Thomas, agent LondonLife h 123 Stewart

Thorndyke A, wks Wm Hamilton

Thorndyke Ada, l 148 Rubidge

Thorndyke Agnes, wks Can Gen Elec Co bds 148 Rubidge

Thorndyke John, carp h 301 King

Thorndyke Robert, lab h 148 Rubidge

Thorndyke Wm A E, moulder Wm Hamilton l 301 King

Thorne Ella, (wid Robert) h 335 Downie

Thorne Millie M, clk J D Armstrong & Co l 382 Stewart

Thorne Robert, wks Can Gen Elec Co l 335 Downie

Thorne Wm, wks Lock Works l 335 Downie

Thornton Easter A, l 65 Harvey

Thornton Melissa, (wid Wm) h 65 Harvey

Thornton Robert, tinner Adam Hall h 67 Harvey

Thornton Theodore, tinner A E Micks l 65 Harvey

Throop George K, butcher Winch Bros h 78 Ware

Throop Williena, dom 682 Stewart

Tierney George, lab l 551 Gilchrist

Tierney Thomas, lab Wm Hamilton h 551 Gilchrist

Tighe George L, janitor Central School h 13 Waterford

Tighe Hugh, harnessmkr B F Ackerman

Tighe James, engr Peterboro Canoe Co h Ashburnham

Tighe Sophronia E, l 13 Waterford

Times Printing Co, W H Robertson Pres 348 George (see adv)

Times The, Times Printing Co Proprs 348 George (see adv)

Timmins Stanley, (S Timmins & Co) bds 360 Aylmer

Timmins S & Co, (Stanley & Thomas Timmins) grocers 360 Aylmer

Timmins Thomas, (S Timmins & Co) h 360 Aylmer

Timmons Thomas, agent Metropolitan Insurance Co

Tindley Clayton, clk Cox & Davis l 589 Downie

Tinkler Wm, storeman George Matthews Co (Ld) bds 184 Brock

Titterson John, clk Hall Gilchrist & Co

Tivey A E, mach Bridge Works

Tobin James S, harnessmkr H Dundas bds Ashburnham

Tobin Kate, dom 195 London

Todd Francis, dressmkr Hall Gilchrist & Co l 717 George

Todd Kity Mrs, housemaid Snowden House

Toms Annie, dom 177 Charlotte

Toms Annie, dom 347 Charlotte

Torrance E F Rev, pastor St Pauls Church h 281 Rubidge

Tougas Joseph, lab Dickson Co h 172 Antrim

Tovey George J, wks Canadian General Elec Co h 471 Sherbrooke

Town Clerks Office, S R Armstrong Clerk cor Simcoe & Water

Tremworth Josepheon, wks Hall Gilchrist & Co bds 391 Smith

Tremain George, carp Wm Donell l 614 Downie

Tremain James, carder h 614 Downie

Tremain Wm, wks A Blade l 614 Downie

Trennum Joseph, barber D Hall bds 527 George

Trent Valley Canal, R B Rogers supt Post Office Bldg

Trickey Warren, h 789 Water

Tripp Wm B, tinsmith A E Micks h 88 McDonnel

Trollope Annie L, dressmkr l 850 Water

Trollope Emma, tlress l 850 Water

Trollope Henry, fireman Auburn Mill h 850 Water

Trollope Henry jr, l 850 Water

Trombly John, lab Wm Hamilton h 442 Charlotte

Trombly Napoleon, carp Dickson Co h 53 Paterson

Trombly Octive, h 388 Sherbrooke

Trotter Annie, waitress White House

Trotter Charles, btchr F T Winch bds same

Trotter Charles L, Mngr Rochester Star Nursery h 555 Downie

Trotter George, mason h 348 Smith

Trotter James Mrs, b 574 Aylmer

Trotter John E Rev, pastor Murray St Baptist h 514 Aylmer

Trotter Linda, wks Peterboro Mill l 352 Smith

Trotter Philippi, (wid Thomas) h 352 Smith

True Hannah, dom 842 Water

True Lizzie, dom 793 George

Tucker Charles, trav l 543 Reid

Tucker D, section foreman C P R

Tucker John T, clk Hall Gilchrist & Co l 543 Reid

Tucker Lizzie S, l 543 Reid

Tucker Thomas C, supt Wm Hamilton h 543 Reid

Tully Annie Mrs, h 223 London

Tully Bella, l 352 McDonnel

Tully James, clk Gough Bros bds 38 Harvey

Tully J D, Druggist 411 George h 352 McDonnel (see adv)

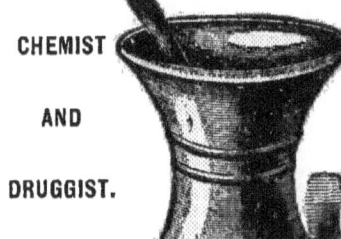

THE BANK OF TORONTO,
PETERBORO' BRANCH, P. CAMPBELL, MANAGER.
BUYS AND SELLS CANADIAN AND FOREIGN EXCHANGE.

PETERBOROUGH CITY DIRECTORY. 133

Tully M ary, (wid Thomas) h 378 McDonnel

Tully Robert, h 277 Stewart

Tully Wm T, carp A A McIntyre bds 16 College

Turcott Albert, wks Lock Works l 10 Cross

Turcott Francis, gardner h 10 Cross

Turnbull John C, Dry Goods, Millinery etc 363 George & 160 Simcoe h 603 Stewart

Turner Adam, wks Auburn Mill h 195 Auburn

Turner Amelia, l 639 Water

Turner C W, clk A E Micks

Turner Edward H, (Turner & Cunningham) h 571 Stewart

Turner Emma, (wid John) l 639 Water

Turner Frank, mldr P Hamilton Mnfg Co bds 113 Rubidge

Turner George E A, clk Robt Fair h 659 Water

Turner Jas, wks Wm Hamilton

Turner John J, (J J Turner & Son) h 283½ George

Turner John J jr, (J J Turner & Son) h 428 Water

Turner Joseph, mach Wm Hamilton b 477 Rubidge

Turner J J & Son, (John J & John J jr) tent, sail & awning makers 283 & 283½ George

Turner Lizzie Mrs, housekeeper H Nisbett

Turner Nellie, wks Auburn Mill l 195 Auburn

Turner Reginald, tent mkr J J Turner & Son bds 283½ George

Manufacturers Life Ins. Co., Toronto, Have :

$282,882.00 - - - Assets.

$545,197.00 - - Insurance in Force

More than any other Canadian Company in the first six years of their existence.

Turner Robert, lab l 195 Auburn

Turner Wm C, clk A Micks h 197 Dublin

Turner Wm R, tinsmith A Hall h 697 Water

Turner & Cunningham, (E H Turner & J P Cunningham) Props Peterboro Music Co 404 George (see adv)

Tyrell Alf, reporter The Examiner

Ullyot Daulton, h 303 Brock

United Fire Insurance Co, W H Hill Agent 400 Water

United States Consulate E E Dodds consul 417 Water

Van Every John, student l 200 Rubidge

Van Every Wm, grocer 200 Rubidge h same

Van Every Wm W, student l 200 Rubidge

Vain Sarah E, l 130 Gilmour

Varnett E, carp Dickson Co

Varnes Harry, car inspector G T R h 293 Bethune

Varnes Louis, l 293 Bethune

Vaseur Emile, bartender Montreal House

Vass Albert, wks Carbon Works l 77 Chamberlain

Vass Alice, wks Carbon Works l 77 Chamberlain

Vass Ester, (wid Wm) h 77 Chamberlain

Vassan Daniel, blksmith P Hamilton Mnfg Co

Vedder Julian, wks Can Gen Elec Co bds 479 Water

Ventress Benjamin, h 213 London

Ventress Ida, dressmkr Robt Hall bds 213 London

Ventress M Miss, mantle & dressmkr Robt Hall bds 213 London

Vernon Margaret, (wid Charles) l 457 Water

Vickers Wm, porter Nicholls Hospital l same

Vinette Agnes, l 29 Union

Vinette Alexander, painter h 29 Union

Vinette Alice, waitress Oriental Hotel

Vinette Eadlor, wks Peterboro Woolen Mill l 10 Lisburn

Vinette Edward, carp h 10 Lisburn

Vinette Emily, l 29 Union

Vinette Francis J, cooper l 29 Union

Vinette Francis W G, clk l 359 McDonnel

Vinette Gabrial C R, millwright h 359 McDonnel

Vinette Lizzie, dom Oriental Hotel

Vinette Margaret, l 29 Union

Vinette Olive, dressmkr Miss Griffin l 359 McDonnel

Von Brocklan Nellie, dom 321 George

Vout Benjamin, lab h over 169 Simcoe

Voysie Patience, dom s s Lansdowne 7 e Lock

Waddell Alex, clk W H Hill

Wade Edward T, contractor h 487 Aylmer

Wade Eliza, (wid Thomas) h 476 Aylmer

Wade Eliza, bds 476 Aylmer

Wade George, wks Lock Wks bds 476 Aylmer

Wade Maggie, l 476 Aylmer

Wade Violet, dressmkr Robert Fair l 487 Aylmer

Wade Wm, lab Lock Works bds 476 Aylmer

Wainright James H, wks G Carton h 75 Romaine

Wainright Mark, grocer 258 London h same

Wainright Mary J, (wid Samuel) l rear 292 Park

Wainright May, l 258 London

Wainright Samuel, wks M Wainright

Wainright Miss, finisher Fairweather & Co

Waldon F A, bookkeeper Dickson Co bds Ashburnham

Walker Herbert A, bicycles 178 Simcoe h Smith tp c l

Walker Joseph, lab Dickson Co

Walker Michael, lab h 319 Bethune

Walker Milton G, clk H A Walker bds Smith tp C L

Walker Pearl, l 390 George

Walkey Wm H, principal Barnardo ave school h 10 Benson

THE BANK OF TORONTO,
PETERBORO' BRANCH, P. CAMPBELL, MANAGER.
HIGHEST RATE OF INTEREST ALLOWED ON DEPOSITS.

PETERBOROUGH CITY DIRECTORY. 135

Wall James, tanner W Paterson & Son h Ashburnham

Wall Maggie, dressmkr Wall & Connall bds Ashburnham

Wall Mary, (Misses Wall & Connall) bds Ashburnham

Wall & Connall Misses, (M Wall & K Connall) dressmakers George

Wallace Annie Mrs, 1 282 Hunter

Wallace David, carp T B Bradburn h 262 Dublin

Wallace George, bricklayer h 37 Dennistoun ave

Wallace James, wks Can Gen E Co bds 407 Wolfe

Wallace John, lab h 584 Downie

Wallace L, ticket clk G T R

Wallace Lillie, dom 570 Water

Wallace Mary, dom 364 Simcoe

Waller Robert J, (Waller & Co) h 168 Charlotte

Waller & Co grocers 168 Charlotte

Walls wks Wm Hamilton

Walsh David, grain h 521 Aylmer

Walsh David, wks Can Gen ElecCo bds 322 Charlotte

Walsh Susan, (wid Thomas) h 186 Antrim

Walsh Wm, (Ormond & Walsh) h 110 Dickson

Walstenholme J H, plasterer h 7 John

Walton Bessie Miss, 1 286 Hunter

Walton Edwin, clk 1 284 Brock

Walton Even C, 1 675 Water

Walton George, fruit etc h 146 London

Walton Jane, (wid John) h 289 Hunter

Walton Robert, h 675 Water

Ward Edward R, mldr Lock Wks h 139 Lake

Wareham Ada, wks Auburn Mill 1 788 Water

Wareham Ellen, (wid George) h 788 Water

Wareham Minnie, wks Auburn Mill 1 788 Water

Wareham Nellie, wks Auburn Mill 1 788 Water

Wareham R, car insp G T R

Warrington Samuel, lab h rear 211 Murray

Warrington Wm C, wks J B Oke & Co h 18 Queen

Warren Miss, dressmaker Miss Geary

Warren Thomas, gardener H RDavis h 35 Weller

Wason James, h 617 Rubidge

Wasson Ernest, jeweler W A Sanderson bds 369 Brock

Waterloo Mutual Fire Insurance Co, W H Hill Agent 400 Water

Watson Admadell, 1 64 Aylmer

Watson Charlotte, 1 64 Aylmer

Watson Hugh W, painter h 64 Aylmer

Watson John, ptr Can Gen Elec Co h 28 Parnell

Watson Ocean, painter h 76 Aylmer

Watson Wm T, painter H W Watson h 32 Parnell

Watt John, Confectioner 366 George h same

Watt Maggie, l 366 George

Watt Mary A, clk Post Office bds 366 George

Watt Richard P, wks J Watt bds 366 George

Watt Wm, clk A McDonald, h 132 Perry

Watt Wm S, mach Can Gen Elec Co h 224 Park

Wease Edward, clk Waller & Co bds Water

Wease Hattie, housemaid Oriental Hotel

Weatherhead Albert, lockfitter Lock Works

Weatherhead Bessie, dressmaker R Fair l 49 Boliver

Weatherhead Robert, lab h 49 Boliver

Weatherhead Wm J, teamster D Belleghem h 239 Hunter

Webb Andrew H, stonemason h 433 Sherbrooke

Webb Edward, bricklayer h 183 Brock

Webster Alfred, tailor P Simons & Co h 14 Aylmer

Webster Effie, tailoress P Simons & Co l 14 Aylmer

Webster Idean, l 14 Aylmer

Webster John, tlr P Simons & Co

Webster Wm, mach Can Gen Elec Co bds 512 Aylmer

Weddell Alexander, clk W Hill l s s Charlotte c l

Weddell Alice M, dressmaker R Fair l s s Charlotte c l

Weddell Isabella B, bookkeeper Hatton & Wood l s s Charlotte c l

Weddell John, gardner T E Bradburn h s s Charlotte c l

Weddell Maggie M, l s s Charlotte c l

Weeks Robert A, wks Auburn Mill h 785 Water

Weese Bryden, wks Can Gen Elec Co bds 324 Water

Weese Ida, dom 302 Reid

Weese James, wks Wm Hamilton h 324 Water

Weir Alfred C, tlr R Weir bds 309 McDonnel

Weir Ann, (wid Wm) l 24 Weller

Weir Annie, dressmkr R Fair l 24 Weller

Weir Jas J, mldr Lock Works h 24 Weller

Weir Maggie, l 309 McDonnell

Weir Maxwell, tlr R Weir bds 309 McDonnel

Weir Minnie, tailoress H Le Brun & Co l 24 Weller

Weir Robert, merchant tailor 158 Simcoe h 309 McDonnel

Weir Sidney B, clk l 309 McDonnel

Weller Charles A, county judge h 371 Reid

Wellington Maggie, (wid Wm) bds 196 Brock

Wells Allen, wks A Hall h 27 Chambers

Wells John S, shoemaker T Rountree h 206 Dublin

Welsh Bridget, dom Morgan House

Welsh Deborah, dressmkr R Fair l 33 Elm

Welsh Edward, teamster h 33 Elm

Welsh Elizabeth, tiress A Mercer & Co h 418 Water

Welsh Ellen, (wid Patrick) h River Rd c l

Welsh Emma, l 418 Water

Welsh Jane, (wid John) h 137 London

Welsh Jane Mrs, cook Balmoral

Welsh Josephine, l 33 Elm

Welsh Michael, clk bds Queens Hotel

Welsh Michael, wks Auburn Mill h 193 River

Wensley Caroline, (wid Wm) l 231 Stewart

Werry Nellie, wks Ensign Corset Co

Wesley Annie, dressmkr R Fair bds 367 Park

Wesley Charles, tlr Hall, Gilchrist & Co bds 367 Park

Wesley Edward, coachman B Jackson h 367 Park

Wesley Jennie, mantle mkr R Fair bds 367 Park

Wesley Walter E, clk Grafton & Co bds 367 Park

West Bessie, clk J W Butcher l 696 George

West Ellen, (wid Robert) h 696 George

West End Greenhouse, Arthur Blade Mngr 465 Park (see adv)

West Maggie, dressmkr Hall, Gilchrist & Co l 696 George

Westbrooke mach Can Gen Elec Co bds 178 Aylmer

Westcott Priscella, bds 74 McDonnel

Westcott Routley, tailor H Le Brun & Co bds 74 McDonnel

Western Assurance Co, Cox & Davis Agents 433 George

Westlake Annie, l 527 George

Westlake Bella, l 527 George

Westlake Charles, carp bds 527 George

Westlake Thomas C, (Westlake & Nesbett) bds 527 George

Westlake Wm G, carp h 527 George

Westlake & Nesbett, (T C Westlake & R H Nesbett) Livery etc 13 Chambers (see adv)

Wetherhead Albert, wks Lock Works l 834 Water

Wetherhead Bruce wks Auburn Mill l 834 Water

Wetherhead Ellen, [wid Thomas] h 834 Water

Wetherhead Richard, wks Auburn Mill l 834 Water

Whalen Mary, [wid Wm] h 221 Park

Wharton James, harnessmkr B F Ackerman bds 332 Water

Wharton John, mldr P Hamilton Mnfg Co h 261 Townsend

Whatley B, condr St Ry Co

Wheeler Annie C, dressmkr 1 229 Edinburgh

Wheeler George, butcher h 718 Water upstairs

Wheeler George jr wks AuburnMill 1 718 Water upstairs

Wheeler Mattie, dom 364 Simcoe

Wheeler Wm, wks Auburn Mill 1 718 Water up stairs

Wheeler Wm, lab h 16ᵁ Charlotte

Wherry Nellie, wks Ensign Corset Co bds 189 Charlotte

Whibbs Mary, dom 515 Water

Whitcroft trackman StRyCobLewis

Whitcroft Lizzie, Binder Times bds 31 Louis

Whitcroft Susie, dsessmaker bds 31 Louis

Whitcroft Wm, lab h 31 Louis

Whitcroft Wm A, wks B F Ackerman bds 31 Louis

White Annie, 1 42 Albert

White A V, draughtsman Can Gen E Co bds 168 Brock

White Ella, 1 42 Albert.

White Elrick H, upholsterer M Belleghem h 344 Charlotte

White Francis, h 430 Water

White Frank, teamster T H G Denne h 21 Ware

White Gordon P, clk Country Treasurar 1 273 Charlotte

White Gus, Clerk White House bds same

White Hattie, (E Melville & Co)bds 273 Charlotte

White Hattie, 1 42 Albert

White House, Robert White Prop 173 Charlotte

White Isabella, dressmaker 1 430 Water

White James, engineer A McDonald h 8 Cresent

White John, 1 White House

White John M, clk Dickson Co h 28 Manning ave

White Joseph, canoe bldr Wm English Canoe Co

White Joseph E, cabinet mkr h 218 Stewart

White Kitty, 1 White House

White Lizzie, dom 338 Rubidge

White Maggie, 1 White House

White Mrs, (wid Samuel) 1 273 Charlotte

White Robert, Propr White House 173 Charlotte

White Samuel, 1 273 Charlotte

White Thos, wks Wm Hamilton

White Wm H, mach P Hamilton Mnfg Co h 193 Dalhousie

White Wm J, clk bds 42 Albert

White Wm Rev, h 42 Albert

Whitechurch John, btchr J Mervin bds same

Whitehair James, moulder Wm Hamilton h 324 Downie

Whitlock Rose, seamstress226Brock

Whitemore Flora, dom 368 Simcoe

Whitney Hellen, dressmkr l 626 Bethune

Whitney Herbert Mrs, l 626 Bethune

Whitney John, gardner h 626 Bethune

Whittaker Wm, lab Dickson Co

Wholton George, Fruits etc 434 George h 146 London (see adv)

GEORGE WHOLTON,
Importer of

Fruit & Confectionery Oysters, Fish & Game.
434 GEORGE.

Wholton Jane, clk Geo Wholton bds Brock

Whyte James, founder h 308 Charlotte

Wild John, condr G T R bds White House

Wilkins Abram, lab h 46 Albert

Wilkins John, lab h 197 Park

Wilkinson Maria, l 25 Division

Wilkinson Mary J, (wid Charles) h 25 Division

Willard Wm, watchman GrandCentral bds same

Williams Albert, lab h 223 Rubidge

Williams Angus, h 71 Cresent

Williams Henry, mach J R Donnel h 363 King

Williams John, gardner l n w cor Lock & Lansdowne

Williams John, baker 406 Sherbrooke h same

Williams John, lab Dickson Co b 67 Chamberlain

Williams Thomas, scavinger h n w cor Lock & Lansdowne

Williams Wm, wks Carbon Works h 73 Chamberlain

Williamson Euphemia, nurse rms 258 Brock

Wills Albert, wks Can Gen ElecCo l 151 Park

Wills Bertha, wks Lock Works l 151 Park

Wills Henry, dray man h 151 Park

Wilson Alvh, carp Cox & Davis h 71 Wescott

Wilson Charles, wks Can Gen Elec Co bds 155 Stewart

Wilson Edward B, b 532 Gilchrist

Wilson James, pedlar h rear 344 Aylmer

Wilson Jane, (wid James) l 556 Aylmer

Wilson Jennie, mlnr R H Kells&Co

Wilson John, moulder Wm Hamilton h 66 Elm

Wilson Macfarlane, Propr China Hall 360 George h 182 McDonnel

Wilson Mary, cook Oriental Hotel

Wilson Mary A, (wid Wm T E) h 625 Aylmer

Wilson Roland, mach Can Gen Elec Co bds 199 Reid

Wilson Sarah, l 282 Edinburgh

Wilson Thomas J, carp h 67 Homewood ave

Wilson Wm, cooper h 282 Edinburgh

Wilson Wm, mach Can Gen Elec Co bds 213 Stewart

Winch Bros, (H C & R J) meat market 328 George

Winch Frederick T, Butcher 460 George h Smith tp

Winch Henry C, (Winch Bros) h 81 Cresent

Winch May, l 247 George

Winch Richard J, (Winch Bros) h 247 George

Windsor Alexander, lab l 929 Water

Windsor Edwin, lab l 929 Water

Windsor Peter, lab h 929 Water

Windsor Thomas J, lab l 929 Water

Winters A Mrs, laundress h 187 Simcoe

Wise Frank, florist 823 George h same

Woffle Louie, dom 324 Rubidge

Woilki Joseph, wks Dickson Co h 95 Elm

Wolstenholme James, plasterer bds 195 Charlotte

Wolstenholme John, eggbuyer h 195 Charlotte

Wolstenholme Robert J, livery 195 Charlotte bds same

Wonham H E C, ledgerkpr Bank Montreal bds Oriental Hotel

Wood Alexander, wks Gas Works h 10 College

Wood Alfred, clk J C Turnbull bds 2 Queen

Wood Alice, nurse Nicholls Hospital l same

Wood Christopher, h over 160 Simcoe

Wood Florence, dressmaker M E Frise l 588 Stewart

Wood Harry, mldr P Hamilton Mnfg Co

Wood Miss, laundress Peterboro Steam Laundry

Wood Robert E, (Hatton & Wood) h 130 Gilmour

Wood Walter, gardener A Stevenson h w s Boundry

Wood Wm, lab Dickson Co

Woodgate H S Miss, Supt Dr Barnardos Home

Woodley John, hostler Balmoral Hotel

Woods Alex, lab Gas Co

Woods Annie, (wid George) h 379 Sherbrooke

Woods Harry, mldr P Hamilton Mnfg Co bds 379 Sherbrooke

Woods Minnie, wks Peterborough Laundry bds 379 Sherbrooke

Workman Thomas, artist 435 George rms same

Worrington Thomas, lab Dickson Co

Wray Frank J, bds 283 Stewart

Wray James G, wks Canadian General Elec Co h 283 Stewart

Wright Charles, wks Dickson Co h 174 Dublin

Wright Charlotte,(wid) h 192 Sherbrooke

Wright George W, carp h 210 Harvey

Wright Gordon, h 36 Bonacord

Wright Gordon jr, mach Moffatt & Co l 36 Bonacord

Wright John, wks Dickson Co l 210 Harvey

Wright Miss, l 174 Dublin

Wright Robert, cooper J Britton

Wright Robert S, harness mkr B F Ackerman h 23 Bethune

Wright Sarah J, school tchr l 36 Bonacord

Wright Wm, mach Canadian General Elec Co bds 123 Stewart

Wrighton E V H Miss, l 106 McDonnel

Wrighton Wm H, grocer 421 George h 106 McDonnel

Wyer James, mldr Lock Works

Wylie Byron M, real estate agent h 270 Dublin

Wynne Charles, saw mill 987 Water h 629 Rubidge

Wynn Charles, contractor h 629 Rubidge

Wynn Henry, wks C Wynn l 629 Rubidge

Wynn Lillian, l 629 Rubidge

Yarnold David, upholsterer J DCraig bds 196 Brock

Yelland Albert E, Physician 147 Murray h same

Yelland Benjamin C, blksmith T Fitzgerald h 403 Sherbrooke

Yelland Frederick J, l cor McDonnel & Bethune

Yelland Joseph H, Carriage Maker 462 George h 466 same (see adv)

Yelland Wm, h cor McDonnel & Bethune

Yenney Henry A, tchr PublicSchool l 95 Weller

Yokome Ferman R, editor The Examiner h 85 Gilmour

Yokome Louise Miss, l 85 Gilmour

York Mary, l 24 College

Youel Frederick, clk bds 579 George

Young Joseph, lab h 187 Perry

Young Matthew, lab Dickson Co h 716 Water

Young Mens Christian Association, J W Bennett Pres 384 George

Young Richard, wks Can Gen Elec Co bds 193 Reid

Young Wm R Rev, pastor George St Methodist h 112 McDonnel

Yule Frederick, mngr Stroud Bros

Y W C A, M L G Barker Secy 414½ George

Zimmerman Rubert J, pastor Bethany Church h 199 Dublin

ASHBURNHAM DIRECTORY.

Abbott Wm T, gardener h n s Woodbine 4 e Concession

Adams Harry, h n w cor Stewart & Stanley ave

Adams Jane, dom n s Elizabeth 4 e Stewart

Adams Samuel, cellarman H Calcutt h n s Robinson 2 e Lake

Agnew John, carp h n s Monroe ave 6 e Concession

Agnew Maggie, wks Auburn Mill 1 n s Monroe ave 6 e Concession

Agnew Thomas, lab h w s Concession 3 n Clifton

Albion Hotel, Patrick Hogan propr s e Elizabeth 3 e Lake

Allen Joseph, 1 House Providence

Anderson Alexander, wks Dickson Co h w s Brown 2 s Douro

Anderson Bruce, bookbinder 1 e s Stewart 1 n Douro

Anderson John, carp h e s Stewart 1 n Douro

Anderson John jr, bkkpr P Hamilton Mnfg Co 1 e s Stewart 1 n Douro

Anderson Susan, wks Auburn Mill 1 e s Stewart 1 n Douro

Armour George, wks Dickson Co h Lumber Yard n w Dickson

Armstrong Albert, lab h n s Euclid ave 6 e Concession

Armstrong James, h e s Brown 1 s Douro

Armstrong John, bds e s Brown 1 s Douro

Baker Robert, dray man bds e s Brown 2 n Elizabeth

Baker Robert jr, mach Bridge Works bds e s Brown 2 n Elizabeth

Barrie Mrs, 1 House Providence

Barrie Wm, upholsterer Wm Faint Peterboro

Baxter, wks Geo Matthews Co Ld h n e cor Mark & James

Beatty E J, [wid Edward] h n s Elizabeth 4 e Stewart

Beatty Lizzie, dressmkr J C Turnbull bds Concession 1 n C P R

Beatty Martha, mlnr R Fair bds Concession 1 n C P R

Beatty Wm, section foreman G T R h w s Concession 1 n C P R

Beauvais Octave, wks Dickson Co h w s Driscoll 1 n Elizabeth

Beavis Maggie, dom Mrs H Burnham

Beer Lottie, 1 W C Beer

Beer Wm C Rev, pastor Mark St Methodist Church h e s Mark 4 e Elizabeth

Begley Joseph, wood turner bds w s Lake 2 s Elizabeth

Begley Minnie l w s Lake 2 s Elizabeth

Begley Patrick, turner J R Donell h w s Lake 2 s Elizabeth

Begley Robert, clk bds w s Lake 2 s Elizabeth

Begley Thomas, prtr Examiner bds w s Lake 2 s Elizabeth

Begley Thomas, bricklayer h s s Douro 1 e Stewart

Bennett Bella, house keeper e s Brown 1 s Douro

Bennett Hettie, tchr Public school l w s Mark 1 s James

Bennett Henry, h w s Mark 1 s James

Bennett Sarah, (wid John) h n s Monroe ave 8 e Concession

Bevis George, teamster Dickson Co h w s Concession 1 n Dickson

Bickell Samuel, cheese box mnfr n s Elizabeth bds Morgan House

Bidgood Wm, l w s Stewart 1 s Stanley ave

Brady B J Mrs, l s s Douro 1 w Concession

Brennan Richard L, miller h s e cor Lake & Robinson

Bridgewater Alexander, wks Bridge Works l s s Dickson 1 w concession

Bridgewater Harry, wks T Bridgewater l s s Dickson 1 w Concession

Bridgewater Thomas, boatbuilder h s s Dickson 1 w Concession

Brown Dorathy, l Dufferin opp Stewart

Brown Faxton, lab h Dufferin opp Stewart

Brownlee Mary, (wid David) h w s Stewart 2 s Elizabeth

Buck Oliver, h Concession 3 s Maria

Burnett Sophia, l J Z Roger

Burnham Edith, l cor Lake & John

Burnham Hetty, (wid Mark) h w s Lake opp Sophia

Burnham John, Barrister h n w cor Lake & John

Burt Bessie Miss, tchr Public School h e s Lake 5 s Elizabeth

Butcher John, musician h e s Stewart 2 s Douro

Butcher Robert, maltster H Calcutt h s s Sophia 1 e Mark

Butcher Rolland, wks brickyard bds s s Sophia 1 e Mark

Butcher Walter, malster H Calcutt

Butcher Wm, carp Wm Wand

Butler James A, teamster J W Moore & Co h e s Lake 1 s Elizabeth

Byshe Ealnor Mrs, h n s James 4 e Lake

Byshe Edith, l n s James 4 e Lake

Byshe Ernest T, mach Can GenElec Co bds n s James 4 e Lake

144   ASHBURNHAM DIRECTORY.

Byshe Percy, mach Can Gen Elec Co bds n s James 4 e Lake

Calcutt Addie, 1 H Calcutt

Calcutt Charles, capt Steamer Daisy bds H Calcutt

Calcutt Clare, steamboat captain bds H Calcutt

Calcutt Henry, Brewer, Maltster etc Lake opp Robinson h s s Robinson 4 e Lake (see adv)

H. CALCUTT,

BREWER, MALTSTER,

BOTTLER, ETC.

Proprietor Calcutt's Line Steamers, &c West side Lake, Ashburnham.

Calcutt Katie, bkkpr H Calcutt bds same

Calcutts Line Steamers, H Calcutt Propr w s Lake opp Robinson

Calcutt Maggie, 1 H Calcutt

Calcutt Susie, 1 H Calcutt

Cadigan John, wks G T R h s s James 4 e Mark

Cadigan Katie, 1 s s James 4 e Mark

Campbell Ann, (wid John) h w s Concession 2 s Sophia

Campbell Wm, lab h w s Concession 2 s Sophia

Carruthers James, gardener J J Lundy bds James

Carton Kate, clk M Carton bds n s Sophia 2 e Lake

Carton M, grocer h n s Sophia 2 e Lake

Castle Charles, lab h n s Maria 2 e Mark

Castle Reuben, lab Geo Matthews Co Ld bds n s Maria 2 e Mark

Chamber Henry, lab Geo Matthews Co Ld h n s Sophia 1 e Mark

Chartren John, wks Bridge Works h n s Euclid ave 4 e Concession

Chrow Wm, wks S Bickle h e s Driscoll 2 n Elizabeth

Clancy Cornelius, wks Lock Works bds Peter Clancy

Clancy Cornelius, blksmith E Clancy 1 e s Stewart 3 s Douro

Clancy Edward, blksmith cor Elizabeth & Brown h e s Stewart

Clancy Edward, clk Wm Collins

Clancy Johanna, 1 Wm Collins

Clancy Peter, h s s Elizabeth 7 e Lake

Clancy Simon, blksmith E Clancy bds e s Stewart

Cleary Timothy, drayman h s s Douro 1 e Brown

Clifford Elizabeth, (wid Wm) h e s Lake 2 s Elizabeth

Clifford Robert, lab h s s Euclid ave 5 e Concession

Clitheroe Thomas J, painter h w s Stewart 3 n Douro

Collins John, clk Wm Collins h e s Lake 2 s Elizabeth

Collins Wm, grocer h e s Lake l s
Robinson

Condon Annie, l e s Driscoll 8 u
Elizabeth

Condon Margaret, (wid John) h e s
Driscoll 8 n Elizabeth

Condon Michael, l e s Driscoll 8 n
Elizabeth

Conroy David, broker h e s Stewart
3 s Clifton

Conroy Edward, l e s Stewart 3 s
Clifton

Conroy John, butcner h Concession
opp Elizabeth

Cook Frederick, sign writer e sDris-
coll 7 n Elizabeth l same

Cook George, painter F Cook l e s
Driscoll 7 n Elizabeth

Cook Minnie, tlress W H Meredith
l e s Driscoll 7 n Elizabeth

Cook Wm,carp h e s Driscoll 7 n
Elizabeth

Cooney Benjamin, wks Bridge Wor-
rks h w s Brown 4 n Elizabeth

Costelle Micheal, agent H Calcutt

Coughlin Richard, agent h e s Concession 2 n Munroe ave

Courtney Edward, cabinetmaker
Elizabeth h w s Concession 1 n
Douro

Courtney Edward H, cabinetmaker
E Courtney l w s Concession 1 n
Douro

Courtney Francis H, wks Auburn
Mill l w s Concession 1 n Douro

Courtney Winnifred, mantlemaker
Hall Gilchrist & Co l w s Concession 1 n Douro

Coveney Elizabeth, l 84 Auburn

Coveney George, brickmaker l 84
Auburn

Coveney Lottie, wks Peterboro
Woolen Mill l 84 Auburn

Coveney Stephen, wks Peterboro
Mill h 84 Auburn

Craig Allen B, wks Bridge Works
l n s Elizabeth 1 w Stewart

Craig Archibald, wks Bridge Works
h n s Elizabeth l e Brown

Craig John T, carriage mkr s s Elizabeth 4 e Lake h cor Elizabeth &
Stewart

Craig John sr, con tractor h u s Elis-
zabeth 1 w Stewart

Craig Joseph B, wks P Hamilton
Mnfg Co h s e cor Stewart & Elizabeth

Craig Rowe, wks Brick Yard bds J
B Craig

Craig Thomas, wks Scott & Hogg
l J B Craig

Crane Wm, miller H A Mulhern h
rear w s Stewart 3 n Douro

Croly Annie, l 66 Auburn

Croly Louis, clk Dickson Co l 66
Auburn

Croly Thomas M D, carp h 66 Auburn

Crouter George, wks Dickson Co h
w s Concession 1 s Dickson

Crowe Charles, wks Wm Hamilton
l n s Monroe ave 5 e Concession

Crowe Charles,lab h s e cor Stewart
& Clifton

Crowe Joseph, section man G T R h n s Munroe ave 5 e Concession

Crowe Sidney, wks S Bickle 1 s e cor Stewart & Clifton

Crowe Wm H, cabinet mkr Peterboro Canoe Co h s e cor Stewart & Sophia

Crowley Wm, bottler H Calcutt

Cummings Wm C, agent h e s Stewart 1 n Elizabeth

Cummins Matthew, butcher h River Rd 1 n Douro Rd

Curry Ernest M, carp h s e cor Robinson & Stewart

Curtis Samuel, h w s Stewart 4 s Douro

Dainty George C, carter h n s Sophia 1 w Mark

Dalton Wm, lab h w s Oxford 3 s Dickson

Davis Charles, wks Dickson Co h w s Stewart 3 s Dickson

Dawson Aggie, 1 Wm Dawson

Dawson Alexander, carp h Ross n w Dufferin

Dawson Alice, photographer P H Green 1 Ross n w Dufferin

Dawson Edwin, telegraph opr G N W T Co l Ross n w Dufferin

Dawson James A, wks Bridge Works 1 Ross n w Dufferin

Dawson John S, Meat Market s s Elizabeth 4 e Bridge h Concession

Dawson Maggie., l Wm Dawson

Dawson Wm, vet surgeon h Concession 4 s Maria

Deacon Emma, dressmkr l n s Douro 2 e Stewart

Deacon Lousia, dressmkr l n s Douro 2 e Stewart

Deacon Wm, h n s Douro 2 e Stewart

Dennie David, lab h w s Concession 1 s Sophia

Dillon Dorothea, dressmkr Miss Mercier l s s Sophia 1 w Mark

Dillon Ellen, dressmkr bds s s Sophia 1 w Mark

Dinne Mrs, 1 House Providence

Distin Thomas, mach P Hamilton Mnfg Co h cor Monroe & Cresent ave

Dixon John, foreman A Hall h e s Lake 2 s Robinson

Dobbin Charles, wks S Bickle 1 rr Oxford s Dickson

Dobbin Frederick, prtr Review l rr Oxford s Dickson

Dobbin Leonard, carp h rr Oxford s Dickson

Dobbin Louis, plumber A Hall l rr Oxford s Dickson

Dobson Mary A, (wid Henry) l w s Oxford 4 s Dickson

Doherty Julia Miss, h e s Mark 3 s Robinson

Donovan Bany, wks Dickson Co l n s Monroe ave 3 e Concession

Donovan James, wks Dickson Co l n s Monroe ave 3 e Concession

Doran Mary, (wid Daniel) h s e cor Driscoll & Douro

Dormer George, wks Bridge Works 1 w s Brown 4 s Douro

Dormer Isaac, lab h n s Douro opp Driscoll

Dormer John, wks Bridge Works h w s Brown 4 s Douro

Dormer Laura, wks Auburn Mill 1 w s Brown 4 s Douro

Dormer Loru, wks BFAckerman 1 n s Douro opp Driscoll

Dormer Maud, wks Auburn Mill 1 n s Douro opp Driscoll

Dormer Robert, 1 n s Douro opp Driscoll

Doupe Bruce, painter bds J Doupe

Doupe Jacob, gardener h s w cor Robinson & Mark

Dover Frederick, clk h cor Elizabeth & Concession

Dover Violet Miss, 1 cor Elizabeth & Concession

Downer AB, h Concession 2 s Maria

Downer Lewis, h Concession s e

Downer Wm, lab h Concession 2 s Maria

Doxsee Jessie H, grocer cor Concession & Carlisle ave h same

Drain James, bkkpr H Calcutt h w s Lake 4 s Elizabeth

Drummond John, wks Bridge Works h n s Douro 1 e Stewart

Dufrain Edward, miller h w s Lake 3 s Robinson

Eano Lue, butcher J Dawson bds w s Concession 1 n Clifton

Eden Benjamin M, h n s Elizabeth 4 e Stewart

Edwards Mathew, wks D Knox h e s Stewart 2 s Sophia

Ellison George, h s s Elizabeth 2 e Bridge

Ellison George A, insurance bds Geo Ellison

Ellison Hattie, comp Review 1 Geo Ellison

Ellison Lena, 1 Geo Ellison

Ellison Martha, 1 Geo Ellison

Ellison Maud E stenogr Edwards & Murray 1 Geo Ellison

Ellsworth Eliza, (wid Orin H) h s e cor Lake & Elizabeth

Emery Mary J, (wid George) h s s James 2 e Mark

Emery Wm, gardener F Mason bds s s James 2 e Mark

Emmerson George, grocer n s Elizabeth h same

Emmerson Hannah, clk Foot & McWhinnie 1 e s Stewart 1 s Clifton

Emmerson Thomas, lab h e s Stewart 1 s Clifton

Eno Annie, 1 F Eno

Eno Frances, Stewart Miss Mills h w s Concession 2 s Maria

Eno John, farmer bds F Eno

Erskin Annie, (wid John) h cor Concession & Carlisle

Erskin Robert, clk Mulholland & Roper bds cor Concession & Carlisle

Eynon Thomas, cooper h n s Carlisle 4 e Concession

Faint Effie, bkkpr Wm Faint bds same

148   ASHBURNHAM DIRECTORY.

Faint Harry, 1 Wm Faint

Faint Wm, woolen mill etc s s Elizabeth 1 e Bridge h same

Farley James, lab h w s Lake 1 s Elizabeth

Fausett Andrew, h w s Stewart s C P R

Ferguson Aggie, dressmkr bds e s Stewart 4 s Douro

Ferguson Ferrington, wks Electric Light Co h w s Brown 5 s Douro

Ferguson Wellington, h s e cor Lake & Sophia

Finlason Catherine, l s s Elizabeth 2 e Stewart

Firman Samuel, lab h e s Driscoll 13 n Elizabeth

Fischer Amelia, wks Auburn Mill 1 107 Auburn

Fischer Mrs, (wid Frederick) h 107 Auburn

Fischer Sophia, wks Auburn Mill 1 107 Auburn

Fitch Harold, lab h s s Carlisle ave 1 e Concession

Fitzgerald Alexander, (Glover & Fitzgerald) h s s Elizabeth 8 e Lake

Fitzgerald John, cigarmkr A Murty 1 n s Douro 3 e Stewart

Fitzgerald Michael, lab h n s Douro 3 e Stewart

Fitzgerald Walter, lab bds n s Euclid ave 7 e Concession

Fleming David, wks Auburn Mill 1 76 Auburn

Fleming Wm, milk man h River rd c 1

Foster Maria, (wid Wm) h w Mark 1 s Robinson

Fowler James, wks S Bickell 1 e s Concession 2 n Euclid ave

Fowler James W, carp h e s Concession 2 n Euclid ave

Fox Maggie, dom Geo Stevens

Frith Wm H, wks Auburn Mill 1 w s Stewart 1 s Dickson

Gainey John, lab h e s Driscoll 3 n Elizabeth

Gainey Maurice, cigar mkr A Murty 1 e s Driscoll 3 n Elizabeth

Galdey Thomas H, painter h s s Smith 1 e River

Geary Margaret, l House Providence

Gibbs Wm, blksmith R Mein h s 1 cor Mark & Robinson

Gillespie James B, wks P Hamilton MnfgCo h n s Elizabeth 2 e Brown

Gillespie Joseph, millwright h s s Carlisle ave 3

Gilman John, lab h e s Brown 3 s Douro

Gilman Robert, wks Dickson Co l e s Brown 3 s Douro

Glover James, btchr Glover & Fitzgerald bds Peter Glover

Glover Jessie, l Peter Glover

Glover Peter, (Glover & Fitzgerald) h Mark

Glover Rolland, wks J R Stratton bds Peter Glover

Left margin (vertical): PLUMBING, STEAM AND GAS FITTING, ADAM HALL, 407 GEORGE STREET

Right margin (vertical): Central Canada Loan and Savings Co

Goodenough Robert, nightwatch

Geo Matthews Co Ld h s s James e 3 Mark

Gooley Annie, dom H C Roger

Gorham Patrick, section man C P R h s s Maria 1 e Lake

Gormally Mrs, 1 House Providence

Graham Christina, 1 Alex Fitzgerald

Graham Elizabeth, tlress A Mercer & Co 1 Alex Fitzgerald

Graham Joseph, lab Dickson Co b w s Lake 3 s Elizabeth

Graham Robert W, lab h n s James 2 e Mark

Gusler L E Mrs, housekeeper s e cor Elizabeth & Stewart

Guy Walter, engr H Calcutt b w s Lake 3 s Elizabeth

Guy Wm, lab H Calcutt h w s Lake 2 s Robinson

Hamilton Albert, wks Mrs M Burnham 1 same

Hamilton Frances, Boots & Shoes s s Elizabeth 4 w Mark h Elizabeth (see adv)

Hamilton Frank jr, mach Bridge Wks h s s Robinson 1 w Mark

Hamilton Frederick W, wks W H Meldrum 1 w s Concession 5 n Clifton

Hamilton Robert, broom mnfr s s Elizabeth 1 e G T R Track h cor Elizabeth & Concession

Hamilton Sarah, school teacher 1 n s Elizabeth 2 e Stewart

Hamilton Wm, wks Bridge Works bds s w cor Stewart & Stanley ave

Hamilton Wm, lab h w s Concession 5 n Clifton

Hamson Wm, wks Dickson Co 1 e s Brown 5 s Douro

Hart John, h e s Stewart 4 s Douro

Hartley David, painter h w s Oxford 2 s Dickson

Hartley Wm, lab h s s Woodbine 1 e Concession

Haws George, brewer H Calcutt bds e s Driscoll 13 n Elizbeth

Hawthorn John, carp h e s Stewart 2 s C P R

Hawthorn Letitia, (wid James) h e s Stewart 1 s C P R

Hawthorn Wm, lab h e s Stewart 1 s C P R

Hayes Thomas, 1 House Providence

Heal John, lab Dickson Co h w s Oxford 1 s Dickson

Hedley Charles W Rev, h n s Douro opp Brown

Heffernan Johanna, dom Wm Scott

Henderson Robert, lab W H Meldrum h n s Clifton 1 w Concession

Hilton Mary, 1 cor Dunlop & River Rd

Hinds Albert W, driver James Donnel h w s Stewart 4 s Dickson

Hogan Patrick, prop Albion Hotel s s Elizabeth 3 e Lake

Hopkins Burt, printer Examiner 1 w s Stewart 2 n Douro

Hopkins Daniel, insurance agent h w s Stewart 2 n Douro

Hoskin Wm, h north end Concession

Hourigan Elizabeth, 1 n s Dufferin 1 w Concession

Hourigan Hanora, (wid Michael) 1 n s Dufferin 1 w Concession

Hourigan James, wks Bridge Works h n s Dufferin 1 w Concession

House of Providence, Mother Vincent superior Stewart s Elizabeth

Huard Stephen, lab Dickson Co h s s Elizabeth 5 e Bridge

Hunter Wm, h s s Carlisle ave 2 e Concession

Huston Martha J, wks Auburn Mill 1 75 1 70 Auburn

Huston Mary J, (wid John) h 70 Auburn

Ingram Absolam, h w s Lake opp Sophia

Jenkins John, bkkpr H Calcutt

Johnston Joseph, plasterer h w s Stewart 2 s Dickson

Johnston Wm J, carp h n s Dufferin 1 w Stewart

Joy Theodore, carp h e s Mark 3 s Elizabeth

Kane Eliza, 1 cor Concession & Maria

Kane Patrick, h cor Maria & Concession

Keating Jane Mrs, h s s Sophia 1 w Mark

Kelly Bernard, lab h s s Maria 1 e Mark

Kelly Bridget, (wid John) h s end Stewart

Kelly John, h Maria 1 e Stewart

Kelly Mary, 1 Maria 1 e Stewart

Kelly Thomas, carp h n s Euclid ave 8 e Concession

Kelly Wm, lab 1 s e Stewart

Kenneally John, 1 House Providence

Kennedy John, 1 House Providence

Kent Wm, wks Dickson Co h e s Concession 1 n Munroe ave

Kerr Annie, 1 n s James 3 e Lake

Kerr Wm, b n s James 3 e Lake

Kinneally Wm, agent H Calcutt Peterborough

Kirk Wm C, trav b s s Elizabeth 6 e Lake

Knapp Marshall, agent h n s Stanley ave 2 w Stewart

Knapp Wm, bookbinder Examiner 1 n s Stanley ave 2 w Stewart

Kylie John, shoemaker n s Elizabeth h same

Laganasse Jerome, engr Steamer Daisey Peterboro

Lapham Wm, carp h s s Woodbine 3 e Concession

Law David, painter h s s Robinson 1 e Lake

Leahy Patrick, lab h n s Munroe ave 2 e Concession

Lehane Michael H, insurance b n s Sophia 1 e Lake

Lemoir Nelson, lab h w s Brown 3 s Douro

Leonard Patrick, l House Providence

Lewarne George, photographer G B Sproule 1 n s Woodbine 5 e Concession

Lewarne John, carp h n s Woodbine 5 e Concession

Lipsett Arthur, wks Dickson Co bds Maple Leaf Hotel

Lipsett George, clk Maple Leaf Hotel bds same

Lipsett George, propr Maple Leaf Hotel n s Elizabeth

Lipsett Prudence, 1 Maple Leaf Hotel

Long Alexander, wks brickyard bds s s Sophia 2 e Mark

Long Fannie J, (wid Samuel) h s s Sophia 2 e Mark

Long George, lumberman h s s Sophia 3 e Mark

Long John B, wks Auburn Mill 1 e s Stewart 1 n Dickson

Long Lizzie, wks Wm Faint bds s s Sophia 2 e Mark

Lowrey Charles M, butcher h e s Stewart 2 n Clifton

Ludgate Theodore, crown land agent h Norwood Rd 1 e Concession

Lundy Bella, 1 cor Lake & James

Lundy J J, h cor Lake & James

Lundy Maggie, 1 cor Lake & James

Lundy Margaret, (wid Wm) 1 cor Lake & James

Lyle James, lumberman bds Maple Leaf Hotel

Lynch Joseph, lab bds n e cor Mark & Robinson

Lynch Margaret A. (wid James) h e s Brown 3 n Elizabeth

Lynch Mary, dressmaker 1 n e cor Mark & Robinson

Lynch Michael, teamster Dickson Co h n e cor Mark & Robinson

McAlpin Ellen, dom Ross n w Dufferin

McAuliffe Catherine, (wid Cornelius) h w s Stewart 2 s Douro

McCabe Annie, l e s Lake 3 s Elizabeth
McCabe Daniel O, prtr The Times bds e s Lake 3 s Elizabeth
McCabe Ernest, prtr The Times h w s Driscoll 2 n Elizabeth
McCabe James, millwright h e s Lake 3 s Elizabeth
McCabe James T, restaurant bds e s Lake 3 s Elizabeth
McCabe John J, wks Wm Wand bds e s Lake 3 s Elizabeth
McCabe Margaret, l House Providence
McCabe Margaret, music teacher bds e s Lake 3 s Elizabeth
McCarthy Allen, house mover h e s Concession 1 n Norwood Rd
McCarty Ann, l House Providence
McCarthy Wm J, miller W H Meldrum l e s Concession 1 n Norwood Rd
McDonald Ellen, l House Providence
McDonald James, buyer Scott & Hogg bds s s Elizabeth 1 e Mark
McDonald Mary, l House Providence
McElroy Samuel, signalman G T R h n s James 3 e Mark
McGrath David, brickmaker h s e cor Dickson & Oxford
McGregor Annie, wks Auburn Mill l s s Douro 1 w Stewart
McGregor David, cooper h s s Douro 1 w Stewart
McGregor Wm, carp l s s Douro 1 w Stewart

McGuire Mrs, l House of Providence
McKewen Maggie Miss, h w s Stewart 1 s James
McKnight, wks Auburn Mill l e s Concession 1 s Woodbine
McKnight Samuel, lab h e s Concession 1 s Woodbine
McMahon Frank, driver J C Sullivan bds c l
McMahon Josephine, dom Albion Hotel
McNair Henrietta (wid Samuel) l D Law
McWha Hugh, wks Dickson Co h s w cor Stewart & James
McWha Maggie, dressmkr bds s w cor Stewart & James
McWilliams John A, carp h e s Stewart 3 s Sophia
McWilliams John W, carp G T R bds e s Stewart 3 s Sophia
McWilliams Thomas G, prtr Examiner bds e s Stewart 3 s Sophia
Mackindo Hugh, grocer h s s Euclid ave 3 e Concession
Malan John, h n s Robinson 4 e Lake
Malan Lizzie, dressmaker l n s Robinson 4 e Lake
Malan Maggie, l n s Robinson 4 e Lake
Manice Bella, l n w cor Mark & James
Manice Jane, (wid Wm) l n w cor Mark & James
Manice John, wks H Calcutt bds n w cor Mark & James
Manice Robert, wks Dickson Co h n s James 1 w Mark

ESTABLISHED 1855. **THE BANK OF TORONTO.** Capital $2,000,000
P. CAMPBELL, MANAGER, PETERBORO' BRANCH.
A GENERAL BANKING BUSINESS TRANSACTED

ASHBURNHAM DIRECTORY. 153

Manice Thomas, wks Dickson Co h n w cor Mark & James

Manice Wm, wks Dickson Co h n w cor Mark & James

Maple Leaf Hotel, George Lipsett prop n s Elizabeth

Marshall John, tmstr Scott & Hogg bds n s James 2 e Lake

Marshall John H, h w s Brown 2 n Elizabeth

Marshall Maud, l Lumber Yard n w Dickson

Marshall Thomas, egg packer h n s James 2 e Lake

Martin John, wks Dickson Co l Lumber Yard n w Dickson

Masters John, engr D Belleghem bds C Wall

Mather Andrew J, lab P Hamilton MnfgCo h s e cor Brown & Douro

Mather John, h w s Stewart 1 n Douro

Matthews Benjamin, farmer h Concession 1 n C P R

Maxwell Wm, lab h e s Concession 1 n Woodbine

May James, lab h w s Concession 1 s C P R

Meade Sophia, (wid Richard) h 62 Dunlop

Meader Samuel, carp h e s Crescent ave c l

Mein John, carp The Canadian Canoe bds s e cor Brown & Douro

Mercier Albert, wks Point St Charles Ice Co bds N Mercier

Mercier Alfred, signalman G T R h n s James 1 w Stewart

Mercier Azedeline, dressmkr R H Kells & Co l N Mercier

Mercier Lydia, l N Mercier

Mercier Narcise, h n e cor Lake & Sophia

Meyett Enos, baker l e s Driscoll 6 n Elizabeth

Meyett Minnie, dressmkr l e s Driscoll 6 n Elizabeth

Milliken Albert E, wks Dickson Co bds s s Ezizabeth 6 e Bridge

Milliken Henry M, wks Dickson Co bds s s Elizabeth 6 e Bridge

Milliken Mary, (wid Joseph) h s s Elizabeth 6 e Bridge

Mills Annie Miss, h e s Concession 1 s Elizabeth

Mitchell George A, lab h e s Brown 1 n Elizabeth

Mitchell Ida, l C T Spilsbury

Mitchell Mary E, (wid Wm H) h s s Elizabeth 2 e G T R

Mitchell Thomas, tmstr h n s James 1 e Mark

Mitchell Wm E, agent bds s s Elizabeth 2 e G T R

Moncrief George, lab h w s Concession 1 s Maria

Moore Charles H, grocer h w s Stewart 1 n Elizabeth

Morgan Ann, (wid Peter) l s w cor Lake & John

Morgan Henry, mach Peterboro Canoe Co, bds e s Mark 5 s Elizabeth

Morgan Margaret, (wid Richard) h e s Mark 5 s Elizabeth

Morrison Richard, lab h w s Driscoll 3 n Elizabeth

Mowry Edgar, clk l w s Brown 1 n Elizabeth

Mowry John H, h e s Lake 2 s Sophia

Mowry Lillie, stamp clk P O l w s Brown 1 n Elizabeth

Mowry Maud, clk W Sailsbury l w s Brown 1 n Elizabeth

Mowry Richard, mach n s Elizabeth h w s Brown

Mulligan Charles, mach bds Maple Leaf Hotel

Munro James, carp h s w cor Stewart & Dickson

Murray Katie, l e s Lake 2 s Elizabeth

Neil Harry, mngr H Calcutt h w s Lake 1 s Robinson

Neild John, carp h e s Lake 4 s Elizabeth

Neild, (wid Wm), l John Neild

Neild Mary, dressmkr R Fair bds e s Lake 4 s Elizabeth

Neild Wm, carp G McWilliams h n s Robinson 3 e Lake

Nesbett Mary, dom J J Lundy

Newall Emma, dom cor Lake & John

Norris Emma M, (wid Lt Col Wm H) l H Spears

Northey Azor, wks Bridge Works h e s Brown 2 n Elizabeth

Noyes Charles, foreman G T R h G T R Track s Maria

Noyes Lizzie, l C Noyes

Noyes Wm, mach bds C Noyes

O'Brien Alexander, lab Dickson Co h n s Monroe ave 3 e Concession

O'Brien Alexander, teamster h e s Driscoll 10 n Elizabeth

O'Brien Daniel, hostler Albion Hotel

O'Brien Edward, lab h e s Stewart 2 n Douro

O'Brien Elizabeth, l w s Concession 2 n Dickson

O'Brien Michael, lab h w s Concession 2 n Dickson

O'Brien Patrick, lab l w s Concession 2 n Dickson

O'Brien Wm, teamster Dickson Co h w s Stewart 1 s Douro

O'Connel Annie, clk l w s Concession 1 n Elizabeth

O'Connel Beatrice, dressmaker O Connel & Wall l w s Concession 1 n Elizabeth

O'Connel Catherine, (wid James) h w s Concession 2 n Clifton

O'Connel David, tailor H LeBrun & Co h w s Concession 1 n Elizabeth

O'Connel Ellen, dressmaker l w s Concession 2 n Clifton

O'Connel John, wks S Bickell

O'Connel Katie, O'Connel & Wall l w s Concession 1 n Elizabeth

O'Connel Lizzie, school teacher l w s Concession 2 n Clifton

O'Connel Margaret, clk J T Stenson bds n s Concession 1 n Stewart

ASHBURNHAM DIRECTORY.   155

O'Connel Mary, (wid Timothy) l w s Concession 1 n Stewart

O'Connel Mary A, school teacher l w s Concession 2 n Clifton

O'Donnell Julia, (wid Patrick) l Lumber Yard n w Dickson

O'Donnell Patrick, lab Dickson Co h Lumber Yard n w Dickson

O'Hanlan Henry,l House Providence

O'Hare Thomas,l House Providence

O'Malley Hannah, l House Providence

O'Toole Wm, caretaker St Josephs Hospital h w s Concession 2 s Elizabeth

Orde Emily, (wid Bertram) h s s Robinson 3 e Lake

Orde Julia, l Mrs E Orde

Osterhout GeorgeB,miller W H Meldrum h n sStanley ave l wStewart

Packenham Walter, millwright h n Douro 1 w Concession

Patterson Alexander A, butcher bds n e cor Lake & Robinson

Patterson WalterJ,mach h n s Elizabeth 3 e Stewart

Patterson Wm, wks Wm W and h w s Stewart 1 Stanly ave

Payne Levi, lab h n s Euclid ave 7 e Concession

Payne Sarah, l Wm Payne

Payne Sarah, mach Wm Faint

Payne Wm,h n e cor Sophia &Lake

Pearce Wm, l n s Woodbine 4 e Concession

Peck A H, h w s Mark 1 s Maria

Peck Edward A, Barrister h s e cor Maria & Mark

Peck Emma, l w s Mark 1 s Maria

Mnfrs. Life Ins. Co., Toronto
"I received your cheque for $10,000 within three hours after I filed claim papers". KATHERINE RIDOUT.

Peck Henrietta,l w s Mark 1 sMaria

Peterboro Navigation Co, H Calcutt Pres & Genl Mngr, R S DavidsonSecy-Treas w s Lake opp Robinson

Peters Absalom, marble cutter T W Moore h é s Mark 4 s Robinson

Peters Angelina, dom s s Elizabeth 2 e G T R

Peters Annie,tchr Public School bds w s Stewart 1 s Elizabeth

Peters George librarian Mechanics Institute h w s Stewart 1 s Elizabeth

Pevoy Benjamin, tmstr h n s Woodbine 6 e Concession

Pevoy Wm broommkr R Hamilton l n s Woodbine 6 e Concession

Phalen Margaret, (wid Peter) h 76 Auburn

Phillips Euphemia, l Jos Phillips

Phillips Harry, bricklayer bds Jos Phillips

Phillips Joseph, bricklayer h e s Mark 1 s Robinson

Phillips Kate, l Jos Phil'ips

Pogue John,lab h s s Euclid ave 6 e Concession

Pollock John, carp l n s Dufferin 1 e Stewart

Pollock Maggie, l n s Dufferin 1 e Stewart

Pollock Robert, plasterer h n s Dufferin 1 e Stewart

Pool Thomas, lab h w s Concession 4 n Clifton

Portway Wm, lab bds s s Euclid ave 2 e Concession

Power James, blksmith h e s Driscoll 6 n Elizabeth

Primeau John, barber h e s Driscoll 9 n Elizabeth

Primeau Joseph H, barber h e s Driscoll 5 n Elizabeth

Pritcherd Margaret, l House of Providence

Quartermaine Thomas, clk h e s Driscoll 1 n Elizabeth

Quinlan Elizabeth, l n s James 3 e Mark

Quinlan Thomas, wks Dickson Co h e s Stewart 2 s Clifton

Quirk Letitia, l Harry Neil

Rackham Maud, l W H Rackham

Rackham Wm H, surveyor h s s Robinson 3 e Lake

Ranton Ellen, (wid James) h s s Euclid ave 2 e Concession

Ranton George, wks Auburn Mill l s s Euclid ave 2 e Concession

Record George, tailor T Dolan & Co l w s Stewart 3 n Elizabeth

Record Richard A, finisher D Belleghem h s s Stewart 3 n Elizabeth

Record Robert, lab h w s Stewart 3 n Elizabeth

Reid Alexander, farmer h w s Concession 1 n Dufferin

Reid Francis, h cor Dunlop & River Rd

Reid Louisa, l cor Dunlop & River Rd

Revoy Wm, broom mkr R Hamilton bds Woodbine ave

Rey Thomas, l House Providence

Richardson John, lab h e s Driscoll 12 n Elizabeth

Ritchie Robert G, carp h n s Dufferin 2 w Stewart

Robertson Lizzie, dom H C Rogers

Rogers David, clk Postoffice bds n e cor Lake & James

Rogers Ethel, l cor Lake & James

Rogers H C, Postmaster h n e cor Lake & James

Rogers J Z, mngr Peterboro Canoe Co h s s Elizabeth 2 e G T R

Rogers Richard B, supt Trent Valley Canal h Douro opp Brown

Rumming David, lab h Munroe ave 1 e Concession

Rumming David jr, wks Peterboro Canoe Co l Munroe ave 1 e Concession

Rumming Henretta, dressmaker l Munroe ave 1 e Concession

Russell Andrew, clk h s w cor Stewart & Stanley ave

Russell Arthur, apiarist l s s Robinson 2 e Lake

Russell John H, dray man h w s Stewart 2 n Elizabeth

St Josephs Hospital, Mother Vincent Superior Stewart s Elizabeth

Sanderson Wm, carp, h e s Lake 5 s Elizabeth

THE BANK OF TORONTO,
PETERBORO' BRANCH, P. CAMPBELL, MANAGER.
BUYS AND SELLS CANADIAN AND FOREIGN EXCHANGE.

Schaffer George L, wks Bell Tel Co h n s Sophia 3 e Lake

Scott Francis, wks G T R bds n s Euclid ave 5 e Concession

Scott George, wks Can Gen ElecCo l n s Monroe ave 4 e Concession

Scott John wks s Bickell

Scott John, wks Geo Matthews Co Ld h n s Maria 1 e Mark

Scott Thomas, wks Waterworks h n s Monroe ave 4 e Concession

Scott Wm, agent H Calcutt

Scott Wm, (Scott & Hogg) h Elizabeth

Scott & Hogg, (Wm Scott & Frank Hogg) Egg Packers G T R Track & Robinson St

Shearer Albert, carp l n s Carlisle ave 1 e Concession

Shearer James K, carp h n s Carlisle ave 1 e Concession

Shearer Richard, carp l n s Carlisle ave 1 e Concession

Shearer Robert, lab l n s Carlisle ave 1 e Concession

Sheehan Ellen, (wid Michael) h s s Douro 1 w Concession

Shelan Johanna, (wid John) h n s James 3 e Mark

Shehan Johanna, l n e cor Mark & Robinson

Shehan Thomas, lab h n s James 3 e Mark

Sheridan Martha, h n s Carlisle 2 e Concession

Sheridan Robert, forman Dickson Co h w s Brown 3 n Elizabeth

Sheridan Sarah, (wid John) l w s Brown 2 n Elizabeth

Smiley Thomas, mach h n e cor Elizabeth & Brown

Smith Ester, (wid John) h e s Stewart 4 n Elizabeth

Smith John H, mach Wm Hamilton h e s Stewart 4 n Elizabeth

Smith Martha, (wid Richard) l M Edwards

Smith Mrs, l House Providence

Smith Wm A, ptr h s s Sophia 1 e Lake

Smith Wm H, carp h n s Concession 2 n Norwood Rd

Spears Hugh, physician etc cor Elizabeth & Mark h s s Elizabeth 9 e Lake

Spears Norman, clk H Spears bds same

Spence Stanley, wks W H Meldrum l n s Dufferin 2 w Stewart

Spence Wm, wks St Car Co l n s Dufferin 2 w Stewart

Spilsbury Charles T, h s w cor Elizabeth & Stewart

Spilsbury Mattie, l C T Spilsbury

Stephenson Bridget, dom cor Lake & John

Stephenson Catherine, tlress H Le Brun&Co bds w s Lake 4 s Robinson

Stephenson John, boat maker rms e s Lake 1 s Elizabeth

Stephenson Jonathan, l e s Lake 1 s Elizabeth

Stevens George, ashery h e s Mark 2 s Elizabeth

Stewart James, h s s Elizabeth 2 e Stewart

Strain George, lab Dickson Co bds Albion Hotel

Strickland Henry T, h s w cor Lake & John

Strickland Minnie, l s w cor Lake & John

Styles Maria A, b e s Cresent Ave c l

Sullivan John C, grocer s s Elizabeth 5 e Lake h Robinson

Sullivan Kate, l J C Sullivan

Swanston Annie, (wid Wm) l cor Elizabeth & Driscoll

Swanston James, wks Dickson Co h w s Brown 1 s Douro

Swanston Wm, baker cor Elizabeth & Driscoll h same

Symonds HerbertRev, rectorStLukes h e s Stewart s Robinson

Taylor John, carp h w s Oxford 4 s Dickson

Taylor Samuel, wks Lock Works l w s Oxford 4 s Dickson

Telford James, lab h s e cor Concession & Euclid ave

Tetterson John, clk Hall, Gilchrist & Co h w s Concession 1 s Elizabeth

Thompson Wm, h s s Dickson near R R Track

Thompson Wm H, wks Auburn Mill l s s Dickson nr R R Track

Tighe Hugh S, harnessmkr B FAckerman bds e s Stewart l s Sophia

Tighe James, fireman Peterboro CanoeCo h e s Stewart l s Sophia

Tighe James jr, carp bds e s Stewart 1 s Sophia

TigheLizzie, dressmaker l e s Stewart 1 s Sophia

Tivey Albert, wks Bridge Wks l s s Stanley ave l w Stewart

Tivey Roland, h s s Stanley ave l w Stewart

Tobin Annie, dressmaker Miss Mercier l n s Maria 1 e Lake

Tobin James, harnessmaker H Dundas bds w s Lake 4 s Elizabeth

Tobin James, engineer Steamer Daisy bds n s Maria 1 e Lake

Tobin Johanna, (wid John) h n s Maria 1 e Lake

Tobin Sarah, dom cor Elizabeth & Concession

Tobin Sarah, l n s Maria 1 e Lake

Torpey Nellie, cook Rev H Symonds

Torpey Wm, school teacher bds Albion Hotel

Valois Charles, lab h n s Woodbine 2 e Concession

Valois Joseph, lab h n s Woodbine 3 e Concession

Waddell Adam P, wks Wm English Canoe Co, h s s Elizabeth 3 e Stewart

Wall Cornelius, lab Wm Hamilton h s e cor Mark & Elizabeth

Wall James, engineer Paterson & Son bds s s Elizabeth 1 e Stewart

Wall Margaret, dressmkr Connel &
Wall bds s s Elizabeth 1 e Stewart

Wall Margaret, (wid Edward) h s s
Elizabeth 1 e Stewart

Wall Mary, dressmaker bds s s Elizabeth 1 e Stewart

Wand Edmund, wks Wm Wand
bds same

Wand Wm, planing mill, n s Elizabeth h e s Lake

Ward George G, captain cor Dickson
& Oxford

Ward Hannah, (wid Robert) l e s
Stewart 2 n Clifton

Weir John R, grocer h e s Lake 1 s
Sophia

Weir Robert J, grocer s s Elizabeth
1 w Mark h Lake

Weir Simon, carp l n e cor Concession & Euclid ave

Westcott Amelia, (wid Wm) h w s
Lake 4 s Robinson

Whatley Arthur, wks S Bickell bds
n s Robinson 1 e Mark

Whatley Robert, lab h n s Robinson
1 e Mark

Whatley Robert, wks S Bickell bds
n e Robinson 1 e Mark

Whatley Wm B, condr St Ry bds n
s Robinson 1 e Mark

White Thomas R, lab h s s James 1
e Mark

Whiteman Joseph, lab h n e cor
Woodbine & Concession

Whitney Grace, (wid Augustus H)
l n s Douro opp Brown

Whittiker Wm, h n s Stanley ave 3
w Stewart

Wigster Jacob, mason h w s Stewart 3 s Douro

Williams Nicholas, wks G T R h n
s Euclid ave 5 e Concession

Wilson Isabella, l e s Stewart 4 s
Douro

Wilson John A, carp h s s Euclid
ave 1 e Concession

Wilson Maggie, nurse Rev H Symonds

Wilson Wm, cooper H Calcutt

Wilson Wm, mach Wm Faint

Wilson Wm, h s s James 5 e Mark

Woodruff Albert J, blksmith h e s
Brown 4 s Douro

Woods John, cook City Peterboro
h s s Elizabeth 1 e Lake

Woods John, town clerk h e s Mark
6 s Elizabeth

Woods Wm, lab h e s Mark 2 s
Elizabeth

Wright Eliza, l e s Stewart 2 n
Elizabeth

Wright Emma, dressmkr l n s Robinson 5 e Lake

Wright George, h n s Robinson 5 e
Lake

Wright John T, h n e cor Elizabeth
& Stewart

Wright Stuart, carp h e s Stewart 2
n Elizabeth

Wyatt Joseph, tlr h e s Driscoll 11
n Elizabeth

Classified Business Directory.

ACCOUNTANTS

Blanchard Alexander, 368 Water (see adv)

AGRIL IMPLTS

MNFRS

Hamilton Peter Mnfg Co, s w cor George & King

AGENTS & DEALERS

Cochrane Thomas, 388 Water

ARCHITECTS

Bartlett Frederick, 140 Murray
Belcher John E, 435 George
Belcher Samuel, 435 George
Blackwell Wm, 374 Water

ARTISTS

Aselstine Samuel G, 348 Water
Hudson Buttle, 134 Brock
Shaw Donald A, 170 Charlotte
Workman Thomas, 435 George

ARTISTS' MATERIALS

Aseltine Samuel G, 348 Water

BAKERS & CONFECTIONERS

Bacon Wm, 485 Park
Barrette Solomon, 28 Park
Bates Walter, 654 Stewart
Craig John C, 426 George
Craig Wm J, 663 George
Cunningham Joesph F, rear 210 Charlotte
Forsythe, rear 641 George
Forsyth & Sons, 641 George
Girard Alphonse, 84 Lake
Hooper Thomas H, 327 George
Lush Nemiah, 599 Aylmer
Lush Thomas, 184 Dublin
McGlynn John, 381 Bethune
Pollard Joseph, 238 Hunter
Schneider George, 521 George
Stock Wm, 283 Sherbrooke
Swarstion Wm, cor Elizabeth & Driscoll Ashburnham
Watt John, 366 George
Williams John, 406 Sherbrooke

BANKS

Bank of Montreal, 360 Water
Bank of Toronto, s e cor George
& Hunter (see adv)
Canadian Bank of Commerce
s w cor George & Brock
Ontario Bank, cor Water & Simcoe

BANKERS

Mulholland & Roper, 142 Hunter

BARBERS

Brousseau P M, 165 Hunter
Cunningham Thomas, 326 Arcade
Guerin & Briou, 349 George
Hall David, 163 Simcoe
Haskill Allen, 164 Simcoe
Lannon Joseph, C P R Hotel
Le Gros Charles, 329 George
(see adv)
Mitchell Joseph, 131 Hunter
Morgan Wm J, 436 George
Primeau Joseph H, 162 Hunter
Robinson Harry, 390 Water
Steel John, 217 Hunter

BARRISTERS, SOLICITORS ETC

Burnham John, 415 Water
Dennistoun & Stevenson, 417
Water (see adv)
Dumble & Johnston, 435 George
Edmison & Dixon, 397 George
(see adv)
Edwards & Murray, 435 George
Gladman Frederick W, 134½ Hunter

AS OTHERS SEE US.

" The Manufacturers' Life is a solid institution".—EMPIRE.

" The Company is evidently in a most satisfactory condition".—THE GLOBE.

" Both the Shareholders and Policy-holders have every reason to be satisfied with the result of last year's business".—THE MAIL.

Green John, 37½ George
Hall & Hayes, 116 Hunter
Hatton & Wood, s w cor George & Hunter
Moore Wm H, 49 Hunter (see adv)
Peck E A, 358 George (see adv)
Poussette Alfred P, 379 Water (see adv)
Roger George M, 375 Water (see adv)
Sawers Campbell W, 39 Simcoe (see adv)
Stone Erastus B, 374½ Water (see adv)
Stratton & Hall, 134½ Hunter (see adv)

BICYCLES

Walker Herbert A, 176 Simcoe

BILLIARD HALLS

Clegg Edward B, 415 George
Ray Samuel, 135 Hunter
Rubidge Geo W, 382 George

BLACKSMITHS

Batten Joseph, 189 Simcoe
Clancey Edward, cor Elizabeth, & Brown Ashburnham
Halpin John, 211 Hunter
Hetherington Wm M, 467 Aylmer

162   CLASSIFIED BUSINESS DIRECTORY.

BLACKSMITHS—Continued.

Hull Robert, 300 Water
Isbister Jacob, 395 Aylmer
Kennedy Wm J, 161 Charlotte
McCall Wm E, 291 George
Murphy Stephen J, 85 Hunter
Smith Frank, 179 Murray

BOAT BUILDERS

Canadian Canoe Co Ltd (The), 439 Water

BOOKS & STATIONERY

Sailsbury & Co, 372 George (see adv)
Stratton A H & Co, 417 George

BOOK BINDERS

The Examiner Printing & Publishing Co (Ld), 419 George (see adv)
Times Printing Co, 348 George

BOOTS & SHOES

Ames James H, 405 George
Carey James W, 450 George
Foot & McWhinnie, 420 George (see adv)
Gough Bros, 375 & 377 George
Hamilton F, s s Elizabeth Ashburnham [see adv]

McNaughton John, 263 Sheridan
Neill Robert, 350, 352 & 354 George
Stenson James T, 364 George

BOOT & SHOE MAKERS

Anthony Wm H, 159 Simcoe
Delaire Patrick, 336 McDonnel
Hetherington John, 523 George
Hickey P J, 178 Hunter
Kylie John, n s Elizabeth Ashburnham
Miller James, 241 George
Miller J W, 438 George
Rountree Thomas, 416 Water

BOTTLERS
GINGER BEER
James Charles, 391 Sherbrooke
SODA WATER
Knox David, 26 Queen

BOX MNFRS
CHEESE
Bickell Samuel, n s Elizabeth Ashburnham
PAPER
The Examiner P&PCo(Ltd), 419 George (see adv)

BREWERS & MALTSTERS
Calcutt Henry, Lake opp Robinson Ashburnham (see adv)

BRIDGE BUILDERS
Central Bridge & Engineering Co Ld 138 Dalhousie

BROOM & BRUSH MNFRS

Gunn Thomas, 557 Gilchrist
Hamilton Robert, s s Elizabeth 1 e
G T R Ashburnham

BUILDERS HARDWARE

PeterboroughLock MnfgCo,
498 Simcoe

BUTCHERS

Conroy John, 213 Hunter
Dawson George S, s s Elizabeth 4 e
Bridge Ashburnham
Denoon John, 561 George
Evens Hugh T, 554 Bethune
Glover& Fitzgerald, s s Elizabeth 5 w Mark Ashburnham (see adv)
Goselin Frank J, 245 George (see adv)
Grady James, 244 Charlotte
Howden John J, 461 George
Laplante & Letellier, 320½ George
McNarn Wm, 236 McDonnel
Mervin John, 234 Hunter (see adv)
Morris & Howden, 133 Hunter
O'Brien Michael, 233 Charlotte
Phillips Charles, 232 Rubidge
Powell George W, 664 George
Redmond Joseph A, 245 Rubidge
Winch Bros, 328 George
Winch Frederick T, 460 George

CABINET MAKERS

Courtney Edward, n s Elizabeth Ashburnham

Mnfrs. Life Ins. Co., Toronto.

"I received your cheque for $10,000 within three hours after I filed claim papers",
KATHERINE RIDOUT.

CANOE BUILDERS

Canadian Canoe Co Ld (The), 439 Water
English Wm Canoe Co, 182 & 184 Charlotte
Peterborough Canoe Co Ld, 290 Water (see adv)

CARBON MNFRS

Peterborough Carbon & Porcelean Co Ld 270 Townsend

CARPENTERS, BUILDERS ETC

Croly T M D, 66 Auburn (see adv)
Stephenson John H, 21½ Paterson

CARPETS & HOUSE FURNISHINGS

Fair Robert, 383 George
Hall, Gilchrist & Co, 130, 132 & 134 Simcoe (see adv)
Turnbull John C, 363 George

CARRIAGE & WAGON MAKERS

Craig John T, s s Elizabeth 4 e Lake Ashburnham
Fitzgerald Tobias, 224 Charlotte & 318 Aylmer
Fitzgerald & Stanger 131 Brock
Logan Wm, cor Brock & Aylmer

164   CLASSIFIED BUSINESS DIRECTORY.

FOR FINE FANCY GOODS,

GAMES AND PLAYING CARDS.

——GO TO——

- SAILSBURY'S -

CARRIAGE AND WAGON MAKERS

Continued.

Mein Robert 57 Hunter
Metheral J & W, 464 Aylmer
Yelland Joseph H, 462 George (see adv)

CARRIAGE DEALERS

Cochrane Thomas, 388 Water

CHEESE EXPORTERS

Cluhlon Wm, 399 George

CHEESE FACTORY SUPPLIES

Moore J W & Co, 351 George (see adv)

CIGAR MNFRS

Murty A, 174 Hunter

CIGARS & TOBACCOS

Clegg Edward B, 415 George
Le Gros Charles, 329 George (see adv)
Ray Samuel, 135 Hunter
Rubidge George W, 382 George

CLOTHIERS

Dolan T & Co, 399 George

Gough Bros, 375 & 377 George
Grafton & Co, 387 George
Le Brun H & Co, 381 George

COAL OIL

China Hall, 360 George

COAL & WOOD

Fitzgerald Tobias, 224 Charlotte & 318 Aylmer
Galvin James, C P R Yard
Stevenson J Coal Co, 368 Water

COLLEGES & SCHOOLS

Peterborough BusinessCollege, 368 & 370 Water(see adv)

COMMISSION MERCHANTS

Oak J B & Co, 356 Water (see adv)

CONFECTIONERY

WHOLESALE
Watt John, 366 George

RETAIL
Job Wm, 169 London
Long Harry, 414 George
Long James, 386 George
McCallum Wm J, 336 George
Potvin Leandre, 425 George (see adv)
Watt John, 366 George

COOPERS

Britton John, 13 Harvey
McDonald Bernard, 21 Queen

Left margin: PLUMBING, STEAM AND GAS FITTING, ADAM HALL, 407 GEORGE STREET

Right margin: Central Canada Loan and Savings Co

CORSET MNFRS

Ensign Corset Co, 176 Simcoe
Gemmell C G, 325 George

CROCKERY CHINA ETC

China Hall, 360 George
Routley Charles B, 379 George

CUTTING SCHOOL

Hawkins Ira Prof, 426 Water

DENTISTS

Manning W H, 146 Hunter
Morrow Robt F, 358 George (see adv)
Nimmo Richard, 420½ George
Pentland Joseph, B, 386 George
Rose & Morrison, 140½ Hunter

DRESSMAKERS

Armstrong Jos & Co, 396 George
Campbell Emma, 285 Wolfe
Davies B Mrs, 499 Aylmer
Delaney E Miss, 403 George
Douglas Ellen, 84 Hunter
Fair Robert, 383 George
Fries Minnie E, 176 McDonnel
Gay Lettie Miss, 376 Water
Geary E A Miss, 371½ George
Graham Margaret, 592 George
Griffin Minnie, 202 Charlotte
Hall, Gilchrist & Co, 130-132 134 Simcoe (see adv)
Keane Ellen, 156 McDonnel
Kells R H & Co, 369 George
Kingdon & Menzies, 374½ George

Manufacturers Life Ins. Co., Toronto, Have:

$282,882.00 - - - - Assets.
$545,197.60 - - - Insurance in Force

More than any other Canadian Company in the first six years of their existence.

Lumsden Libbie Miss, 426½ George
McCaulley Matilda Mrs, 125 Brock
McFadden Annie, 365 George
McIntosh Tena, 142 Murray
Mann Sarah Mrs, 434½ George
Morgan Selvia, 147 Hunter
Northcott Sarah, 189 Charlotte
Nevin Mary A, 213 Simcoe
O'Brien Lizzie Miss, 386 George
O'Brien Maggie, 355 George
O'Reilly Maggie Miss, 420½ George
Rae Elizabeth, 146 Simcoe
Robertson Sadie, 178 Simcoe
Turnbull John C, 363 George
Wall & Connall Misses, George

DRUGGISTS

Lynch James, 168 Hunter
McKee John, 384 George (see adv)
Macdonald Hugh S, 402 George
Madill Wm, 142 Hunter
Nugent John, 389 George (see adv)
Ormond & Walsh, 362 George
Schofield George A, 408 George
Spears Hugh, cor Elizabeth & Mark Ashburnham
Tully J D, 411 George (see adv)

DRY GOODS

Armstrong Jos & Co, 396 George
Delaney E Miss, 403 George

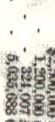

DRY GOODS—Continued.

Dickson A G, 395 George (see adv)
Fair Robert, 383 George
Hall, Gilchrist & Co, 130-132-134 Simcoe (see adv)
Hall Robert, 395 George
Johnston W W, 410 George
Kells R H & Co, 369 George
Kelly Thomas, 365 George (see adv)
Rudkins K Miss, 412 George
Turnbull John C, 363 George

DYE WORKS

Parkers Steam Dye Works, 177 Charlotte (see adv)

ELECTRIC CO S

Peterboro Light & Power Co, 417 Water

ELECTRICIANS

Greer Johnson H, 134 Brock (see adv)

ELECTRICAL SUPPLIES

Greer J H, 134 Brock (see adv)

ENGINE BUILDERS

Best & Metheral 419

Hamilton Wm, Mnfg CoLd 470 Reid

ENGINEERS

CIVIL

Belcher John E, 435 George
Belcher Samuel, 435 George
Hay Thomas A S, Bank Commerce Bldg

FANCY GOODS

Armstrong S J Miss, 390 George
Bentleys Fair, 340 George
Brown Ellen, 162 Simcoe
Butcher John W, 378 George
McEachern Charlotte Mrs, 422 George
Melville E & Co, 424 George
Routley Charles B, 379 George
Sailsbury & Co, 372 George (see adv)

FISH

Mercer Frank, 376 George
Ostrom M T, 418 George
Wholton George, 434 George (see adv)

FLAG MNFRS

Turner J J & Son, 283 George

FLORISTS

Blade Arthur, 489 Park
Jordan Bros, 43 Argyle (see adv)
Mason Francis, 440 Water
West End Greenhouse, 465 Park (see adv)
Wise Frank, 823 George

FLOUR & FEED

Brisbin James W, 161 Hunter
Brown Charles N, 139 Simcoe
Denne T H G, 135 & 137 Charlotte
Glover & Fitzgerald, s sElizabeth Ashburnham (see adv)

FLOUR MILLS

Meldrum Wm H, Water

FRUIT

WHOLESALE

Oke J B & Co, 356 Water (see adv)

RETAIL

Anthony Frank, 387 Aylmer
Locco Philip, 172 Hunter
Marino Frank, 228 Hunter
Mercer Frank, 376 George
Ostrom M T, 418 George
Romano Antonio, 445 George
Smith Charles B, 166 Charlotte
Wholton George, 434 George (see adv)

FURNITURE

Begley Robert, 380 Water
Belleghem Daniel 188 Hunter
Clegg Abraham, 427 George
Comstock Aaron, 300 George (see adv)
Craig John D, 441 George
McFadden Martin, 186 Hunter
Newton Henry, 432 George

FURRIERS

MNFG

Lech W & Sons, 413 George

SOLID PROGRESS DURING 1893:

New Business Issued, — $2,490,210
  (Increase over 1892) — 407,960
Gross Cash Income, — 287,340
  (Increase over 1892) — 45,525
Assets 31st December, 1893, — 673,738
  (Increase over 1892) — 137,071
Surplus on Policyholder's Account — 164,598
  (Increase over 1892) — 30,922
Showing a total insurance in force at 1st January, 1894, of nearly NINE MILLION DOLLARS

Mills Bros, 374 George

GRAIN DEALERS

McBain John J, 237 Charlotte
Wrighton Wm H, 421 George

GENERAL STORES

Giles John, 315 George

GENTS FURNISHINGS

Dolan T & Co, 399 George
Le Brun H & Co, 381 George
McComb James, 138 Hunter

GLOVE MNFRS

McComb James, 138 Hunter

GROCERS

WHOLESALE

Carton Michael, 206 Simcoe

RETAIL

Alexander Charles A, 559 George
Allison Andrew, 877 Water
Armstrong John F, River Rd c 1
Armstrong John & Co, 129 Hunter
Bradshaw Wellington, cor Hunter & Aylmer
Brady Thomas, 442 George
Braund Ralph C, 111 Park

168   CLASSIFIED BUSINESS DIRECTORY.

GROCERS—Continued.

Brown Bros, 394 George
Bullen Wm Mrs, 241 Rubidge
Burns May Mrs, 313 McDonnel
Cahill Annie Mrs, 262 Simcoe
Cameron John, 392 George
Card Walter D, 99 Hunter
Carton George, 321 George
Carveth Henry, 212 Hunter
Collins Wm, n w cor Elizabeth &
     Driscol Terrace Ashburnham
Collins & Co, 225 Hunter
Connal Peter & Co, 380 George
Crowley M Mrs, 108 Lake
Dawson Alfred, 355 George
Delaney Kate Mrs, 853 Water
Detcher Wm, 1 Victoria ave
Donovan John M, 356 Charlotte
Doxsee Jessie H, cor Concession &
     Carlisle ave Ashburnham
Drake Rosa Mrs, 87 Hunter
Dunn Justus, 163 Charlotte
Dunsford M J Mrs, 240 Rubidge
Edgcumbe James, 682 George
Elliott Alex, 353 George
Emmerson George, n s Elizabeth
     Ashburnham
Fleming Andrew Mrs, 113 Rubidge
Fowler George, 481 Aylmer
Fowler W G & Co, 159 Hunter
Geroux Timothy S, 208 Charlotte
Hall Wm J, 355 George

Hallihan P Mrs, 181 Reid
Halpin M H, 39 George
Hamilton Wm H, 138 Simcoe
Hartley Charles, 547 George
Henry Bros, 839-341 George
Hill M Mrs, 292 Park
Laing George, 182 Simcoe
Lane & Hunter, 144 Hunter
Lewis Thomas, 352½ Water
Lynch John J, 387 Park
McIndoe Hugh, 718-720 Water
Martyn Ipsa, 285 George
Mason E F & Co, 429 George
Michiel Thomas, 167 Simcoe
Miller James, 241 George
Minicoli Phillips, 67 Elm
Minicolo Philip, 206 Charlotte
Mitchell Fred J R, 141 Hunter
Moore J W & Co, 351 George
     (see adv)
Porter John, 292 Dalhousie
Potvin L Mrs, 73 Lake
Quirk Rebecca S, 236 Charlotte
Reid M A Mrs, 189 Dublin
Rickey George, 120 Aylmer
Sanderson George, 235 McDonnel
Smith Jason, 332 McDonnel
Squres W J Mrs, 79 Albert
Sullivan Daniel, 297 Rubidge
Sullivan Daniel, 639 George
Sullivan Patrick, 949 Water
Sullivan John C, s s Elizabeth 5 e
     Lake Ashburnham
Timmins S & Co, 360 Aylmer
Van Every Wm, 200 Rubidge
Wainright Mark, 258 London
Waller & Co, 168 Charlotte
Weir Robert J, s s Elizabeth 1 w
     Market
Wrighton Wm H, 421 George

GUNSMITHS

Terrill Lyman H, 82 Hunter

HARDWARE

WHOLESALE

Peterborough Hardware Co Ld, 368 George & 140 Simcoe

RETAIL

Hall Adam, 407 George(see adv)
Kingan & Allen, s w cor George & Simcoe
Micks Alonzo E, 137 Hunter
Stethem Geo & Son, 134 Hunter

HARNESS

WHOLESALE

Ackerman Benjamin F, 204 George

RETAIL

Denne T H G, 135 & 137 Charlotte
Devlin Wm J, 160 Hunter
Dundas Harry, 166 Simcoe
Gunsolas Charles, 346 Water
Metcalfe Wm, 140 Brock
Quinlan Michael H, 180 Hunter
Shortly Benjamin, 37½ George

HATTERS

Fairweather & Co, 361 George (see adv)
Lech W & Sons, 413 George
Mills Bros, 374 George

HIDES, ETC

Appleby Alexander B,cor Simcoe & Bethune

HOSIERY MNFRS

Elliott Thomas C, 382½ George

HOTELS

Albion Hotel,s s Elizabeth 3 e Lake Ashburnham
American House, 184 & 186 Hunter
Balmoral Hotel, cor Charlotte & Water
Carew House, 219 Hunter
City Hotel, 331 & 333 George
Commercial Hotel, 440 George
Croft House, 402 Water
C P R Hotel, 170 & 172 Simcoe
Grand Central Hotel, 345 & 347 George (see adv)
Kindred Wm A, 69 Hunter
Little Windsor, 144 Brock
Live Oak Hotel, 201 & 203 Hunter
Maple Leaf Hotel, n s Elizabeth Ashburnham
Montreal House, cor Aylmer & King
Morgan House, 123 Hunter
Oriental Hotel, 167, 169 & 171 Hunter
Peterboro House, 189 Hunter
Phelans Hotel, 181 Simcoe
Pullman Hotel, 339 George
Queens Hotel, cor Charlotte & Aylmer
Snowden House, 190 Charlotte
Southern Hotel, 295 George
White House, 173 Charlotte

HOUSE FURNISHINGS

Stratton A H & Co, 417 George

ICE

Point StCharles Ice Co, Point St Charles (see adv)

INSURANCE AGENTS

Boswell John S, 161½ Simcoe
Bradburn T Evans, 336 George
Cox & Davis, 433 George (see adv)
Cluxton Wm H, 399 George (see adv)
Errett Richard W, 392 Water
Faulkner Sylvester, 379 Water
Hanratty J J, 336 George
Hill W H, 400 Water (see adv)
Hoskins George J, 134½ Hunter (see adv)
Lindsay & Might, 326 George
McMullen Wm, 374 George
Meharry Hugh B, 161 Simcoe
Rush Thomas O, 374 Water
Smith Henry J, 172 Hunter

JEWELLERS

Calder Wm H, 428 George (see-
Clarke & Gibson, 136 Hunter
Everett Henry T, 161 Simcoe
McClelland John, 388 George

McClelland Joseph, 323 George
Sanderson W A, 367 George (see adv)
Schneider Frank S, 391 George

Junk

Doig David, 214 Hunter

KNITTING WORKS

Elliot Thomas C, 382½ George

LADIES FURNISHINGS

Armstrong S J Miss, 390 George
Byrne James Mrs, 452 George
Gemmell C G, 325 George

LAUNDRIES

Lee Sam, 169 Simcoe
McGrath Thomas B, 390 Aylmer
Peterborough Steam Laundry, 179 Charlotte [see adv]

LIME ETC

Rehill Bros, 149 George

LIVERY & BOARDING STABLES

Connor Bros, rr 303 George
Fitzgerald Tobias, 224 Charlotte & 318 Aylmer
Gibbs Robert, 25 Chambers
Jones Fred E, 193 Hunter
Leary Robert H, w s Water 1 s Hunter (see adv)
Mosley Ashton E, 193 Simcoe
Nesbitt R H, 13 Chambers

Reynolds John, 272 Simcoe

Sloan R A, Simcoe

Westlake &Nesbett, 13 Chambers (see adv)

Wolstenholme Robert J, 195 Charlotte

LOAN & SAVINGS CO

Central Canada Loan &Savings Co, 407 George (see adv)

LOCK MNFRS

Peterborough LockMnfgCo, 198 Simcoe

LOCKSMITHS

Redner Thomas, 443 George

LUMBER

Dickson Co Ld, 47 London

Irwin James M, 435 George

Rathbun Co The, 248 Murray

MACHINISTS

Best & Metherel, 419 Water

Elves James, 232 Hunter

Frost & Heath, 287 George (see adv)

Morvy Richard, n s Elizabeth Ashburnham

MALTSTERS

Calcutt Henry, Lake opp Robinson Ashburnham (see adv)

MARBLE WORKS

Coughlin Bros, 209 Hunter

Moore T W, 317 George

MARRIAGE LICENSES

Green Wm J, 145 Hunter

MATTRESS MNFRS

Faint Wm, s s Elizabeth 1 e Bridge Ashburnham

MERCHANT TAILORS

Dolan T & C, 399 George

Green Wm J, 145 Hunter

Hall, Gilchrist & Co, 130-132-134 Simcoe (see adv)

Le Brun H & Co, 381 George

Mercer A & Co, 401 George

Meredith W H, 393 George (see adv)

Simons Pete & Co, 416 George

Turnbull John C, 363 George

Weir Robert, 158 Simcoe

MILLINERY

Armstrong S J Miss, 390 George

Cassidy Margaret, 423 George

Delaney E Miss, 403 George

Fair Robert, 383 George

Hall, Gilchrist & Co, 130-132-134 Simcoe (see adv)

Hall Robert, 385 George

Kells R H & Co, 369 George

Turnbull John C, 363 George

MODEL MAKERS

Frost & Heath, 287 George(see adv)

MUSICAL GOODS

Peterboro Music Co, 404 George (see adv)

NEWSPAPERS

The Examiner, 419 George (see adv)
The Peterboro Review, 164 & 166 Hunter, (see adv)
The Times, 348 George,(see adv)

NURSERYS

Rochester Star Nursery, 415½ Water

OPTICIANS

McClelland John, 388 George
Sanderson W A, 367 George (see adv)

PACKERS

EGG

Scott & Hogg. G T R Track & Robinson Ashburnham

PORK

Carton George, 321 George

Matthews Geo Co Ld (The), 356 George

PAINTERS

Cook Frederick, e s Driscoll 7 n Elizabeth Ashburnham
Shevlin John P, 229 King

PATENT SOLICITORS

Ranney & Innes, 372½ Water

PHOTOGRAPHERS

Early George J, 374½ George
Green P H, 140½ Hunter
Sproule George B, 170 Charlotte

PHYSICIANS

Bell Robert W, 494 George
Bingham James, 473 Water
Boucher Robert P, 543 Water
Brennan Frederick H, 217 Brock
Burnham George, 513 Water
Caldwell Wm, 212 Brock
Carmichael Duncan N, 132 Brock
Clarke John, 166 Brock
Fife Joseph A, 631 George
Goldsmith P D, 190 Brock
Greer Thomas N, 357 Aylmer
Halliday James T I, 457 Water
King Richard, 290 Charlotte
McGrath Edward, 539 George
Pigeon Henry, 270 Charlotte
Scott Wm, 176 Brock
Spears Hugh, cor Elizabeth & Mark Ashburnham
Yelland A E, 147 Murray

Left margin (vertical): PLUMBING, STEAM AND GAS FITTING, ADAM HALL, 407 GEORGE STREET

Right margin (vertical): Central Canada Loan and Savings Co

PIANOS & ORGANS

Crosby J W, 342 Water(see adv)
Jackson & Co, 378 Aylmer
Peterboro Music Co, 404 George (see adv)

PICTURES & PICTURE FRAMES

Aselstine Samuel G, 348 Water
Stratton A H & Co, 417 George

PLANING MILLS

Donell James R, Dicksons Raceway
Donell Wm, 165 Dublin
Wand Wm, n s Elizabeth Ashburnham

PLATED WARE

China Hall, 390 George

PLUMBERS

Hall Adam, 407 George (see adv)
Micks Alonzo E, 137 Hunter
Noble & Co, 214 Hunter

PORCELEAN MNFRS

Peterborough Carbon & Porcelean, Co Ld 270 Townsend

POTTERY

Allin John F, 19 Cresent

PRINTERS & PUBLISHERS

PeterboroughReviewPrinting & Publisling Co Ltd (The)164 & 166 Hunter(see adv)

The Examiner P & P Co 419 George (see adv)
Times Printing Co, 348 George (see adv)

PUMP MNFRS

Condon John, 196 King
Owens Henry, 124 Simcoe
Payton Edward H, 174 Charlotte
McWilliams George, Dicksons Raceway

REAL ESTATE

Boswell John S, 161½ Simcoe
Lindsay & Might, 326 George
Morrow Thomas, 134½ Hunter

REFRIGERATOR MNFR

Croly T M D, 66 Auburn (see adv)

REPAIR SHOPS

Frost & Heath, 287 George (see adv)
Hudson Edmund, 138 Brock

RESTAURANTS

Brown Gavin, 386 Water
Craig J C, 426 George
Le Brun & Brown, 344 George
McCallum Wm J, 330 George
McGregor Cecila, 350 Water

Right margin (vertical): CAPITAL SUBSCRIBED, $2,500,000.00 / CAPITAL PAID UP 1,230,000 00 / RESERVED FUNDS 223,007 57 / TOTAL ASSETS 3,053,033 09

174   CLASSIFIED BUSINESS DIRECTORY.

RESTAURANTS—Continued.

Potvin Leandre, 425 George (see adv)

Powell Otho, 344 George

SADDLERY

WHOLESALE

Ackerman Benjamin F, 204 George

SAIL MNFRS

Canadian Canoe Co Ltd (The), 439 Water

Kingscote Alfred, 344 Water (see adv)

Turner J J & Son, 283 & 283½ George

SALOONS

Dunn Thomas, 189 Hunter

SAWMILLS

McDonald Alfred, Point St Charles

Wynne Charles, 987 Water

SEEDSMEN

Brisbin James W, 161 Hunter

SEWING MACHINES

Mitchell German A, 420 Water

Peterborough Music Co, 404 George (see adv)

Singer Mufg Co, 430 George

STAIR BUILDERS

Croly T M D, 66 Auburn (see adv)

STEAM & GAS FITTINGS

Hall Adam, 407 George (see adv]

STEEL RANGE MNFRS

Hall Adam, 407 George (see adv)

STOVES & TINWARE

Best Henry, 324 George

Breeze & Jones, 437 Water

Hall Adam, 407 George (see adv)

Hutchinson George, 140 Hunter

Micks Alonzo E, 137 Hunter

Murty James, 174 Hunter

Spry Lewis, 214 Stewart

SURVEYORS

Ranney & Innes, 372¼ Water

TAXIDERMISTS

Elcome R Edwin, 176 Harvey

Hudson Buttle, 134 Brock

TANNERS

Paterson Walter & Son, 412 Aylmer

TEAS & COFFEES

Stroud Bros, 370 George

TENTS & AWNINGS

Kingscote Alfred, 344 Water (see adv)

THE BANK OF TORONTO,
PETERBORO' BRANCH, P. CAMPBELL, MANAGER.
HIGHEST RATE OF INTEREST ALLOWED ON DEPOSITS.

CLASSIFIED BUSINESS DIRECTORY. 175

Left margin: **ADAM HALL, MNFR. STEEL RANGES, 407 GEORGE STREET**

Right margin: **Central Canada Loan and Savings Co.** — MONEY TO LOAN ON EASY TERMS. DEPOSITS RECEIVED.

Turner J J & Son, 283-283½ George

TICKETS

Cox & Davis, 433 George (see adv)

Hurley J P, 433 George

TOBACCONISTS

WHOLESALE

Henry Bros, 341 George

UNDERTAKERS

Belleghem Daniel, 188 Hunter
Clegg Abraham, 427 George
Comstock George, 300 George (see adv)
McFadden Martin, 186 Hunter

UPHOLSTERERS

Peate Bros, 197 Simcoe

VESSEL OWNERS

Calcutt Henry, w s Lake opp Robinson Ashburnham
Peterboro Navigation Co, w s Lake opp Robinson Ashburnham

VETERINARY SURGEONS

Beatty John, 180 Simcoe
Johnston Thomas, 13 Chambers
Poole Bernard R, 352 Water

WALLPAPER

Stratton A H & Co, 417 George

SOLID PROGRESS DURING 1893:

New Business Issued,	$2,490,210
(Increase over 1892)	407,960
Gross Cash Income,	287,340
(Increase over 1892)	45,525
Assets 31st December, 1893,	673,738
(Increase over 1892)	137,671
Surplus on Policyholder's Account	164,598
(Increase over 1892),	30,922

Showing a total insurance in force at 1st January, 1894, of nearly NINE MILLION DOLLARS

WATER WORKS

Peterboro Water Works Co, 253 Hunter

WATERPROOF CLOTHING

Turner J J & Son, 283-283½ George

WEAVERS

Barclay John, 583 George
Curray Wm S, 273 McDonnel
Lowry Samuel W, 172 Hunter

WINDOW SHADE MNFRS

Green Edward, 326 Water

WINES & LIQUORS

Brown Bros, 394 George
Elliott George, 353 George
Henry Bros, 339-341 George
Sullivan J C, s s Elizabeth Ashburnham

WOOLEN MILLS

Auburn Woolen Mill, Auburn
Faint Wm, s s Elizabeth 1 e Bridge Ashburnham
Peterborough Woolen Mill, Water n

Peterborough Street Guide.

ABBREVIATIONS:—e. east ; n. north ; s. south , w. west; bet. between; ave. avenue ; st. street ; rd. road ; opp. opposite.

ALBERT, runs w from 111 Park

ALFRED, runs s from 116 Albert

ANTRIM, runs w from 677 Water

ARGYLE, runs w from 827 Water

AUBURN, runs n from Black Bridge foot of Smith

AYLMER, runs s from Smith bet Bethune & George

BABBS LANE, runs n from 76 Gilmour

BARNARDO AVE, runs w from 785 George

BELMONT AVE, runs s from Weller bet Park & Walton

BENNETT, runs w from Barnardo ave 1 n Wolsley

BENSON AVE, runs e from 20 Benson St

BENSON, runs n from 162 Smith

BETHUNE, runs s from Smith bet Stewart & Aylmer

BOLIVER, runs w from 211 Park

BONACORD, runs w from 485 Park

BOUNDRY RD, runs n & s dividing town from n Monaghan

BROCK, runs w from 40 Sheridan bet Hunter & Murray

CAMBRIDGE AVE, runs n from Cedar

CEDAR, runs w from 401 Park

CHAMBERLAIN, runs w from opp 86 Park

CHAMBERS, runs n from 166 Hunter

CHARLOTTE, runs w from 322 Water

COLLEGE, runs n from 68 Murray

CONGER, n & s from Barnardo ave 1 w George

CRESENT, runs s from Perry 1 e George

CROSS, runs n from Cedar

DALHOUSIE, runs w from 204 George

DENNISTOUN, runs n from opp 91 Smith

DICKSON, runs n from 84 Murray

DIVISION, runs n from 184 London

DONEGAL, runs n from 370 Hunter

DOWNIE, runs n from 348 Charlotte

DUBLIN, runs w from Waterford to Park bet Edinburgh & London

DUNLOP, runs e from Auburn

EDINBURGH, runs w from 639 George

ELM, runs w from 389 Park

GEORGE, runs n from Lake to Smith bet Aylmer & Water

GILCHRIST, runs n from 388 Murray

GILMOUR, runs w from 285 Park

HARVEY, runs n from 106 McDonnel

HOMEWOOD AVE, runs w from Belmont ave bet Weller & Gilmour

HUNTER, runs w from River bet Brock & Simcoe

INVERLEA, runs s from 788 Water

JOHN, n from 68 Boliver

KIRK, runs w from opp458 Rubidge

KING, runs w from 281 George

LAKE, runs w from 9 Cresent

LANSDOWNE, runs e from Lock 1 s Ware

LISBURN, 1 s River rd

LOCK, runs s from Romaine at Junction of Cresent

LONDON, runs w from River to Park bet McDonnel & Dublin

LOUIS, runs n from 214 King

LUNDY, runs w from Monaghan rd 1 s Chamberlain

McDONNEL, runs w from opp 124 Dickson

MANNING AVE, runs e from 690 Aylmer

MURRAY, runs w from Dickson to Park bet Brock & McDonnel

PARK, runs s from w end of Smith to Romaine

PARNELL, runs w from 61 Park

PATERSON, runs w from 159 Park

PERRY runs w from opp 2 Cresent

QUEEN, runs s from 99 Hunter

REID, runs n from 409 Wolfe

RINK, runs w from George bet Townsend & Perry

RIVER ROAD, runs n from Concession 1 e Auburn

ROMAINE, runs W from Lock 1 s Westcott

RUBIDGE, runs s from Smith bet Reid & Stewart

RUTHERFORD AVE, runs s from opp 66 Paterson

SCOTT, runs w from opp 372 Rubidge

SHERBROOKE, runs w from 241 George

SHERIDAN, runs n from 82 Water

SIMCOE, runs w from River bet Hunter & Charlotte

SMITH, runs w from Black Bridge

STEWART, runs s from Smith bet Rubidge & Bethune

TOWNSEND, e from 124 Rubidge

UNION, runs n from 192 Dublin

VICTORIA AVE, runs w from 867 Water

WALNUT, runs w from Cambridge ave

WALTON, runs s from 93 Weller

WARE, runs e from Lock bet Cresent & Lansdowne

WATER, runs n tron Sherbrooke to city limits 1 e George

WATERFORD, runs n from 74 McDonnel

WELLER, runs w from 367 Park

WESCOTT, runs w from foot of George bet Romaine & Lake

WILLIAM, w from 24 Boliver

WOLFE, runs w from George bet Dalhousie & Townsend

WOLSLEY, runs w from Barnardo ave

Miscellaneous Directory.

COURT HOUSE & GAOL, George-st, bet Murray & Brock.—

Judge of the County Court, C A Weller.
Clerk of the Peace and County Crown Attorney, R E Wood.
Sheriff, J A Hall.
Clerk of the County Court and Registrar of Surrogate Court, John Moloney.

THE BANK OF TORONTO,
PETERBORO' BRANCH, P. CAMPBELL, MANAGER.
FARMERS' NOTES DISCOUNTED,

Treasurer and Clerk, E H Pearse.
School Inspector, J C Brown.
Jailor, H Nesbitt.
Turnkey, R Rae.
Registrar, B Morrow.

PUBLIC HALLS & BUILDINGS.—

Water Works, 1000 Water-st.
I. O. O. F. Hall, cor George & Hunter-
Temperance Hall, 376 Water
Police Court, 355 Water.
Foresters Hall, 180 Simcoe.
Town Hall, 127 Simcoe.
Post Office, cor Hunter & Water.
Fire Hall, 133 Simcoe.
Custom House, cor George & Charlotte.
Opera House, 338 George.
Court House and Gaol, George bet Murray and Brock
Masonic Hall, 354½ Water.

GOVERNMENT OF THE TOWN OF PETERBOROUGH.—

James Kendry, Mayor.
S R Armstrong, Clerk of Police Court & Secy of Board of Health.
Chas McGill, Treasurer.
D W Dumble, Police Magistrate.
E B Edwards, Town Solicitor.
J E Belcher, Town Engineer.
B Cumming, Tax Collector.
Geo I Roszel, Chief of Police, Sanitary Inspector & Truant Office.
Robt Pope, Street, Bridge & Building Inspector & Relief Officer.
A E Yelland, M D, Town Physician.
J Clarke M D, Medical Health Officer.
James A Hall, E A Peck, Auditors.
W Aldridge, T B McGrath, J J Hartley & Thos McKee, Assessors.
Thos Rutherford, Chief; J D Craig, Ass't Chief; Jas English Engineer, Fire Brigade.

180   MISCELLANEOUS DIRECTORY

BOARD OF ALDERMEN.—

Ward No 1.—Thos Cahill, H Best, W H White.
Ward No 2.—Thos Kelly, E H D Hall, George Stevenson, J L Hughes.
Ward No 3.—A Dawson, G M Roger, Edw Sutton.
Ward No 4.—W H McElwain, F Mason, Thos Brady.

STANDING COMMITTEES FOR 1894.—

FINANCE—Councillor Cahill, (Chairman).
STREETS & BRIDGES—Councillor Best, (Chairman) and Councillors Dawson, Cahill, Kelly, Winch and McElwain.
COURT OF REVISION—Councillor Roger, (Chairman)
FIRE WATER AND LIGHT—Councillor Kelly (Chairman)
CHARITY—Councillor White, (Chairman)
HEALTH—Councillor Hughes, (Chairman)
APPOINTMENTS TO OFFICE AND SUPERVISION OF POLICE—Councillor Best, (Chairman)
LICENSE—Councillor Hughes, (Chairman)
PROPERTY—Councillor Dawson (Chairman)
PRINTING—Councillor McElwain, (Chairman)
JOINT COMMITTEE—Councillor Cahill, (Chairman) and Councillors Stevenson, Bradburn, Dawson, Dennistoun and Kelly.
MARKET—Councillor McElwain, (Chairman)
MANUFACTURERS AND RAILWAYS—Councillor Hall, (Chairman)
SEWERAGE—Councillor Best,
BOARD OF HEALTH—J J Hartley, Chairman, Mayor Kendry, Henry Denne, Robert Innes, Dr McGrath, Wm Blackwell, C E B Shortly, Adam Hall, C Stapleton, John Kincaid.

POLICE DEPARTMENT—D. W Dumble Magistrate.

George I Roszel Chief.
Constables. Robert H Adams, Charles McGinty, Joseph Stewart

FIRE DEPARTMENT.—

Thomas Rutherford, Chief
John Craig, Ass't Chief
C Rutherford, Secy Trea
Jas English, Engineer
E Lawrence, 1st Driver
Jno Montgomery 2nd Driver

THE BANK OF TORONTO,
PETERBORO' BRANCH, P. CAMPBELL, MANAGER.
BUYS AND SELLS CANADIAN AND FOREIGN EXCHANGE.

MISCELLANEOUS DIRECTORY. 181

BOARD OF EDUCATION.—

STANDING COMMITTEE FOR 1894—

FINANCE—Mr W G Ferguson, Chairman; Messrs Denne, Hayes, Wrighton, McBain & Hill.

SUPERVISION—Mr Jno McKee, Chairman; Messrs Hamilton, Hill, Boucher, Edgcumbe and Caldwell.

PROPERTY—Mr Peter Hamilton, Chairman; Messrs Stevenson, McBain Hartley, Law and Wrighton.

COMMITTEE ON APPOINTMENTS—Mr W H Hill, Chairman; The Whole Board.

Dr. Burnham, Chairman

W G Morrow, Sec.-Treas.

SEPARATE SCHOOL BOARD.—

Dr. Brennan, Chairman.
John Corkery, Secy. Treas.
Rev. Father Collins, Local Superintendent.

SCHOOLS.—

Public School, cor Mark & Robinson, R G Dean, Principal. Ashburnham.
Barnardo ave School, W H Walkey, Principal.
Separate School, Lake St, Sisters of St Joseph.
3rd Ward School cor Park & Cedar, Jas McCreary, Principal.
Notre Dame Convent & Separate School, cor Rubidge & Scott, Sister Veronica Lady Superioress.
Rubidge Street School, cor Rubidge & Serbrook H A Yenney Principal.
Murray St Separate School, bet George & Aylmer, Wm Burke Principal.
Central School, Murray e of George, Wm Smith Principal.

PETERBORO COLLEGIATE INSTITUTE.—Murray Street e of George

PRINCIPAL—CORETZ FESSENDEN.

TEACHERS.—

John Jeffries, Jas. A. Fife, Wm. John Drope, H R Kenner, Sophia Marty, Michael O'Brien.

MUNICIPAL OFFICERS FOR THE COUNTY OF PETERBOROUGH.

Ashburnham Villiage, John Burnham, Esq., Reeve.
Havelock Villiage, Samuel Joyce, Esq., Reeve.
Lakefield Villiage, Wm H Casement, Esq., Reeve.
Norwood Villlage, Joseph B Pearce, Esq., Reeve.
Asphodel Township, John Walsh, Esq., Reeve.
    "   "   Samuel Scott, Esq., Deputy Reeve.
Belmont and Methuen, John Brown, Esq., Reeve.
    "   "   J L Aunger, Esq., Deputy Reeve.
Burleigh and Anstruther, A Brown, Esq., Reeve.
Chandos, William Hales, Esq., Reeve.
Douro, John Moloney, Esq., Reeve.
    "   Wm Jno Bullock, Esq., Dep. Reeve.
Drummer, Edward Hawthorne, Esq., Reeve.
    "   Henry A Moore, Esq., Dep. Reeve.
Ennismore, Wm Crough, Esq., Reeve,
Galway and Cavendish, Michael Mansfield, Esq., Reeve.
Harvey, Robt Shaw, Esq., Reeve.
North Monaghan, Joseph Forster, Esq., Reeve.
Otonabee, Wm Anderson, Esq., Reeve.
    "   T J Johnston, Esq., 1st Dep. Reeve.
    "   J Lancaster, Esq., 2nd Dep Reeve.
Smith Township, James Middleton, Esq., Reeve.
    "   "   Wm McIlmoyle, Esq., Dep Reeve.

POSTOFFICE, Cor Hunter & Water.—

H. C. Rogers, Postmaster.
John Corkery, Asst Postmaster.
Clerks—Walter Bourn; Miss Mary Watt; Miss R Nethercutt; D. M.
    Rogers; Sidney Mitchell; John Irwin, Caretaker.

CUSTOM HOUSE, cor. George and Hunter

C. H. Clementi, Collector.
C. Snyder, Deputy Collector.

INLAND REVENUE, cor George and Charlotte.—

J J Hall, Collector.
Thos. Cahill, Deputy Collector

NEWSPAPERS.—

"REVIEW," Peterboro Review Co Prop'rs, Daily & Weekley (Conservative 166 Hunter.

"EXAMINER," J. R. Stratton, Propr, Daily & Weekly, (Reform) 419 George.

"TIMES," W. H. Robertson, Propr, Daily & Weekly (Independent)348 George.

"PARISH WORK," J. R. Stratton Publr, 419 George

BELL TELEPHONE CO.—

J. S. Knapman Mngr 332 George.

TELEGRAPH COMPANIES.—

G. N. W. Telegraph Co, 433 George, Cox & Davis Agents.
C. P. R. Telegraph Co, 322 George, T. E. Boddy Agent.

MILITARY.—

C TROOP 3RD REGIMENT, Prince of Wales Dragoons.—

Lt. Col. H. C. Rogers.   Lt. E. B. Loucks.   Lt. W. H. Bradburn Capt. Stapleton, Quarter Master.   T. Johnson Veterinary Surgeon. D. J. Johnson Adjutant.

57TH BATTALION PETERBOROUGH RANGERS, City Corps, Drill Hall Murray St. in Central Park.—

Staff, J. L. Rogers, Lt. Col.; R. W. Bell, Sen. Maj.; E. B. Edwards,

Jun. Maj.; I. Howard, Major Paymaster; Capt Mason. Capt. & Adjutant; W. Langford, Capt. Actg Quartermaster; Surgeon, J. T. J. Halliday, M. D.; Asst. Surgeon, V. Halliday, M. D.

COMPANY OFFICERS.—

A Co., Capt. R. M. Dennistoun. B Co., Capt. Schofield. Lt, Eastwood C Co., Capt Hill, Lt. A. Stevenson.   D Co., Capt. Lech Lt. Hayes. E Co., Capt. Miller, 2nd Lt. Matthews.   F Co., Capt., Brennan, 2nd Lt. Mills.

CHURCHES.

George St Methodist Church cor George & McDonnel Rev W R Young B. A. Pastor. Sunday Services, 11 a. m. & 7 p. m. Sunday School, 2 30 p. m. Wednesday Prayer Meeting 8 p. m.

Bethany Church, Opera House Block, R J Zimmerman Service Pastor Sunday 11 a. m. & 7 p. m. Thursday 8 p. m. Sunday School 3 p. m.

St. Johns (Church of England), Hunter opp Queen Rev J C Davidson Rector Sunday Services 8.30 & 11 a. m. & 7 p.m. Sunday School 3. p m. Wednesday 8 p. m. Friday 7.30 p. m.

Charlotte St. Methodist Church cor Charlotte & Reid Rev Joseph J Rae Pastor. Sunday Services 11 a. m. & 7 p. m. Sunday Schoo' 2. 30. p. m. Wednesday Prayer Meeting 8 p. m.

St. Peters Cathedral (R. C.) cor Hunter & Reid Right Rev R A O'Connor Bishop of Peterboro Ven Archdeacon Casey Rector Rev's D O'Connell, D J Scollard, S Collins. Sunday Services Mass 8 & 11. 30. a. m. Vespers 7 p. m, Sunday School 2.30 p.m.

St. Andrews Presbyterian Church cor Rubidge & Kirke Rev. Andrew MacWilliams Pastor. Sunday Services 11 a. m. & 7. m. Sunday School 3 p. m. Wednesday Prayer Meeting 8 p. m.

Mark St. Methodist Church Rev A C Beer Pastor. Sunday Servi s 11 a. m. & 7 p. m. Sunday School 2. 30. p. m. Wednesday Prayer Meeting 8 p. m.

St Lukes (Episcopal) e s Stewart St. Rev. Herbert Symonds Pastor. Sunday Services 11 a. m. 7 p. m. Sunday School 3 p. m. Friday Evening Services 7. 30. p. m.

Murray St Baptist Church. Rev. J Trotter Pastor. Sunday Services 11 a. m. 7 p. m. Sunday School 3 p. m. Wednesday Prayer meeting 8 p. m.

St Pauls Presbyterian, cor Water & Murray. Rev E F Torrance M. A. Pastor. Sunday Services, 11 a. m. & 7 p. m. Sunday School 3. p. m. Wednesday Prayer meeting 8 p. m.

Salvation Army Barracks, 223 Simcoe, Ensign Alex McDonald

ESTABLISHED 1855. **THE BANK OF TORONTO.** Capital $2,000,000
P. CAMPBELL, MANAGER, PETERBORO' BRANCH.
A GENERAL BANKING BUSINESS TRANSACTED

MISCELLANEOUS DIRECTORY. 185

SOCIETIES.

MASONIC.

Moor Preceptory & Priory No 13 Knight Templars.
Meets last Tuesday in Jan, Feb, Apr, May, Nov & Dec, and the 11th day of March

Em Sir Kt D Spence, P Preceptor.
" " " C Cameron, Registrar.
" " " B Shortly, Treasurer.

Corinthian Chapter R A No 36 meets 3rd Tuesday. D Spence Z, Jno McKee H, J M Shaw J, Dr Carmichael S E.

Corinthian Lodge No 101 A F & A M, meets Wednesday before full moon. R M Dennistoun W M, W D Parker S W, W F Johnson J W, A Stevenson Secy, T A Hay Treas.

Peterborough Lodge No 155 meets alternate Mondays in I. O. O. F. Hall. R Logan W M, W H Walkey S W, A Gibson J W, W J Drope Secy, R S Davidson Treas.

I. O. O. F.

Canton Peterborough, No 10 meets 1st Wednesday each month. Jos Kidd Com, C Moffat Lieut, J Mein Ensign, J Fanning Clk.

Mount Hebron Encampment No 56 meets 2nd & 4th Tuesdays. Wm Hill J P C P, J H Smith C P, J A Davidson H P, T Hooper S W, R Mulligan Scribe, W H Dayman Treas.

Hiawatha Encampment No 66. meets 2nd & 4th Fridays. W C Springer J P C P, R M Armstrong C P, J Nugent H P, W G Howden S W, J A McGill Scribe, J W Butcher Treas.

Peterborough Lodge No 111, meets every Thursday. J White J P G, T Hooper N G, Jos McClelland V G, A McFarlane R S, W J Green P S, S Clegg Treas.

Otonabee Lodge No 13, meets every Monday. D G Armstong J P G A Rutherford N G, J A Tully V G, A Rose R S, M Mowry P S, W H Meredith Treas.

All Lodges meet in I. O. O. F. Hall cor George & Hunter Sts.

FORRESTERS.

I. O. F. Court Chemung meets 4th Friday each month in C O F Hall M A Morrison C R, G S Ames V C R, H Fife Fin Secy, W H Meldrum Treas.

C. O. F. Court Langton No 344 meets 2nd & 4th Wednesday each month. W A Patterson P C R, H Evans C R, I Isaacs V C R, R R Hall Treas, C Robertson Secy, W C Morris Fin Secy.

Court Little John No 92, meets 1st & 3rd Wednesday. Wm Kemp P C R, J Perrington C R, W Kemp S C R, G W Rose Treas, F H Dobbin Fin Secy, J Green R Secy.

Court Peterborough No 29, meets 1st & 3rd Friday in Forresters Hall J Alexander, P C R, D S Harvey, C R, G Dredge, V C R, H Nesbett, F S, C Curtis, R S, F Adams, Treas.

A O F Court Stanley No 7680 meets alternate Fridays cor Simcoe & George Sts, W J Craig, C R, Geo Tremain, S C R, George Record Secy, R F Morrow, Treas

Catholic Order Forresters, St Peters Court No 229, meets 1st & 3rd, Monday in Hall Hunter St, J Bogue, C R, B Laroque, V C R, J C Bryon, R S, J O'Shea, F S, R Gough, Treas.

Royal Arcanum No 735 meets 2nd & 4th Thursday, D W Dunber, Regent, E A Peck, Secy-Treas.

A O U W Peterboro Lodge No 135 meets 2nd & 4th Tuesday in Forresters Hall, T G Gillespie, Recorder, J Mulholland, M W, J W Brisbin, Receiver.

S O C Peterboro Cabin No 13 meets every Wednesday S O C Hall George St. J W Kennedy, Pres, W Comstock, Treas, W C Mudge F S, T W Meredith, R S.

Sons of England Lansdowne Lodge No 25 meets 1st & 3rd Monday in each month in Hall Hunter St, T H Martin, P Pres, Geo Carpenter, Pres, D Curtis, V Pres, F Mitchell, Treas, E A Peck, Fin Secy, W J Squire, Rec Sec, Rev H Simons, Chap.

CATHOLIC MUTUAL BENEFIT ASSOCIATION.

meets in Hall George St 2nd & 4th Tuesdays, Dr Brennan, Pres, T Dolan, V Pres, A Vinette, 2nd Vice Pres, W J Devlin, Fin Secy, T J Doris, Rec Secy, J Kelly, Treas.

YOUNG MENS CATHOLIC ASSOCIATION.

A J Gough, Pres, W Rudkins, Vice Pres, Wm Burke, Secy, M Lahane, Treas, 435 George.

K. O. T. M.

Tent No 69 meets Sons of Canada Hall, W H Meldrum, Com, S W English, Lt Com, Jas Patterson, R K, R Sloan, F K.

I. O. G. T.

City Lodge No 404 meets every Thursday cor George & Simcoe Sts, Bro Simpson, C T, Bro J Stubbs, P C T, Sister Cromie, V T, Sister Stubbs, Chaplain, BroSmith, Marshall, Sister M Kindred, Deputy Marshall, Bro G S K Munro, Secy, Bro Hetherington, Fin Secy, Bro Gates, Treas.

ORANGE LODGES.

County Orange Lodge, Samuel Stenson, W M, E Kemp, D W M,S B Weir, Secy, Dr Burgess, Treas.

Peterboro District Lodge, J A Williams, D M, H Armstrong,DDM; W J Green, R S.

Royal Black Knights of Ireland, Preceptory No 261, meets 2nd Thursday in Orange Hall, Jos Saunders W P; W J Green, Registrar.

Royal Scarlet Chapter for the Court West Peterboro, S Stenson W C C, S B Weir C S; J Batton C T.

Young Canadian Lodge, No 49, meets 1st Thursday each month, S B Weir, P M; J C Hamilton, M; A Armstrong, Secy; R Weir, Treas.

Diamond Lodge, No 80, meets 1st Tuesday each month, J A McWilliams, M; W J Green, R S; W J McGregor, Treas.

SOCIETIES—Continued.

Col Sanderson Lodge, No 321 meets 2nd Tuesday, each month, J A Murray, M; G Horsefield, R S; J Saunders, Treas.

Nassau Lodge, No 457 (Nassau), meets 1st Mondy each month H S Armstrong, M; E Kemp, R S.

Jubilee Lodge, No 178, (Smith) meets 1st Tuesday each month, S Stinson, M; J Archer, R S.

All Lodges, meet in Orange Hall.

L. T. B. A Queens Own Lodge, No 48, meets every Monday, in True Blue Hall, F Reynolds, M; E Dormer, Secy.

Scns of Ireland, Protestant Association, meets 1st & 3rd Thursday, in each month, in True Blue Hall, Simcoe Street, W H Armstrong, Pres; Ed Dormer, Treas; Wm Fowler, Secy.

EMERALD BOARD.

meets 2nd & 4th Thursday 433 George St, J J Lynch, Pres, E Ward, V P, J Hickey, R S, J Carveth, F S, J Primrose, Treas.

R. T. of T.

Peterboro Council No 97 meets every Tuesday in Hall Water St, C L Trotter, S C, Mrs G J Early, V C.

PETERBOROUGH LAW ASSOCIATION.

Court House, E B Edwards, Pres, J W Bennet, Secy. A Stevenson, Treas.

CHILDRENS AID SOCIETY

Sherriff Hall, Hon Pres, Hampden Burnham, Hon Secy-Treas.

PETERBOROUGH WORKING MENS BUILDING & SAVINGS SOCIETY

T Cahill, Pres, J Lynch, Vice Pres, J P Hurley, Secy-Treas, Dennistoun & Stevenson, Solicitors Directors J S, W H Hill & F J Lewis.

Y. W. C. A.

Mrs Dr Scott, Pres, Mrs R Fairbairn, 1st V P, Mrs W Walsh, 2 V P, Mrs J McKee, Secy of Board, Mrs Dr Bell, Treas.

Y. M. C. A.

J W Bennet Pres, G J Early, V P, Madill, Treas, A L Grover, Rec Secy.

ST VINCENT DE PAUL SOCIETY.

A Vinette, Pres. T Cahill, Secy. Thomas Kelly, Trea.

PROTESTANT HOME, 470 Stewart Street.

Mrs Vernon, Pres. Mrs Hall, Vice Pres. Miss Roper, Secy Miss Roger Trea Miss E Londerville, Matron.

DR. BARNARDO'S HOME. George Street near Smith

Miss H S Woodgate, Supt.

HOSPITALS.

Nicholls Hospital, Mrs M O'Donovan Supt Argyle Street
St. Joseph Hospital & House of Providence Stewart street Ashburnham Sister Vincent Superioress.

MECHANICS INSTITUTE, 377 Water Street.

Dr G Burnham, Pres. F J Lewis, Vice Pres- John Corkery Secy Trea George Peters Librarian.

190 MISCELLANEOUS DIRECTORY.

CENTRAL CANADA LOAN AND SAVINGS CO (Of Ontario, Limited)

DIRECTORS:—

PRESIDENT—Geo A Cox Esq, Toronto.

VICE-PRESIDENTS:—J R Dundas Esq. (of Messers D Gunn, Flavelle & Co), Toronto; Richard Hall, Esq. (of Messers Hall, Gilchrist & Co), Peterborough.

Bobert Jaffray, Esq. (Director Imperial Bank), Toronto; Edmund S Vindin, Esq. Port Hope; F C Taylor, Esq. Lindsay; D W Dumble, Esq. (Barristers, etc) Peterborough; Henry J Le Fevre, Esq. Lakefield; Wm Cluxton, Esq. Peterborough; James Stevenson, Esq. M P Peterborough

MANAGER,—F G Cox

SECRETARY,—E R Wood

INSPECTOR,—A A Cox

SOLICITORS:—

Messers Dumble & Leonard, Peterborough:

BANKERS IN CANADA:

The Canadian Bank of Commerce, The Bank of Toronto The Ontario Bank.

PETERBOROUGH & ASHBURNHAM STREET RY CO LD.

T E Bradburn Pres & Genl Mngr, Fred Nicholls Vice Pres, A P Pousette Secy & Treas. Office 336 George.

PETERBOROUGH LIGHT & POWER CO.

T G Hazlitt Pres, T E Bradburn V P, A Stevenson Secy.

PETERBOROUGH WATER CO.

J Burnham Pres.

PETERBOROUGH CENTRAL EXHIBITION.

OFFICERS OF 1894.—

Geo E Elliott Esq, President.
Wm Rutherford Esq, First Vice-President.
James Davidson Esq, Second Vice-President.
W J Green Esq, Secretary.
C McGill Esq, Man'r Ontario Bank, Treasurer.

DIRECTORS.—James Kendry, Mayor Peterboro, Jas Stevenson, Esq
M P P, Peterboro, A P Morgan, Esq, Peterboro, H C Winch Esq
Peterboro, J R Stratton M P P, Peterboro, Robert Vance Esq,
Ida, Dawson Kennedy, Esq, Peterborough, Thomas Hall Esq,
Smith.

PETERBOROUGH HORTICULTURAL SOCIETY.

Pres Dr Burnham, 1st Vice-Pres, J Stephenson, M P, 2nd Vice-Pres
D W Dumble, Secy P Henry, Treas F J Lewis; Directors—Rev
V Clementi, Messrs J R Stratton, M P P, Col H C Rogers, J H
Roper, W H Hill, W H Manning, Adam Hall, J Cobb, John
Burnham, M P, T A Hay.

ST ANDREWS SOCIETY.

Pres R M Dennistoun, 1st Vice-Pres, Dr Carmichael, 2nd Vice-Pres
W J Hamilton, Treas D Caldwell, Secy W Menzies.

PETERBORO DRURY CLUB.—

R A Morrow, E E Bradburn, G W Hatton Geo Horkins, E Brown

PETERBORO RIFLE ASSOCIATION.—

President Dr Bell.
1st Vice President, Rev V Clementi
2nd Vice President, R A Morrow.
Sec Treas, F Bartlett.
Council, Chas Curtis, Geo Fitzgerald A Blade.

192   ADVERTISEMENTS.

R.F.Morrow, L.D.S

Office over China Hall, PETERBOROUGH.

Gold Medalist and Honor Graduate

STAR

REFRIGERATORS

——MANUFACTURED BY——

T. M. D. Croly,

66 AUBURN STREET.

THESE Refrigerators are Spruce Lined, Dry Air Cold Storage in their construction, and have received the highest awards.   Made to order for the trade.   Family sizes always kept in Stock.

Correspondence promptly replied to.

T. M. D. CROLY,

Box 198, Peterborough.

STAIR BUILDING ATTENDED TO.